THE

DARK
ABOVE

A NOVEL

JEREMY FINLEY

ST. MARTIN'S PRESS
NEW YORK

Published in the United States by St. Martin's Press, an imprint of St. Martin's Publishing Group

THE DARK ABOVE. Copyright © 2019 by Jeremy Finley. All rights reserved. Printed in the United States of America. For information, address St. Martin's Press, 120 Broadway, New York, NY 10271.

www.stmartins.com

Designed by Omar Chapa

Library of Congress Cataloging-in Publication Data

Names: Finley, Jeremy, author.
Title: The dark above / Jeremy Finley.
Description: First edition. | New York : St. Martin's Press, [2019]
Identifiers: LCCN 2019007958| ISBN 9781250147288 (hardcover : acid-free paper) | ISBN 9781250147295 (ebook)
Subjects: LCSH: Paranormal fiction. | GSAFD: Science fiction. | Suspense fiction.
Classification: LCC PS3606.I55345 D36 2019 | DDC 813/.6—dc23
LC record available at https://lccn.loc.gov/2019007958

Our books may be purchased in bulk for promotional, educational, or business use. Please contact your local bookseller or the Macmillan Corporate and Premium Sales Department at 800-221-7945, extension 5442, or by email at MacmillanSpecialMarkets@macmillan.com.

First Edition: July 2019

10 9 8 7 6 5 4 3 2 1

For Rebecca,
Who can summon the storm,
but prefers to command the sun.

ACKNOWLEDGMENTS

I am deeply indebted to Paul Stevens at the Donald Maass Literary Agency, for his calm and steady guidance. To the entire staff at St. Martin's Press, especially my brilliant editor, Peter Wolverton, who knew he wanted a sequel from the very beginning. My additional thanks to the talented Jennifer Donovan, Joe Brosnan, Sarah Bonamino, Hannah O'Grady, Sophia Dembling, Norma Hoffman, and Niko Eickelbeck.

To Lauren Szurgot with the William Morris Agency, who shares the vision.

I cannot express my gratitude enough to the bookstore owners and staff, the book clubs, and my family and friends who embraced these novels. And to the writers who've offered support along the way, especially Michael Koryta, J. T. Ellison, and Hank Phillippi Ryan, I am forever thankful.

To Kathleen and Steve Morris, family who are our closest friends. Thank you for bringing Peter and Nick into the world so I could write about redheads.

To Michael Morris, for the fact-checking.

To Todd Wrubel, for helping to develop a character that proves there is good even in the most notorious of troublemakers.

To Todd Doughty, an extraordinary publicist and an even better friend.

To my brother Jason Finley, for your edits and extensive knowledge of aliens.

To my daughters Eve and Charlotte. You make me proud to be your father.

And to my wife, Rebecca, whose grace, kindness, grit, beauty, intelligence, and love proves in the story of my life, the hero is a woman.

THE
DARK
ABOVE

PROLOGUE

The monster in the mountain was awake.

Even outside, under stars drowning in a dark North Dakota sky, the little girl felt it stir. She waited to see if it would come for her; steal through the dark and drag her back.

Standing in the dust from her escape, she felt it move within the stone and become still.

A mournful hooting interrupted the silence. The girl looked away from the towering stone to stare across the vast emptiness illuminated by a shy moon peeking out just enough to reveal land formations in the distance, thick and blocky. She wanted to run to them, and whatever lay beyond, and never stop.

Instead, she slowly turned back to the mountain, knowing what she left behind. It hurt so badly, she felt she might die on the spot.

But she was only nine years old, and she wanted to live.

She'd almost forgotten about the outside world, having been asleep inside the mountain for so long. But then a man had appeared in her dark dreams and reminded her that there was, in fact, a real world to which she belonged. He looked as frightened as she.

She wanted to reach out to him and never let go, as she once had the small velvet bag containing her meager possessions. There hadn't been much in that bag, just a plastic ring, a marble, and a top that blurred the color of the rainbow when it spun. She'd loved that bag, even slept with it, holding it close to her chest, until the night came that never ended, and the monster emerged from the black.

The girl had no idea how she'd escaped, where to go, or what to do. She thought of the man, with his kind face and thick hair that swirled in waves. He'd seen her, too; she knew it. He'd seen the awful things that had happened in her dreams. He'd shown her she wasn't alone. All she knew was that after he'd appeared, she found a way out.

She had to find him, even if it meant leaving behind what mattered to her most in the world.

"I promise," she whispered.

Feeling the aching breach in her heart, she turned from the mountain and began to walk.

ONE

Her Birkenstocks, with straps nearly identical in color to her turquoise bracelet, scooted along the cobblestones. Every third paver or so, she would eye a raised edge or a bit of moss, both of which she knew would surely result in a terrible slip and a broken neck.

"Would it kill you to just put in a concrete slab?" Roxy grumbled.

She knew the answer. Lynn would sooner place one of those cowboy silhouettes tilting his hat before she would dig up her carefully plotted cobblestone path.

The entire garden lacked practicality, and it expanded every spring. It was way too much for a widow in her late seventies, Roxy liked to remind her. Still, Lynn had recently planted a row of delphiniums, despite their dislike for hot summers.

"Those are going to die, you know," Roxy had warned her last month, carrying over a metal watering can.

"We will see," Lynn had responded, tossing a scoopful of Miracle-Gro into the water. "And if you insist on scuffling when you walk because you're afraid you're going to fall and a break a hip, let me remind you that you walked the Tomato Art Fest 5K last year and came in first in the sixty-and-older division."

Roxy had made it a point to skid her shoes loudly each time she walked past Lynn since she'd made that comment. This morning was no different, just in case Lynn was in the kitchen and could hear her approaching. She passed the delphiniums with their stately white blooms reaching for the sun. They shouldn't flourish like this here. They should be wilting. Their garden club had included them on their "DO NOT PLANT" list because of their preference for cool climates.

As always, Lynn Roseworth had proved them all wrong.

Roxy reached the porch, wincing on the stairs. The pain was bad this morning. It was bad every morning. Women don't get beaten in their mid-sixties and then decide to start taking up tennis. But the pain lessened as the day went on, and she wasn't going to start taking those opioids that doctors seemed to give out like Reese's cups at Halloween.

So I have some pain, big deal. And a big, ugly scar to go with it. It's not like I'm entering Miss Tennessee this year.

"Lynn!" she called out as she entered the kitchen. "I've got it! The Happy Hookers! Get it? I know Gladyce will object, but she can pull that walker of hers out of her ass. We can get bowling jackets with the name on the back and wear them in Gatlinburg. We'll be the stars of the fall rug-hooking conference."

Roxy went straight for the coffeepot, delighted that it was still warm. "Did you make the reservation for it yet? I prefer a cabin with a pool table. Hey, where are you hiding the sugar these days? I'm not using artificial sweeteners anymore. They say it causes dementia, and I can't afford to lose any brain cells."

She found the sugar stashed on the lazy Susan in the corner cabinet, mumbling that it was the least accessible place in the kitchen. Lynn had kept it in a sizeable wooden canister for decades, ready for her to dip in to at a moment's notice should her husband come home cranky from DC. The smell of a freshly baked apple pie was always the best way to detox from the Beltway, Tom always said with a wink.

Roxy gently placed the small glass container on the counter, her hands trembling a bit. Grief was sneaky like that. Comes up like a thief, waiting for you to feel comfortable, even happy, then jabs in the knife.

Tom, she thought, closing her eyes. *You stubborn, set-in-your-ways politician. I miss you.*

You wouldn't know it, given how we bickered. But I was part of the package when you married my best friend. You didn't like that I knew more about cigars than you did, and I didn't like your unwavering stance on the death penalty. We were supposed to argue for many, many years to come. You weren't supposed to die at seventy-eight.

She'd been prepared for Ed's passing. Her sweet, quiet husband, living so long with colon cancer. Of course she sobbed that morning when she woke to find him blissfully silent, after so many weeks of the hospice workers giving him painkillers that dried out his mouth and scratched his throat, forcing him to make the unmistakable sound of approaching death.

But Tom, even with his smoking habit, always seemed so solid and healthy that death wasn't a possibility. Lung cancer, however, disagreed.

"Lynn?" Roxy's voice was quieter when she called out again. She really was trying to be a bit less blunt these days, more compassionate. Age was supposed to soften people naturally. Roxy was waiting for that to kick in.

She walked through the kitchen and down the hall to Tom's study, swallowing her desire to kick aside the oriental rugs that lined Lynn's wood floors throughout the house.

You don't get it, she thought as she carefully avoided the curled edges of the runners. *If I fell or tripped, and truly hurt myself, I couldn't bear the thought of you always alone in this big old house, wrapped up in your secretive work and worrying about your family. You are the strongest person I've ever known, Lynn Roseworth. But you need me up and mobile.*

The door to Tom's study was closed, signaling that Lynn was deep into whatever she was working on.

Roxy wanted to pound on the door in irritation, but instead took a deep breath and quietly knocked. "Hey Sis, I've been calling for you. Can I come in?"

When there was no response, Roxy tried the handle. If it was locked, she would have no choice but to make a minor scene. Lynn might have her headphones on, with Yo-Yo Ma blaring, oblivious to anything from the outside world.

When the handle turned, Roxy peeked in. "Lynn?"

The room smelled so much like Tom, a mix of tobacco and books, that another wave of sadness brushed over her. She understood why Lynn chose to spend so much of her time in here. Roxy often found herself going into the basement of her own home, carrying whatever she was reading at the time, to walk past her husband's workbench. Beyond Ed's woodworking tools and amongst the last of the scattered shavings of pine, she would sit in the maroon recliner she'd banished to the underworld of their house. She'd inhale deeply, open the book, and find the words blurred by tears.

Entering Tom's study, Roxy could see the aging desktop computer was humming with no fewer than twenty open internet searches and a Word document. She fought the urge to peek at it, but remembered the time Lynn had caught her flipping through files when she was supposed to be looking for the remote to the TV in the den.

"Never, ever, are you to know what I'm doing," Lynn had said. "You're already at risk and have been unfairly scrutinized because of me. I can't drag you down further. Promise me, Roxy. Promise me."

Roxy had begun to protest and accidentally hit the side of the desk. It was like pouring gasoline on the fire of the nagging pain in her hip from where that Colorado thug had struck her and tossed her into the snow. She'd grimaced and said something about being tougher than old rawhide—with the skin to match—but she'd grudgingly vowed.

She'd felt better knowing that Lynn wasn't alone in her work, that after some significant time and discussions shared only between them, Tom turned over his study to his wife. Even after a lifetime seeing the wrinkles on his forehead deepen from handling crisis after crisis, domestic and international, she'd never seen him look as grim as he did after Lynn allowed him to join in her research. It was no wonder he made the decision he did, as much as it shocked the country and, ultimately, fractured his family.

Roxy's attention was caught by a small video in the corner of the screen, playing on a continuous loop that reset every few moments. Roxy looked closer, putting on her glasses, which hung from a multicolored lanyard around her neck. The video was from an entertainment news show. It had a broad, dramatic headline beneath the image of a handsome, redheaded young man: "WHERE IS WILLIAM NOW?"

Roxy sighed and turned away. She knew exactly where Lynn was.

Through the house she marched, out the porch door, and into the garden once again. She swept past the Rose Peddler, hoping Lynn's oldest daughter, Anne, would be late in arriving this morning to open the garden shop at ten. Especially fragile these days, it always made Anne nervous to see her mother emerge from the woods.

Roxy cleared her throat, to prepare to yell. It was her only option, given that her friend was deep within the trees, separated from the outside world by the sky-high iron fence. Not long after they'd returned from Colorado all those years ago, Lynn had the fence erected to surround the entire woods. No one, not even Tom, knew the pass code to enter through the hidden gate.

As she rounded two large boxwoods that Lynn had planted strategically to block any view of the gate, Roxy sighed in relief to see a blond-haired woman standing at the fence line, her hand on one of the iron posts. *More white than blond these days,* Roxy thought. *But aren't we all.*

"There you are," she said. She watched as Lynn turned slowly, her hand remaining on the fence. "It's a bit early to be tromping about in the woods."

As she approached, she could see that Lynn was trembling. The binoculars that hung on a strap around her neck rose and fell with heavy breathing. When Lynn teetered, it became immediately clear that she wasn't casually leaning on the fence, but rather clinging to it to keep from falling.

"Lynn!" Roxy rushed forward, grabbing her friend. "Lynn, what's wrong?"

Even when supported by Roxy's arm, Lynn still clung to the fence. "Roxy . . . you have to go away."

"What are you talking about? Come on, let's go to the shop and sit down."

"Are my ears bleeding?" Lynn turned her head.

"No, not at all."

"My head isn't hurting. I don't feel pain . . ."

"Honey, let's go inside. I'll call the doctor—"

"No," Lynn shook her head. "You have to go. Right now. And don't let Anne come to the shop. Close it. No one comes anywhere near the property."

"I'm not going anywhere. What the hell is going on? Do you feel like you had a stroke? Does your chest hurt?"

Lynn closed her eyes. "I'm afraid it's happening. After all this time . . . it's happening."

Roxy lifted her chin. "Well, let it come, then. I've had a good, yet increasingly strange, life. And if it ends standing outside the damn woods with you, so be it. But I can tell you, I feel just fine. Maybe irritated that I haven't had enough coffee, but I'm not dying."

"Roxy, please. It could be happening—"

"Look at me. I'm fine. No one is dying, OK. Start with explaining to me why you think . . . after all this time . . . you've been triggered."

The words still felt heavy, difficult to say. Even after everything she'd learned, everything she'd seen that Colorado night that haunted her, Roxy still struggled with discussing it: a nightmare that should disappear in the morning light but proved to be just as real as the grass they stood upon, the branches above, the very air around them.

They all carried the burden. All of them who survived that frantic escape from Argentum. How do you pay the gas bill, clean your windows, go to Bunko, go on living a normal life, knowing what's beyond the night sky?

"Just talk to me," Roxy said softly. "Why did you go into the woods this time?"

She watched Lynn take a deep breath. "You really feel OK?" Lynn said. "No pain, nothing strange at all?"

"I think you know there's a whole lot strange about me. But nothing unusual. I know you were watching some video about William. Don't be mad, I just glanced at it on your computer screen when I was looking for you. I promise I wasn't snooping."

Lynn's fist covered her mouth, her other hand bracing her elbow. "I don't want the shop opening today. I have to call Anne. In fact, we need to leave *right now*."

"Anne won't be here for another three hours to open the shop. You need to take a deep breath and just explain what's going on. I know this has something to do with that video."

"I have to know when anything is reported about William. Turned out to be just the same rehashed theories of where he might be. But that wasn't why I came out here. I was right to be worried."

As Lynn turned once again to the trees, Roxy followed her gaze. The morning's humidity swam like a river around them, seeping through the iron fence and throughout the burr oaks beyond. Not a half mile into the trees was the site that prompted Lynn to wall off the woods from the world.

"I woke up with this horrible feeling. You know how it is when you're supposed to do something important, then you forget it, and when it comes back to you, it hits you like a Mack truck?"

"We turn eighty next year, Lynn. I am well aware of the sensation of forgetfulness."

"This was worse than that. It was like a neighbor calling to say that smoke is coming out of your house and remembering that you left the gas burner on. Take that horrible feeling and times it by a thousand. I was in a panic. When the video proved to be nothing new, I searched for anything about him or Kate. There was nothing. That feeling, though . . . of something horrible remembered . . . wouldn't go away."

Lynn continued to look through the fence. Roxy had only been to the abduction site a few times, and that was when William first disappeared. She'd found nothing remarkable about it all those years ago. Just a small grove amidst the trees where, unlike most of the woods, grass actually thrived in places, thanks to gaps of sky amongst the canopy of leaves. That summer, everything the sun encouraged to grow was flattened by the feet of searchers and police. Surrounded by crime-scene tape even in the winter months, it became desolate.

The fence prevented anyone, except for Lynn and the few she allowed to enter, to reach the site. Upon learning its history, tied to the disappearances of so many, Roxy understood her friend's fierce commitment to conceal it. Privately, she worried how often Lynn returned.

"Why did you say you were right to be worried?" Roxy prodded.

Lynn did not respond at first, careful, as always, to mask her reasons. "I didn't even like Tom going there. I fought for so long to keep him from even stepping foot there. But Tom gave up so much . . . and was such an asset to my work . . . that it was unfair to stop him. And when I'm lost, or frustrated with my own deep failings, I can't help but go there, to see if I've missed something. And I was right to go there today. We have to leave. Right now."

Roxy allowed Lynn to drag her away. "I know you enjoy keeping me in the dark, but if there's truly something dangerous—"

"I have to find William. I have to."

"Lynn, we all want to know where he is. I've told you time and time again that he's a grown man now, and he's just working his way through this—"

"He's not. He's hiding. And I understand why. But he can't hide anymore. I have to tell him."

"Tell him what?" Roxy planted her feet. "Even though I am in desperate need of air-conditioning right now, I need an explanation."

Lynn once again touched her arm. "Then come and see."

Moving around the boxwoods and across the lawn, Lynn led her out into the sun that hit them with the ferocity of a Tennessee summer morning.

Roxy winced, pulling her "I ♥ PBS" T-shirt loose from her chest. "Can we stand in the shade at least?"

"No. Right here." Lynn took off her binoculars and thrust them into Roxy's hands. "Hold them up. Follow where I point."

"Can I go get my sunglasses?"

"No."

Roxy sighed and lifted the binoculars to her eyes. "Great. I see leaves."

"Look up higher," Lynn said, gently lifting the binoculars. "Follow my finger."

"All I can see is white. I can't see your finger through these things. Wonderful, more white. Wait. Is that a rain cloud? If I'm lucky, it will burst open and drench us and complete this marvelous morning."

"That's not a cloud."

"Of course it is," Roxy lowered the binoculars, squinting. The sky was piercingly white, awash in thin cirrus clouds. The strip of razor-thin dark could have been easily missed. "What is that? Birds?"

"No," Lynn said, the pitch of her voice dropping. "Ladybugs."

The dread that hit Roxy was like suddenly realizing there was a semi truck in her blind spot. While she knew little about her friend's research, Lynn had explained to her the swarming of the beetles at the time of William's disappearance, and how even the government kept them in canisters at the hospital in Argentum to serve as a warning of what was to come.

"Are you sure? They're so far above trees. I didn't think insects could fly that high."

"Neither did I," Lynn said, walking towards the house. "But once I saw them again in the sky this morning, I knew there was a reason I feel that awful . . . foreboding. It's so much stronger this time . . . I feared it was finally happening."

"You mean you've seen them in the sky like that before?"

"Just once." Lynn was quickening her step. "Not long after William left. I thought at the time it was just the anxiety of realizing he was gone again, even if it was of his own choosing. I wasn't surprised that I woke up the next day a bundle of nerves and ended up in the woods again, looking for something to help me understand what happened to us. Here, watch the stairs. They're wet from the sprinklers."

"At least you finally are worrying that I'm going to wipe out. But I'm fine. Go on."

"It wasn't even cloudy that morning," Lynn said, holding open the screen door. "But when I entered the clearing, I immediately noticed something was casting shadows on the ground. That's when I looked up and saw it. So many of them . . . far above . . . so thick that I didn't understand, at first, what I was seeing. Then, I saw the ladybugs everywhere, thousands of them. I ran inside to get my phone to document it, and thankfully also grabbed Tom's old Canon."

Lynn ushered them through the kitchen, down the hall, and into the study. "Sit at the computer."

"At long last."

"Maybe I shouldn't. I probably shouldn't. . . ."

"Because you think it might shock me? I think we're past that point."

Lynn's hand hovered over the mouse. "I'm sorry, Roxy. Just in case I haven't said it lately. I'm sorry for dragging you into all this."

Roxy placed her hand on top of Lynn's. "If you recall, I shoved and pushed and corralled my way in. You would have left me back at the train station fifteen years ago if you'd had your way. I chose this. I've held back on demanding answers to what you've been up to because I know you worry that it could end up harming me. But I want to know. So get that mouse moving."

Lynn sighed. She reached into her pocket, withdrawing a flash drive.

"Do you routinely walk around with those in your pockets these days?"

"I keep them in Tom's gun safe. It was the first thing I grabbed before I headed outside. I wanted it on me just in case. . . ."

Just in case you died. That whatever is in you was activated and your ears bled and you died or went into a coma, like all those people in that terrible hospital. We would have found your body and ultimately that flash drive. Your last secret to reveal.

Roxy patted her hand. "Show me."

Lynn plugged in the flash drive and typed a long security code. A series of folders emerged on the screen.

The cursor moved to one labeled "SWARM."

Inside were dozens of photographs, and Lynn scrolled through them, clicking on one.

"These are from Tom's camera. The lens is much better than my phone's camera."

Roxy put her glasses on and leaned in. A tree in the photo looked as if an infection had overtaken it; a red mass covered every inch of its trunk.

"Those are all ladybugs?"

"Yes. Look at this next picture. They swarmed up the tree. Covering every inch of it. Now, look at this."

She closed the folder and opened another labeled, "IN THE SKY."

Even taken with the excellent lens, the photograph just showed a mass of black dots against a blue sky.

"I don't get it."

Lynn pointed to the photograph. "They started to move, like a wind had blown them off the tree. They just kept drifting upward. Now, this is the picture I took when they resettled."

She opened another photograph that showed the beetles had begun to make a formation, moving into clear curves.

"How can they do that? I know birds know how to fly in formation, but bugs? But it's not like they're forming an arrow pointing to the grove or anything. What is it?" Roxy asked. "And what are these other folders? Michigan, London, Argentum—"

Lynn opened another folder. It was an illustration, clearly taken from a scientific journal. She moved the graphic to sit directly beside the photo of the formation the beetles had made in the sky.

"My God," Roxy said, covering her mouth with her hand.

"It's what they did to us," Lynn said. "It's why I have to find William."

TWO

Sweat surged down his face, soaking his T-shirt, despite the best efforts of the box fan from Walmart pointed directly on him. It was a fairly new purchase, given that he'd run the last one from Goodwill so consistently at night that it ultimately burned out.

With a temporal vein bulging across his forehead, he could not move, paralyzed by the kind of fear usually reserved for children caught in the throes of nightmares, crying out for their parents.

He, however, was twenty-two years old.

Rubbing his aching shoulders, he sat up. It was not uncommon for him to be unable to stand after the dreams, his calves burning and even his feet throbbing from his fiercely curled toes. When he woke, there was no part of his body that wasn't tense.

He swung his long legs over the bed and gingerly touched the floor, anticipating pain. Instead his legs only trembled, which meant he could get the ibuprofen without feeling like he was walking on nails.

The distance to the bathroom was a short walk across carpet that twenty years ago was a stylish shade of deep red. In the dark, the stains from coffee and God knows what else were blessedly hidden.

Even in dim, filtered light, the pill bottle was easily found, for it was always in the same place on the corner of the sink. He had considered moving it permanently to his nightstand, but stashing it in the bathroom meant he would have no choice but to get up after the dreams. And if he'd learned anything, it was the importance of not lying in bed in a state of shock. It was better to move, to remind himself that what he dreamt was not real, that his subconscious was simply reacting to nagging fears, that there was a difference between worry and reality. It was why, even knowing exactly where the bottle rested in the dark, he turned on the light.

His reflection appeared in the mirror, revealing hair so ridiculously unkempt that he almost laughed. His brothers certainly would if they could see it. The higher the hair, the closer to God, their mother would say, running her fingers through his churning locks, which grew like crabgrass in a wet spring. Jabs would be made about pulling the WeedWacker out from the shed, and certainly the ruler stashed in the junk drawer would be seized to see if the height had reached a new record. His dad would wrap his arms around him, pretending to hold him in place while the ruler rested on his scalp, his brothers and mother delighting in counting the centimeters, cheering if the height stretched past seven. One summer, it reached to twelve, which was noted with a red Sharpie on the ruler, an exclamation mark drawn next to it.

He wished he could dream of them.

Twisting open the pill bottle cap, he tossed back three pills. Then he turned off the light and lumbered across the bedroom, rotating his shoulders to increase the blood circulation. He leaned his six-foot-two form against the frame of the room's solitary window, parting blinds to squint at the early morning light.

You are surrounded by cotton in the middle of nowhere. You are not even close to what you're dreaming about. What's irrefutable is that you need to get your butt ready for work.

But it always felt so real. He could practically taste it.

And this time, there was something more.

As always, the nightmare had started in a storm. The blistering rain had barreled around him, beating him with stinging winds. Torrential rain soaked him, making his clothes a second skin.

Raging waters rushed like an army towards the city in the distance, crashing into levees, seeking crevices, cracks, anything to slip through to further erode the stone. What it couldn't break it would bypass altogether, to pummel the electricity-stripped buildings and homes beyond.

He tried to look away from the bodies in the mud-clogged waters, knowing they hadn't anticipated the storm would arrive so fast, or with such fury. But on this night, when he wrenched his gaze away, he saw them: two specks of white in the swallowed city, tiny stars in the engulfed night. In all the hundreds of times the dream had come, he'd never seen them. They felt like a stare, a gaze, directed at him.

Then the dream shifted. He was surrounded by people, shoving and shouting. The anger from the crowd seeped into him; their heat like an iron an inch from his skin.

Many held signs that blurred in the fight, some crashing down in the swirl of bodies, others pounded against the pavement as if intended to stab through the very earth.

When the bullets started whizzing past, it was as if a shock wave rolled over the crowd; people covered their heads or ducked. And he saw them again: eyes, watching the massacre, then turning to him.

Overwhelming heat came next. Not anger, but embers and ash and flame. Trees fully engulfed, like a city of skyscrapers on fire. Yet someone was there, someone was surviving all this, and their eyes watched from beyond the flames.

The smell of the hospital came a moment later, both fetid and sanitized. Bleach applied over and over again across tiled floors on which gurneys rushed, carrying people covered in plastic.

It wasn't just the doctors and nurses wearing masks, but the attendants at the help desk, and the panicked family members trying to find their loved ones. Some covered their mouths with scarves or their hands.

He heard the high-pitched beeping of the sinking heart rates, the suctions pumping stomachs.

Once again were eyes. But this time, they didn't watch from behind the doctors, the hospital walls, or even the windows. They were in the far distance, almost miniscule amongst the towering stones that lined the horizon.

Suddenly, those eyes were right in front of him.

He was in the rock itself, encased in the dark, unable to move or to breathe, trapped, with something slithering across his skin—

He snapped the blinds shut.

He could still feel the wretched smoothness of the scales, the sensation of being encapsulated within the rock. It was always what ended the nightmares, his mind unable to stand the feeling of the encompassing swirling of the snakes around him.

But this time, those eyes—those different, haunted eyes—felt like some-one stabbed through his chest to his heart.

His hand drifted from rubbing his forehead to his closely cropped beard. A necessity, now, if he were to be unrecognizable.

If there was any doubt, the dreams reminded him of the reason why he had to run. Why he had to stay away.

He knew he wasn't supposed to know about it; he had eavesdropped on a conversation he was never supposed to hear, made in the worst of circumstances. But he'd heard it, there was no denying it, even if he didn't truly understand what was said. He'd made the decision that any man who loved his family would make.

After all, she'd risked everything for him. Her reputation, her marriage, the exposure of her secrets, all to find him. To save him.

His grandmother, who went from mildly famous to internationally infamous, faced the kind of scrutiny that would make most people turn away from the world. But not his grandmother. She was stronger than anyone he'd ever known.

I'm trying to be brave like you. To risk everything for my family. It's why I can't tell you where I am.

He hated causing her to once again relive the pain that she—and all of his family—endured more than a decade ago. Despite everything they'd gone through since then, he knew all they wanted was for him to be home.

But you are alive. Without me, Nanna isn't a danger to anyone. But if I return, you could all die.

From now on, his memories would have to suffice—of the family that loved him and that he loved so much in return.

William Chance had no choice but to never see them again.

The most famous boy in the world was dead.

William repeated the words in his head like an invocation. He'd waited in the Jeep in the parking lot until the kid, dragging his mother in a faded Razorback tank top and balancing a cigarette and a toothpick in her mouth with the skill of a juggler, emerged with a grape slushy. When they got into their Mini Cooper and pulled out, only a rusted Honda Civic with the bumper sticker, "I Miss Bill," remained.

The stifling air, void of a trace of a breeze, propelled through the vents in the Wrangler. He'd taken the doors off in the absence of air conditioning that had cut off about three months ago. When the Jeep came to a halt, even at a stoplight, the summer heat rushed in, threatening to drown him in his own sweat.

This was his chance.

The most famous boy in the world was dead.

He turned off the engine and slid out, pulling the rim of his St. Louis Cardinals ball cap down low, and walked through the doors.

"Welcome to Uncle Steve's Food Mart," a girl at the checkout said with the enthusiasm of a deflating balloon. William imagined a manager sending out a memo, maybe stapling it to the paychecks: *Every customer must receive a greeting at the door—a warm greeting means hot business!* William nodded in sympathy.

The entire back wall was beer, waving at him like a teenager seeing her boyfriend for the first time since he left for college, his texts and calls dwindling by the day. *I've been waiting for you!* the Corona panted in the cooler. William snatched up a twelve-pack of Dr Pepper instead, practically hearing the coolers whine in outrage.

The pleasant door chime announced the arrival of three people, all heading directly for the counter.

Are you kidding me?

An older man pointed outside and proclaimed loudly, "Pump one!"

"We only take cash, machine's down," the girl responded.

Holding out a credit card, the man tilted his right ear towards her. "You said what, hon?"

"We. Only. Take. Cash."

"Still don't understand you," he said, touching his hearing aid.

"You don't take credit cards?" the woman next in line demanded.

"Only cash."

"Don't nobody carry cash anymore." The woman jutted out her hip.

"What did you say?" the old man practically leaned across the counter.

Scratching underneath his hat, William scanned the room. The aisles faced the front, allowing whomever was working to keep an eye out for shoplifters. Only one row was positioned horizontally to the checkout counter.

He slid over to the aisle and peered over the top. The old man was slowly pulling out his wallet. He could hear the woman on her phone, calling her sister to bring some cash. The last man in line was intently reading whatever was on his phone.

One side of the aisle was peanut butter and chocolate bars masquerading as protein bars, and the other was lined with magazines. William set down the Dr Pepper and reached for one of the magazines. A headline in red letters on a black cover stood out among the rest, just as its designers intended it to do, knowing their magazine would be surrounded by an actress's seventeenth pregnancy announcement; an exclusive on the luxury fallout shelter hidden in the Hollywood Hills for a family of reality stars; and a lifestyle guru, whose name William couldn't remember, leaning forward thoughtfully, her glasses resting on the tip of her nose, encouraging meditation.

"YEAR OF TURMOIL," *Time* magazine proclaimed. The cover was split into four sections, displaying flooded streets of New Orleans, miles of burned trees in California, a hospital somewhere surrounded by hordes of people trying to rush in, and smoke from gunfire before the Supreme Court.

In the center of the photos were words in stark white:

RELENTLESS STORMS.

FIRES.

INCURABLE DISEASES.

BLOODSHED.

HOW THE NATION IS FALLING APART.

William put the magazine back. He watched the news nightly and listened to NPR almost constantly during work, so he didn't need a recap of the disasters. Was it any wonder he had nightmares every night? That he carried around the constant fear like a lead blanket?

Hey, chill out, chili dog. Don't get your panties in a wad.

Roxy's voice came out of nowhere, and William couldn't help but smile. It's exactly what she would say if she were standing next to him, followed by a twist of her finger to his rib cage or a gentle tug on his earlobe. While his parents showered him with compassion and his grandparents taught him resilience, it was Roxy who infused in him the importance of laughing—and making an obscene gesture towards—the face of adversity.

Don't try and fool me, Willie boy, he imagined her saying, picturing her in her favorite T-shirt, which read "Squad Goals" with a picture of the Golden Girls beneath. *I know all you truly want to read is that magazine with the floozy on the hood of that Mustang. Just remember: Venereal disease is the gift that keeps on giving.*

The last was actually one of her favorite sayings to him, whispered both before he left for prom and when that picture of him passed out cold nearly naked in a girl's bed on the third floor of his freshman dorm set social media on fire for a solid week. His family had been horrified. Roxy had simply set it as the screen saver on her phone.

When three tabloid reporters were busted recording his high school graduation, Roxy had snuck outside to smear Vaseline on the inside of their door handles. After he was relentlessly taunted in the fifth grade by the Jolton twins for being the redheaded-stepchild-from-space, Roxy sat him down and made him repeat one saying until he got it right: "Hey Joltons: My other ride is your mom." When he delivered the line while sitting on his bike after baseball practice, even the twins laughed. The teasing stopped.

When he mooned an entire trove of photographers who showed up at his lacrosse tournament, Roxy taped the published photograph on her refrigerator.

Find the humor, kiddo. Make 'em laugh. Sometimes it's all we've got.

OK Roxy, he thought. *What's that runner's magazine with the columnist that shares funny stories about crapping his pants during race day . . . ?*

He scanned the covers and saw his own face.

He flinched as if a snake had just dropped from the ceiling and landed on the pop star with whom he shared the cover of *Hello!* magazine. She got the full-page treatment, drunkenly getting into a car with the words, "Rock Bottom!" Tucked up in the right-hand corner, next to the magazine's famous red-and-white lettering, a photograph showed him wearing a black tie with a solemn expression. "WILLIAM FOUND ALIVE?" the headline asked.

The tie had been one of Grandpa Tom's. "He'd have liked you to have worn it," Nanna had told him, her age-spotted hands trembling as she helped him with the knot before the funeral. "Your grandpa had classic style."

He'd taken her hands in his own and held them until they had both stopped shaking.

William hesitated, staring at the cover. It would be a mistake to look. After all, he'd managed to elude them all for a year.

The most famous boy in the world is dead, remember?

He snatched the magazine, flipping to the story and wincing at its two-page layout. The headline shouted across both pages, "The Disappearance of William Chance."

The first paragraph was equally cringe-worthy.

"The most fascinating story of the century has taken another twist, as the young man, who many believe is proof of UFO abductions, has yet to be seen in public in a year. Sources say even William's grandmother, Lynn Roseworth, doesn't know where he is and fears he may have been abducted again. There have been multiple, unconfirmed sightings of him across the country, from New York to Los Angeles. One entertainment outlet has set up a toll-free hotline and a cash reward for any information leading to proof of his whereabouts–

"Don't I know you?"

William looked up, his heart in this throat. He was still alone in the aisle.

Then he saw himself in the security mirror in an upper corner, above a row of hand sanitizers. The checkout girl, leaning on the counter, was also in its reflection, staring at him. He'd been so preoccupied that he'd zoned out, failing to realize the store had emptied.

"You work with all those Mexicans who mow the lawn at the Methodist Church in the Quapaw," she said.

Finally breathing, he picked up the Dr Pepper and a bag of Cheetos, slipping the magazine beneath the orange bag.

"Yeah," he said, rounding the aisle and sliding the magazine facedown on the counter.

"I've noticed you after church. You always have that hat on. Your hair sticks out like duck feathers," she said with a smile as she flipped over the magazine and scanned the bar code.

"I need it cut," he said, quickly sliding the magazine into a plastic bag and taking the chips to cover it up.

"I just can't get over how familiar you look." She handed him the Dr Pepper.

Make them laugh.

He kept the brim of his hat low. "Not many gingers on the mow team. We burn too easily in the sun. We're basically albino sausages on a grill."

She smiled, biting her bottom lip.

"So how much?"

"Oh, sorry. Eight twenty-five. That your Jeep out there? You live just down on Ripper, right? I seen it parked at that trailer."

"I stay there when my home in the Hamptons is under renovation. Have a good one."

"See ya."

William tried not to scramble out of the store, even though he would smash through the glass if it meant getting out quicker. No more coming back to Uncle Steve's.

He jogged past the pumps and set the soda and the bag on the floorboard, cranking up the Jeep and gunning it out onto the road.

She was just flirting. He downshifted to second gear. *She's bored and likes guys in Jeeps. Nothing to worry about.*

Third gear and dust started flying. It hadn't rained in a week and a half and nothing was tamping down the grit. The handle of the plastic bag whipped out the absent door, and he reached down quickly to throw the bag in the back to keep it from blowing out. He wanted to pull over and tear open the magazine inside, but the trailer was just a quick left away on Ripper Road.

The beat-up and heavily leaning sign on the corner actually read "Lee Road," but the Little Rock police never came out this far, and everyone drove it like Bristol. William tore around the corner.

As cotton on both sides of the dirt road rushed by, the Dr Pepper twelve-pack thumped around on the floorboard in the back. He'd have to let it settle before he cracked one open. If he stepped it up, he might beat Carlos and have a few minutes to read the speculation about where he was.

When the cotton briefly broke and the trailer came into view, he saw an old F-150 on the gravel driveway, hitched to a large trailer carrying two mowers. So much for beating Carlos.

At the Jeep's approach, a Hispanic man, his already dark skin made leathery from constant sun exposure, slid out of the truck cab, a notebook in his hand. Carlos still did it old school: He liked to write down all their yards for the week and who was assigned to which address. He kept a special red pen for the people who hadn't paid.

"Where you been Nick?" he said as William came to a stop.

"Got hung up at Uncle Steve's."

"Ticktock Nickie! Mrs. Goff wants you there at 6 a.m. tomorrow, and we've got a shit ton more after that to schedule."

"Why don't you take Goff and I'll take the Lion's Club?" William grabbed the soda and the bag.

"Because she doesn't like *Mexicanos!*" Carlos grinned and then spit out his chew. "She wouldn't even use us if that nice little Caucasian wasn't part of the crew. She thinks you're mute. Always gives extra tip for the white boy because she's convinced you're special needs. Why else would you mow lawns with a bunch of illegals?"

"I never see that tip." William jangled his keys and opened the trailer door.

"These mowers don't run on air, my man." Carlos followed him in.

The window air-conditioner hummed as William headed straight for the fridge, sliding in the twelve-pack and tossing the chips and magazine into one of the cheap wood-paneled cabinets. Maybe Carlos will need to take a leak and give him a few seconds—

"Throw me one of those DPs." Carlos sat down at the table, sliding over the stack of books piled on top, and flipped open his notebook.

"All shook up from the ride. Unless you want to wear it."

"Why don't you get a decent car? Something with doors. Something with air-conditioning."

"My boss doesn't pay me enough."

"You know, I don't get it Nick," Carlos said, holding up his pen.

Here it comes. "Can you save me the same old speech—?"

"You're smart." Carlos pointed the pen at him. "My best worker and my accountant—"

"We agreed not to talk about that."

"I'm not planning on telling the IRS. You're a freakin' whiz with numbers. And look at this place." Carlos waved to the books stacked on anything that wasn't moving. "It's a damned library in here. *East of Eden*? *Never Let Me Go*? You should be in college. Getting laid by sorority girls. And yet here you are, living in this shithole and making minimum wage. I don't get it."

Because my name isn't Nick Peters. Because I am not from Lonoke, Arkansas. Because I needed a job where I wouldn't talk to or see anyone. Because no one would ever think to look for me here.

"You trying to get rid of me?" He forced a smile.

"Hell no. Just trying to finally figure you out. Remember when you first stopped me and asked if I was hiring? You didn't talk again for about four months. Just nodded all the time, wouldn't even look me in the eye. Then I had you hold my notebook that one time, and you quietly pointed out that I was double billing Ron Neil. You failed to mention you're a genius with numbers."

"Hardly a genius." *A Catholic school education with accelerated math is all it was.*

"Ok, let's see who gets a trim tomorrow."

William sat down and looked over at the notebook. "Right off the bat, this is wrong. We did Eddie three days ago. His grass will burn if we cut it again."

"No, that was Mrs. Hoffman—"

"Hoffman lives down the street. We did her two weeks ago. She's due. You're off."

"Just do it." Carlos slid the notebook across the table. "Hey, I hired those two guys from the Pancake House."

"I don't suppose they have papers."

"Just focus on getting us on track please." Carlos stood and walked over to the fridge.

He'd been on Carlos to hire the two young men who hung out in front of the restaurant. They were obviously fresh off the truck that had successfully snuck by Homeland Security to transport them from Texas to Arkansas. That ride, and getting across the border, had certainly cost them everything they had.

"You're running a booming enterprise," William said.

"My vast empire is growing, thanks to you."

Grandpa Tom would be proud of his miniscule efforts for job creation. "The Democratic party has lost their way, Willie boy," he often said, pointing his finger at William. "We've got to return to the working class. Focus more on creating good jobs and realizing people are desperate to get here because of what America stands for. Sure, we need strong protection at the borders, but do people really think that illegals are sneaking in and taking all the well-paying jobs?"

Nanna would usually tried to change the subject then, and his brother, Brian, would announce, once again, that he was voting Republican. And the kitchen would erupt in chaos.

William closed his eyes. *Is it always going to hurt this bad—?*

"You got ice?" Carlos opened the freezer. "Damn, this is frosted over!"

"Told the landlord about it two weeks ago."

"Can't drink hot Dr Pepper," Carlos walked back over to the table. "You got us figured out?"

"You were just off on addresses. You're good now. Ready to take on the overgrown lawns of Little Rock."

"Good man, Nick. Then I'm out. Mrs. Gonzales told me to come by and see her after work. I got just enough time to take a shower and shave. She likes a clean workspace." Carlos winked.

"Go on with your bad self."

"What are you gonna do? Sit in here and read? No man is an island, Nick."

Not true. "Cards play the Reds tonight."

"I'm gonna see if Mrs. Gonzales has a daughter for you." Carlos swatted him on the shoulder.

As soon as Carlos closed the door, William walked to the cabinet and pulled out the magazine. The badly needed shower would have to wait.

He leaned against the counter, flipping to the article.

William's last appearance in public was at the funeral for his grandfather, former U.S. Senator Tom Roseworth. Since then, sources say, William failed to return to Belmont University, where he was to finish his senior year.

"He no doubt moved to a smaller college and is laying low," said a source close to the family. "He just needed time to grieve."

If only it were that simple.

He looked up from the magazine, sliding open another drawer. The Cricket phone inside was dark. It would need to be charged before he could send the texts.

Afterwards, he'd quickly destroy it. Using a ghost number, he would text his parents, brothers, and Nanna. *I'm OK*, he would type. *Just need space.*

He'd add that he loved them too. They'd all know it was definitely him, as the message was an inside, morbid joke. "The boy back from space just needs space," William would quip to his parents when he was in a rotten mood.

When he sent the monthly texts, they were always followed by a flurry of calls and texts. *Where are you? This has gone on long enough! Just call us! We'll come get you! Don't you know that you're making this worse?*

Nanna's texts were less demanding. *Please come home.*

He'd then immediately smash the cheap phone so it couldn't be traced. Even the sight of it brought on a familiar unease in his stomach. He slid the drawer shut and resumed scanning the article.

The piece picked up as they always did, with the same damn recap.

How the world watched him grow up, clamoring for details of how he'd been found by his grandmother, Lynn Roseworth, the wife of a US senator and vice presidential contender, who hid from her own family that at one point in her life she was a researcher of UFOs.

The paragraph broke to feature a screen grab of the now-infamous video of his grandmother meeting with extraterrestrial researchers in Illinois. Once, a few years ago, he'd gotten on YouTube to see how many views it had received. At that point, it was more than two hundred million.

The article went on to detail how his grandmother never publically discussed how she found him or what happened in the town of Argentum, only saying at a brief news conference afterwards that a great government conspiracy was hiding the truth from the public about extraterrestrial abductions.

Almost immediately, the man suspected of abducting and killing William, Dr. Steven Richards, was released and was never seen in public again. His alleged accomplice, Barbara Rush, was also freed, but refused to talk to reporters.

The world held its collective breath after the town was locked down for three months by the Department of Homeland Security. Despite the isolated and brutal conditions of the area, the network news divisions set up temporary bureaus outside. Families of missing people arrived from across the globe, holding an almost constant vigil.

When the government finally allowed the media in, the experience for the reporters was a disappointing and resounding thud. No spaceships, no alien bodies, no Roswell. Only a sad little broken-down town, with hardly any residents, who knew nothing about what had occurred. In interviews, they were mostly agitated that their streets were lined with satellite trucks and just wanted to go back to living off the grid, thank you very much.

Their main complaint was that after the military occupation, the only hotel in the town had shut down when the well-liked front-desk girl skipped town.

"How she did it when the rest of us couldn't leave is really the only mystery we've got," grumbled a former occupant, who said he was forced to move in with his girlfriend and now had to clean his own room.

The government encouraged everyone in the town to do interviews, including the staff at the hospital, who claimed William was simply never there. Despite rumors that other abducted people were brought to the town, the doctors explained they were basically a small research clinic for people with amnesia and had very few patients, given the dwindling population of the town. They preferred the isolated location because the quiet and calm was soothing to their troubled clients. They'd considered shutting down for years after their prime source of income, a private donor whose wife had suffered from amnesia, had died.

"Perhaps," the lead doctor had told reporters, "Mrs. Roseworth is deeply troubled."

The article explained how that quote was prominently featured in the ad campaign for the eventual movie that followed. Next to the paragraph was the poster for the film adaptation of the international bestseller, *The Senator's Wife*, showing a beautiful British actress in her mid-sixties—who'd mastered a southern accent enough to land her an Oscar nomination— standing in the snow, thrusting out a pistol and holding tight to a red-haired boy while a looming shadow of a massive alien fell upon her.

In quotes at the bottom of the dramatic scene were the words, "Perhaps Mrs. Roseworth is deeply troubled."

The official government report was equally as damning. It prominently listed the cost of the occupation of Argentum as more than $10 million, resulting in no proof of any extraterrestrial life or abductions. It also cited repeatedly that neither Lynn Roseworth nor her companions, Roxy Garth and Don Rush, would agree to interviews with government investigators.

When reporters confirmed that Don had, in fact, been reported missing decades ago, and that the trail led to his sister, Barbara, who had already been revealed to be a UFO researcher, the condemnation by lawmakers had been swift and merciless.

"LYNN'S LIES," read the subhead, as the article continued. Congressional inquiries followed, in which Lynn and her companions invoked the Fifth Amendment.

"What we are seeing is a sick, twisted ploy by this obviously troubled woman to use her grandson to inflame the public into believing something that simply isn't true, and costing taxpayers millions of dollars," said Senator Jake Hondal, the chairman of Senate Appropriations Committee, following the conclusion of the last hearing. "It is the belief of this committee that Mrs. Roseworth staged her own grandson's disappearance using her equally troubled friends to pull it off. It is, in my opinion, one of the great scams of the 21st century. It is no wonder why Senator Tom Roseworth had made his decision."

A photograph of Grandpa Tom at a podium, looking weary, was included. He was announcing his retirement from the Senate. After thanking the Democratic Party for inviting him to be part of the presidential ticket, and declaring his love for the country and Tennessee, his grandfather made a statement that sucked the air out of the room.

"And let me be clear on this: I believe my wife."

It was the last public remarks the retired senator ever made, the article noted.

The senator and his wife both refused repeated interview requests, even when his middle daughter and former chief of staff, Kate Roseworth, once again ignited the controversy by announcing she would seek to fill her father's seat.

Another photograph showed his Aunt Kate at the first press conference announcing her decision, her blond hair pulled back, glasses on her beautiful face. "As for my mother and father's claims, I will only address this once and never again: I love my family. Nothing will ever change that. But I have read the government's investigations. I have spoken to the director of the hospital in Colorado. Let me be clear: I do not subscribe to my family's theories about my nephew's disappearance. And I never will."

"THE ROSEWORTHS' THORN," read the next subhead, followed by how his Aunt Kate barely won the election. And how, in the past decade, she slowly had become just as influential in Congress as her father, despite the fact that he never campaigned with her. Multiple sources confirmed privately that she was estranged from her family.

At last, a slice of truth in this article, William thought.

He grimaced at what followed. Another subhead: "WILD WILLIAM."

He started to skim. The familiar photographs were republished: him drunk at fifteen, being carried out of a bar by his brothers; his face reflected in police lights after being pulled over for riding a motorcycle that later proved to be stolen by a friend; and the tabloid favorite shot of him nearly naked, sleeping in that college girl's bed.

His fingers laced behind his head, he began to pace. The tingling had already started in his fingertips. He tried to ignore the trembling, the heaviness in his chest.

Inside the fridge was the remainder of the Rolling Rock. He was so thirsty that he could slam three or four easily. The other option was the horribly beat-up and dirty pair of running shoes by the door.

Drunk or run? Drunk or run?

He had about a minute to decide before the panic attack was in full swing.

After a six-mile run and a day spent mowing lawns in the heat of a Little Rock summer, he showered till he couldn't stand the cold water anymore. He'd hoped the running would kill the anxiety, at the very least give it a decent wound. But with every heel strike on the dirt roads among the cotton fields—he didn't dare run anywhere where someone might drive by—he'd think about the magazine article. Even after a freezing shower, the embers of worry still churned hot.

William knows he suffers from extreme anxiety, his longtime therapist had advised his parents. *He's still battling trust issues.*

That emergency family session was supposed to be a turning point after he had to be rushed to the emergency room when he felt like he was having a heart attack and couldn't breathe. He remembered the looks of fear on his parents' faces, and it both crushed and comforted him. It wasn't that they overtly coddled or spoiled him or his brothers, but they had stood on the cliffs of utter despair once and had never truly recovered themselves. After all, their youngest child had disappeared for nearly six months; and their middle child, Brian, who had witnessed the disappearance, had become despondent and mute. Greg, their oldest, had sunk into a deep depression.

Even when Nanna brought him back, Brian once again began to speak, and Greg emerged from his cocoon of despair, there was the reality that William didn't know any of them. His only bond was to his grandmother and Roxy. Even though they too were unfamiliar people to him, Nanna exuded safety, and Roxy made him laugh. It took painful years to learn to trust, and eventually love, the strangers who were his parents, brothers, aunts, and grandfather.

It did not help that his memories of Colorado faded as he aged. Just fragments now, of ever-present snow, the anxiety of not even knowing his name. Of an old woman with a crooked finger who barked commands but gave strong hugs. A strange woman, not as old as the first, showing up and saying she was his grandmother. Running with her in the dark.

And what emerged from it.

Just a sliver of a memory, a shadow that struck him with such horror that he couldn't breathe. Then, a moment later, a strong feeling of euphoria that replaced the fear with joy. Being jostled away by the nice old woman. The sound of gunshots. Eventually waking up in a stranger's truck. The lights of the news photographers' cameras stinging his eyes.

His therapist had advised that his mind was suppressing whatever trauma he endured and that, in time, he might find clarity.

He'd repeatedly, over the years, pressed for clarification of his memories. Nanna's routine response was to say that she, too, was searching for explanations. When she had them, she would tell him.

Once he had lashed out at her, saying if she'd only tell him what happened in Colorado, reveal what she saw and had uncovered in her work since then, then maybe he wouldn't feel so anxious all the time.

She'd worn a white shirt that day, the collar turned up, her sunglasses resting on the curls on the crown of her head. She'd looked regal to him, like a furious queen.

"That is my burden to bear and mine alone," she'd said, pointing her finger. "I do not have the answers. But when I do, I will tell you everything. And when my time here on earth is over, you will carry the burden. But I take my vitamins and walk every day and I intend to be here for a long time. So for now, my gift to you is normality. Do not waste these years. At one point, you will long for them. Just as I do."

William stretched his calf muscle, leaning on the counter, watching the crust of the frozen pizza begin to darken in the oven.

You did what you thought was best to protect me, Nanna. Now I'm doing the same for you. Truth be told, I'd give anything to be in your kitchen right now for Sunday dinner.

Mom would be helping add the fried onions to your orzo pasta. Dad would be on his phone, pointing out to Brian and Greg that the Cardinals still had a chance at a wildcard spot if they'd just beat the Reds in the series. Roxy would stand before the pantry for at least five minutes, complaining that it was impossible to find the Doritos with all the gluten-free healthy junk everywhere. Maybe Aunt Stella would FaceTime in from New York, letting everyone know for the hundredth time that the kitchen was bigger than her entire apartment.

The oven dinged.

Just because I dropped out of college doesn't mean I can't eat like a college student. William used a heavily stained oven mitt to pull out the pizza. *But you're safe, Nanna. As long as I'm not near you. And that's what matters.*

The pizza clanged on top of the scorched cooktop. After slicing it in half and piling it on a plate, he walked over to the table, looking for the remote. The Cards game would have started by now.

His hand hovered over the power button. Especially after this carb coma and being broke-ass tired, the lull of the announcer would certainly slip him into a deep sleep.

The dreams would be waiting.

Nope. Not yet. Let's put that off a bit, shall we?

He bypassed the TV to kneel on the floor by the stack of his latest haul from the library. Among all of the techniques his therapist had suggested to combat the anxiety, only two had truly stuck: running and reading. Of every material possession he left behind, he missed his paperback of *Huckleberry Finn* the most.

After scanning his options and shoveling down the pizza, *The Sword of Shannara* won the draw. He slumped into the couch, feeling the busted spring jab him in the familiar spot on his right shoulder. It would soon poke through the cloth and give him a wicked scrape. The pillow he'd bought for a dollar at Goodwill was serving as his shield.

Just as Flick Ohmsford's descent into the valley began, the knock came at the trailer's cheap metal door.

He strained his neck over to the table. Carlos's notebook rested there where he had left it. Again.

"You're killing me, compadre." He climbed out of the rapidly collapsing couch and snapped up the notebook.

He slumped over to the door, turning the handle. "I swear I'm going to chain this thing to your belt—"

The light outside the door momentarily blinded him. Wincing, the first thing he could see were the professionally bleached teeth of a woman standing with a microphone pointed towards him.

"William Chance? The whole world has been looking for you," she said, shooting the words at him as fast as major league pitcher.

She licked her lips. "I'm Stephanie Stiller with Hollywoodextra.com. We have been trying to find you for a long time. Let me say what a relief it is to know you're alive and OK!"

His chest constricted so hard that the woman might as well have reached in and squeezed his heart, her French manicure puncturing the upper chambers. The heavy, humid night air rushed into his lungs as he tried to breathe.

"I only want to be able to tell your side of the story," she continued, holding the mic closer.

Never slam the door. Whatever you do, don't slam the door.

That was Aunt Stella's guiding words after a tabloid videographer had snuck up to the front door of his parents' home, barking questions on the tenth anniversary of his disappearance. *Watch*, Stella had instructed, pointing to the video online. *It will play a million times on a loop if you get fired up. And for God's sake, never, ever hit the camera. A slow, painful close of the door makes for bad television. And if you think of it, look sad. Makes people feel for you, and the network gets slammed by angry viewers. It's why us honest journos never ambush innocent people.*

"Please, William, I just need a moment—"

He'd heard the pitch a million times. The request was usually accompanied by, "I want to be fair to you and your family."

After he slowly closed the door, he rushed to the windows, drawing the vinyl blinds, seeing the photographer outside zooming in on his every move.

Why does this keep happening? he'd lamented to Stella after a janitor at his high school was fired for carrying around a hidden camera. The man had later admitted that a magazine had offered to pay him more for those photos than he would make in a year. *When is this ever going to stop?*

Blame the genes from your parents, she'd answered, gently holding his face. This mug sells tabloids; it gets ratings, it gets clicks. Sad truth: If you weren't six foot one with those dimples and built like a swimmer, they'd have lost interest a long time ago. Go eat more donuts.

The girl at the gas station. It had to be.

It was stupid of him to buy that magazine. She'd obviously walked back over to the rack, looked at the issue he'd bought, and quickly put two and two together. The words from the article snuck in like a sucker punch: *One entertainment outlet has set up a toll free hotline and a cash reward for any information leading to his whereabouts—*

He scrambled for his keys and snatched the phone from the drawer. Knowing the back door creaked, he slowly unlocked it and gingerly stepped down the wobbly wooden stairs leading to the ground.

Creeping around the back to the side of the trailer, he peered around to see the reporter talking excitedly into her phone. "He's here! He's inside! We got video!" She was practically shouting while her photographer chewed his gum.

Thankfully, his landlord didn't spring for exterior lights, so he moved in the dark to the Jeep. He awkwardly climbed over the stick shift and shoved the key into the ignition.

Knowing the photographer could be focused in on him in a second, he fired up the engine and threw the Jeep in reverse.

He was barreling down the road a heartbeat later. He looked back to see the reporter frantically pointing in his direction.

There was simply no way they could catch up with him, especially given how he knew to navigate the back roads. Confident now that the top light on the camera couldn't capture a single frame of him, he extended his middle finger and drove.

If the news crew had been able to keep up to see where he ultimately stopped, they would have drooled.

William ignored the government sign indicating that the Toltec Mounds Archeological State Park closed at dusk, pulling into the visitor parking lot. Arkansas wasn't exactly flush with money, and the budget didn't include constant monitoring of state parks. It meant for the teenage couple hoping to get laid, and anyone on the run trying to survive a panic attack, there was ample ability to do so in the privacy of one's own vehicle.

You are not dying.

He killed the headlights and his eyes adjusted. Away from the meager lights of downtown Little Rock and thanks to a swollen moon, he could make out the hills.

Focus on them. Distraction helps. You've gotten through this before.

The first time he'd stolen his brother's laptop, he'd typed in "alien abductions" in Google, and coverage of his own story, Area 51, and the Toltec Mounds in Arkansas were right at the top.

The websites claimed the hidden purpose of the mounds, and the reason for the disappearance of the ancient people who built them, were obvious. From the skies, the hills corresponded with certain clusters of stars. A map reflecting the heavens on earth.

How could a prehistoric society know to do that without guidance from beings from beyond? the websites wondered, and theorized that the mounds were designed to be landing sites for ships, and on their last return to earth, they took the worshipping people on the ground back to the stars.

Maybe not the best place to overcome an anxiety attack.

He reclined the seat, taking long, deep breaths. The reporter didn't have much, but it was enough. Aunt Stella had long ago put him through a media boot camp to prepare for a lifetime of attention. Having moved from a local news station to write investigative pieces for sites like ESPN and Politico, she was deeply plugged in and understood how all the organizations operated. He knew the reporter wasn't with one of the TV stations, so she would download the footage to a private video-sharing site and get it back to promotions ASAP.

He'd never heard of the TV show. Hollywoodextra, did she call it? Some junk like that. Given the scoop, he knew from what Stella had taught him that the promotion would run for days, using only the video of his face, providing no other location information so as to not tip off competitors. Stella had even educated him on the ratings months of the year, when sales generated their ad rates and the networks released their new episodes. Be especially cautious in those months, she'd warned. Overnight ratings have changed the game to some degree, she'd explained, but everyone still wants their blockbusters in November.

Regardless, he had two days, tops, to get out of town. As soon as that story aired, the hordes would come like an invading army.

He'd wait to return to the trailer at dawn. If he was lucky, they'd stake out his house all night, but eventually give up when he didn't return. They'd come back quickly, though. He'd only have a short time to pack up what he could, drive to Carlos's place to leave a note apologizing for his sudden disappearance, and flee.

The thought made his stomach churn. Where would he go now? The renewed media attention would make him even more recognizable wherever he went. When he'd decided to disappear a year ago, he'd simply hopped on the interstate. No reporters trailing him. He was gone an entire day before even his family realized he was missing.

As soon as this story aired, the entire world would know where he is, and if he weren't out of town by then, there would be nowhere left for him to hide.

"Take a chill pill. Everyone needs their lawns mowed, and every town has a trailer park. Just take your pick," he imagined Roxy advising, sitting in the passenger seat and hooking a rug pattern of a frowning pug. "I know this sucks, kiddo. But your Nanna went through hell herself to find you and bring you back. Find another small town, buy some Just For Men, and go brunette for a while. But for God's sake, don't go blond. You'll look like your grandmother in drag."

What would you really say if I called you, Roxy? If I told you what was happening, and that I can't find anything funny about it. You'd certainly be at Nanna's house—you always claim it's for her own good—and vow to help me in private, while waving over my grandmother and writing down exactly where I am. The wheels in your head would be full tilt, figuring that you could cram in a car with Nanna with Mom and Dad and be in Little Rock by 2 a.m.

"I know how dangerous I am," is all I would have to say to you to stop your pacing. "I overheard you and Nanna, Roxy. I know."

You would feign ignorance, but you're a terrible liar. Even you would have no clever comeback when I explained how I eavesdropped on you and Nanna in the most raw of moments.

No one wanted Nanna to be alone with Grandpa Tom in those final days of hospice care. He'd been brought home from the hospital to spend his last days in his own bed. Of course we knew that Nanna wouldn't be alone, as Roxy had practically moved into the guest room, refusing to go home until she was thrown out.

It was after midnight. Grandpa had long since stopped speaking, having been given the powerful palliative sedative that eased cancer patients through their last moments, spoon-fed to him lovingly by his wife. No one knew how long he might live, so Aunt Stella had gone home with his parents and brothers, trying to figure out how to notify Aunt Kate when none of them had spoken to her in years. Roxy and I had kept a vigil with Nanna upstairs, sitting in the dim light while the clock ticked loudly. I'd dozed and I guess started to snore. Roxy told me to either go get some caffeine or she was going to put a clothespin on my nose.

I'd gone downstairs to make coffee and laid my head on the old farm table, and the next thing I knew, I woke to a stiff neck and the digital clock on the microwave reading 3 a.m., the coffee now cold. I trudged up the stairs, hearing their voices and quiet crying from where the door was slightly open. I'd reached for the handle when I heard Nanna say, "He was the only one who knew what we're capable of doing."

My hand had hovered. "Hon, don't go there just now. Give yourself a moment to just say goodbye," Roxy said, her own voice broken.

"I said my goodbyes to him a hundred times over the past few days. He'd become so sweet, you know, especially after he got sick. Death does that, the doctors said. It softens a person, knowing the end is near. I told him every hour how much I loved him, and apologized for everything I'd done all those years ago. All he would do is hold my hand and say how important it is that I keep up the work. Our work. Now that he's gone, I can't imagine doing it without him."

"Shhhh. Come on, now. Let's call hospice, and you need to tell the girls—"

"I need to tell them everything. Everything. And William deserves to know. What I can do. What he can do. What they did to us."

"Lynn, you still don't know what they did to you—"

"It's there. Inside me. Inside William. Even if we don't know what it is, I know what I read in those computer files and saw in those interviews. I know what I saw underneath the hospital, with all those people. What we're capable of doing. And once it comes—the pain, the bleeding in the ears—it means we're activated. Not long after, we'll die, and so will anyone near to us."

"Lynn, don't do this now. You know nothing has happened in fifteen years. You wouldn't have remained by your family if there was any hint that you were dangerous. No one's been activated or anything like that—"

"And William. He's different. He has it in him too. He's the conduit. I don't even know what that means, but he's the final stage; the trigger to activate all of us."

"This isn't the time. You're exhausted—"

"Tom kept telling me that it was important that we just lived our lives. That William knew he was loved. And he was right. . . ."

He could hear Roxy move in to comfort her. I'd stepped away from the door, feeling numb.

The binge that came next lasted a few days. Everyone thought I was just grief drinking. Maybe I was. Grief for my grandfather, and grief knowing I could be the one to ultimately cause the death of my own grandmother—

William realized his hands had stopped shaking. His body temperature had calmed. Funny thing about anxiety attacks—they kick your ass when they show up, but you don't notice when they've slipped out the back door. *Or maybe I've found a way to trump whatever disaster I've encountered at the moment by reminding myself that something even worse could be happening at any moment.*

"Is this is a pity party for one or are guests invited?" the imagined Roxy said, looking over her glasses at him.

Truth be told, I don't feel sorry for myself. I'm just angry. With the tabloid reporters, with my stupid and repeated mistakes, and with not knowing the truth after all this time.

After eavesdropping on Nanna and Roxy's conversation, and knowing his grandmother was in a deep stage of grief, William had stifled his nagging questions. He'd saved his frustrations for the blowout with his brothers after his drunken arrival at the funeral, a version of the same fight they'd had almost their entire lives. Greg had torn into him about his lack of respect. Brian then stepped up to the plate, calling him irresponsible, complaining how everyone coddled him. He even went so far as to say that if William hadn't run off into the woods that night he and Greg were camping, their lives would be completely different.

Then came the shoving and a toppled lamp, William chastising Brian for never taking his side, saying that his brother knew the truth too. Brian had seen the light, he'd seen what happened.

Brian had picked up the lamp and hurled it against the wall, asking how long he was supposed to feel guilty, that he had been just a kid too, who was completely traumatized about seeing his brother disappear in what seemed to be a bolt of lightning.

He'd held his index finger inches from William's face, saying how tired he was for feeling responsible for him, and that he needed to take ownership for his actions for once in his damn life.

William had told both his brothers to go to hell and jumped in his Jeep. He'd meant to drive to the suburb of Bellevue and the condo of a girl he'd casually dated—dating being a prim word for it. But instead he'd passed her exit and kept driving west.

He'd realized it, then—how the weight of the world slowly lifted from his shoulders with every mile. The farther away he drove, the more he understood that the anxiety had a message for him: Get the hell out of Dodge. It had plagued him for months: a nagging feeling to escape, to move on. It was bold and determined, starting with a whisper and then shouting that he was in the wrong place and needed to leave. He'd tried to ignore it, but once he succumbed, he was almost euphoric.

He'd practically leapt off the interstate when he'd reached Little Rock. *This is it*, every membrane of his body had hummed. *This is where you're meant to be.*

Even broke, with no job and no prospects, he'd felt the calmness. The sensation stayed with him, despite the longing for his family and living in a crappy trailer making minimum wage.

And who was he kidding? For the first time in his life, he was free. Free of speculation about what happened to him, free of the stares, free of the burden of being *that* UFO guy.

The nightmares, however, reminded him that some things you can't outrun. Whether it was guilt for abandoning his family or the troubling headlines of the day soaking into his subconscious, the dreams were inescapable. But at least—unlike the anxiety and panic attacks that were always waiting and could linger for an hour—when he woke, it was a clean cut. And he had a job to go to that filled up the days, and books and baseball at night.

Now that life was over.

I've done it once. I can do it again, he thought. He'd rest until first light. Once he got what he needed from the trailer, mostly the cash he'd kept hidden in his closet, he'd head further south, maybe to Louisiana. Especially with all the storms they've been experiencing, it would be easy to get lost in New Orleans.

William put his hands behind his head. If the dreams did come tonight, at least there would be no one to hear him scream.

She could hear the footsteps of the knockoff Allen Edmonds echoing loudly across the marble floors of the Dirksen Senate Office Building. She knew without a doubt that it was Frank, and that meant he would be wearing the cheap shoes, designed to look expensive but with thin soles that would wear out soon because he wore them every single day. Even when he stood on the other side of her desk, sliding across the latest research on human trafficking in Tennessee, she could smell his feet.

Frank sweated a lot in her presence.

Kate Roseworth hoped to have several hours alone, given that a looming budget battle in the upcoming fall session promised yet another government shutdown. Her secretary and staff, including Frank, had gone home some time ago, which meant she could play some Leon Bridges and try to focus without interruption. She'd actually made some serious headway and was on the trail of what seemed to be some common-sense budget cuts that would be appreciated by her constituents. Her calculator was deep into an equation when she heard the footsteps.

"Come in, Frank."

He could not hide the astonishment on his face that Kate had been able to identify him before he had even stepped inside. Her index finger diminished the volume just as Leon and his background singers were crooning into the first chorus of "River." When she looked up to see that his eyes had changed from surprised to full-on puppy dog, she sighed.

She knew the look and the variations of it. The interns were the worst, the ones who elbowed their way to try and score a semester or two working for Washington Barbie. It was her least favorite of all the nicknames they didn't think she knew about: Tennessee Tornado, Killer Kate and the Devil Wears Prada Pantsuits. Even with a master's in public policy from Brown, a career as a policy wonk in Washington, and now a decade of service as a US senator, she still heard the whispers about herself behind the backs of her colleagues' hands.

Kate knew how she appeared to Frank right now. Late night, sexy music, hair in a ponytail, glasses, and chewing on a pen. *Hot For Teacher*, she once found scrawled on a colleague's fiscal notes, with an arrow pointing in the direction of her desk in the senate chamber.

Yes, Frank, that's why I'm here so late. To seduce you. Come on over here and let's read through some budget appropriations to really turn up the heat.

"What is it, Frank?" she said, turning back to her calculator.

He cleared his throat. "They found him, Senator."

"Found who, Frank?"

"Your nephew."

She saw him visibly flinch when she blinked and looked over her laptop at him. She didn't mean to have *the look*; her mother always said it was a genetic trait she inherited from her father. It meant she gave a laser focus to whoever was speaking, her eyelids closing ever so slightly, with daggers glinting in her pupils.

"How do you know this?"

"Came across in an alert." He held up his iPhone.

She glanced at her own phone. "I don't see any alerts from the *Post* or CNN."

He swallowed. "It wasn't a news alert. It's from . . . Hollywoodextra."

The look changed now, and she saw him almost wince. That website had an almost criminal obsession with her family, frequently romantically linking her to actors and athletes, all of whom, in reality, requested meetings with her to discuss their environmental causes.

"Where is he? Is he OK?"

Please say he didn't get a DUI.

"Little Rock. They didn't say. It only read that they found him."

Please say he's not in jail.

"How? Did they source police?"

"No. It just reads that it's an exclusive. The alert said that the site would broadcast their findings at midnight."

Good to know that a high-priced private investigator couldn't find him, but some crap entertainment website could.

"I just knew you'd want to know," he said softly.

"Thank you Frank. I appreciate it. I'll handle it from here."

"Is there anything—?"

"I'll see you at seven. I'd go straight home, tomorrow will be a mess. No detour to the Blackfinn."

He nodded once and stepped out, barely concealing his disappointment. He was obviously giddy with excitement to gossip with the other staffers still at the bar. They'd lean in, ties loosened or hair let down after long days at the hill. *How did she react when you told her, Frank? Was she pissed?*

Yes, Kate thought, sitting back in her chair. She is pissed.

A familiar twist came from her stomach. *Do you know yet, Anne? I should call you, right now. He's your son, after all. I know you and Chris must have been agonizing this year, and Brian and Greg too. Once Mom finds out, she'll be so upset. Or is this just part of a plan—*

No. Keep your distance. That's the past. Focus on the present.

Her fingers toyed with the handle of her right-hand desk drawer. She pulled it open, fished around under a sea of pens, and found the business card, stashed where she'd put it a year ago, when she'd thrown the disgusting man out of her office.

She held up the card.

Flynn Hallow. Agent. Division of the FBI.

The rest of the FBI had no interest in locating the grandson of a deceased senator, who had vanished again, this time of his own accord.

As much as she hated it, she picked up the phone, quickly dialing the number. It was near midnight. There's a chance he'd be asleep—

"Hello?" came an extremely alert voice, full of phlegm, which immediately broke into a cough.

"This is Senator Kate Roseworth. I'm assuming you've heard the news?"

"Of course. We dispatched our agents as soon as it came out. It's good that you called—"

"It's actually not." She pivoted in her chair. "I don't want to be making this call. I don't want you to think I want anything at all to do with you. If this call is being recorded, I'll have you sued. Let me remind you we are a two-consent state. And I *do not* give my consent. But I think you know what this phone call means."

"I do."

"I want this contained. Do you understand? I don't want to see him on the news. I don't want to see my family interviewed. I don't want there to be a single dose of coverage beyond the fact that he was found. And more importantly, I want him safe. Can you absolutely guarantee to me that you can contain this and bring him in?"

"We will do our best, Senator."

"This is all off the books, Agent. Bring him in, and I'll meet with your director. But if you botch this, then all bets are off. I want him unharmed. I don't care if you have to scorch the earth around him, but I want my nephew brought to me."

THREE

William swerved the Jeep so hard to the right that dust and rock billowed like the aftermath of an explosion beneath his tires. He slammed the gear into park, placing one foot on the rusted metal step outside the absent door to stand, leaning on the frame of the Jeep. He could barely see above the rows of cotton.

"Oh shit," he muttered.

In the still dark hour of five a.m., he counted the lights of ten satellite trucks on the road before his trailer. Accompanying the massive white vans looked to be forty—no, fifty—cars. The top lights of the cameras revealed photographers lining the dirt road like paparazzi on a red carpet, along with a crowd of people, many holding signs. He watched as three vans more raised their masts.

William sunk back into his seat.

He pulled out the phone from his console and got online, grinding his teeth at the sparse Wi-Fi that meant the search bar moved at a crawl. Hollywoodextra, the reporter had called it, yet nothing came up for a television outlet. What did appear was a website.

He shook his head. Hollywoodextra.*com* is what she had actually said.

Everything in the media world has changed, his Aunt Stella had cautioned during her tutorials. TV will still wait and promote a story for days trying to build hype and ratings. But don't think a camera crew is just for television anymore. If a story is big enough, it becomes all about clicks. Get it verified and get it online, get it on Twitter, get it on the app. Don't waste a moment.

When the website loaded, it practically screamed the headline: "WORLD EXCLUSIVE: WILLIAM CHANCE'S SECRET LIFE IN ARKANSAS." At the top of the accompanying story was an icon revealing it had been shared six thousand times—

From around the bend of the field behind him came the sound of tires tearing down the dirt road. The doors of the Jeep were still stored inside the trailer, along with his hat. There was no way to conceal himself from whatever news crew was approaching.

He turned to his console, hunching completely over and pretending to look for something. *Please, please let that photographer not have gotten video of his Jeep for people to recognize it.*

He almost exhaled in relief as he heard the car fly past. But then rubber squealed, followed by an abrupt U-turn. William jammed his key into the ignition, but the car had already pulled up directly beside him at a sloppy angle. The only way to drive past now would be to barrel through the cotton or hit the car itself.

He expected the bright call letters of a local station on the side of the car, or perhaps a generic Honda rented from the airport. Instead, the sleek curve to the roof, along with the vent just above the back wheel, made it apparent that someone was driving a $200,000 Porsche on the back roads of Arkansas.

The driver-side window rolled down. "Are you freelance? I'm trying to find the house where that Chance kid is living . . . oh crap."

William fired up the Jeep, whipping his arm around the headrest of his passenger seat to back up.

"Wait, wait, I'm not a reporter!" The man threw open his door, squeezing through the narrow distance between their vehicles. It wasn't easy for him, his husky build revealed in the tightness of his custom-made suit. A brilliant red pocket square practically glowed in the faint morning light.

"I swear to God, I am not a reporter." For a big guy he moved fast, resting his hand on the soft top of the Jeep.

William clenched his jaw. He had to get in the trailer and grab the essentials and his stash of cash or he wouldn't be able to even afford the gas to get out of town.

"I hate the media, they're always on my ass too," the man continued.

He couldn't drive around the guy, and this was the closest he could get without being spotted. He looked over at the fields to his right and climbed over his stick shift, slipping out the opening on the other side.

"Hey William, seriously, I'm here to help. I'm a fan of your grandmother. I know she was telling the truth. The media can be a real pain, I know all about it. I'll show you how to get past them—"

"I know how," William said, jogging into the nearest row of cotton.

"Dude, these shoes are Italian leather! I'll bust my pants trying to keep up if you're gonna run like that!"

Exactly.

There was no doubt who the guy was, or at least which camp he fell into. The ones who sent his family bushels of letters; showed up at his high school soccer games, taking selfies as he walked by; stopped him in grocery stores and whispered, "I believe too."

They were the same people now standing outside the trailer with homemade cardboard signs. If history repeated itself, many would be teenage girls, raised on a steady diet of his pictures in memes.

"You're basically a reality star who doesn't have a reality show or any discernable talents," his brothers liked to joke. "Famous for being famous."

He almost halted at the realization that Brian and Greg could be in the crowd, maybe even with their parents. All would be in the van with tinted windows they bought years ago, baseball caps pulled low, so as not to be recognized themselves. At the first sign of him, they'd practically burst into the trailer, regardless of how the media would swarm around them.

They wouldn't bring Nanna and Roxy, though, as much as they'd want to come. That would be the equivalent of pouring gasoline on what promised to be a media dumpster fire.

Please let his family either be disconnected or completely unaware. Even if they wake up to the news, it was still at least a five-hour drive from Nashville. He had to get in, get out, and be long gone before they would arrive.

He rushed at a crouch. The cotton stretched to six feet, but he could still clear it with his height. He started moving through the rows, doing his best not to make the stalks completely shake. It was not out of the question to suspect that drones would be launched at daylight. He once opened his dorm room window only to hear the buzzing of a tricopter hovering outside.

It meant passing through row after row, holding the shafts to keep them from quivering too much, even if it meant scrapes from the bolls.

He finally emerged at the edge of the yard, where he could see the frame of the trailer outlined by the lights of the cameras. The farmer from whom he rented the place dumped it among the crops intentionally; he'd told his wife he needed a place for him and his workers to cool off in the worst of the summer heat. In reality, he'd moved his girlfriend in for lunchtime visits, until his wife one day showed up with Chinese takeout. Needing to make some extra money to pay alimony, he'd advertised for a renter.

The photographers' lights were focused on the front of the trailer, leaving enough darkness in the back for him to slip through to reach the back door.

William fumbled with his keys, thankful for the landlord's lack of interest in providing security or outdoor lighting.

He quietly closed the door and turned around to see a small shape sitting on the couch.

The lights from outside, set on stands to brighten the faces of the reporters preparing for the morning news, shone through the blinds to reveal a girl, her legs barely touching the floor. Her hair was done up in braids with white hair ties.

William gaped for a second. "How did you get in here?"

"Mr. Chance, please forgive the intrusion."

He jumped at the woman's voice. She stood up from where she was sitting on the edge of one of his mismatched chairs, thick round glasses pushed up to contain a mane of curly hair, wearing a dark vest with some kind of emblem. "I am so sorry to bust in here like this. I cannot get her to leave. For a little girl who has barely made a peep in the last twenty-four hours, she's a stubborn one. When we pulled up down the street just a few minutes ago, she got out and ran through the fields. I could barely keep up. She just walked around the back and let herself in. Lily said she could find you, and she was right."

He wanted to pound himself on the forehead. In his haste to leave last night, he'd never locked the back door.

"I don't know who you people are, but you've got to get out of here," he said.

The girl stared at him without blinking, the whites of her eyes contrasting sharply to her dark black skin. She wore shorts and a T-shirt with a cat on the front and the word "cool" written above it.

"Again, I am so sorry," the woman continued. "We wanted to call you but there was no number—"

William moved past her. "You've got to go."

"I'm Lois Jumper." She followed him down the hall. "That's Lily in your living room. I'm an agent with the Investigative Services Branch of the National Park Service—"

"Lady, I'm going to need you not to follow me," William said as he entered his bedroom, closing the door.

"I know this is unorthodox, it certainly is for us," she said through the door. "But you have to understand. Rangers found that girl in the middle of the national park in North Dakota less than two days ago. Mr. Chance, we have no idea where she came from. She barely speaks. It's like she just appeared out of nowhere."

He'd heard so many stories like this over the years. People at Target, in the line at Bobbie's Dairy Dip, in the beer garden at M.L. Rose. People with fantastical or bizarre stories, from sharks with two heads to the Taos Hum. The worst was always the stories about a missing loved one. *Do you think it's aliens?*

His mother would always respond like an angry lioness, all five foot two of her. *Please don't*, she would intervene. *Please don't bother my son.*

He'd had his own disastrous exchanges, especially when people insulted his family. Once some frat guy at a bar had pointed his finger at his brother Brian, slurring, "Aren't you the one who stopped talking for like a year? You missed the aliens by *this much*." William had hit him squarely in the jaw, and Brian had yanked him out before police had been called.

"You have to leave. Please," William called out. He stuffed some jeans and T-shirts into a backpack and reached under the bed to pull out the wad of cash he kept stashed in a plastic bag.

"Mr. Chance, Lily has barely spoken beyond saying her first name. We've tried to figure out where she came from. When I took her to my office, she was given a phone to play a game while we began our investigation, and she suddenly started talking. She showed us the alert about your appearance and kept saying, 'He knows, he knows.' Over and over. She said she could find you. Given the seriousness of this, I got the authority to fly us here on a red-eye. Sir, you've got to understand that you're our only hope at this point. And there's more. I don't know if you're following what's happening in North Dakota—"

William slid the bag onto his back and opened the door, breezing past her. "Lady, I've never seen that girl in my life—"

He almost ran into the girl, who was standing at the end of the hallway.

"Excuse me," William said, moving around her and heading for the door.

"Mr. Chance, please. She can describe you with incredible detail. She knew how to get into this trailer. We need to understand what she's talking about. She won't elaborate, but indicates you know her—"

"Lady!" William turned around to find the girl now standing just two feet behind him. "I cannot help you. I have no explanation for you. You are breaking and entering, and I could call the cops."

"I am a cop, Mr. Chance. I'm a federal criminal investigator, and right now, you're our only lead in the case of a little girl found in the middle of an empty canyon that happens to be the center of a major disaster—"

"I wish I could help. I've never been to North Dakota, and I've never seen her before. And unless you've got a warrant, you can't be in here."

Lois hustled towards him as he opened the door. "She also keeps repeating the same thing over and over that troubles us even more. Mr. Chance, please don't make me use my arrest privileges—"

"I come from a long line of lawyers, ma'am," he said, stepping out. "I know what it takes to make an arrest, and you don't have it. . . ."

His words choked in his throat. On the far eastern corner of the yard, a group of shapes began to step out from the cotton.

Crap. People are starting to sneak around through the fields.

"This is private property!" he called out, sprinting down the stairs. "You're trespassing!"

"Mr. Chance, stop!" Lois ordered.

Another voice, deeper and definitely male, yelled his name.

This is now completely out of control, he thought as he leapt through the cotton. At least the emerging crowd was coming from the east and the Jeep was parked beyond the western edge of the fields.

You can get to the Jeep. You can get to the Jeep.

He ran, heedless of trying to pass through undetected. Halfway through the fifth row he heard the sound of someone following behind and hissing through their teeth at the pain.

He turned to the little girl, pulling one of the hard bracts from a cotton boll off her shirt.

"Lily!" he heard a call from several rows back.

"No!" William held up his hand. "Kid, stop right now. You're gonna hurt yourself. I can't help you, OK? You've got to stop."

He took off running down the row, still hearing little feet coming after him. He tore through a cluster of cotton to head down another dirt path, zigzagging back and forth.

After a wicked scrape on his arm, he stuck to a single row and headed for the road, emerging still too far from the Jeep. Knowing he'd be too exposed to just run out in the open, he stepped back into the row, only to find the girl and the woman emerging from the cotton.

"Get out of here," William said, now seeing lights flashing in the fields as the people from the yard tried to follow, obviously trying to get video or photos on their phones. "Just please leave me alone."

"Mr. Chance, this girl obviously knows you," Lois said, trying to catch her breath. "I'm going to have to take you into custody—"

He practically sprung through another row, the dried bristles snagging so fiercely, he knew his T-shirt would be ripped. He again heard the girl behind him and Lois yelling at them both to stop.

Go five more rows. Four. Three. Two. He had to be close enough now to make a run for the Jeep.

When he busted down the row and broke from the field, the man in the expensive suit was still leaning on his Porsche.

"Hey William, seriously, give me a second—"

Ignoring him, William reached the Jeep. He was about to toss his backpack in when he saw the girl climb into his open passenger side, looking at him in desperation. Before he could speak, Lois gasped in exasperation, stumbling to catch up.

"Mr. Chance, get that girl out of your car—"

The hissing sound came just as the Jeep shuddered, then slowly began to sink on the back. A pop, a series of dings, and the front of the jeep too began to lower as well. Even in the dark, William knew his tires were rapidly deflating.

He scrambled to inspect when he saw Lois fall to her knees and then thud to the ground.

"Hey," he said, sliding over to her. "Hey, lady. Are you OK?"

The answer was revealed in the headlights of the Porsche that shone on the blood gurgling from the wound in her neck. Her eyes were unblinking.

"My God," he whispered. He knew he should apply pressure to her wound to stop the flow, but it was horribly clear that she wasn't breathing.

He looked up to the deflated tire beside her. There were three bullet holes in the corner panel not far from where the girl had jumped in.

"No," he said. "Kid! Are you alright—?"

She immediately climbed out, apparently unharmed, staring at the dead body of the agent.

"Mr. Chance."

At the edge of the cotton, a man now stood, a pistol still pointed in their direction. From the rows came more people, all with weapons raised.

"Mr. Chance. I need you to remain calm. This is a dangerous situation and we need to get you out of here," the man said.

"What the hell is going on?" the Porsche driver called out from where he was crouched by his car. "Seriously, what the—"

"Mr. Chance, for your own safety, you need to come with us. Now," the man continued.

"Did you shoot that woman? She's a federal agent!" William bellowed. "What the hell are you doing?"

The cotton behind them began to shiver and then sway. In an ever-increasing wind, lights from the center of the field flickered on, and the unmistakable sound of helicopter blades whirred in the near distance.

"Now, Mr. Chance," the man said. "We are here to protect you."

"You need to put that gun down," William said.

Instead, the man took a step forward, brandishing his barrel towards him. "Let's go. We need you to come with us now—"

His words ended in a choke.

With a surprised look on his face, he clutched his throat. As he began to violently shake, he dropped his pistol, collapsing to the ground. As if on cue, the others shapes began to gasp as well, reaching up for their throats, falling one by one.

"Holy shit," the driver of the Porsche said, sliding around his car to climb in. "Holy shit!"

Two of the last men standing began to shoot as they fell. William raised his arm towards the girl to cover her, but shuddered to a halt when he saw her face.

Lily's chin was raised, her eyes had narrowed in rage. Her hands were tight fists, her arms like trembling sticks, and she was staring hard at the two men remaining standing. Only when their bodies hit the ground did she flinch, her expression changing from fury to astonishment.

The winds from the approaching helicopter began to tear at their faces and clothes. William jerked back to the field, seeing once again the flashing lights approaching.

Those aren't phones. Those are scopes on guns.

The Porsche's engine roared through the night. Clearly with one foot on the gas and the other on the brake, the driver rolled down his window, "Get in! Get in, William!"

William's hands rose to the back of his head, frantically looking from the series of unmoving bodies to the dead woman lying at his feet. For a moment, he thought he was caught up in another horrible nightmare.

Wake up! Wake up!

The approaching helicopter above the thrashing cotton was a slap of reality. With more lights approaching and his Jeep slumped to the dirt, he scrambled towards the car. He reached the door and threw it open, almost stepping in.

He then stopped, turned around and ran back.

"What the hell! Dude, I'm not waiting!"

William stumbled around the Jeep, seeing the girl in what appeared to be a state of shock. He snatched her up, carrying her in his arms just as more people emerged. He quickly glanced back, fearing they would start firing. Instead, they began to drag the unmoving bodies into the rows.

Wait, are they all wearing suits?

"Come on!" the man yelled through the Porsche's window.

One of the men, who had seized Lois' body and begun to pull her into the field, looked in their direction.

William ran for the backseat and slid in, the girl holding tight to his neck.

"Go!" he shouted.

"No way man, not with that kid—"

"Do you want to get shot too?"

The driver's response was a collection of curses as he let his foot off the brake and slammed the pedal to the floor.

FOUR

"Lynn."

Her first reaction was not to respond to Roxy's voice but instead to reach over to the phone on the nightstand. Her friend's tone beyond the door was the first signal flare, which became more alarming when Lynn realized she'd accidentally set her phone facedown, meaning there had been no flash on her screen to jar her from sleep. As she slipped on her glasses and saw the multiple, brightly colored alerts, her stomach dropped.

The words from the local NBC station alert came into focus. "DISTUR-BANCE AT WILLIAM CHANCE'S ARKANSAS HOME."

"Lynn?"

"I'm reading it now," she said, pressing the link.

"You need to turn on the TV," Roxy said, opening the door. "And turn on the damn light, who knows where you tossed your shoes for me to trip on. Where's the remote?"

Lynn barely heard her words, frantically reading the article.

"Arkansas? He's in Arkansas? All this time?"

"Seriously, I can't see a damn thing. Brace yourself, I'm hitting the lights. Jesus, what's the wattage on these bulbs? I'm practically blind now. OK, there's the remote. I'm opening up the cabinet. You need to see this."

"When did this come out?" Lynn slid out from her covers, still reading.

"I know I look so beautiful that you're surprised to know I just woke up too. I just saw it myself when my usual five a.m. internal clock began its usual punishment. It's the top story on all the early morning news shows. I came up as soon as I saw it. Best stay sitting down."

Lynn remained standing as the TV flared. "Is he OK?"

"I don't know," Roxy said, coming to stand beside her.

The concerned expression of the news anchor spoke volumes.

". . . we're still gathering information from the scene, so it's unclear exactly what happened."

"But clearly something has," noted the anchor's male counterpart.

"Thank you, Captain Obvious," Roxy muttered.

"It's now 5:15," the female anchor continued. "And if you're just now joining us, we're continuing to monitor the situation in Little Rock, Arkansas, where there are reports of some kind of disturbance outside the mobile home that local media are reporting is the home of William Chance."

A photo of William, taken from a distance during Tom's funeral, then flashed across the scene alongside a live feed of a trailer lit up like a Christmas tree by the lights of the news crews. "Chance is, of course, the grandson of the late Senator Tom Roseworth. As a boy, Chance went missing fifteen years ago and was discovered by his grandmother under what government officials now describe as questionable circumstances."

"There's no question that they're assholes," Roxy added.

The male anchor jumped in. "We want to remind you that none of what is coming from that location in rural Arkansas has been confirmed by local police. This is all from the journalists stationed on the road in front of the trailer, who reported hearing what they thought were gunshots far behind in the field. The Associated Press is now reporting that police have yet to respond, as Chance has never been reported as a missing person. In fact, there have been no sightings of Chance himself this morning. The only confirmation that he was ever in the home was from video from an entertainment website that shows him inside the trailer last evening—"

"Of all the nights to have my phone turned over!" Lynn said.

"You were exhausted last night. It's my fault. I kept you up too late with questions, and you got all worked up and insisted on vacuuming the guest room for me even though there's not a speck of dirt—"

Her cell phone rang, causing them both to jump. "It's Anne," Lynn said. She pressed the speaker icon.

"Mom? Are you watching?" It was clear her oldest daughter was on Bluetooth.

"I just saw it. Are you in the car?"

"Me and Chris are headed to Arkansas right now. Brian is driving over to Greg's to pick him up, and then they're coming too."

"It's best that you stay behind, Lynn," Chris chimed in. "And Roxy too, once she finds out."

"Too late, she already knows," Roxy practically shouted.

"She spent the night," Lynn explained, motioning for Roxy that she didn't have to yell.

"Screw that, Chris. We're on our way as soon as we throw on some clothes," Roxy said, heading for the door.

"No," Anne's husband ordered. "It already looks like a circus there. If you two show up, we'll have no chance of slipping by to try and get to him. Plus, neither of you should be driving in the dark."

"We're old, not blind," Roxy said.

"Mom, can you stay by the TV? The reports on the radio are sporadic and the live streams on the apps are hit and miss," Anne said. "I need you to call me as soon as anything new comes on. Can you do that, Mom?"

"I will."

"Lynn, if you have heard anything from William recently, this is the time to come clean," Chris said.

"You know I would have told you, Chris, if I had."

"Mom?" Anne's voice broke into a higher pitch. "Do you think he's alright? Why would he be there? In Arkansas, of all places? All this time, he's been that close and never told us. And why are the reporters there saying they heard gunshots?"

"I don't know. But y'all just be safe. I know you're all going to speed, especially Brian and Greg, but it doesn't do this family any good if there's an accident on the way to try and find him. You need to call Stella. Tell her what's going on. I promise to stay right here and keep watching. I will call the second there's an update."

"Don't think about getting in the car, Roxy," Chris yelled before hanging up.

"He knows I'm just a faster driver than he is." Roxy waved her hand as Lynn ended the call. "I'll go make the coffee."

She paused, looking out the window towards the trees lost in the dark. "Is there a reason this is all happening at the same time? Do you think they're still out there? The ladybugs?"

"We will see at daybreak. I need to call Don and Barbara. They need to know. William needs to know. I may be forced to remain in front of this TV, but I'll be damned if I'll sit here and do nothing."

"What the hell just happened?"

With the girl clinging to his neck so fiercely it was starting to hurt, William strained to look back.

"Seriously, what the hell?" the driver of the Porsche yelled again. "One minute I'm twiddling my thumbs waiting for you to come back, and the next thing I know you're running out with a freakin' parade behind you and people start dying—"

"Can you just keep driving?" William said, prying the girl off. She let go but immediately sat directly beside him.

Here it comes. He knew his fair skin was already a flushed red. His chest was constricting, his fingertips tingling.

When the attack comes on, recognize it for what it is, observe it like you're watching it happen to someone else, his therapist advised. That detachment will help you stay calm and realize whatever's happened isn't that bad—

Oh, it's bad, doc. There's a dead federal agent back there, killed by people who stepped out of the fields and blew out my tires. And it sure as hell looked like when that little girl stared at them, they started to die.

"And who were those people with the guns? I mean—wait. Wait a second. Wait a damn second! They were wearing suits! Black suits! Crap on a stick, that was my proof! Why the hell didn't I get out my phone?" the driver said, thumping the steering wheel.

Breathe in, breathe out. Long, deliberate breaths. Block out everything. It will pass. Focus on what you can control—

"Man, I needed that video! If I hadn't hauled ass from Atlanta, I would have totally missed it!"

Missed it. We wouldn't miss that turn if I were driving—

"Turn left!"

The Porsche swung hard, barely avoiding another row of cotton to head down the intersecting road. "Dude!"

"Pull over and let me drive," William said.

"A bit more heads up next time, OK? Man, I'm going to be kicking myself for a long time that I didn't get that video. Of course, I also didn't want a bullet in my butt either. So what's the story? Have they been after you for a while now? Is that why you've been on the run?"

"Pull over right there. I know these roads. I need to drive."

"Buddy, this is a 2019 Porsche 911 Turbo. I'm not happy that it probably has a few dings on it—"

William leaned forward and pointed. "If you don't pull over right now, I'm going to puke all over your back seat."

"Jesus, fine! OK! Hold it in, Linda Blair."

Taking a long deep breath as the Porsche came to a sudden stop, William looked down at the girl. "Are you OK?"

She just turned to him, her eyes wide. *Is she in shock? Did I just see you do what I thought you did?*

"We'll get you someplace safe," William said, opening the door. The girl made a small whining sound and clamored after him. "You've gotta sit back here. Put on your seatbelt."

He stepped out as the driver hustled around the hood, pointing to the back seat. "We've got to ditch that kid and get to the airport pronto. I called the Cessna on the way here. I can get us out of here fast."

William began to slide in the driver's seat when he looked over the field, seeing the helicopter hovering over the section where the Jeep was stranded. He jumped in, his foot on the brake, throwing the gear into drive.

"Whoa, dude! Gotta wait till I'm in the car! You can adjust the seat, OK, looks like you've got that handled. I guess you think they're still coming for you?"

The car tore down the road, William glancing in the rearview mirror.

"I'm guessing by your expression that even you don't know exactly who they are, right? I knew it, I knew it, I knew that's why you've been hiding. Am I right? It's all real. It is all real! And I saw it! Why did I not get out my phone? Me, the king of phones, and I didn't even think to whip it out—"

"Were you joking that you have a plane at the airport?"

I can lose you there. Leave the girl outside in a crowd.

"No joke. You know I'm good for it."

William looked in the rearview mirror again, catching a glimpse of Lily's worried face. "How would I know that?"

"Well, at least there's one person in America who doesn't know who I am, no thanks to the photographers at LAX. Quincy Martin, Mr. Chance.

Hey, what we saw back there is just another example of what the government can do, am I right? If they can pull off Roswell, they can cover this up easy. So what the hell happened? Why did they shoot that lady? I saw them dragging those bodies. Damn! Hiding your shot-up Jeep will be harder though, especially if the newsies get video of it—"

The man spoke like a machine gun, becoming more animated by the second. *Mom and Dad will hear about the Jeep. They'll panic. So will Nanna. I have to find a way to tell them that I'm not hurt.*

He swallowed the bile in his throat, thinking of the dead woman. She could have a family too—

"We've got to ditch that kid, whoever she is. Once we get to the airport, she's out. I told my board I came here to make a business deal, but there's a whole lot more I've been wanting to talk to you about. We shouldn't be too far, right?" Quincy held up his phone to look at the map on the screen. "Yeah, yeah. Left here—whoa, son. Can't off-road in a Porsche. Ok, then we take this to that crappy frontage road. Then interstate, then airport—"

"Call 911," William ordered.

"Listen, think about that—"

"A woman was shot and killed back there, and we saw them drag her body into the fields. Call the police."

"Hey. Don't you get it? We need to get out of here. *They will cover this up.* They'll come up with some kind of story that you shot up your own Jeep, and given my personal history, they'll drag me into it, and how we staged it all for publicity. We'll be discredited, just like your grandma was. . . ."

William's temples pounded. *If my family is waiting outside the trailer, I can't risk them being anywhere near this. So follow me all you want, you bastards. I'll drop off this girl and this crackpot somewhere safe, and you can chase me to the ends of the earth. But stay away from my family.*

He looked over his shoulder and, as if right on cue, saw a helicopter in the distance do a complete 180 and head in their direction. As it flew over the center of the field, another quickly rose from the cotton to hover and turn towards them as well.

"Don't sweat that," Quincy said. "It's not like this is an LA car chase. I doubt those TV helicopters are broadcasting this live."

William looked back and forth from the road to the black helicopters, vacant of any of the bright call letters he'd seen on media vehicles his entire life.

"I don't think those are from television."

"Aw, man, you're right!" Quincy whipped out his phone, shifting his weight to extend his arm over Lily to the back window. "I've paid more money than I care to admit to try to prove they exist. And it's happening right now! Smile boys!"

"Use the phone to call police, not to record video!"

"Screw that man. I came to make a deal. I never expected to get to see proof of the freakin' Men in Black! But there they are! It's still so dark everyone on the ground will think they're just cops."

They aren't cops. Cops don't kill federal agents. Cops don't drag bodies into fields.

All his life he'd heard the whispers. Had he and his grandmother been brainwashed by crazy conspiracy theorists? Or had some shadow government, in the form of men in black suits, really had him all that time?

He took another hard right to speed down Ripper Road. As they drove, William could see the media trucks still camped out around the trailer. While most remained unmoving, a single set of headlights barreled away from the horde towards them. Had one of the photographers caught on to what had happened?

"Lily," William said. "Just hang on. I need people to know what happened to the woman who brought you here. Can you get into my backpack and get out my phone?"

"Dude, think long and hard about that one," Quincy warned, trying to focus his phone.

William heard Lily fumble with the backpack on the floor, and a small hand squeezed past Quincy's considerable stomach to deliver the cheap phone. William whispered a quick thanks and held it up, only to realize it was dead.

He reached back and snatched the phone out of Quincy's hand.

"Hey, man!"

William tried to navigate the complicated screen. He'd never seen anything like it. It looked more of a tablet, with 3-D apps and several buttons on the sides.

"Careful with that, it's a prototype," Quincy said. "And don't lose my video!"

"I just need to know how to make a call."

"The icon is right there—the blinking app of the voice box. You're gonna regret that 911 call. There's going to be a recording of your voice that's broadcast on every TV station and website in the world."

Let there be a damn record of what I saw.

William dialed the three digits and immediately got a busy signal. He tried again, with the same result.

"Am I dialing this right? It's just busy."

"That phone has the latest hologram software that's not even available anywhere yet. So yeah, it can make a call."

"It's constantly busy."

"Are we too deep in the sticks? We're on a frontage road. It shouldn't be a problem. Look, it has bars. Maybe it's a sign. . . ."

William dialed again and the busy sound responded. "How can that be? I can even make a call from my crap phone at my house."

"Sorry son. Damn, that helicopter is close now! Give it back. I'm getting more video."

William let him take it, seeing the exit ramp to the interstate quickly approaching. The rearview mirror showed headlights coming up fast behind them. The height and spacing of the lights suggested the news crew was in a van.

He pulled onto the exit, watching as the helicopter continued to trail them. There was nothing coming over a loudspeaker with commands to stop. *That's what police would be doing right now.*

"Who the hell is that behind us?" Quincy asked. "They're getting so close they're gonna block my shot."

"They came from the trailer."

"Well, reporters can't follow us where we're going. You're heading to the airport, right? If you can call that Tinkertoy setup an airport."

And you're getting shoved out of the car at the terminal, and Lily will be dropped off in the closest crowd. Then I'm gone.

"The Cessna is parked on the private strips. Don't go to the main terminal. You know where the private planes land, right?"

No. I don't fly in private jets. This guy is a perfect addition to this crapshow of a twenty-four hours. You'll have to walk to your jet, if it even exists, from where I dump you off—

Wait. The reporters in that van. The news crew won't leave a kid stranded on the road.

"I think I've seen a sign for a private strip near the airport," William said. *Keep thinking that's where we're headed. I need this car.*

"OK. I know there's a basically an AH-64 Apache on our ass, but we need a McDonald's in the worst way to drop her off. She is not part of this deal."

"There is no deal," William snapped.

"I don't know what happened back there, but I am seriously freaked out. Drop her off and she can order a Big Mac and call her parents."

"I don't know . . ." William looked to the back seat and Lily's frightened face. His voice quieted. "I don't know if she even has parents."

"I get it. You're sensitive to kids in peril. But she scares the hell out of me. Hey, the airport is coming up. Once we get there, we're out of here."

"I see it," William said, seeing the one-mile sign for the airport. *But I'll be leaving here solo.*

He'd have to act fast once they got off at the exit. There would be a sudden stop at the entrance road to the airport, and if he was lucky, the helicopter would have to circle around and buy him a few seconds.

He'd walk out and wave the reporters over. Quincy would get out in frustration, and William would help Lily out of the back seat. Once they were away from the car, he could sprint back and be gone fast—

"Hey asshole, we see you! Back off!" Quincy yelled, motioning to a large gray van that had pulled up alongside them. William realized that the headlights in the rearview mirror were gone, and the van had moved into the other lane.

The window rolled down. Even in the dim light, it was clear the van was several decades old. A bald man was waving frantically, motioning them to get off the road.

"You sure can attract them," Quincy said. "You're like a crazy magnet."

William rubbed his forehead as he exited the interstate. The Porsche's engine easily allowed him to shoot past the van. So much for ditching them with surprised reporters.

"They're freelancers, probably. Or just another nutso just wanting an autograph," Quincy said. "Hey, the helicopter is pulling back. They know they can't fly in this restricted airspace."

Look for a bus stop. Get him out of this car. Then find a place for Lily. Move. Move. Who knows how long the helicopter will hold off—

"Hey, turn left. That sign points to the private airstrip. I'll call and tell them we're coming."

It's not even six in the morning. He could dump Quincy there easily.

"Crap. I can't make a call either. Must be my phone. Good thing I paid two million for the patent. But my guys know to be waiting for us. My security team is there too, just in case crazy town in the van decides to try and join the party. And that's one thing a helicopter can't keep up with: a jet."

"Is there private security at the gate?" *Drop them off there and throw it in reverse.*

"That's why you fly private. No one to ask any questions. OK, there's an open gate. Nice. Ok, see it? See it there? It's got the big Q on it. That's it."

William did a double take. There, sitting among a few smaller planes on the mostly barren runway, was an enormous Cessna with a giant "Q" painted on its side in a bold red swirl.

"Who the hell are you?" William asked.

The man in the passenger seat grinned. "Just a man who believes, Mr. Chance."

Drive up, act like you're getting out, and once he's out of the car, drive away. You can find another place to leave Lily.

"And as I expected," Quincy said, looking over his shoulder. "Creeper Van is following us in. So just pull up right to the plane and get inside as fast as you can. I'd call my security again, but obviously my deep financial investment in this certain model of phone has a major flaw. But don't think this isn't worth your time, I'll get the bugs worked out. You'll want to be on board for this new model. Wait till you see what it can do. Just so you know, I'm packing, but it's just a pistol. Once my guys see me whip it out, they'll do the same. No one in that van will think about stopping . . . wait . . . wait . . ."

"What is it?" William asked, hearing the change in Quincy's voice.

As they drove up to the Cessna, they saw men standing on the stairs leading to the door.

"My guys don't wear suits," Quincy said.

As William slammed on the brakes, the men began to run in their direction.

"They're on my damn plane!"

William saw it, then: the landing skids of a helicopter on the other side.

"Turn around, turn around!" Quincy yelled.

William attempted a U-turn as the now-familiar sound of whizzing and popping resounded outside the car. The Porsche lurched perilously to one side.

"Drive on the rims if you have to!" Quincy yelled.

William grabbed the back of Quincy's headrest to back up, only to slam on the brakes.

"What are you doing—" Quincy began.

Through the rear window William could see another black helicopter landing, its tail blocking the entrance through the gate.

"Oh shit," he whispered.

The gray van, which had obviously hesitated as the men in suits rushed from the plane, now bounded across the pavement to drive up directly beside the Porsche.

The passenger side door opened, and a man wearing a ski mask jumped out, carrying a long rifle.

"Aw, come on!" Quincy said, fumbling for his glove compartment. "Who is that?"

The man in the mask yanked William's door open, motioning with the barrel. "Unless you want to disappear forever, move your ass. Get in the van."

"What the hell is this?" William asked. Through the windshield, he could see the men in suits were now halfway between the plane and the van.

"Now!" the man yelled, prodding him in the shoulder.

"OK, OK," William held up his hands, sliding out. Lily scrambled across her seat and opened her door.

"Lily, don't—"

"Everyone get out of the damn car!" the man yelled. "And drop the pistol, sir. It won't do you much good against a semiautomatic."

"Screw you, man," Quincy yelled. "I'm not—"

Another man wearing a Richard Nixon mask had jumped out of the van's side door, brandishing a revolver and running around the back of the Porsche.

"Whoa, whoa!" Quincy pointed at the plane. "I've got armed security right in that plane—"

"If you haven't figured it out, your security is worth crap now." The man in the Nixon mask yanked open Quincy's door.

William stepped out and Lily immediately embraced him at the waist. "Lily, get back in the car—"

The ski-masked man pushed them towards the open door of the van. "Get inside!"

"Put your hands up and drop your weapons!" a voice from a bullhorn echoed through the air.

The men in suits had stopped, their pistols aimed. "I repeat: Put your hands up where we can see them and drop those guns, or we will have no choice but to open fire. . . ."

The voice began trailing off.

William realized the girl's arms were no longer wrapped around him.

As in the cotton field, the men began to fall, one by one. With one hand still clutching his pant leg, Lily had raised her other and pointed. As she swiped across them, the men violently shook and crumbled.

"Holy Mary, Mother of God," the man in the ski mask said.

For a moment they stood in stunned silence between the incapacitated Porsche and the van, staring at the unmoving bodies littering the airstrip.

"Let's go!" yelled a female voice from inside.

"Move," the ski masked man said. "Move, now!"

He practically shoved William inside but made no move towards Lily. She scampered after in a daze, still holding on to William. The other masked man used his pistol to move Quincy quickly in as well. As they fumbled into the seats, the door slammed shut.

"What just happened out there?" a woman yelled from the driver's seat.

"Just go! Go!" Even muffled by the ski mask, the man's voice was clearly rattled.

"Go where?" She was looking back, her mouth covered by a bandana. "The gate is blocked!"

"Ram it. Don't let them shoot the tires!"

"Do not ram anything!" Quincy said, his hand bracing himself as the van began to spin around. "Whatever you want, I'll pay it. Just stop and let us out—"

"Shut the hell up!" the ski-masked man said, pointing the rifle inches from Quincy's face. "Go! Go!"

William leaned over to look out the windshield as the van wildly swerved, a pinging sound cutting through the air.

"Get down!"

The bullets then suddenly stopped as the van headed directly for the helicopter's tail. The men in suits that had piled out were now scrambling away.

The van made a horrible crunching sound as they smashed into the tail, the helicopter blades still whirling above. The rotor blade came dangerously close to slicing into the roof.

The woman gunned the engine, continuing to push the helicopter. As soon as it had moved far enough, she spun the wheel, and propelled the van forward through the open gate.

"Don't stop!" the ski-masked man yelled, sliding down the aisle to the back. The back doors of the van flew open, and William watched as he scrambled with something in a metal box and threw it out.

The chain flew out wildly into the air and crashed onto the road. "Hope your tires like that, you fuckers," William heard him say.

Quincy jammed his hand into his suit coat pocket. "Name your price. Whatever you want, I will pay. Just let us go."

"Please shut up," the man in the Nixon man said, pointing his pistol at him. "And get your hand out where I can see it."

The woman called out from the front. "Rudd, are we heading—"

"You know where to go, Neve. Anyone trailing us yet?" The man pulled off the ski mask, revealing the face William had seen frantically waving at them to pull over on the interstate.

"Not yet. But Rudd, what the hell . . ."

"Plan B. We go to Plan B right now," he said.

"Already there," the man in the Nixon mask said, pulling out a metal box from under the seat. From inside, he brought out plastic bags and threw one to the bald man in the back.

Taking off the Nixon mask, he fumbled with the bag in his hand. For a moment, William saw a flash of a vial and some thin plastic tubes.

"Wait," William began. "What are you—?"

The man spun around with such speed that he had the needle in Lily's leg before William could block him. She gasped in pain.

William leapt forward, grabbing the man's arm. He ripped the syringe from the man's hand just as he felt a needle slide into his own arm, followed by a swirl of hot pain.

William swung back, hitting the bald man who had come up from behind. The world immediately began to fade.

"What . . ." William's voice slurred.

"What the hell are you doing?" he heard Quincy yell.

"Don't . . . hurt . . ." William fell to the floor.

"Not to worry, Mr. Chance." The man who once wore with the Nixon mask leaned down, patting his cheek roughly. "Your grandmother gave specific orders."

FIVE

The rain splintered the view outside the window of the town car, blurring the beginnings and endings of the warehouses. Developers had salivated over the district along the Potomac for years, dreaming of demolishing the old buildings and slamming shiny condos in their place. Yet the industrial stain along the river remained, the owners clutching to their decades-old property deeds that promised sales that would one day pay for beach houses along the Gulf Coast. In cash.

I'll give them this, Kate thought: It's a hell of a place to hide.

She tapped her fingers on the armrest, her other hand holding her iPhone, frantically scrolling through her news feed.

"BREAKING: Jeep belonging to William Chance found near home in Little Rock, tires shot out."

"DEVELOPING: Maintenance crew outside private landing strip at Clinton National Airport report hearing gunfire."

"TIMELINE: What we know at this hour about the discovery of William Chance—"

Kate leaned forward. "Is it much farther?"

"We're actually here, Senator," the driver responded.

She'd had her misgivings even entering the Lincoln town car when it arrived at her townhouse as scheduled. But it had the standard government plates, and the driver flashed a proper security badge. When she questioned the location, knowing that no government agencies were housed that far from DC's central corridor, the driver had referred to the paper-work delivered to her by a process server containing the official seal with a raised emblem that included the address. It had been signed by the agency's director, Mark Wolve.

She'd done her due diligence, finding the obscure branch of the FBI in the encrypted database provided to her first thing in the morning. But even in those internal records, it was simply listed as the SSA. Everything checked out, except for the glaring fact that no one had ever heard of it.

The driver came to a stop in front of yet another nondescript ware-house. He stepped out and opened her door, umbrella ready. It was a short walk to a lone metal door. The driver reached out with a key.

A key? That's the security for a supposedly top-secret agency?

He inserted it into a weary lockbox next to the door. A turn of the key revealed a keypad within. He flashed his security badge at a small screen, punched in a code, and leaned down to do a quick retinal scan. Finally, he placed his thumbprint on the screen. She heard a series of heavy locks re-lease inside.

"I stand corrected," she murmured.

The small front lobby featured no furniture. A woman wearing a black suit similar to the driver's sat behind a window, sliding it open without a word. She requested both their security badges, examined them, and made a quiet phone call. She then asked for the umbrella, which the driver pro-vided. She simply nodded towards the only other door in the room. "I can buzz you through—"

"I can handle it." The driver proceeded to wave his badge again.

"I don't think the FBI even has this redundancy for security," Kate said.

"We're not the FBI, ma'am."

"According to budget appropriations, you are."

"Technically, I suppose," he said, opening the door. "Please follow me."

Kate's eyes immediately had to adjust to the darkness of the room be-yond, which was lit only by hundreds of computer monitors and televi-sions that filled the space. The light from the screens revealed intense expressions and wrinkled foreheads.

They passed through without a single employee looking in their direc-tion. Kate slowed her stride to try and see what they were all so intently studying, but when the driver did not, she was forced to keep pace. She did catch a glimpse of what appeared to be the latest video of hurricane damage in New Orleans, with the worker drawing circles on a monitor with a red digital pen.

The driver led her into a small room where a receptionist smiled and nodded. They passed through into a windowless office, lit this time with dim fluorescent lights. No one was sitting at the immaculately clean desk at the far end of the room.

"Am I not to be meeting with Director Wolve?" Kate asked.

The driver walked to the desk and sat down, touching the pad on the laptop to bring it to life. "You are. I'm Mark Wolve."

"Excuse me?"

He typed quickly, obviously entering his pass code. "Have a seat, Senator."

"You never thought to introduce yourself?"

"You never asked. You assumed I was the driver. I've learned in this life never to assume anything." He continued to look at the screen intently.

Well played, Kate thought as she sat. *Already getting the upper hand by making me look unaware and pretentious.*

He reached for the phone. "Terri? Can you send in Mr. Hallow?"

"I was under the impression that we would be meeting privately, Director. I did not—"

"Director, Senator," said the man walking into the room. The smell of cigarettes preceded him, and Kate felt the all-too-familiar need for a smoke. She'd officially kicked the habit two years ago, but the desire never truly went away.

Yet at the sight of Flynn Hallow, the smell actually repulsed her. The man's skin had a yellowish tint, and his comb-over barely covered his age-spotted head.

She hadn't liked him when she kicked him out of her office at the beginning of the year.

"I understand the two of you have met," Mark said, still reading the computer.

"Yes. I'm sorry it didn't end well at our last meeting," Flynn said.

"No, it did not." Kate rested her hands on her lap.

"But perhaps now you see what I was saying?" Flynn asked.

She eyed him coolly. "My stance has not changed. You asked me to share with the president a series of conspiracy theories—something which I have fought against my entire political career—and in return you promised to find my missing nephew. You not only did not find my nephew—an entertainment reporter did that for you—but I will not clutter the leader of the free world's desk with unproven fiction."

"Your mother obviously believed; even your father did at the end—"

"I will not be discussing my family with you or anyone else."

"Senator, Mr. Hallow," Mark closed his laptop. "We need to keep this civil. We have a real crisis on our hands over which we've got to get control."

"Get control?" Kate leaned forward, showing the screen of her phone. "I'm sure your phone is lighting up just like mine. I said I would meet with you if you brought in my nephew safely. Obviously, that has not happened. But I'm told now that you have intelligence to share with me. That is the only reason I am here."

"Let's get right to it, then. We are afraid he has been taken."

"Taken? By whom?"

"We don't know. We suspect some kind of fanatical group."

"I need facts, Director Wolve, not your suspicions. I am frankly tired of hearing about this agency's wild suppositions—"

"Perhaps you'd like to see the videos."

Kate blinked. "Videos?"

The director turned his laptop to face her. She moved in closer, seeing dark, rapidly moving body camera footage.

"What is this?"

"One of our agents was wearing a camera. Your nephew was living in a trailer on some farmland, and when he snuck back in to gather something inside, we tried to bring him in. He ran from us, and we pursued. You can see at this moment—there—the agent emerges from the cotton—"

"Is that gunfire? Your agents are shooting!"

"He was about to drive away and they shot out his tires. Unfortunately, there was a casualty."

"Someone died?" Kate's fist now curled on the desk.

"An accidental shooting. We don't know who these people were, but a woman and a little girl were seen leaving the trailer with him. By the way, he was also running from them; it appears they were not welcome. The woman moved into our agent's line of fire and was shot. I am not happy about it."

"Was my nephew hurt?"

"No. He's fine, we think."

"You *think?*"

Kate heard Flynn clear his throat behind her. Even in the frantic, dark video, she could see that the agent wearing the camera quickly turned to his right. One by one, his colleagues began to convulse and fall.

As that agent whipped his gun back to the Jeep, the camera began to shake wildly, and then both toppled to the ground.

"What's happening?" Kate demanded.

"Look here," Flynn walked up and pointed to the corner of the screen. The camera was now still and tilted from where the agent lay unmoving on the ground. From the brake lights of another car, the small figure of the girl was revealed.

"Director, can you flip the video and zoom in?" he asked.

"I already had it edited," Mark said, reaching around and punching a key.

The video turned and moved in on the girl. She appeared to shake as she looked, one by one, to the agents. The brake lights from the car then fell off her, and she was bathed in black.

Kate watched as headlights then briefly flashed over her. She was still standing and trembling in exertion. A figure flashed in the dark and picked up her up, carrying her away.

"Wait, was that—"

"It was your nephew," Flynn said.

"I don't understand. What was that girl doing? What happened to your agents?"

"She's one of the four, Senator."

Kate turned to the agent. "You're still fixated on that theory?"

"I think this video proves it's much more than a theory." Flynn pointed to the screen. "She killed those men just by looking in their direction."

"We're doing detailed autopsies on them now," the director said, his chin in his hand. "But already our physicians are confirming they died of cancer."

"No one just dies suddenly of cancer," Kate said.

"They do when they've been attacked by someone implanted with the ability to kill with disease," Flynn said.

"For Christ sake." Kate stood. "This is what got you thrown out of my office last year."

"And you refused then to even hear me out that it was starting again. But it's worse this time. The deaths, the storms, the sicknesses, the bloodshed. We knew the abducted were returning again—"

"I can't listen to this bullshit again." Kate reached for her phone, which she'd left on her chair.

"After what you've just seen, after what your own mother and father believed, how can you continue to doubt—"

Kate pointed at him. "Because I read *your* parent agency's own reports of what happened in Argentum. I devoured them, and the Homeland Security reports. I questioned the authors of both reports. I reviewed every single bit of available information. And the conclusion was unquestionable: There was no proof of any mass abductions or their return. This comes from *your* government agencies—"

"Not mine. You never read the reports from the SSA," Flynn said with a scowl.

"Because until five minutes ago, I didn't believe that you even existed."

"Flynn, thank you for delaying your trip. You should have been in the air an hour ago." The director motioned to the door.

The agent looked at Kate for a moment, clearly wanting to say something, and then walked out.

As the door shut, Mark said quietly, "Senator—"

"I will not waste a second more of my time on these theories. I want to know who has my nephew."

"There's a second video. Please take a moment to watch."

As she exhaled, he reached around to his keyboard and opened another window. This time, the video came from a steady camera showing a landing strip.

"The camera was mounted on one of our helicopters. Watch that Porsche driving up and the van behind it. I'll zoom in. Our agents shot out the tires, so don't be alarmed by the bullet sound."

Kate held her breath, her arms folded across her chest. She watched as the van pulled up to the stalled Porsche and a man in a mask with a long rifle jumped out. He forced open the door, and another man, also wearing some sort of mask, held up a gun to the front seat.

"Who the hell is that?" she demanded.

"We don't know."

Moments later, a tall man with red hair emerged from the car with what looked to be the same little girl from the earlier video. As the agents scrambled towards them, the girl pointed in their direction.

Kate watched as once again, they began to twitch and fall.

"My God," she said.

A moment later, William and another man from the Porsche were practically shoved into the van, with the girl scrambling to follow.

"Wait a minute," Kate said, pointing to the screen. "Is that—?"

The director paused the video. "Quincy Martin. Yes."

"What in the world is he doing there? Is he in on this?"

"We are actively reaching out to his company to find out. We know that *Wired* magazine is reporting that Mr. Martin has been privately voicing to investors that he's wanted, for a long time, for your nephew to endorse his latest version of a hologram app. Turns out his competitors are scrambling to release their own. Apparently, he's been frustrated by his inability to find William."

"He also happens to be a complete conspiracy nut who regurgitates abduction theories."

"We're aware."

"Please keep playing the video."

Kate reminded herself to breathe as she watched the van spin around, seemingly waffling as to what to do, and then ram into the tail of the helicopter that had landed behind it. After pushing the helicopter, it drove out of the gate.

The director then closed the laptop. "What you don't see is that someone in that van then threw out spike strips to slow anyone chasing them. But unfortunately, we had no ground pursuit. And by the time we got our helicopter that was still operational in the air, they were gone."

Kate knew she was trembling. "My God. All those agents . . ."

"Their bodies, and those from the field, were recovered and placed in our helicopter before anyone in the media could make it there," Mark said.

"That girl . . ."

"It's why we had to show you, Senator. So you understand."

"And there's a dead civilian killed by live fire from our agents—"

"She was also recovered before the media arrived. I promise you a full investigation is underway into that terrible mistake."

Kate began to pace, looking back at the screen. "What the hell did I just see, Director?"

"There's much we need to discuss. Please take a seat."

"We have God knows how many dead federal agents, an active kidnapping of my nephew, and apparently a nut-job billionaire. And I just watched a little girl kill those agents without touching them."

"You understand our concern."

"The most important question: Where are they now?"

"We don't know. We are scrambling to get agents on the interstates and side roads. It's a somewhat isolated area for us. We sent most of our agents in the helicopters, never anticipating it would go . . ."

"This badly? Because it's bad, Director. I know very little of your branch, but surely you've made the FBI director aware. Even if the media doesn't know—at the moment—about the deaths of these agents, they will soon. The FBI has its fair share of leakers. My God, the president needs to know as well."

"The FBI director is well aware of the dire situation at hand. But as you know, he and the president don't see eye to eye on most things. Which is why, frankly, we need *you* to understand just how serious this has become."

"I think all the director has to do is show that video to the president and he will be quite alarmed."

Mark began to click the pen in his hand. "Do you recall what happened when Agent Hallow came to you with his theories?"

Kate remembered vividly throwing him out of her office personally, and telling her secretary never to allow him to return. The agent had left his business card and yelled something about calling him when she'd realized the truth.

She motioned to the laptop. "I don't even know what to make of it. But if federal agents are dead, then the president must know immediately."

"We're hoping you will be the one to show it to him."

"And tell him what, exactly? I don't even know how to explain what I saw. I've spent the last fifteen years stamping out the ridiculous theories surrounding my family."

"We will fully brief you on what we know. Now that you've seen the video, and your nephew is involved, you know the stakes. And frankly, it has to happen right now. In fact, neither the president nor any of his cabinet even know about the SSA. And there's a reason for this—"

"I don't even know what SSA stands for, for Christ sake."

"Sky Surveillance Agency. Truman created the agency and ordered it to act independently of our government. That was when they started keeping the files."

"The files?"

The director reached into his desk and pulled out two thick binders. "And I want you to read these in particular."

"What are these?"

"Copies of the files of everything we know about your family."

Kate suddenly felt hot all over.

"You have files on my family?"

"We have files on all the abducted."

She looked at the voluminous black folders as if they were venomous snakes. "I'm sorry, but how can these even exist after everything I've been provided from the FBI that contradicts that notion—"

"We are independent, as I stated before. Please begin with this one. It's about your mother. Unfortunately, it lacks some important documents, which were stolen."

"Stolen?"

He slid the folder towards her.

"We don't just have to contain your nephew and that girl, Senator," he said. "We must find them all. Your mother must be brought in as well."

The sound of her cell phone ringing brought on a brief moment of relief. Lynn stood from her vigil in front of the television in Tom's study and walked to the door. Roxy leaned back in her chair, looking at her questioningly.

"It's Don."

"Just take the call in here," Roxy said.

Lynn walked out, hearing Roxy mutter something about already being in deep. She answered when she'd reached the kitchen. "Don?"

"Hello there, Miss Lynn."

She couldn't help but smile, thinking immediately of the first time she'd met him. Even in those terrible dark days in Argentum, desperate to find her grandson and knowing her deepest secrets had been exposed online, the smile and twinkling eyes of the proprietor of the town's general store was a reminder that kindness could surface even in the bleakest of circumstances. Without Don Rush, none of them would be alive today.

"Thank you for calling me back so quickly," she said.

"I would have done it sooner, except for our cell service out here is no good."

She paused, closing her eyes, her stomach dropping. "So you've done it, then?"

"Successfully off the grid."

"You felt it, then."

"Yes ma'am. Woke up yesterday morning and thought for sure this was it. My whole body felt like I'd been rung like a bell, and that any minute it would start happening. I tried to sneak out, but you know I'm an old man, so I knocked over the dang cane just getting out of bed. Barbara came in to see what had happened. I guess the expression on my face, and the fact that I told her to run out of the house and not stop running, did not help matters."

"Barbara is with you?"

"Right over there in the driver's seat." Lynn heard a soft voice speak in the background. "She says hello, Lynn."

"Tell her . . ." Lynn stammered. Offer an apology? But, of course, it had been Barbara, all those decades ago, when they were both young women, who willingly entered this world of shadows and secrets to try and find her missing brother.

"She knows, Lynn. I tried to convince her that I needed to go off on my own for the time being, that the safest thing was for me to put as much distance between me and anyone with a heartbeat. But she's stubborn, this sister of mine. So we're out here in the middle of nowhere. Did you do the same?"

She exhaled. "I wanted to, but . . . circumstances have prevented me."

Don chuckled. "I bet one circumstance is an ornery woman with a fondness for quilted vests and cuss words."

"Roxy is part of it. But . . . I won't burden you with the rest. If you've truly unplugged . . ."

"I haven't read any news in days. Blissfully unaware, except for the fear that it's finally happening, after all this time. But . . . your ears aren't bleeding, are they? No headaches? And I assume no one is dying around you?"

Lynn shook her head. "No. Nothing. But . . ."

"I know. It's there. No doubt about it. It's back. That damn feeling that I could never understand before, like I was always being watched. Had it all my life, until the bastards took all the others away that night in Argentum.

Then, it was gone, and I felt free, for the first time. Now that it's back, boy do I hate it. Any word from William?"

Lynn swallowed. "No."

"Well, I can tell in your voice that something's up. I could usually find out on my own, but we've taken the camper and there's zero internet access out where we're going. I hate to not be of help to you, Miss Lynn. After everything you and Roxy and your husbands did for me."

"Funny, I was just thinking of how indebted we are to you."

"Please. You gave me back my life. Roxy and Ed opened up their home to me, until Barbara finally dragged me up north. I began to think maybe we'd just all die of old age and those fears we had were bunk. I had a flicker of it about a year ago, but it went away pretty quick. But now it's here . . ."

"And it's not going anywhere. I know."

"It's easy for me to skip town. No wife, no kids, just a very protective twin sister who refuses to *let me go on my own*."

"Hush," Lynn heard Barbara say.

"But I know it's harder for you, Lynn. You can't exactly run off can you? Not with all those daughters and grandsons and people so reliant on you. If Roxy knows something's up, though, then I doubt she's left your side."

"She's in the other room. I'm just trying . . . to protect her. Although I suppose it's moot at this point."

"And I know you're worried about Will. If we're feeling this . . ."

I'm more worried about him than anything else.

"Yes. I'm frankly terrified."

Don sighed as the cell phone cut out briefly. "I think, my dear lady, we're getting deep into no man's land. I'm gonna lose you. I guess this is goodbye."

The tears that sprang to Lynn's eyes surprised her. She struggled to keep her voice from revealing the sudden wave of grief. "You take care of yourself, Don. And Barbara too."

"I'm sorry that Tom is gone, that you're facing this without him. But you're not alone. Both my sister and your friend know what they've signed up for. Sooner or later, we're going to have to explain this to them."

"I just wish I could."

"Lynn, you're worlds smarter than me. Haven't you realized it yet?"

Lynn blinked. "I honestly don't know. I can't describe it."

She heard Don cut out, but then his voice returning with urgency. ". . . control."

"You broke up, Don."

". . . I didn't realize it . . . all those years . . . until it was gone. That's why the last fifteen years . . . been so great . . . the weight lifted . . . now it's back. What we're feeling . . . control. Something's controlling us."

SIX

Once again, he was in the storm.

The wind struck with such force that it burned. William's ears rang from the muscular howls, forcing him to want to cower. But his limbs refused to move, like the pole of a battered flag enduring the worst of a churning squall. He immediately regretted looking down, for among the choppy whitecaps, something slithered, spreading out like black veins in the deep.

In the far distance, as always, was the bracing city. And even from this distance he could see the hint of white, the eyes of someone watching the impending catastrophe.

He blinked, and was in flames. The hills upon which he stood were scorched of any life, blackened and beaten by the flames. A closer examination did reveal movement among the ashes. Something writhed and twisted, moving like moles beneath the ash, rushing towards two singular eyes that stood out like missing pieces in a puzzle of smoke that was void of any colors but black and gray.

He knew what came next. Brutal violence, the sound of gunshots, tears of pain and fear, around another set of eyes.

Then gurneys rushing with unmoving bodies, desperate pleas for help. Through the windows of the hospital he could see towering rocks on the horizon.

A moment later he was inside that stone, as scales slid across his arms and legs and around his neck, moving over his chin and nearing his lips.

Barely, he could see the eyes, full of fear and horror, lost in the creeping, shining tendrils—

His own scream brought him from the dream, and to a frantic face looking down at him. Ash blond hair fell down shoulders to meet a bandana hanging around her neck. His last glimpse of the woman had been behind the wheel of a van, frantically driving through the predawn light.

"What's wrong?" she demanded.

He tried to catch his breath. It always took him a few minutes to fully awaken after the dreams.

"Calm down." She placed a firm hand on his chest, holding him down. "There's nowhere for you to go at the moment."

It all came back: the sharp pain in his arm, the collapse of Lily, and then Quincy fighting in the seat behind him.

"You drugged us," he managed to say.

"Had no choice," she responded in a quiet voice. "The sedative must have given you some hell of a nightmare. But it's over now, and we need you to be quiet. Don't want to wake up the others."

He looked over to see another double bed in the room, where Quincy and Lily lay side by side.

"Don't panic," she said. "It's important she stay asleep until we can figure out how she's able to do what we saw. And nobody wants to hear Quincy Martin's crap at the moment, so it's just fine that he keeps sleeping too. We have no intention of hurting anyone."

"You'll understand that's hard to believe."

"Well, we had strict orders to bring you in unharmed. And we needed some time to process what happened out there. So it was just best that you slept on the road."

He vaguely remembered the last words of the man in the front seat.

"My grandmother . . . she knows about this?"

"She does," said a whisper from the window. The man with the shaved head stood peering out through blinds, a long rifle in his hands. "And we intend to deliver you in one piece. Thus the necessary constraints."

"Who are you?" he said, sitting up despite the woman's pressure.

"You're stronger than I thought," she said.

"My grandmother would never, ever condone a kidnapping. Not of me, and never of a little girl."

"Your grandmother didn't see that little girl just kill federal agents by looking at them. And if she thought you were in danger at all, then believe me, she would have authorized it."

He began to demand to speak with his grandmother when he saw the guns lined up beneath the window. Six AK-47s, four with bump stocks. Two large black bags sat before the guns, obviously used to carry the weapons into the motel room. The man had a pistol on his waist, as did the woman with the bandana, who walked over to continue watching from the other side of the window.

William knew nothing about his grandmother's work or who was ever on the other end of those secretive phone calls in Grandpa Tom's office, who sent the mail that arrived for her with no return address, and who she thought of when she silently watched the trees behind her home.

But this? These people? No. Not his grandmother.

He looked over to Lily. Then again, nothing made sense.

"Are you Researchers?" he asked.

The man raised an eyebrow. "Do we look like academics?"

"Then who are you?"

"Neve, keep watching for Kevin. He should have found a place to stash the van. We got lucky that no one was outside when we snuck 'em in. I know Kevin's trying to be cautious."

The woman nodded, fingering her pistol to take off the safety.

The man came to kneel in front of William. "What do you know about this girl?"

"Maybe you could start by explaining who you are—"

"We were dispatched by an organization to which your grandmother, shall we say, belongs. When word surfaced of your appearance, we were sent to keep you safe. And given what we saw, it's a good thing we came."

William narrowed his eyes. "You knew something would happen?"

"Keep your voice down. Let's just say we had reason to be concerned. Let me ask you: Has Lynn Roseworth ever mentioned the SSA? Anything about them?"

The thick packages that arrived with "URGENT," usually in red marker, arriving at his parent's house. Swells of people that surrounded him in public bathrooms, asking for just a minute of his time to answer some questions. The social media pages run full-time by strangers that stole his picture and sent out warnings about government conspiracies. All part of the hysteria he'd hated his whole life.

The man before him reeked of it.

"What you've just seen should let you know that there's a whole lot more going on than what you've ever known of. I can also see that you don't believe me. Well, you tell me, then—you tell me why those federal agents were trying to take you. Why they had two helicopters filled with agents ready to bring you in at gunpoint, both at that trailer and then the airport. Agents who all wore black suits. All at the same time a little girl shows up with the ability to kill on the spot. You tell me what's going on."

"I don't have a damn clue."

"I think you do, Mr. Chance. I don't think you're stupid. I think you need to explain to me what you know about this girl and how Quincy Martin is involved."

William did not miss the fact that the man continued to keep his finger on the trigger.

Stay calm. Keep everyone calm.

"Listen. I don't know who she is. She somehow ended up in my trailer with an agent from the federal park service. I don't really understand why they came. The agent said the girl insisted on finding me. I have no idea how those men died at the airport and the field—"

"What do you mean the field?" Rudd asked. "You mean it didn't just happen at the airport?"

"I don't know what happened. And then that guy—Quincy—who drove the Porsche, was there. He wanted to run, and I couldn't just leave her there. So we took off."

The man pointed angrily. "Why was Quincy Martin there?"

"I don't know. I don't even know who he is. All he said was something about wanting to make some kind of deal."

"Are you kidding? Swooping in on all this trying to make a buck? Not that he needs it. You really don't know who he is? I don't think it's by chance he showed up at the same moment those agents moved in. He needs to be removed from this scenario. And fast."

"Listen. No one gets hurt, understand?" William said. "I understand you think you're keep me safe, but you have to let us go—"

"You don't get it. We let you go, and the government gets you, and you disappear forever—"

The sound of a pistol resounded from outside, followed by another.

"Rudd!" Neve said, peering out the window. "It's Kevin, he's running!"

"What's going on . . ." Quincy muttered from his bed. Lily too began to stir.

The bald man turned his eyes, streaked with reddening vessels, back to William. "Stay away from the windows. Can you keep the girl calm?"

"I don't know—"

"I suggest you try," the man said, running to the door.

William hurried over to the bed while keeping an eye on the man. Those bloodshot eyes were now peering through the peephole, his finger was on the trigger of the gun. Neve, too, had her pistol raised in preparation.

William gently brushed the girl's forehead and face. "Lily, can you wake up . . ."

Her eyes popped open in panic, her voice raspy. "There's a monster in the mountain."

"It's OK, Lily—"

"There's a monster in the mountain," she frantically repeated. "She's there. We have to go!"

"It's OK, it's OK," he whispered. "Don't talk right now, OK?"

Quincy began to groan and tried to sit up. "You've got to keep quiet, too. These people are heavily armed. Something's happened outside—"

Rudd pulled open the door, and William recognized the man who injected Lily. His thick shock of black hair was flattened somewhat by the Nixon mask he'd worn before.

"What happened?" Rudd asked, quickly shutting the door.

"Drone. I had to shoot it down. Hovering over the other end of the parking lot. Couldn't take a chance on it getting video of us," the man said, holstering his pistol and picking up one of the semiautomatics.

"Every man in a midlife crisis has one of those," Quincy said, holding his head. "What the hell is wrong with you people—?"

"Quiet!" Rudd commanded, pointing the rifle at Quincy. "I am not screwing around here!" He then held up his hand at Lily, cautiously. "We're here to protect you too, honey."

The girl scooted towards William on the bed.

"It's just a matter of time now. Neve, how much longer on that SUV?" Rudd asked.

"I only dared to make one call on that landline. I don't want to call again. They said it could be any moment. Might not be soon enough if the cops respond to a shot-up drone."

"I'll keep watch. Turn on CNN. See what they're reporting. Hopefully they still don't have a clue where we are. And the Memphis TV stations surely won't respond to the shooting of a drone." Rudd peered out again through the peephole.

Memphis, William thought. Halfway home to Nashville. Is that where we're ultimately headed?

The TV flared on. Neve flipped till she found CNN, with the banner at the bottom reading, in bold red letters, "THE ABDUCTION OF WILLIAM CHANCE."

"That should read 'Part Two,'" Quincy muttered.

William frowned at him, watching the anchorwoman, who sported a hairstyle that could be seen on networks across the country, share the screen with video of both his trailer and of the Clinton National Airport.

". . . it is still unclear the connection, but here's what we know at the top of this hour. Following reports of gunshots being fired in a field surrounding the mobile home where it is believed that William Chance was living in central Arkansas, there were also calls of gunfire near Clinton National Airport. We are hearing from federal agents on the scene that there is growing concern that Mr. Chance has been taken hostage by armed abductors and is now missing."

"And the spin begins," Rudd said.

The anchor continued breathlessly. "We have team coverage of this breaking story, beginning with Maurice Muller at the mobile home just south of Little Rock."

A reporter who looked like he had just graduated middle school but with a jawline straight out of a J. Crew catalog pointed to the trailer cordoned off by crime scene tape. "Kit, this continues to be a very active scene. At some point early this morning, many of the reporters here trying to get a comment from William Chance heard what sounded like bullets being fired on the other end of this cotton field. I can show you video of what our photographer captured before police moved us all back."

The screen cut to shaky video taken from a distance down the road, quickly zooming in on William's sunken Jeep. "This Jeep is believed to belong to William Chance, and the tires have been shot out. A short while ago, a spokesman from Little Rock police gave us a brief update. Take a listen."

A tired-looking officer in glasses came onto the screen. "We can confirm that a Jeep parked not far from the trailer was fired upon. We are working in conjunction with federal investigators on the scene to determine what happened. But there is no evidence of anyone being hurt."

Rudd shook his head. "Bastards. Moved the bodies before the cops arrived."

The reporter was back on camera. "We can also tell you that two helicopters took off not long after the gunshots, and it's believed those are federal agents."

"Maurice, do we have any idea at this point why William Chance was even living in Little Rock? How long he had been here?" the anchorwoman asked.

"We don't. But I can tell you, minute by minute, the crowd here continues to grow. One group of women tell me they drove all night from Idaho to see if it was true that Chance had finally surfaced."

The anchor tossed her ever-so-perfectly curled hair slightly. "Thank you Maurice. The answer to why federal agents are on the scene of what appears to be a random shooting may be answered by what happened at Clinton National Airport. We continue our team coverage now with Susan Strandon outside the airport with the latest there. Susan?"

The reporter, whose version of the anchor hairstyle was growing limper by the second due to the humidity, motioned to the airport.

"It's still unclear, Kit, why William Chance ended up here. All we can tell you is the FBI has released a photograph of a van that they say Chance was forced into."

A photograph, clearly taken from the video mounted on one of the helicopters, showed the gray van as William, Lily, and Quincy were entering. Rudd, in his ski mask, was waving them in.

"Federal agents say men wearing masks seized Chance and forced him into the van. A FBI spokesman said they fear Mr. Chance is in real danger. And there is another astonishing element to this. If you look closely at that photograph, it appears that's Quincy Martin. If his name sounds familiar, it's because he's the billionaire creator of all those new hologram functions on smartphones, and more recently, the 'Beam Me Up' app. The video shows he's being forced into the van along with a little girl. And we've con-firmed his private plane was parked nearby."

Video then came up showing Quincy at the New York Stock Exchange, ringing the bell among cheering investors. For a brief moment, the video included images of a green hologram of Quincy beaming from the light of a smartphone.

"Susan, do we have any idea why Quincy Martin is there? And who this little girl is?" the anchor asked.

"We don't."

"Alright, thank you Susan. We want to bring in now Stephanie Stiller with Hollywoodextra.com, who broke the news of William Chance living in Arkansas, to talk about this whirlwind twenty-four hours—"

Neve muted the TV. "Well, the narrative is set."

"Kevin, tell me you parked the van far away from here. Everyone and their brother is looking for it now," Rudd said.

"I did. We need that SUV. Like an hour ago."

"Keep your eyes up. The second somebody sees that SUV, we're out of here."

As the three continued to look out the window, Quincy moved closer behind William, whispering. "This might be a good time for little thing here to summon the dark side and kill them before they kill us."

Lily turned her head into William's shoulder and buried it.

"We don't have much time," Quincy said. "This cannot end well. Who are these nut jobs?"

William tilted his head and whispered back. "I don't know."

"Well, I do. I know plenty of them. Not all true believers are as stable as yours truly. I just didn't know they came in a Fast and Furious version."

"All that matters now is we remain calm and get out of here," William responded.

"Hey, angel. Can you just make 'em collapse or something?"

"Knock it off," William said. "Nobody's killing anybody—"

Lily pulled back. "There's a monster in the mountain!"

"What did she say?" Quincy asked.

"Lily, shh . . ." William reached out for her shoulder.

"There's a monster in the mountain!" she pleaded.

"Screw this," Quincy said, standing up. "Hey, whatever you shot us up with has really messed up this kid. She needs a doctor."

"Sit down," Rudd said, pointing the gun at Quincy.

"Rudd." The woman motioned to the window. "Cops."

The word sucked the oxygen from the room. Rudd made a slicing motion with his hand.

Minutes passed in silence, the three at the windows nervously fingering their weapons.

"Shit, here he comes," Neve said.

Rush the door. Yell for help. William took a step forward when Rudd turned back to him, his palm raised in yet another angry, silent order.

A firm, loud knock rattled the door. "Memphis police. Please open the door."

Rudd exhaled loudly, waiting a few moments. He then leaned on the door. "Hi officer, what's going on?"

"You can't shoot down drones. You've ruined a kid's birthday. Open up."

"Nicely done," Quincy muttered.

"Just getting on my shoes, sorry," Rudd said, flashing Kevin an angry look. "I'm really sorry about that. Drones aren't supposed to fly over people. I am just a stickler for rules, don't think it's fair when they're broken. But I promise it won't happen again."

They could hear the high-pitched beep of the officer opening up his radio. Once he was done talking, his voice was considerably calmer.

"You could have hurt someone seriously. We need to talk about that. I understand you're not alone in there. The boy said it looked like some people were being carried in. Have you got a little girl with you?"

Rudd's eyes grew wide. "Like I said—I'm really sorry. I will pay for a new drone once I find my wallet. It's just me and my family. My daughter's actually in the bathtub right now."

Rudd pointed his finger at Neve and then to the bathroom. She nodded and hurried to the back of the room, motioning with her gun for William and Quincy to bring Lily.

"Never a good idea to shoot a loaded gun around a kid," the cop said through the door. "You need to open up right now."

The woman rushed the three into the bathroom. The uncomfortable tightness of the room was revealed in the dim light from a single bulb in a double socket, and a window with a frosted pane.

Neve slid back the shower curtain and kneeled in front of Lily. "Listen, honey. I know this seems really strange. But we're doing all this to protect you and William from getting hurt."

"Including drugging you," Quincy said.

"You," Neve said, again displaying her pistol. "See if you can quietly get that window open."

"That's your exit strategy? I couldn't begin to get my fat ass through there."

"Wouldn't that be a loss. Now move," she said.

As Quincy grumbled something about bleach while inspecting the window, Neve leaned on the counter, tapping the countertop and trying to listen through the door.

"You can end this right now, you know," William said. "You have no proof that my grandmother sent you. Just let us leave and go with that officer. He's just a local cop; he's here on a nuisance call. No one has to get hurt."

"You don't get it, do you?" she said. "Even after everything you've seen. You go with that cop, and eventually you and this extraordinary girl would end up in federal custody, which means no one will ever see you again. They've seen what she can do. They'll take her away forever, get it? We're trying to keep that from happening."

"All I'm worried about now is that no one gets hurt, and you have filled this room with guns. I swear to you that I will make it clear we were not harmed by you—"

"Just shut up," she said, and then forced herself to calm, looking at Lily. "I shouldn't have said that honey, we're all just a bit stressed right now. I need everyone to stay quiet. Please. No more talking. And get that window open."

For several minutes, they watched Quincy struggle. The window, coated in years of grime, clearly hadn't been opened for some time.

"It's stuck," Quincy said.

"Help him," Neve said, motioning with her chin.

William slid by the woman. "Take that corner, and I'll do this one. On the count of three."

As they both pushed, the window slammed open so roughly that the glass cracked.

"Nice place you chose here," Quincy said, peering outside. "Even nicer view of the alley. Is this where your ride is coming?"

"Is it big enough for us all to get through?"

"If I really sucked in my gut," Quincy said.

"You're the least of my concerns. Now we wait."

Lily moved over to where William sat on the edge of the bathtub. Quincy unrolled a ridiculous amount of tissue and spread it out on the toilet lid, wincing as he sat.

"How much you guys going to ask in your ransom?" Quincy asked.

"I'm serious about shutting the hell up." Neve came to lean on the door frame. "I need to hear—"

The sound of splintered wood came from outside, and then the breaking of glass. Heavy footsteps rushed across the room.

"Stay down!" Rudd yelled.

"What's happening?" Neve asked, yanking open the bathroom door.

Rudd had his hand on his forehead, breathing loudly as he leaned against the wall.

"The cop. They shot the cop."

"Who shot the cop?" Neve demanded.

"They're outside. They must have heard the cop on the scanner. How'd they get here so fast? They're gonna make it look like we shot through the door at the cop and he fired back. Shit . . . Kevin . . ."

"What about Kevin?"

"Stay in there, Neve—"

She pushed her way past him and then gasped. "Kevin!"

"Neve, don't—" Rudd rushed after her.

"Now," Quincy said, pointing to the window. "We've got to get out now."

William nodded, reaching for Lily. "Come on."

She immediately came to him. He began to lift her up when the sound of more bullets riddled the front room, along with the crashing of glass, followed by a scream.

"Lift her out!" William said, sliding to peer around the doorframe.

The front door was splintered with holes, the window nearly shot out. Kevin lay in the sunlight streaming through, covered in blood. Neve slumped, unmoving, on the floor in front of the bed, where she clearly had run into the line of fire.

"My God," William whispered. Bodies on the floor. Bodies at the airport, in the field.

Rudd kneeled in the back corner with a AK-47, sweat pouring down his shaved head.

"They've got to have snipers out there," Rudd gasped. "We can't get out. Where's the damn SUV?"

Neve's hair was a matted dark red. Kevin's clothes were stained the same color, his neck tilted unnaturally to the side.

William thought of Lois and her unblinking eyes in the headlights. The agents' faces as they died, their skin turning yellow, their cheeks sinking, their bodies convulsing in pain.

He turned to Quincy. "Get Lily out that window and run."

"William—!"

"I'm in here!" William yelled, coming to stand before the window. "I'm not hurt! Don't shoot! I'm coming out!"

"William!" Rudd was standing now, running for him.

But William got to the door quicker, ripping it open and immediately shutting it. Fighting back the bile that rose to his throat at seeing the dead officer—*more bodies*—he stepped over it and lifted his hands into the air.

The heat from the deserted Memphis street was immediately oppressive, rising like smoke as if the pavement were on fire. The blight was everywhere, from the outdated apartment complex across the street to the abandoned gas station next to it. On the roof of the complex, William could see dark figures, their guns pointed at him.

He slowly walked out and then took a sharp right, heading down the street.

"Stop!" came a command from a dark vehicle parked at the gas station. Another man, dressed in all black, was kneeling beside the driver's-side door, his pistol aimed at him.

William continued to walk. Out of the corner of his eye, he saw a white flash. An SUV passed on the intersecting street, turning behind a rundown tire store and down the alley stretching behind the motel.

"Stop! Right now!"

William kept on walking. *Get out that window, Quincy. Get her out.*

"Do not shoot!" William yelled. "Do you hear me? I am William Chance! There are innocent people in there! Do not shoot!"

He then calmly laid down on the street. *She had to be out now. Quincy could fit through. Go. Go. Get in and don't stop.*

He knew no one anticipated this. The agents or police, whoever they were, were frantically talking about what to do. But the gunfire had stopped.

"Do not shoot!" William cried out.

A few moments later they were on him, all wearing dark sunglasses, their weapons drawn. He heard the squeal of tires and the car from the gas station was beside them.

One of the men reached out and patted him all over. Feeling nothing, they rushed him up and into the car.

Once inside, they forced off his shoes, inspecting them thoroughly, patting him down once again.

The car took off with such force that William had to steady himself. "I'm OK—"

The entire car then violently shuddered as it pulled around the corner. William whipped his head around to look out the back window.

Smoke poured through the windows of the hotel room, the door flying off its hinges as the room exploded in a rain of fire.

The mass of beetles swirled above the treetops. Lynn had come out to observe them as they hovered, dipped and soared, thinking of Don's last words as the signal dropped out.

"Something is controlling us."

It continued to send shivers through her like a fever, an ailment finally diagnosed.

It had been so long since she'd experienced it that she'd forgotten. She liked to pretend that she had imagined it, like a barely recalled moment of a nightmare that seemed so real that only the morning light through the curtains could prove it was false. That she'd been wrong to even think it ever existed.

She'd realized its absence not long after she'd returned from Colorado with William. Even in the chaos and uncertainty of that time, she'd felt different: lighter, warmer, like a burden had been lifted.

She could have easily dismissed the vacancy, believing it had been replaced by relief that her grandson was alive. That his return, at last, relieved her of the dark lining she'd carried with her all her days. Something she never even recognized was there until it was gone.

Lynn often tried to explain it to Tom, but struggled with the words. How does one describe that throughout your entire life, a shadow existed within you, on the periphery of your vision, on the verge of everything; something as familiar as blinking and breathing? And then, with her grandson returned, it was gone.

In the many years that followed, she'd forgotten it. After all, there was a new life to build. Trust to rebuild. Protection to give. Wounds to heal. Work to continue.

But now she knew it had never left her. It had been asleep and suddenly woke.

One person might understand, but she wasn't about to call the man who began her descent down this frightening path. She hadn't talked to Dr. Steven Richards in more than a decade. She had to close that door firmly, to salvage her marriage.

She'd convinced herself that fear and secrets no longer ruled her life. It was no wonder that the shadow she'd never even realized hung on her like a heavy coat was gone as well.

It now returned with a wicked oppression. The chains on all of them had returned—

"Lynn!"

At the sound of Roxy's voice, she rushed back through the screen door to see her emerge from the study, pointing. "Come right now."

Lynn practically ran inside and down the hall, seeing billowing smoke smearing across the Memphis skyline on the TV screen.

"What's happening?"

"They just broke in with this. They say William is in Memphis. They say he was in some motel room and some witnesses said they saw police rush him out. There's been some kind of explosion . . ."

"Explosion?" Lynn walked up to stand directly in front of the screen. "But you heard he's got out?"

"That's just what these people said. They live in an apartment nearby and they say they saw him lay down on the street and the police got him. My God, Lynn. I can take a lot, but this . . . I just want him home."

"Where's my phone? I think my purse is in the kitchen. We can be in Memphis in three hours. I'm not sitting around anymore."

Roxy clapped her hands. "That's my girl. There's your phone. Looks like it's blowing up."

Lynn picked up cell on the desk, seeing multiple texts from Anne and Brian.

We're heading to Memphis, Mom. We heard what happened. Please keep watching the news.

Don't come, Nanna. It's a circus. You can't be here. Don't let Roxy convince you otherwise.

"Why am I always made out to be the bad influence?" Roxy asked, reading over her shoulder.

Please be careful. Please keep me posted, Lynn texted back.

"Lynn, what in the world is going on?" Roxy said, following Lynn out of the study. "Is this maybe the time to call the Illuminati, see what they know?"

"The Corcillium, Roxy. This is exactly why I can't tell you anything."

"Sorry. Old habits. Could they know something? Or would you even tell me?"

"I can't reach them. I've tried. Where is my purse? My keys are in there."

"You probably left it upstairs. So you do still speak with them, then? I'm just trying to come up with anything that could help. Remember that I know *nothing*."

"You know that I trust you implicitly. But what's happening with William right now is exactly why I can't drag you in even further. You have to stay here."

"You can't tell by my face, but I'm laughing inside. So I sit in front of the TV and call you every five minutes? He may not be my blood kin, but I feel like he's my own grandson. Chris's parents are dead. I'm the other de facto grandmother he never asked for."

"I think I left my purse in the pantry."

"I was just in there looking for the Oreos, it's not in there. I'm telling you it's in your bedroom. I don't want to stress you out any more, but I guess we've crossed that threshold. I don't suppose you've heard from Kate? Surely her connections in Washington could get you some answers."

As they clambered up the stairs to the bedroom, Lynn's chest tightened. It hurt every single time when she thought of her oldest daughter. Her strong, stubborn, brilliant girl. The last she'd spoken with Kate was Tom's funeral, and even at that, she'd come to the mass at the cathedral, sat with the family but did not speak, and left with just a kiss on Lynn's cheek, saying, "I'll always love you, Mama." Then, she was gone. She was so much like Tom that with his passing, it felt like two of the great loves of her life were dead to her.

"I've tried to call her. She doesn't pick up."

"Stella?"

"She's trying her law enforcement sources. But no one, even in the FBI, seems to have any answers."

"Well, not to make this day even more of a mess, but I think the reporters have found you," Roxy said, stopping at the window on the stairs. "Did you take down that no trespassing sign?"

"No," Lynn said, squinting. "I didn't."

"Then call the cops—"

"That's a town car. Now there are two."

"Could it be Kate . . . ?"

A third dark town car pulled up. Then, all the doors opened at the exact same moment, and men in black suits began to step out.

"Oh crap."

"Go upstairs and lock the door," Lynn ordered.

"Hell if I'm hiding up there."

"Forget the bedroom. Where do you park the truck—?"

"I traded it in for the Honda, remember? Couldn't climb it in anymore. It doesn't matter, Lynn. I'm not going anywhere."

As they hustled down the stairs, Lynn pointed down the hall. "Go out through the back door. Right now!"

"Good luck with that—"

They heard the kitchen screen door open and a deep voice call out. "Mrs. Roseworth?"

Lynn waved Roxy down the hall, but instead, Roxy practically tripped on Lynn's heels.

"Mrs. Roseworth—"

"You are not able to enter this house without a warrant!"

"You aren't under arrest, ma'am. May we enter?"

"You may not," Lynn said, stopping at the end of the hall to stand at the door of the kitchen.

The screen door swung open. Three men entered, all taking off their dark sunglasses. Outside the door, more men stood waiting.

She rose her arm before Roxy, who was holding out her phone like a weapon.

"Don't take one more step, sucker. I'll stream all this on Facebook and you can kiss your pension goodbye," Roxy said.

"I'm not worried about Facebook at the moment, ma'am. I'm sorry for the intrusion, but this is a matter of national security."

"Dammit," Roxy swore, repeatedly thumping her phone. Lynn watched as the Facebook app failed to open. Roxy tried to swipe the screen to the phone icon to dial 9-1-1, to no avail.

"You need to leave my house immediately," Lynn said.

"We intend to leave, ma'am, as soon as you are packed and ready to go."

"I won't be going anywhere. This is my house. You have no right to come in here—"

"Ma'am, this is an order from the director of the FBI." The man held out a sealed envelope. "Please read it in its entirety. We have a plane ready to take you to Washington."

"So is that who you claim to be with these days? The FBI?" Roxy asked. "I still have the aches and pains from my last tango with you assholes."

Lynn strode across the kitchen, with Roxy pumping her arms to keep up. Lynn seized the letter, breaking the government seal.

"What is this crap?" Roxy said, peering over her shoulder. "*For the greater good of the nation, it is imperative that you come under the protection of the federal government.* She's eighty years old, you jerk offs. What do you think she's going to do? Let loose the bombs she's got stashed in the pantry?"

Lynn could barely hear Roxy's continued berating of the agents, as all of the words began to blur together. Beneath the name of the director of the FBI was penmanship so familiar that she ached to read it.

The order was co-signed by U.S. Senator Kate Roseworth.

SEVEN

William didn't have to strain to see the smoke. Even though they were half-way across the city at this point, it gushed across the sky.

"It's a very good thing we got you away from those people when we did, Mr. Chance," said the man in the front passenger seat.

"There was a child in there!" William exploded.

"Hostage situations can sometimes end very badly."

William couldn't take his eyes off the smoke. Had that been the SUV that the woman, Neve, had talked about? Could Quincy and Lily had gotten out safely in time?

"Give yourself a moment, Mr. Chance. You've been through a lot. You cannot blame yourself for this. We feared this would happen. They were not going to let you go. Obviously they had explosives in there. There's strong reason to believe the park employee, who brought that girl to you, was linked to your captors. We believe it was all just an elaborate trap by some fanatical people. The girl and Mr. Martin were just unfortunate casualties."

"You can save that bullshit."

"But you are safe now, and you need some time to process all this. We're going to take you to a place where you can rest and speak with a counselor—"

"Enough." William held up his hand. The gesture caused the agent beside him to pull back his coat, displaying the gun holstered on his side.

"It's not unusual for captives—even if they've been with their captors for a brief amount of time—to believe their lies. Maybe even sympathize with them. You just need time now to recover. But at least the world knows you're safe. The family who witnessed your rescue was kind enough to tell the media that they saw you walk out and were rescued by our team. That will calm a lot of people after the explosion."

"Why," William's teeth were clenched. "Why—"

"You were in danger, Mr. Chance. You were being held by clearly unstable people. When you surfaced, we feared they would find you. And we were right. That poor girl was simply dragged into all this."

All this time, everything he did to try and keep his family safe, to keep himself from hurting innocent people . . . Look what had happened instead.

"I'll make this clear right now: You can feed all that crap to the reporters at your press conference. But the one thing you can't do is keep me from telling what really happened. And I will."

"We're going to give you all the time you need to recover. Process what happened. Really analyze what you *think* happened."

"No amount of brainwashing will change what I saw, I promise you that."

"OK, OK," said the agent sitting on William's right side. "Listen, kid. We just want to keep you safe and alive. Until we can figure out what's happening."

William turned to him. "And that's why you blew up that motel?"

The anger in the agent's face was obvious. "We all have bosses that make decisions we don't agree with. All I'm telling you is this: If you're with me, you're safe."

He gave William a reassuring nod. "Take the west garage, Stan."

Through the windshield William saw they were approaching a tall building, the flags of the world waving outside, the gray sign reading "Clifford Davis/Odell Horton Federal Building." They turned and began to head down a ramp.

"Safest place in the world for you right now," the agent beside him said. "We have agents awaiting—Jesus Christ!"

The driver swerved. William braced himself, seeing a white shape pull up dangerously close.

The SUV was only inches away, close enough for William to see the back seat window lower and a tiny face look out.

William's heart leapt to his throat.

Even though the windows of the agents' car were deeply tinted, he could see Lily looking straight at him. Through the dark windows, her black skin made her face almost disappear, with only the whites of her eyes truly visible.

The man driving the car began to lurch suddenly and convulse. The agent in the passenger side reached for the wheel and then began to shudder himself, his skin turning a putrid shade of yellow.

The car veered wildly, sliding with a painful crunching against a stone wall, over a curb and directly into the corner of the front of the garage.

William was thrown forward with such force that he landed between the two front seats, his head crashing into the dashboard.

His vision spun, squinting to see the driver's face rest on its side, his eyes open, bloodshot. His cheeks were sunken in, his hair drifting from his head in clumps.

William felt a strong hand grab the back of his shirt, and the agent from the back seat yanked him, trying to force him into the back seat. "Stay with me, son! When I give the count of two, we run—"

The back door was thrown open, and Rudd was there, pistol raised. Over his shoulder, William could see Lily's face. Her worried expression turned to one of anger, seeing the agent with his arm protectively around William.

No, Lily. No.

The girl blinked, her furious expression immediately fading.

"Don't move, asshole," Rudd said.

"He didn't hurt me," William said. "Listen—"

"Get down on the floor and cover your head. Now!" Rudd ordered. "William, let's go!"

The agent's grip loosened and let go, his hands up in the air.

Everything spinning now, William felt like he could throw up. He stumbled from the car into the opened door of the SUV, where Lily was reaching for him.

He slid inside, clutching his head.

"William, are you OK?"

He tried to focus his eyes, seeing Quincy's face come into view.

"Go!" Rudd yelled, jumping into the front seat. The driver, a black man in a Memphis Grizzlies hat and sunglasses, began to back out of the ramp.

William looked to Lily. "You got out."

"Barely," Quincy said. "One minute later and we would have been burnt toast."

William saw Rudd turn angrily to the windshield. "Don't speed, for God's sake. Make it seem like we're out for a leisurely drive. We were pretty far down that ramp, maybe nobody saw what happened back there. That agent stayed on the floor. If we're lucky, he didn't see the license plate . . ."

Rudd rubbed his eyes. William could see the sleeve of his shirt was singed.

"Do we need to get you to a doctor—?"

"What we need to do is get you out of here," Rudd snapped.

"How . . ." William began. "How did you even know where I was?"

"We didn't," Quincy said, motioning to Lily. "Looks like you have your own personal tracking device—"

"Can you all just be quiet?" Rudd said. "Please."

William felt the girl slide up against him. He lifted his arm and she leaned against his chest.

"I'm a monster," she whispered.

She looked up at him, the proximity to her bringing forth a sensation, almost a jolt, that threatened to take his breath away.

"I'm a monster in the mountain," she said.

She then snuggled up closer to him and closed her eyes.

He stared at her in stunned realization, almost reaching down to place his finger under her chin, lifting so she would have to look up.

He was wrong to think that Lily looked familiar when he found her inside his trailer. Nothing about her—the tightly-pulled hair, cheeks still round with baby fat, the dimpled chin—was recognizable.

But he knew her.

In his nightmares, a pair of eyes watched each disaster, including the dying people at the hospital. Doctors rushing, gurneys wheeling, sunken skin and faces ultimately covered by white sheets, all observed from another who was somehow inside the stone formations in the distance.

Each time, he went from witnessing the horrors himself at the hospital to being trapped within that stone. There, in the dark, with something slithering across his skin, his only companion was that singular pair of eyes.

I'm a monster in the mountain.

Eyes belonging to the girl beside him.

The helicopter's blades tossed the flags of the federal building, the last light of day falling across the building's hundreds of windows. Without an official helipad, the helicopter had to circle the building to position itself to land in a small grassy courtyard.

Circle for hours if you want, Kate thought. Circle for days.

She needed more time to think, to attempt to process what she'd read. The few hours hadn't been enough.

A lifetime might not be enough.

You were wrong. You have been wrong the entire time.

She felt like an elephant had settled onto her chest. She'd made many difficult decisions in the past fourteen years, from calling for a congressional investigation into a prominent member of her own party using taxpayer dollars to take luxurious trips overseas under the guise of business development, to approving a budget that increased welfare benefits and military appropriations but sank the country further into debt.

Centrist Democrats is what we are, her father often said. And we vote with our mind, but lead with our guts.

But no decision, no maneuver, no judgment came anywhere close to the agony of declaring herself a nominee for father's vacant seat without discussing it with him, knowing she could no longer associate with her own family.

Yes, she was infuriated by what she'd read in the government investigation into Argentum. But what very few knew is that she privately went to the town herself, to question the staff at the hospital. Hearing denial after denial, a sliver of doubt wormed its way into her heart, which had always aggressively protected her family. And when her own mother—her rock, her guiding star, her dependable foundation—refused to even discuss what happened with her own family, citing her desire to protect them all, that sliver began to expand.

Her father's abrupt decision to step away from the Senate had been the final straw. She'd lashed out at him, saying he was officially destroying what was left of the family's good name. Her father, always strong to the point of being defiant, seemed different now. Older. Weary. He'd listened to her furious words saying he was being caught up in a ridiculous conspiracy.

He'd simply said, "I believe your mother," and was committing all his time to her work. She'd left the office that day vowing to not speak to him for an entire day until she cooled off.

Instead, she'd gone directly to meet with trusted strategists. A day turned into weeks and months. There was the campaign, and then the election, and then assembling her staff. Her work was all-consuming. Her dedication to her constituents and her country earned her a reputation as a tireless public servant. The corridors of power had slowly opened up to her, extending the type of access most politicians dream of: to the oval office and a second-term president.

It only cost her a family.

When her father died, she'd realized their fight over his decision to leave politics was the last time they'd ever spoken.

After reading the files on her mother and nephew on the flight from DC, she kept thinking about her father's face that day of their final conversation. She couldn't pinpoint then if he was just exhausted from having to make such a monumental decision. But she recalled thinking she'd never seen him look that way.

Having now examined the records from the SSA, she understood. She'd never seen her father look that frightened before.

How much her mother had revealed to her father about what happened in Argentum, Kate didn't know. But if her mother had told him half of what was contained within the files, then she understood why he was so afraid.

Kate wished she could have seen the videos referenced in the pages herself, of the interrogation of her mother when she was a little girl, and of William at seven years old. All she had was the transcript, but what both of them described, especially William, of why they were returned, and what frightening abilities rested within them, made her physically ill.

She also desperately wanted to know why a large portion of the file on her mother was missing. Stolen, the SSA director had said. An internal problem that we're still looking into.

But she had seen the videos of the little girl and what she'd done in those moments in the field and at the airport before those fanatics took them all.

"It's happening again, Senator," the SSA's director had said, leaning on his desk. "All you have to see for proof is on any news network's website."

He'd then turned around his laptop to reveal CNN's front page, showing the next burgeoning hurricane on the coast of New Orleans.

"Take your pick. Hurricanes on the coasts of twelve countries now. Wildfires too. Uprising in violence and hospitals suddenly overrun with people dying rapidly of diseases. Over and over. But faster and more powerful than before. And when you look at this," he said, calling up the surveillance video from the airport, "you understand why."

She'd told him she needed time to examine the records. He'd allowed her to take copies of them home, and arranged for them to have a conference call at seven. By midafternoon, the news about the disaster in Memphis and William's appearance broke, and she'd called, demanding to speak with him. Director Wolve was already dispatched to Memphis, she was told. But he had staff coming to her at that very moment.

When the men in suits arrived, they had with them a signed order from the FBI. Having read and reread the files repeatedly at that point, she'd co-signed the document, and accepted the agency's offer to fly her to Memphis.

As the helicopter finally began to descend, Kate took a long, deep breath. She had always been decisive, able to take command and feel confident about her decisions, even if they were painful to make. Now, she hated the waffling within her, born from the reality that she was going ever deeper, entwining with an enemy she had fought against her entire political career.

As soon as the whirling began to diminish, the doors opened and the suits were waiting. A tall man with short gray hair followed her as she brushed past them, his long legs allowing him to keep up with her brisk pace.

"Where exactly did it happen?" she demanded.

"On the east side, on a service ramp, I'm told. Luckily no one heard or saw it."

"No one heard a car crash and an agent get shot outside a federal building?"

"I asked the same question. It's Sunday. If anyone is in downtown Memphis on the weekend, it's on Beale Street. There's also the distraction of a motel on fire at this moment."

"Director Wolve, I cannot imagine how this could have been handled worse," she said, walking into the building, the door held open for her by the accompanying agents. "And all I want to know is the location of my nephew."

"Agent Hallow knows to give us a full briefing."

"And my mother? Is she safe?"

"She's been brought in. On her way to Washington now. She was not pleased. And as you anticipated, she was not alone. The woman . . ."

"Roxy Garth."

"She had to be taken in as well. She threatened to put it all on social media."

"And she would have. As I stated before: They are to both be treated with extreme care. Anything they need, they get. They'll be furious that they are under constant watch, but as soon as I've addressed the mess you've made here, and made sure my nephew is safe, I'll go to them."

"That is the deal, Senator."

"This way, ma'am," one of the agents said, directing her to the elevator.

"And trust me on this," Kate held up her finger as she stepped in. "My family will not stand for this. My sister is a well-connected journalist. My brother-in-law is a hell of a lawyer. We're in for a battle on this one once they figure out my mother has been taken in. And just exactly how am I to explain this to them? That my nearly eighty-year-old mother is a potential deadly threat to all those around her?"

"You know what you've seen, Senator. We just have to determine why she hasn't been activated like the others."

The doors opened, and the agents led them down another empty hallway. At the end, they reached another office, where a man with an earpiece stood.

"Director, Mr. Hallow would like to see you for a moment—"

"He can see us both," Kate said, striding over to the only other door in the room. "I assume he's in there?"

"Ma'am—"

She opened the door to what had clearly become a war room in the last six hours. Along with multiple white Styrofoam coffee cups, laptops beside large monitors littered the room. Agents clustered around the screens.

In the midst of the chaos, Flynn Hallow rose, brushing his thin strands of hair across his forehead.

"Director Wolve," he said. He looked over to Kate. "Senator."

"Bring us up to speed, Agent Hallow. Everyone, continue your work, I want those people found," the director said.

As the conversations continued at a much more subdued tone, Flynn walked through, brandishing an iPad.

Before he could begin to speak, Kate stepped forward. "Begin with where you think my nephew is at this very moment."

"We believe with the same fanatics that took him in Little Rock."

"How can that be, when you obviously blew up an entire hotel room to stop them?"

"Let me be clear that we are investigating at this very moment what caused the explosion, that it could very well have been these true believers—"

"Don't bullshit me," she said. "Spin it any way you want it to cover yourself, but don't attempt it on me. While I wholeheartedly disagree with your methods, including the danger you put many innocent Tennesseans in, I have read the files. I understand that you believe this girl, even my nephew, pose some sort of danger—"

"Not some sort," Flynn said.

"Agent Hallow, please explain to the senator what happened here," Mark said.

"The car driving your nephew crashed and he is now missing. Three of our best agents were in that car."

"How in the world did that happen?" Kate asked.

Flynn swiped the screen of his iPad, and turned it around. "The girl happened," he said.

Kate covered her mouth at the sight of the photograph of two agents slumped over in the front seat of the smashed vehicle, their skin splotchy, their hair having fallen out in massive clumps.

"One of our agents survived, though. And verified what this video shows. There was a camera posted on the parking garage ramp."

He swiped again, and surveillance video appeared on the screen. It showed the agents' car suddenly speeding up and crashing into the side entrance. A white SUV pulled up alongside, and a man jumped out.

Kate held her breath as the man pulled her obviously disoriented nephew from the car and led him into the SUV. For a brief moment, a little girl could be seen reaching for William as the door shut behind him.

"An APB has been put out for that SUV," Mark said.

"Only on private channels to law enforcement," Flynn added. "We suspect they've already changed out the license plate, even though the agent who survived was unable to see it. But we're monitoring cameras throughout the city, and social media. We are holding off putting it out to the media until we develop a next course of action."

Kate frowned. "I want to make one thing very, very clear. I want my nephew found, but I will not have innocent people in my state—or any other state, for matter—put in danger. Blow up another building in Tennessee, and I'll shut down your entire operation."

Flynn's face flushed. "You can't—"

"I can and I will. I did what you asked in signing that order with the FBI. But I'm now going to be included in all your briefings. Is that understood?"

"Senator, we need time—"

"You have two hours to come up with a course of action to find him. We'll meet again at nine o'clock. I'm issuing a statement that I am closely monitoring the investigation by the FBI. I won't hover, but I won't be far either. Find my nephew, gentlemen. Bring him in safely."

"Ma'am, please realize there is much more to discuss," Flynn said. "All this needs to get to the top levels—"

"When my nephew is unharmed and safe and I know exactly where he is, we can discuss more. He needs to be your top priority. Am I clear?"

Kate did not wait for their response before walking away and reaching for her phone, glad that her back was to them so they could not see how badly her hands were shaking.

EIGHT

William felt hands on his shoulders, shaking him, Quincy's voice repeatedly asking what was wrong. When he opened his eyes to the familiar feeling of his throat scratchy from crying out, he could see the driver of the van had pulled over to the side of the road and was looking at him in astonishment beneath the brim of his hat.

Rudd turned around in his seat, wearing an annoyed expression. "Again with the screams?"

A soft hand rested on William's own. Lily looked up at him, sitting so close that her eyes were only inches away from his.

In his nightmare, he saw those eyes trapped in stone.

"Seriously, are you OK?" Quincy asked from where he sat forward in the back seat. "You sounded like someone set you on fire. What the hell were you dreaming about?"

"It's OK," William said. "Just a nightmare."

"Well, get yourself together. We're almost there." Rudd motioned for the driver to keep on.

Lily removed her hand. William wiped his eyes and leaned in towards her. "Lily . . . you have to talk to me."

As she had done in each of the several attempts he'd made in their overnight travel south, she once again turned away but scooted up next to him. She'd proven that she physically couldn't get close enough to him, like a nervous child to a parent, but refused to communicate.

I'm a monster in the mountain, she'd said.

Lily's eyes in stone. Eyes in the mountain? People dying in a hospital nearby. People dying as Lily watched.

Once they got wherever they were going, he would find a way to get her alone. She had to explain what she meant by those words. Why she had made the national parks investigator bring her to Little Rock. How she had tracked him from the motel to the federal building.

And, more important than anything else: How she wielded the power to kill.

"We're here," Rudd said.

The expansive oaks claustrophobically close to the windows were another reminder that their final destination was Florida. If the windows hadn't been locked, he could have reached out to touch the Spanish moss hanging in the branches.

The narrow road opened out to a vast clearing, still surrounded by the same sprawling trees. If it weren't for their massive trunks, it would be difficult to see where one ended and the other began.

In the midst of the yard was a house; a mansion, to be more accurate. Antebellum in design, sweeping white pillars with upper and lower porches. Bright pink azalea bushes spread across the front.

"Where are we?" William asked.

"Right now," Rudd said, taking out his pistol and engaging the safety button, "the only safe place in the world."

They pulled up to the front, keeping the engine running.

"Last stop," the driver said.

Rudd reached over and gave him a hearty handshake. "Thank you, my friend. I know this wasn't what you expected when we needed a ride out of Memphis."

"Just doing my part for the cause. Give Miss Blue my best."

As Rudd slid out and opened the back seat passenger door, motioning for William, Lily, and Quincy to exit, the driver turned around.

"You keep little miss safe, you hear?"

William nodded. As soon as they stepped out and the door was closed, the SUV pulled away. They watched it leave the clearing and disappear on the shadowy road.

"If I took off running, how long would it be until an alligator ate me?" Quincy asked.

"Feel free to try and find out." Rudd began to climb the stairs to the house.

"What are we doing here," William asked. "Where are we?"

"Where she told us to bring you."

"She? Who is she?" Quincy asked.

Nanna? She couldn't be here. Could she?

"My grandmother? Is she here?" William asked.

"Your grandmother?" Quincy whispered, keeping pace with Lily. "Really? Here?"

When Rudd didn't respond, William shook his head in frustration. "I don't know."

They entered the front doors into a hallway with a stairwell surrounded on both sides by murals depicting peacocks and other birds nestled in billowing bushes and trees. A tall, stately grandfather clock stood guard next to a writing desk.

Rudd marched past it all to approach the two men standing by another set of double doors. Both wore pistols in holsters at their waists.

"She's on the porch," one of them said.

"It's too hot right now for her out there, even with the fans on," Rudd said.

"Go 'head and try to convince her of that," the other responded, opening the doors.

They followed Rudd onto a sprawling back porch. Boston ferns sat in urns overlooking a carefully manicured lawn with a reflecting pool. The sound of waves echoed in the distance.

Observing it all was a woman sitting in a domed rattan chair. Beside her was a wheelchair, with a file resting in the seat. She turned to them as they stepped out.

William swallowed his disappointment. It never made sense that his grandmother would be here, that she was behind all of it. But there was a part of him that had hoped at the end of this bloody and frantic journey, she would be there to somehow make sense of it all.

The woman was, without a doubt, the oldest person he had ever seen. The hand she reached out to Rudd was small and frail, her cotton-white hair was pulled up in a tight bun. Thin glasses sat on her tiny nose.

Even as Rudd knelt before her, she did not take her eyes off William.

"You lived," she said to Rudd, her eyes remaining fixed. Even at a distance, William could see they were a deep shade of blue.

"Barely," Rudd said, holding her hand.

"I'm so sorry," she said, at last looking to Rudd. "About Kevin and Neve. I know better than anyone what the Suits are capable of doing."

"They knew the risks, just like all of us do."

"Still . . ." She paused, looking at his singed arm. "You all must be exhausted. Rudd, make sure that burn isn't serious. You know where we keep the first aid kit. The rest of you, we'll have food brought up to you. We've laid out clothes for you in your rooms. All except for Mr. Chance. I need to speak with him."

"Actually, I need to hear this too," Quincy said. "I need some goddamn answers—"

"Show some respect." The men from the doors moved in closer behind them.

"Respect to who? Where the hell are we? Who the hell are you people?" Quincy asked.

"Mr. Martin is right to ask," the woman said. "You may have come to find William to make money, sir, but it has led you on a dangerous path, one you now cannot veer from."

"I'm the only driver on my path, Ancient One," Quincy said. "You can't keep us here."

"Show Mr. Martin to our finest accommodations," she said.

Quincy was practically spun around into the house. With a slight shove, he was inside, the sound of his complaints echoing from the hallway.

"Rudd, you can't risk infection."

"I'm fine, Miss Blue."

"Just go make sure that wound is clean. Come right back. When William and I are done here, I'll need a full debriefing from you."

Rudd nodded and went to leave, holding out his hand to Lily. "I bet you're hungry." Lily shook her head and clung to William.

"I figured as much. She never leaves his side," Rudd said.

"That's just fine," the woman said, her eyes crinkling at the girl. "Miss Lily, you are welcome to stay if you'd like."

The remaining guard brought forth two chairs and sat them before the woman. He then walked away and, crossing his arms across his burly chest, leaned on a pillar on the far end of the porch.

As William and Lily sat, the woman clasped her hands on her lap.

"I am sorry for what you've both been through."

William leaned forward. "Once you tell us what you can, you need to let us go."

"I wish I could, sweet boy. Well, you aren't a boy anymore, are you? I know your family wants to know you're alright. And pretty girl, I wish I knew of anywhere safe to send you. But there is nowhere safe now, for either of you."

"I don't even know who you are."

She sat up surprisingly straight for someone of her age. "Everyone here calls me Blue. My eyes are the only thing about me that hasn't dulled. Tell me, William, how much did your grandmother tell you about the Researchers? Did she ever mention a group called the Corcillium?"

"My grandmother never spoke of her work. I only know what I've read; that they researched unexplained disappearances."

"She was smart not to tell you. She wanted to protect you. She's a . . ." Blue's voice trembled for a moment. "She's a good girl, your grandmother."

"So you're one of them, then? Rudd said it was my grandmother who summoned him and the others to find me. Are you taking orders from her?"

She took a deep breath. "We claim her as one of us, even though she only communicates with one of our members. The Corcillium wanted her to join us, but she refused. She trusted no one. I certainly cannot blame her."

"What is this . . . Corcillium?"

"It's actually the name of this house," Blue said, looking around. "The family who owned it considered it the heart of their family—corcillum means "heart" in Latin. Ultimately, it was inherited by one of our first members, and it became the center of the group that took its name. The Corcillium is like a council that directs the work of the Researchers. About fourteen years ago, I joined that council. But before that, I worked for the same shadow agency that wishes to take you and never let you go."

"You mean . . . you worked for those men in suits?"

"I was with the SSA for most of my entire life, until something happened, shall we say, that showed me the truth. And now I lead the Corcillium. Which is why, when I learned that you had surfaced in Arkansas, I sent my people to protect you. Leaving your family was a dangerous move. You were safe with them, in the protective bubble created by your parents and grandparents. You have no idea what danger you put yourself in by going on the run."

Blue looked to Lily. "And when Rudd and the others told me about you, Miss Lily, I knew we had to keep you both safe. I've lived more than one hundred years without dying, but I felt like I almost would when I heard of the motel exploding. And yet, you survived. And at last, you are here."

"So it's all been a lie, then," William said. "My grandmother wasn't behind all this."

Blue leaned forward. "Tell me, what do you know about your mother's family? Her mother and father?"

"Why does it matter?"

"It matters greatly."

William raised his eyebrow. "Not much. Only that they built the house where my grandmother lives. My great-grandfather was a landscaper. And my grandmother's mother died when she was just a child."

Blue reached over to the file in the seat of the wheelchair, her hands trembling, to open it and pull out a small photo. "I don't even know . . . if your grandmother has any photos of her mother."

She passed a small black-and-white photograph to him. The edges were yellowed and torn on one corner. It looked to be an ID of some sort, as the woman in the picture was not smiling.

"Do you recognize your great-grandmother?" she asked.

"Honestly . . . I think my grandmother has one photo in her bedroom, of her mother holding her as a baby. But I never really looked at it. Are you saying this is my great-grandmother? And how, may I ask, do you have it?"

"Her name was Freda Stanson, isn't that right?"

"Yes. What does this have to do with anything?"

"Look closely at it. In fact, focus solely on that picture until I tell you otherwise. Hold it up, right there. Think of nothing but that face."

"Ma'am, please—"

"Please, William. It's the beginning of the explanation as to why you're here."

He sighed, holding up the photo before his eyes. Even in the black-and-white photo, he could see she had the same blond hair as Nanna, a trait passed along to his aunts but not his mother. She had other features like his grandmother: a graceful neck, the small ears, the curled hair. How many times had he heard Nanna grumble about how often she had to pull her own curls from her face, muttering that the only time it was ever controlled was when it was tightly curtailed in a bun—?

He dropped the picture. In the seconds that he'd stared at the photo, Blue had pulled out the few pins in her hair, letting it now fall in curls around her face. She was also extending her own neck to reveal its natural state before age took its toll.

No. It can't possibly be—

"She didn't die, William," she said. "Despite all she's seen and done, she is still alive. And she is very happy to, at long last, meet her great-grandson."

William had not wanted to go when Rudd returned to the porch, right on cue from where he had been waiting, directing him to follow. He'd stammered something about not moving a muscle, staring at Blue's face, astonished at the growing resemblance to Nanna, even his own mother. Blue's eyes were filled with happy tears as Rudd had placed his hand on William's shoulder, saying there were things he needed to see.

"Go, my boy," Blue had said. "Read our family's history. You need to see it for yourself. I've waited all my life for this moment. I'm not going anywhere."

Rudd's grip had been insistent. Blue turned to Lily and said she'd love to get to know her a little better, and the little girl had warily watched William stand and leave in a haze of astonishment.

Once in the hallway, he'd stopped and turned back to the porch. "No, I've got to talk to her—"

"You will. But she wants you to see something first. You'll understand. And then you can come back," Rudd beckoned.

Down the hall and then a turn into a butler's pantry, where a heavy set of double doors stood. Directly beside them was a small painting of a woman standing behind a greyhound. Rudd moved the painting, which hung not on a hook but by hinges, opening it like a cabinet door to reveal a keypad underneath.

After he punched in a code, a loud, mechanical sound echoed from the wall. Rudd opened the doors to reveal a concealed elevator.

It was a short one-floor ride downwards. The basement that opened up before them was a stark contrast to the airy, antiques-filled rooms above. The walls and floor here were all concrete, with rows of shelves stocked with files and folders. A long metal table with a lamp stretched out in the center, with a thin stack of papers in the center.

"It's all ready."

The voice was deep but scratchy with age. The back of a man's head, almost bushy with stark white hair, was barely visible in a corner table, where he sat in front of a laptop.

"Thank you," Rudd said.

"Is she doing alright?" the man asked. "I do not want her overextended."

"Good luck telling her to go take a nap."

The man chuckled, returning to study the computer screen.

"William, have a seat," Rudd said.

"What is all this?"

"The most valuable assets we have." Rudd pulled out a chair, motioning to sit. "The research of the Corcillium. Into all the cases of the missing, gathered from around the nation. Each one has a file. This is your grandmother's."

A photocopy of a letter rested on top of the stack. "These aren't the originals; those are stored in the shelves around you. But we've taken the copies and put them in chronological order so you can understand."

"Copies of what? I don't even know what I'm looking at."

Rudd crossed his arms. "Not even your grandmother has seen the letters that her parents wrote about her disappearance."

"Letters to whom? The Corcillium?"

Rudd shook his head. "To fully comprehend what you're facing, you need to read every word. I'm going to leave you to it. It's not that we don't trust you—but our friend there in the corner will keep an eye on you. He'll let me know when you're done."

William leaned forward as Rudd walked away, his steel-toed boots crossing the floor to the elevator.

He looked at the letter on top, seeing immediately it was a relic of a different age, the handwriting not just precise, but also elegant. The gentle sweep of the *y*, the supple *o*, the gentle dots above the *i*, all written by a hand not yet ravaged by age.

CLASSIFIED SSA
AUTHORIZED READERS ONLY
LYNN STANSON FILE

October 26, 1951
YUCATAN, MEXICO

I will use what is left of me to write this. This is the time to do it, as I am as numb as a magnolia branch in December, bending but not yet broken by the ice. Do not take me for an unloving mother or wife who is able to methodically dictate the loss of my daughter and husband. My heart has already broken, along with much of my body, and I cannot ever recover. If this exercise assists in determining what's happening to other families like mine, then so be it. This is for them. It will not help me.

My name is Freda Stanson.

I'd only meant to lay down for a minute the night my daughter disappeared. But the rain was an undeniable lullaby.

The flash was so bright I could see it despite my closed eyes. I sat up to see a section of the woods momentarily illuminate and then go dark. The rain had stopped, long enough for the screen on the window to dry. I must have drifted a bit more, because I only truly woke when I heard Bud's calls from outside.

Immediately I was on my feet and running down the hall. I pushed through the screened door, spotting my husband on the edge of the woods, his hands cupped around his mouth, calling for Lynn.

He'd answered my question before I could ask it. They'd dozed off, watching the fireflies that our daughter loved so much that she spent nearly every night trapping them and then delighting in letting them go. He'd woken to find her gone. He'd searched the house and the yard. He'd noticed then that the fireflies were heavy in the trees after the rain.

He'd directed me to get the flashlight from the greenhouse. She'll see the light and come back, he said. She just got turned around. She's a country girl. She's not afraid of the woods.

I'd run to the greenhouse and found the silver Rayovac where Bud had left it after trying to chase away a coyote that had wandered too close to the property line a few weeks ago.

I thought of the creature, its eyes reflecting the flashlight. I'd stood on the porch, watching Bud waving his arms to spook it. It had examined him for far too long, in my opinion, before slipping into the dark.

I'd reminded him of the coyote when I hurried back. He ran into the woods.

The light winked between the dark trees as I'd yelled out, telling Lynn to follow the flashlight to Daddy. I could see the other flickerings from the fireflies as well, and felt one dart in front of my face, another bounce off my ear. I anticipated their illumination before me, but none appeared. Even in the night, I could see them zig-zagging, with one or two landing on my neck.

I pulled them off, gentle as I taught Lynn to do if they landed on her. They popped in my hand, and yet as I opened my fingers, no tiny glow emerged.

I felt a few on my legs now, and knew, the way they clung to me without piercing or irritation, that they were Bud's ladybugs. He'd had them shipped in to eat the aphids in the gardens, but they were supposed to rest at night.

They were everywhere now, and I thought of how I'd have to search through Lynn's curls later to make sure none got entangled. She would laugh if I brought one from her hair, like a magician pulling a dime from behind her ear.

I kept walking to escape their swarm, following Bud's light as he went deeper into the woods. I then saw the light stop, and I held my breath, waiting for him to call out that he'd found her.

The light came towards me with a rapid pace. When he at last emerged, I could see he was alone, his face sunken in the harsh light, holding out one of our daughter's shoes.

I need to take a break now. I will wait for the pain to subside.

William read the letter twice, his hands trembling.

He was not the first of his family to disappear in the woods behind their homes.

Flipping to the next page, he saw distinctly different handwriting, as different from Freda Stanson's as possible. There was a practicality to it, written without flare.

Nov 1, 1951

Lynn,

This is foreign to me. I am a man who writes only for purpose. Receipts. Plant orders. Bills. I have had no use for it in my life. I barely finished high school, after all. I attempted to write your mother a love letter once. She read it, corrected my spelling, and folded it in her Bible. In the same place she keeps a lock of your hair.

Kept. She kept it there.

It is still hard for me to think of her as gone.

As I write this, I am watching you sleep. You resemble her so much, with your long eyelashes and curls. When you sleep, it is one of the few times when I can get close to you. My heart breaks a bit more every morning when you wake and look at me with confusion. But it is the fear that hurts the most. You do not believe me when I tell you that I am your father.

Dr. Martin isn't a medical doctor, but he's a very smart man. He tells me that in time your memory might return. That whatever they did to you could be reversible. I truly, though, just want you to remember your mother.

And that is why, my girl, I write this. Because I want you to know who your mother was and what she did to save you.

When you disappeared that night, we were in such a panic. We looked all night. We were waiting for morning to ask for help, as we didn't dare leave the trees. Then a truck pulled up in the drive. You have to know how strange that was. We don't get many visitors out here except for customers.

Your mother ran to the truck, and that's when the strange man with glasses stepped out. I remember thinking I had misunderstood him. He asked something about if lightning had struck near our house.

This is harder than I thought. The words don't come easily to me. But I will do this for you. I will do anything for you, my girl. And I will wait as long as it takes for you to call me father.

Love,
Daddy

CLASSIFIED SSA
AUTHORIZED READERS ONLY
LYNN STANSON FILE

October 27, 1951
YUCATAN, MEXICO

Terrible pain. The pain medication helps, but today is difficult. Keep writing, Freda, they tell me. It will take your mind off it. I know why they tell me that. They want a record of it, while it's still fresh in my mind. What they really want is for me to tell it just in case I don't survive. So be it.

We'd searched all night. Nothing. No trace of her. Only the shoe. Bud had gotten his shotgun and entered the woods while I just stood and cried, calling for her until daylight.

There was nowhere to go for help. We agreed Bud would leave at dawn. We didn't know our neighbors well, and we were really scattered far apart. But I'd stay here and look while Bud tried to wrangle some people up. That's when the old Ford pulled into the drive.

I ran over in desperation, begging the man who stepped out to drive to the police or find the county sheriff and report Lynn's disappearance. I must have sounded insane, saying that our phone lines were crackling so badly that I couldn't get through last night and we didn't dare stop searching to go drive for help.

He'd introduced himself as Dr. Rex Martin, and asked us a singular question that I remember stopped me in my tracks: had my daughter vanished after lightning struck?

I'd remembered it, then, the flash of light. I must have stammered that I'd seen it.

He was so calm.

I think I know where your daughter is, he'd said.

William's brow furrowed. The letter from Nanna's mother ended suddenly, as if the rest of it had been cut and replaced. The next page was another letter from Nanna's father. Why had they removed—

Then he remembered what Rudd said, about how they had been placed in chronological order.

The letters obviously came from different sources and were written about a year apart. His great-grandmother's letters were labeled "classified" with that acronym—SSA. Both Blue and Rudd had mentioned them in correlation with agents in black suits. Her letters even bore an official stamp. His great-grandfather's letter, however, had no such distinction.

Nov 2, 1951

Lynn,

Not a good day for us, baby. You were especially skittish today. I know it's so hard for you, not knowing who I am and just the two of us here at this house. I keep showing you the picture of your mother and me on our wedding day. I keep pointing out how much you look like her. I think you see it, too, but you're still not convinced. If it takes a lifetime, I'll point it out every day.

It's especially difficult to see you look so afraid. It's an almost identical expression to your mother's on the night you disappeared and that morning afterwards, when that man showed up in the driveway.

He gave us his name, Dr. Rex Martin—a professor from some university in St. Louis. Said he had been fishing up at the Land Between the Lakes in Kentucky when he was listening to radio reports of storms that passed through Nashville and how farmers on the west side of the county said that the lightning continued after the rain had passed. He kept talking about how he broke every speed limit to get here, stopping at every house to see if they'd seen any lightning actually touch down.

Your mama told him that there had been lightning when our daughter disappeared.

I'll be honest with you, I started getting mad. The man said he needed to make a call, and I'd pointed out that we'd tried to use our phone but the reception was so bad we couldn't get through. I told him that he needed to get in the car and go for help. He kept saying he had to make a call right now. I said any phone call that worked would be used to find my girl.

He then ran back to his passenger seat and pulled out a map, flattening it out on the hood. He motioned us over, showing us a map of the gulf. He pointed to what looked like the flipped-up tail of Mexico. He said something about a town not on the map, called Olvidar. He said if he was right, that's where our daughter was.

I'd put my arm in front of your mama, getting her to back up. I suspected, at that moment, that he'd had something to do with your disappearance. I started walking towards him, demanding to know what he'd done with our girl. He held up his hands, talking real fast, repeating that he was a meteorology professor, and that he'd been working with a man in the Yucatan to document cases of people vanishing after lightning strikes when storms are over.

I was about to swing when your mama said something about the girl's gravestone in the woods.

The letter ended suddenly, and when William flipped to the next, someone had typed at the top of the next page, "Continuation of Freda Stanson's recollection from October 28, 1951."

Dr. Martin had explained how he was doing research, with some man in the Yucatan, of all places, about how people disappeared after strange lightning following storms. I know my husband: he was ready to pounce. Bud had always been scrappy, and it was really what first attracted me to him. At that moment, Bud was exhausted, scared, and now very angry at this man who came out of nowhere. But when Dr. Martin mentioned the lightning, I remembered something. About the girl, and her gravestone in the woods.

I must have said it quietly, the name Amelia Shrank.

I'd watched my husband's face, ruddy from hours of yelling and hurrying through the trees, drain to pale.

Dr. Martin had asked who Amelia Shrank was. Bud hadn't interrupted me, and that let me know that he must have passed her gravestone in his frantic searches and tried not to think about what it meant for Lynn.

I'd explained that there was a gravestone in the middle of the woods. For a little girl named Amelia. Bud had found it by accident while deer hunting two years ago. I'd asked Martha Jacobs about it. She lived a few farms over, and she told me that the girl's parents had put it there before they packed up and moved away. Martha said it had been so long since the girl vanished that she didn't remember the details, something about Amelia going into the woods after her dog when it got loose after a big rain. But Martha did point out she remembered quite clearly how another man, Josh Stone, had died in the woods about ten years ago. He drowned in the creek after a storm, she said. They think he got struck by lightning and fell in. They never found his body.

Dr. Martin had taken a deep breath. He spoke about how his colleague in Mexico said that in the town there, when lightning strikes after a storm, people show up on the beach. People who have no memory. It's happened for so long that the town actually took its name from it. Olvidar means, "to forget" in Spanish.

I'd looked at Dr. Martin. Call it a mother's intuition, call it a lack of sleep or quiet desperation, but I'd motioned him for him to follow. Bud looked to me with anger, but I'd held up my hand to him to stop. My husband knows not to push me. And the truth be told, I wanted to see for myself if the phone was back working so I could start making calls for help.

We ran inside, Bud practically right on top of the man. I picked up the phone, and found the static gone. I'd told Dr. Martin that I needed to have the operator call the police, but he'd practically begged me to try to make the call first.

It hadn't been easy standing there. I quickly grew frustrated at the minutes ticking by as he'd argued with the operator about how to make an international call to Mexico. Bud banged the wall. Just when I'd finally demanded that he give me the phone and stop this nonsense, he held up a finger, saying there was a connection.

CONTINUATION OF LETTER BY BUD STANSON

Dr. Martin let your mama and me gather close to listen when a man answered, with a thick Mexican accident. Dr. Martin was relieved, and covered up the bottom of the phone for a moment to explain it was his friend in the Yucatan. His name was Antonio.

The man sounded frantic to me. Said he'd been trying to reach Dr. Martin at his house and office for a few hours. That there had been a storm there that morning and he'd found them. He kept saying that: I found them.

I remember Dr. Martin telling him to slow down. Who did he find?

The white people, the man said. On the beach. Three adults, one child. The adults don't remember anything. They don't know their names. But the little girl does. She knows who she is.

I don't think I breathed, baby girl. I was so confused, but even my simple mind started to dare to hope.

Dr. Martin asked what the girl said. His friend said that she'd been up in the sky with scary people and she wanted her Mama and Daddy. That she had blond curly hair and overalls.

She said her name was Lynn.

CONTINUATION OF DOCUMENTATION OF FREDA STANSON

I just screamed. Over and over again. Asking where was my daughter? Where was my daughter?

The man, Antonio was his name, said he'd gathered them up and told them he was taking them to get help. They were in the other room at the apartment he had been renting.

I demanded to talk to her, and I heard him call out for her, to come to the other room.

I've never cried tears before that burned my eyes, but they came, hot and gushing, when I heard my little girl get on the phone and ask for me.

I'd asked her if she was all right. She said she was, but she was scared. She asked where her daddy and I were.

I told her to stay right there, that Daddy and I were coming right now to get her. I told her that I loved her and not to be afraid. That we were coming for her.

Antonio had gotten back on the phone and said that Lynn appeared just fine aside from some kind of pain on the back of her head. I begged him to keep her safe, which he promised to do.

Then, he paused. I heard it too, even over the phone. The loud knocking on the door.

CONTINUATION OF LETTER FROM BUD STANSON

And then he got you on the phone. I heard your voice and I couldn't help but cry in relief. We told you we were coming for you. Then we heard something at the door.

The Mexican man whispered that someone was outside. He went to go check and came back and said there were men in suits at the door.

Dr. Martin told him to hide, right now. To take you and the adults and hide.

We just stood there, waiting. I shouted for him to tell us that you were OK. But there was only silence.

I need to stop now. I'll write more tomorrow, if my heart can take it. I pray, maybe tonight, you'll dream of your mother.

Love,
Daddy

CONTINUATION OF LETTER BY FREDA STANSON

To have that kind of hope, that kind of relief, of knowing that your missing child is alive and apparently well, and then in the next moment have it all plunge into deeper fear and confusion, is an experience I would not wish on the devil himself. But that's exactly what happened. Antonio had gone to check to see who was knocking, said it was men in suits at the door, and then nothing.

We'd frantically had the operator call the number again. But each time, she said the line was dead. The glimpse into the welfare of my daughter had closed.

Bud had exploded, and I hadn't blamed him. Shouting, demanding an explanation for what the hell just happened, ordering me to go pack a bag and that Dr. Martin would get in his truck and drive us to our daughter right now.

Dr. Martin tried to remain calm, explaining that the man on the phone was a journalist he trusted who had grown up near Olvidar and had heard stories of people showing up on the beach without memories after lightning storms. That he'd moved there to write a book about the town, but when he started inquiring about it, his house had burned down.

I kept fighting the urge to do as Bud instructed, to throw our things together and just get on the road. Mexico, I kept thinking. How will we ever get to Mexico?

Dr. Martin could clearly see we were panicking and cut to the chase: Antonio had read an article he'd written, about his theory that lightning strikes were incinerating people and making them look as if they disappeared. Antonio had written him about the strange occurrences in

Olvidar, how he thought the theory was wrong. That they'd begun to talk by phone. And together, they'd come up with the idea that people weren't burning so quickly that there was nothing left of them, but rather vanishing. And reappearing in Mexico.

I am going to ask for some more of the medication and try to sleep now. It's the only time I have peace, when the drugs deafen the pain and rid my brain of the ability to remember.

CONTINUATION OF LETTER FROM BUD STANSON

Nov 10, 1951
Lynn,

You smiled at me when you woke today! It was a real breakthrough. You asked for honey on your toast. I told you I would get you anything you wanted. Could it be that maybe—just maybe—that there is hope for us as a family?

Every time I start feeling bad, feeling sorry for myself and missing your mother so much that it hurts, I think about how your mother heard your voice on the phone and that it went dead. I thought that it would be the last time we would ever hear or see you. But now, you are in your bed asleep and I can reach out and touch you. You are real and here with me. It is worth reliving this so you can one day know what your mother did to bring you home.

I know what Dr. Martin must have thought of us that morning. Practically kids ourselves, just nineteen when we had you. Could we even begin to understand what he was saying? I'll admit, my mind is like a fog sometimes, it takes me a minute to understand some things. But not your mama. She is as sharp as a tack. He learned that fast.

CLASSIFIED SSA
AUTHORIZED READERS ONLY
LYNN STANSON FILE

October 30, 1951
YUCATAN, MEXICO

Sometimes they allow me to leave my windows open for a brief amount of time, so I can feel the breeze off the ocean. It's never for long—

they worry it will get too humid in the room despite the fans, that I will sweat too much under all these casts and bandages. It's one of the first things I ask for each day, to open the windows. It reminds me of the first day we landed in Mexico, when I still had hope.

They ask me to detail as much as I can about Dr. Martin, and the organization he belongs to. But the truth is I know very little. He never discussed them by name, and I was never privy to his quiet phone conversations with them. I only know they must have had a wealthy member, or maybe several, otherwise we wouldn't have had access to the small propeller planes that took us from Nashville to New Orleans. And finally, to Mexico, after an agonizing two-day wait, while Martin's colleagues scrambled to find another plane.

We landed, and headed directly for the beach at Olvidar. I had to keep reminding myself that this wasn't some sort of lagging nightmare, that this was all really happening. That my little girl was here somewhere, taken from our woods and dropped somehow in this poverty-stricken piece of the world.

Bud had grown so quiet at this point I knew he was at the breaking point. Most of our communications were had when I reached out for his hand, and he held it with a fierceness that renewed my strength.

In broken Spanish, Dr. Martin repeatedly asked anyone if they knew Antonio Borges. Even I, who could not comprehend their words, could tell by watching their faces that they didn't want to answer.

We made our way to the beach, a sprawling stretch of emerald and blue spilling onto white.

It was empty. No people, no witnesses.

Then I saw the children. They were sitting in the shade of several palm trees, watching us. I gave them a small wave, and they didn't respond.

Dr. Martin approached them. I feared they might sprint at the sight of three strangers approaching.

Almost frantically reading through the pages, William flipped to the next and stopped. The handwriting was different, and the letter was addressed this time to Bud Stanson. The return address was from St. Louis, Missouri, and the name of the sender was of the professor so often mentioned in his great-grandparents' letters: Dr. Rex Martin.

Bud Stanson
1 Evelyn Road
Nashville, TN 37205

Rex Martin
St. Louis University
1 North Grand Boulevard
St. Louis, Missouri 63103

Dec 1, 1951
Bud,

I will continue to write you, even if you do not respond. This exercise may be more for me at this point. To detail this so there is no loss of memory. I have not been feeling well as of late.

It is horrible on my part that I do not remember their names. But they were clearly brother and sister. The boy answered almost immediately that he knew Antonio, his sister shaking her head, telling him to be quiet. I think the silver pesos from my pocket helped.

They wouldn't get into the car, so it meant we had to walk. Even with my limited Spanish, I could understand the girl was chastising her brother. He ignored her, as all brothers do their older sisters. I asked him if he ever saw people show up on the beach. White people, like us. The boy nodded, saying two words over and over, pulling at his shirt.

Traje negro, traje negro. Over and over. I pulled out the Spanish dictionary.

Black suit.

CONTINUATION OF LETTER BY FREDA STANSON

I suppose it was the money, in the end, that got the children to take us to the house of the journalist. Bud didn't like the idea of leaving the car parked at the beach, but he eagerly followed. For him, it was the first proof he'd seen for himself that at least something Dr. Martin had told us was true, that this Antonio Borges existed. I know Bud believed me that I'd spoken to Lynn. But it's different, I know, when you see a grain of truth for yourself.

I wanted to run. I kept walking as close to the children as possible, hoping my urgency would propel them faster. But they walked slowly as all children do in the heat, even those who had known nothing all their lives other than the oppressive humidity.

When they finally took us to the house off a dirt road, I learned there are no limitations on how many ways your heart can break. All that was left was charred beams and a collapsed roof.

The boy had just pointed.

Dr. Martin had knelt down to him, shaking his head, saying no, not the house where Antonio lived before. I need his new house, where he lives now.

The boy continued to point and speak in Spanish.

The little girl then quietly responded, surprising us by speaking in broken English, telling us that this is where Antonio stayed. Like his first house, this one burned down too.

Dr. Martin asked her how she knew all this.

She'd said because it was her family's home.

They're closing my window now. They say it's too hot in the room. Maybe they're right. I don't feel like writing any more.

CONTINUATION OF LETTER BY DR. REX MARTIN

I know the mention of black suits didn't mean anything to you and Freda, but it sent a chill down my spine. I know what their arrival means.

I knew when we arrived that the house would be burned. It crushed us. I knew that it was more than just an erasing of proof, it was a clear message to any of the people in the area not to snoop around.

The sister of the boy turned out to have better English. I think seeing her burned home made her angrier, a bit freer to speak. The home had been her father's, who was friends with Antonio and allowed him to stay with them while he did his research. After the home burned down a few days ago, their father had disappeared too. She and her brother had been at the beach when it happened, or otherwise they certainly wouldn't have survived.

The poor things. Homeless and without a parent. I remember pointing at you and Freda and saying that their daughter was taken to the house by Antonio, and we were looking for her.

I asked if they had any idea what had happened here. They spoke so frantically in Spanish, remember? It was so hard to understand them.

Please tell me you do remember, Bud. Your memories are just as valuable as mine.

Rex

CLASSIFIED SSA
AUTHORIZED READERS ONLY
LYNN STANSON FILE

November 1, 1951
Yucatan

I will not survive this, I know this now. The doctors keep telling me that the antibiotics should treat the infections, but my fevers keep spiking. I also know that's why they keep urging me to write. They want it down on paper before I die. Keep writing, Freda, the nurse tells me. I try not to get angry about it. If I were in their shoes, I might ask the same of someone like me, to help determine what's happening.

I understand why the houses had burned down. I understand, because I know what happened to us.

Those two poor children. I don't even know if they survived. I doubt they did. So many people died in that storm. It wasn't only my family who got wiped out.

I wasn't interested in finding shelter when the storm started blowing in—a storm that just came out of nowhere. The children had agreed to take us to where Lynn and their father may have been taken. I didn't care at that point about anything but finding my daughter.

The building wasn't far away. I was surprised; the trees ended and suddenly there was this concrete building in the middle of nowhere. And there were men in camouflage scurrying everywhere, trying to cover up the windows with large boards.

I remember feeling such relief—the military! Men in army fatigues! They have to be American. They'll help us. But Dr. Martin had held me back as I went to leave the woods and call out for them. I could see Bud was wary too, especially seeing how the children were hesitant to go forward.

How to describe the storm at that point. It just dumped on us. I mean, the skies went from gray to black. And the rain. It fell like the ocean had overturned, and the wind nearly knocked us off our feet.

What I did was reckless. But I just knew Lynn was inside.

I ran. Even in the chaos from the storm, the soldiers saw me coming, with Dr. Martin and Bud behind. One of them rushed up to me, and I just cried out that my daughter was in there. That I was an American citizen and my daughter was in there.

The soldier took me, and called out for the other soldiers. They'd come for Bud and Dr. Martin too, and rushed us inside. I heard them lock the doors. I remember hearing the hollow sound of multiple dead bolts sliding.

Then they pulled their guns on us. Bud had stepped in front of me and held up his hands, repeating that we are Americans. That there were children outside that needed to be brought in too.

I can't explain the strange sensation of how it feels to step inside a building to escape a storm, only to realize it was inside as well. That's the best way for me to say it. It's like running from a tornado into a cellar, only to find that the wind was coming from beneath the earth.

The winds hit the soldiers, and then us, so hard that we all fell down. Someone had failed to block a door, I thought at first. Somebody go shut that door.

But the winds weren't coming from one direction, but instead from the hallways around us. And then, it started to rain. Inside.

The soldiers were terrified too, and kept yelling at each other, asking what to do.

Bud grabbed one of them, shouting: Where is my daughter? Where is my daughter?

I could see the soldier's face. He was young. And he was scared. I'd begged him, yelling too now above the winds. Where is she?

He pointed down the hall to the only door on the right.

The winds knocked us all down again, but Bud caught me. Dr. Martin was being held back by one of the soldiers. Bud and I just ran.

We'd reached the door and rushed in, finding the winds and rain were inside there too. There were beds everywhere, with people lying on them, all hooked up to tubes. They looked like they were sleeping. They were all drenched in their slumber, their white bed sheets soaked, sticking to their unmoving bodies.

In the corner was Lynn.

I recognized her little body. I'd screamed to Bud, who pulled me through the wind. Like the others, she was sleeping. As we reached her, the stand holding a bag of clear solution that seeped through the tube into her body blew over on top of her.

Bud knocked it off and swept her up into his arms. I was sobbing at that point, kissing her face, telling her that Mommy and Daddy were here. That we'd found her.

But she didn't respond, as if we were holding a rag doll. I know I must have screamed: what was wrong with her? The needle attached to the tube had been yanked out of her arm, and she was bleeding.

Bud just grabbed me and we headed for the door. We knew we had to just get out.

The door flew open, and Dr. Martin stumbled in. I saw for a moment his eyes open in alarm at seeing Lynn limp in our arms.

The three of us ran back out into the hall. I started to ask about what happened to the soldiers when a gust of wind hit us so strong that we fell against the wall.

It was like the soldiers were leaves tossed in the air. They came from an intersecting hallway, thrown with such intensity that even in the howling winds, I could hear their bodies crash against the floor.

We couldn't stop, though. The only way to the door was to run across that same intersection. Bud gave me Lynn, motioning us to stay behind him. Dr. Martin was actually taller and bigger, but not as strong.

We intended to run and not stop, but we all made the mistake of looking down the other hallway as we moved past.

That's when we saw her. The woman, at the end of the hall, dressed in the same white medical gown as Lynn. Even with the debris and rain flying around her, I could tell her eyes were closed, her hands on her ears as if they were in terrible pain, blood seeping through her fingers. The soldiers who attempted to reach her were tossed away by the winds like paper dolls.

She opened her eyes.

Somehow, the wind, the chaos, was coming from her.

I heard a massive crack, and the walls themselves started to peel away; chunks of concrete and wood barreling in all directions, including ours.

As we ran, the floor itself began to crumble. I saw Bud reach the door and pull, but the winds were so hard pushing against us that it wouldn't budge. He cried out in anger and fear, and forced it open.

For a brief moment, I could see outside. The winds and rain were blowing, but paled in comparison to the storm raging around us.

When the slivers of wood sliced into my legs, I had one singular thought. And I knew I alone had it.

Do not misunderstand me: fathers are the pillars of all families. They are the strength, they are the foundation. But it is the mother who is always one step ahead, who sees what must be done before all else.

I screamed at Bud to go out and hold the door, thrusting Lynn at Dr. Martin, ordering him to take her outside. They'd both obliged, just as a block of concrete slammed into me. I could feel my back break.

I'll never forget Bud's face as he turned back for me, trying to hold the door open. I was able to scream for him to run, and then immediately slam it shut, preventing everything crashing and barreling into my body from following them out the door.

I'd wanted to save them. I know now it was a futile effort.

My hand aches, but I've done it. I am going to rest. If I'm fortunate, I won't wake up.

Nov 12, 1951

Lynn,

I have not written as I vowed to do. I have changed my mind.

I do not want you haunted by what happened to us in Mexico, to your mother. I am determined for you to know her as I did, and I speak of her every day. We even set her picture beside us at breakfast, lunch and dinner. You ask if Mama would have liked the food we were eating, the pumpkins in the field? Yes, I tell you. Yes, she would.

I will keep these letters, in case I change my mind. But for now, I want you to live a lie, and that hurts to even write those words. A normal life is what I want for you. And when you are grown, I want you far from these trees, never to return.

Love,
Daddy

Dec 10, 1951
BUD STANSON
1 EVELYN ROAD
NASHVILLE, TN 37205

REX MARTIN
ST. LOUIS UNIVERSITY
1 NORTH GRAND BOULEVARD
ST. LOUIS, MISSOURI 63103

Bud,

I realize that I've also been a complete narcissist and have failed to inquire about Lynn. I hope that her memory condition has changed. I knew she'd been heavily drugged; it was obvious by her lethargic state as we'd made that awful flight back to the states. But she was alive, and didn't appear to have any physical injuries, and that alone gave me hope. How the three of us escaped from the collapsed building without injuries astounds me.

I still have nightmares about it: Freda slamming the door, you running to open it, the entire structure vibrating. It was if a bomb had gone off inside and everything was about to blow.

I know you think it was cowardly of me to run. But I didn't want to die. I didn't want your daughter to die. I will be brutally honest with you: I couldn't risk losing her. I'm a terrible son of a bitch, I know, that my first thought wasn't of Freda's sacrifice. It was that this child has to get out of there.

I didn't even look to see if you were behind me. But even now, in your hatred for me, you know what Lynn represents: the only proof of extraterrestrial abductions. I never even stopped running when I heard the building collapse. It was remarkable what happened next: the sky almost immediately began to clear. The sun peeked through the clouds.

I could hear you screaming my name. I know it was the only reason you would leave Freda. You would have chased me to hell and back. Even in her lifeless form, she was your daughter. To both of us, she was the most valuable thing on earth.

Has she exhibited any physical abnormalities at all?

I know Rick, my doctor friend, gave her a clean bill of health, except for, obviously, the memory loss. Thank God he saw us when we'd shown up at his home when we'd landed. If we hadn't been friends since the second grade, he probably would have reported us to child services. Two men, unshowered, unshaved, obviously exhausted, showing up at a doctor's home on a Sunday with a limp child.

I can only imagine if my heart broke when she woke and didn't recognize you, that yours must have shattered.

Damn this cough, keeps me from writing. Please, Bud, write back and let me know about Lynn.

Rex

Dec 15, 1951
REX MARTIN
ST. LOUIS UNIVERSITY
1 NORTH GRAND BOULEVARD
ST. LOUIS, MISSOURI 63103

Rex,

I don't want to ever see you again. Your letter is just another reminder of why I will not provide you any updates on my daughter, as she is none of your business.

Do you even realize what you did? Running away from that building with my wife trapped inside? I couldn't even try to look for her. I had to go after you. And you kept saying Freda's dead, Bud. She's dead. She couldn't have survived that collapse.

I think you knew. I think you knew the danger in Mexico. And you used us to go down there. You said you still don't understand how that woman was causing the storm inside that building, but I don't believe you. We were your way in. You'd been looking for a family just like ours.

I should have stayed in Mexico, found a doctor, even though you said the medicine wasn't good enough there to help Lynn. You said we were lucky that the private plane hadn't left or been damaged in the hurricane, and that we needed to leave now before the pilot changed his mind. I know now you just wanted to get Lynn out so you could study her.

My wife died, alone, in the rubble of a building, because of you. You shouldn't have taken Lynn and run out. You should have stayed inside and let her escape.

Do not contact me again.

Bud Stanson

Feb 21, 1952
BUD STANSON
1 EVELYN ROAD
NASHVILLE, TN 37205

REX MARTIN
ST. LOUIS UNIVERSITY
1 NORTH GRAND BOULEVARD
ST. LOUIS, MISSOURI 63103

Bud,

It's cancer. I feared as much, even when I was writing to you last year. I know you asked me not to ever contact you again, and I promised myself I wouldn't. Because I thought I had time. Time enough to change your mind over the years.

But I don't have time. The cancer is stage four. I won't live, I don't think, past the summer.

If you won't further corroborate what happened, then I beg you to let some of my colleagues come and study the site in your woods where Lynn was taken.

Please consider it. Someone from my organization will be contacting you shortly. I am not well enough to make the trip myself.

I know I told you about my son. I've been a disappointment to him, because of how often I've been away and the priority I've given my career. He's a young man, already soured about what he calls this nonsense work of mine. I cannot blame him. But he has opened his home to me in my final days, and I have learned, too late, that nothing is more important than being a good father.

I pray that Lynn grows up to be just like her parents.

Rex

CLASSIFIED SSA
AUTHORIZED READERS ONLY
LYNN STANSON FILE

November 15, 1951
YUCATAN, MEXICO

The doctors are suggesting some kind of medical coma. I'm no fool, I know what that means. My injuries are so severe, the infection so great, that they hope putting me in a coma will help me survive. At least not live with constant pain. I think they're trying to be kind.

I will not live through this, and I have made peace with that. I do not wish to live. When you are told that you have barely survived being buried under a building, and that your daughter, your husband, and a kind professor, who only tried to help us find her, were all killed in the storm along with so many others, the will to live isn't strong.

I tried to save them. I did. But it was a fruitless gesture. Nothing could have saved any of us. So many people died that day.

Our neighbors in Nashville will wonder what happened to us. How we just took off and never returned. Bud and I have no close family. No one there will ever know the truth.

But to the people who will study my file, in the hopes of understanding what's happening, I want you to know this: I loved my daughter, and my husband. I am happy to join them now.

They are coming with the medicine to put me to sleep. I hope to dream of them.

Freda Stanson

William sat back, almost having to force himself to look away from the pages.

"Are you finished?"

The voice came from the man in the corner, still facing his laptop, who cleared his throat immediately after he spoke.

William realized that the screen of the laptop was black, and that it was angled so that the man could monitor William while he read the letters.

"I am, but . . . I just need a moment."

"That's understandable. I've also put it all on a flash drive, in case you want to review it later. It's something I should have done a long time ago. I think the time has come, at last, for me to deliver on something I vowed to do fifteen years ago."

The man turned around, picking up the laptop. Even in the dark of the corner, it was clear, despite his advanced age, his hair was still thick, with a hairline that would be the envy of even young men. He stood with a tremble, but walked with ease. When he stepped into the light of the table, William blinked in recognition.

"How do I know you?"

"I've waited my entire adult life to meet you, William. My name is Dr. Steven Richards." He then placed the laptop in front of William. "And do brace yourself, son. There are some videos you need to see."

NINE

They emerged from the elevator to a house draped in the pinkish light of a sunset. The old man shuffled into the kitchen instead of veering down the hall to the porch. "I think, perhaps, you need a drink."

"Sir, I need to see—"

"She's not going anywhere, I promise you that."

William followed him into the kitchen, its white countertops and cabinets soaking in the hue of the light that poured from the front windows. Dr. Richards took out two glasses and hunched over, struggling a bit to lift something out of a bottom drawer.

"Can I help—?"

"My doctor said I need to move as much as possible. Helps the blood flow. Heart needs all the help it can get. Which is why," he held up the long bottle with a musky brown color, "we need whiskey."

He poured and slid a glass across the counter to where William stood. As William raised his glass, the man reached over and clinked his glass to it with a wink. "To your grandmother," he said, tossing it back.

My grandmother. Who was taken, just like me. Who was returned, just like me. Who I just watched be interrogated by government agents, just as I was. And we both have something within us that could kill—

William swallowed the drink in one gulp, hoping Dr. Richards would refill the glass as quickly as possible.

"I'm guessing you have some questions?"

Let's see . . . So everything I suspected about myself being a danger to my family is true? Why you, the central figure in my disappearance, would be in the same house with my great-grandmother, who is somehow still alive, despite that letter that seemed to indicate she was about to die?

"You're him," was all William could mutter.

"Well, I guess that depends on what you've heard. Steven Richards, the man who the FBI tried to say kidnapped and killed you fifteen years ago? Steven Richards, the mad scientist in the tinfoil hat? Anything else I'm missing?"

William scooted the glass across the granite countertop. "Another, please."

"I'll join you. But I'm serious, son. Anything else you know about me?"

The man's eyes were a bit cloudy, perhaps from cataracts. His hands shook slightly as he poured them another round, but he did not spill. "All I ever knew is that my grandmother worked for you when she was young. And then you were cleared of the criminal charges and disappeared."

Steven's face looked a bit crestfallen, but he held up the glass one more time. "To your grandmother again. And her secrets."

William took a long, slow drink, feeling the heat in his throat spill down to his chest. Steven set his glass on the counter. "I know this is a lot. It's why she wanted to meet you. She could hardly wait. For obvious reasons— but she also wanted you to read the letters that she and your great-grandfather, along with Dr. Martin, wrote about Lynn's disappearance. And also for you to see the recordings where you were both questioned. So you could start at the beginning and perhaps begin to understand how it's all tied in to what's happening now."

"And what is that, exactly?"

"Let's have that conversation with Miss Blue. After all, she's our expert. She may be the oldest woman I've ever known, but her mind hasn't dulled at all. Even I, who have spent my whole life researching this—and I'm old too—don't know as much as she."

"How is she even alive? And how are you here with her? Does my grandmother even know?"

Steven's mouth twitched. "It's complicated, William. But the short answer is no. Lynn—your grandmother—doesn't know."

William leaned forward. "She doesn't know her own mother is alive?"

Steven shook his head. "Sadly, she's never even read the letters."

"You've got to be kidding me. How can the Corcillium have them and my grandmother does not? Especially given that my great-grandfather, Bud, didn't even want to communicate with Rex Martin."

"Bud did later have a change of heart. But only because he later needed the Corcillium's assistance."

"I don't understand."

"After Rex Martin died, the Corcillium continued to reach out to Bud to try and study the abduction site where Lynn was taken. They repeatedly reminded him that he would not have his daughter if it weren't for Rex Martin and his research. So Bud, at last, conceded and allowed a group of Researchers to come to the property. Apparently Lynn witnessed the Researcher's arrival, and Bud swore to never allow them to come again until she had moved away. When Lynn married Tom and left for Illinois so he could go to law school, Bud learned he had liver failure. It was at that point he asked for the Corcillium's help."

"Help?"

"To keep Lynn away from the woods. If we assisted in making sure she never moved back, he would allow access to the site, and give the letters he wrote for Lynn to the Corcillium, as well as his correspondence with Dr. Martin. As you can imagine, the Corcillium certainly made sure a job opportunity was presented to Lynn. I became one of Bud's contacts at the university. No one, including myself, could have imagined what would happen next."

Steven rubbed the back of his head. "I shouldn't delay your time with Blue a moment longer. But listen, son. You seem like a nice young man. Raised well. I know you've gone through hell in the last forty-eight hours. But this is a lot for someone of her age. Hell, it's a lot for me, and I'm a kid compared to her."

Steven rounded the counter and William followed him through the butler's pantry, down the hall, and through the porch doors, where the two burly guards were still stationed. William stepped between them and stopped immediately in the doorframe.

Quincy sat directly beside Blue, with Lily standing on her other side. Both had changed clothes, Lily to a blue dress and Quincy into an ill-fitting shirt and pants. At William's arrival, Blue clasped her hands together, Lily shyly smiled, and Quincy stood up.

"William! She's your great-grandmother!" Quincy said, pointing to Blue.

"Mr. Martin, a bit of decorum, shall we?" Blue asked.

"Come on girl, we're old friends now," Quincy said, reaching down to gently pat her hand. "One believer to another, right?"

"He knows?" William asked, looking at Quincy. "You told *him*?"

"Of course she did. She knows who I am. She doesn't know my taste in clothing or my actual pants size. She figured this is the size I would wear, which means a serious juice cleanse is in my future."

"You decided to let him out?" Steven asked.

"More like he complained his way out." Blue looked up to Quincy's grin. "Miss Lily and I were having a nice talk when all we could hear was stomping and cursing upstairs. So I sent for him."

"Against all of our better judgments," Rudd said, from where he leaned against the pillar.

"Now wait a minute. Wait a damn minute," Quincy said, walking towards Steven. "I know you! You're Steven Richards."

"Mr. Martin. Let's give them a minute," Rudd said. "You said you were hungry. I will happily stuff your mouth with anything to keep you from talking for five minutes."

"No way. This is a gold mine right here. Everything I knew was real, is right here before my eyes. It was almost worth almost getting my butt blown off."

"Let's go." Rudd took him by the arm. "Let them talk. I don't agree with you knowing *anything*, but now that you do, I'll be keeping a close eye on you."

"Let it be known," Quincy said, holding up a finger as Rudd led him to the door, "I spent half my fortune on trying to unravel the truth. I know my phone got either blown up or tossed somewhere, but give me a way to call and I'll have a jet here within the hour. I can get us somewhere truly safe—"

Rudd closed the doors behind them.

"I know you disagree, Steven, I can tell by the look in your eyes," Blue said. "But you know why he's been on our radar all these years."

"And there are reasons why the Corcillium ultimately never reached out to him," Steven responded. "Enthusiasm is one thing. But he's a glorified cell phone salesman. Who just happens to have made millions on a nifty hologram idea with a horrible name. But he's in deep now. Even he doesn't realize how deep. There's no turning back for him. For any of us."

"William, will you help me into my wheelchair? I need to move," Blue said, reaching up with her hands.

He walked over, seeing the delight in her eyes. *Nanna's mother. My God.*

She seemed as light as the pages he'd just flipped through, as fragile as bone china. There was a fierce grip to her, though, as he lifted her from the rattan to the wheelchair.

"You're so handsome. Even more so than you are in all those pictures in the magazines," she said, placing her hand on his bearded cheek as she settled into the chair. "You resemble your grandparents so much."

He heard Steven clear his throat again. "Do you want me to push you, Blue?"

"No. I want my great-grandson to push me," she said. "Lily, want to come with us out into the yard? Go see the dragonflies at the fountain? Take the ramp right there, William."

He took the handles of the chair and guided her across the wood floors and down the ramp onto the grass. The wheels bumped a bit on the uneven soil, but Blue didn't seem to mind, reaching out for Lily. The little girl took her hand.

"Go on, run now. We can talk more in a bit."

Lily scampered across the grass. She hesitated a bit, seeing the flurry of red-and-green dragonflies hovering above the water.

"They won't hurt you, honey, I promise," Blue said.

She walked to the edge of the fountain, climbing to stand on the stone. Slowly, she began to walk the perimeter, making a loop around the water, grinning at the hovering insects.

"Watch your step!" Blue said.

Lily waved slightly.

"Remarkable girl, that one," she said. "I can't imagine what she's been through. But look at her. That's the wonderful thing about children: Despite whatever's happened to her . . . she's playing. Smiling. She's just a regular child."

"There is nothing regular about her," Steven said, walking beside William.

"No. And she didn't ask for it. Just like my daughter didn't ask for it. Or you, my boy." She reached over her shoulder to pat his hand.

"I've got a lot of questions."

"I know you do. Let's rest right over there. By the Knock Outs," she said.

He wheeled her over to where a flourishing set of rosebushes were contained behind a knee-high iron fence. Three Adirondack chairs with thick cushions were situated before it, facing the fountain.

As Blue reached over to smell one of the blooms, William sat, watching her. "I just . . . I just can't believe . . ."

"That I'm alive?" She laughed in a tone so similar to his grandmother's that goose bumps raised on his arm. "It's a good question, one I've asked myself more than once. I honestly wished to die so often as a young woman that maybe I cursed myself, hoping death would come for me. But I'm certainly glad it ignored me. Because here you are. I just wish your grandmother were here too."

"She needs to know that you're alive."

Blue looked past him. "I've wanted to call her every day for the past fifteen years. As soon as I found out she was alive. No family should have endured this. But it appears this is the burden of ours."

She turned to him. "You thought you knew her story; how your grandmother's mother died young and she was raised by her father. Now, you've read what happened when we found Lynn in Mexico. We placed the letters in chronological order for obvious reasons; you see that my husband and Dr. Martin obviously believed I had died when the building collapsed. In turn, I was told they died in the hurricane. But the truth is quite different."

"How *did* you survive?" he asked.

"I didn't want to. Everyone I loved was gone. I had no extended family; my parents were already dead and I had no siblings. My body was crushed, I would certainly never walk again. Even if I wanted to leave and return home, I couldn't. But I kept hearing their whispers, their suggestions. You may find in life, my boy, that anger can keep you alive."

"Whispers? Suggestions? From whom?"

She folded her hands on her lap. "From the very organization that is hunting you. The same agency that constructed the building in Mexico, that collected the abducted who were returned. They are not characters in a movie or comic book. They are very real, with a very real purpose. And I became one of them."

William's ears flushed. "You joined them? Even though they knowingly took your daughter? And then gave her something that erased her memories?"

"And now you know they did it to you as well. And I know that must make you angry."

William frowned. "I don't think angry comes close to how I feel about it. It took years for me to adjust to the strangers who claimed to be my family. I just . . . can't understand why you would join a government operation responsible for what they did to your daughter."

"The SSA isn't just a US government operation. It's in every country in the world. And yes, I did. And I know you're angry. But trust me, your anger doesn't begin to compare to mine when I realized what had been kept from me. I lost out on an entire life with my daughter and husband."

The anger building within him began to quell at the bitterness in her voice. "I don't mean to blame you. I'm just confused."

"Understand that I was told that my family was dead, but that I could help others like me. I could devote my life to a cause that was trying to understand why people, like my Lynn, were being taken and returned to earth. That I could avenge her, and my husband, by seeking the answers. All this planted in me by the extremely encouraging agents who routinely visited me in my recovery. It lit a fire within me. Ultimately, it gave me a reason to live. Ultimately, they were successful in keeping me silent."

She motioned to the wheelchair. "My legs were shattered. But in time, the rest of me healed. Enough for me to quietly be wheeled into the new, tiny, research facility in Mexico run by the SSA. Everyone there spoke Spanish, so it took me a long time to learn the language. But I did. And my life's work began."

"All this time . . . you've been in Mexico?"

Her lips pursed. "It's strange, now, to think back on all those years. A simple but fulfilling life. I lived alone, did my work in the archive division. Since I had no family, I naturally yearned to create another. 'The widow of the library,' the agents called me when they didn't think I could hear. They all became my children, and many treated me with kindness. I was grateful that I had a job that supported a disabled woman with no education, and that I was allowed to be a surrogate mother and grandmother to my co-workers. They appeared grateful to have me, and I focused all my energies on the abduction cases in Mexico."

"But how could you have not known about my grandmother?" William asked. "She was married to a US senator. Her picture was in newspapers and certainly online. And if you researched abductions, surely you came upon . . ."

"I quickly learned in order to survive, the past would have to die. Freda Stanson died when her family did. When the agents started calling me Blue, because of my eyes, it became my new name. Mother Blue, then, as I aged, Grandmother Blue, then Great-Grandmother Blue. My office in the Yucatan was covered in hundreds of pictures of my agents' families. I had to fill a void. And it meant completely and utterly shunning anything that had to do with the United States. In time, it became a foreign country that conjured up too much pain to even think about. And it was the greatest mistake of my life. And if it hadn't been for the Rapture, I would still be there now."

"The Rapture?"

She took a deep breath. "The SSA's code name for when the ships returned to Argentum and to all the bases where the abductees were contained all over the world. Including the rebuilt location in the Yucatan. When they were all taken up, you can't imagine the internal chaos. The SSA thought they'd contained it all, but they didn't count on your grandmother. Everyone at the office was whispering about it. For the first time, I got online to a US news website and read about the one case that had gone public."

Blue shut her eyes and slightly shook her head. "I did not know that your heart could heal and break all at the same time. I realized then the great tragedy of my life. That it had all been a lie. They'd kept me in Mexico to silence me. And I knew, very soon, they would make certain that the widow of the library had finally gotten too old to live.

"So here I was: an old woman without working legs who needed to go on the run to find her daughter. I wanted to try to call her, but I knew all of our phones were constantly monitored. I learned about the Researchers in the article and the YouTube video they'd released. So I reached out in desperation with an encrypted message to them, and they responded.

"The days that followed . . . were among the most frightening of my life. I had stolen the files on your and your grandmother's cases and copied the videos. I hid the best I could, jumping at every noise outside the motel room where I'd disappeared to. I knew the agents were searching for me, desperate to recover what I'd taken. When at last I heard a knock at my door, exactly in the manner the Researchers said it would be, I opened it to find another face that had become plastered across the world's news organizations."

She looked over to Steven.

He nodded once. "Once we were able to decipher her message, I was determined to get her out and bring her home. Lynn needed to know her own mother was alive. Rudd, with his military background, was essential in coordinating the effort. And we almost slipped her out without notice."

"Almost?" William asked.

"We were discovered. We lost two good people. The SSA lost more. But we succeeded in getting to the private plane. As soon as we landed in Florida, we took her into hiding."

Blue shook her head. "We had to wait two months before we felt it was safe to even leave Steven's house. It isn't far from here, but still very remote. Once again, Dr. Richards came to my rescue."

Steven smiled wearily. "We old people have to take care of each other. For your daughter, it was the least I could do."

"I don't understand . . . you never reached out to my grandmother? After all that . . . you never told her you're alive?"

"Trust me, my boy. It has pained me every single moment since I returned to US soil," she said. "But that terrible escape from Mexico made me realize that the closer I got to Lynn, to your mother, and her daughters, and even you, the more danger you all would face. If they learned I had gotten to her . . . there would be a freak gas explosion, or car accident, or something awful. I couldn't risk it."

"It weighed heavily on all of us," Steven continued. "All I ever wanted was for your grandmother to know the truth. But I'd seen too much as well. I know what the SSA is capable of doing; no one, and I mean no one, is safe when they determine you know too much. They've been permanently removing witnesses of abductions for decades. We didn't just keep ourselves from your grandmother, but from everyone and everything. We've lived in isolation."

William let that sink in. "So ever since my grandmother found me . . ."

"I've been watching. From afar. As long as life appeared to go on as normal for you and your family, and I never surfaced, the SSA wouldn't dare touch you. As I began to share with the Corcillium what I knew about the abductions, including the files I stole on your mother and yourself, I became an asset to them."

"More than an asset," Steven said. "For the first time in the history of the Corcillium, we had someone with direct knowledge of how the SSA worked and their purposes. To us, there is no one more valuable in the world."

"And also dangerous," she added softly. "And we all knew that no one, save for a few of our members, would know who I truly am."

"Listen," William began, "I know people have died, and I'm truly sorry for that. But the fact that my grandmother was unaware of all of this—"

"I actually extended an offer to your grandmother to join the Corcillium," Steven said. "I even told her that letters existed from her father that she hadn't read. I fully intended on her having it all. And when I first learned that Blue might be alive, I only told Lynn that I was trying to find something of significance to her. But when Mexico went so badly, and we knew the SSA would be desperately searching for Blue, we had no choice. To protect Lynn, she had to think the Corcillium—including myself—had disappeared."

Blue trembled. William reached out and took her hand, cold even in the summer heat. "I'm sorry. I'm sorry for what you've had to go through."

She smiled through her tears, her voice choking. "But here you are. My great-grandson. My whole life, all I've been awarded with is time. And now that I need it, we have none."

"What do you mean?"

Blue looked across the yard to Lily, now sitting by the fountain, trying to convince one of the dragonflies to land on her finger. "It stopped, you know. After the abducted vanished from Argentum and the others sites, the disasters ceased. The diseases slowed, even the violence. And the numbers of missing people dropped dramatically. But last year, the fires out west started without a clear ignition source. Hurricanes in the south started churning, one after another. Increased violence on the East Coast and widespread, unexplained diseases in the upper Midwest. Similar disasters are now unfolding in every country. And we knew."

"Rudd is a talented hacker," Steven continued. "With Blue's assistance in unraveling their security codes, we've kept tabs on the SSA. And a year ago, they detected four single beams of light from the sky on a single night in every major country around the world. Then, a day or so later, it happened again. But not in Argentum, or the Yucatan, or the other locations where you and the other abducted were returned."

Blue motioned slightly to Lily. "What do you know of her?"

William watched the girl for a moment. "I only know what an agent with the parks service told me: She was found somewhere in a national park in North Dakota just a few days ago, wandering alone. I can't get her to tell me anything else. She just tends to repeat one saying, over and over."

"And what is that?" Steven asked.

William exhaled through his nose. "Something about being a monster in a mountain."

Blue tilted her head. "What does that mean to you?"

William stood, wincing as a final beam of sunlight cast across his face. The pained look on his face remained as he moved from the light.

"Let us help you unravel this," Steven said. "You saw the video of your interrogation when you were a child. You know how you, your grandmother, and the others who were abducted were implanted somehow with technology that we still don't understand. To be used as weapons to be tested on the people of this planet. And you . . ."

"I'm the conduit. Yes. I heard it in that video. And my grandmother said the same."

"She did?" Blue asked.

William turned back to her. "She would never talk about Argentum or what happened. But in a very bad moment after my grandfather died, I overheard her tell her friend that I was a conduit of some kind. That if triggered, I could cause her to do something terrible to the people around her. It's why I had to run. I couldn't risk her safety, or our family's."

"That must weigh heavily on her," Blue said quietly.

"She doesn't know that I overheard her. She probably assumes I figured something out. I hated isolating myself, but if anyone would understand, it would be her."

Blue slowly looked over to Lily. "If she knew about that little girl over there and had the chance to talk to her like I did . . . she would certainly come to the same conclusion. In my talks with Lily—and she is still extremely guarded—she explained that she's desperate to protect you."

"Protect me?"

"Rudd debriefed me on everything that happened. Quincy filled in the rest of the blanks of what happened in that cotton field. Poor Lily, she won't talk about it. But she did say some things. She doesn't understand why she's able . . ."

"To kill," William said.

"She says she isn't doing it intentionally. The way the bodies of those agents were described to me by Rudd . . . she's making them sick. In an instant. So sick that they're dead within moments. What the abducted from before were implanted with . . . is nothing compared to what Lily is able to do. She told me she does it because she thinks she's protecting you. She says you want her to do it."

"But, I'm not . . ."

Blue reached out for his leg. "She says she felt it at that cotton field and at the airport. Even in the agent's car in Memphis. All she knows is that she feels your fear and anger. She told me what happened when you were in the back seat of the agent's car. She says she saw him holding you, and she was going to kill him to save you. But she heard your voice, telling her to stop."

William watched Lily dip her toes in the water. "I think I did. That particular agent seemed like he honestly wanted to protect me. I didn't want him to die."

Blue smiled sadly. "Your connection with her is extremely strong."

William exhaled. "It's stronger than you know."

"What do you mean?"

"I dream of her."

"You do?" Steven asked.

"Just her eyes. About a year ago, I started having these nightmares when I moved to Little Rock. I dream of awful things, in different places. Fires, storms, shootings, people suffering. But just days ago, in the nightmares, I started seeing the eyes. A different single pair at each disaster. I often see people dying at a hospital, and when I do, one pair of deep brown eyes watches as well. Lily's eyes."

"My God." Blue's hand cupped her chin. "William, this is important. Just one pair of eyes? In each disaster?"

"I think so."

"That's what we've theorized," she said.

"Here's what we think," Steven said. "The original people who were abducted and were later taken away by those ships . . . we think they were ultimately determined to be . . . flawed. You read the letter Blue wrote as a young woman, about the woman causing the hurricane, how her ears seemed to bleed?"

"I read about it in so many other cases. It was horrible seeing what became of them once they were triggered," Blue shivered. "Once their abilities were unleashed, they were vegetables afterwards. Comatose. Those ships arrived in Argentum and in every place in the world where the SSA had collected them. Those people were picked up like broken toys and taken away. What happened to them, we may never know. But seeing Lily . . . we think we understand the next phase."

"The next phase?"

"You've seen Lily—her ears don't bleed, she doesn't cry out in pain. She's *enhanced*. As soon as she's triggered, she ignites without warning, as easily as batting an eye. And then she continues on, as if nothing happened. We believe those lights from the heavens a year ago were the abductions of *new* people. The subsequent lights a day or so later were them being returned. Lily came from North Dakota, which is at the center of the spike in diseases. I believe here in the South, another is causing the hurricanes. Another is causing the uptick in violence on the East Coast, and yet another the fires in the West. And you, William, were drawn to the center of them all. You are the conduit."

William rubbed his forehead. "And this is all happening through me."

"We don't know that for sure. But you're obviously connected to them. It's why the SSA wants to bring you in," Steven said.

"And they should." William placed his hands behind his head. "We're all dangerous. They should lock us up and throw away the key."

"No," Blue said. "That's not the answer. After talking with Lily, and knowing your connection to her . . . I wonder if *you* are the answer. The way to stop it all."

"How can I stop it if I'm starting it?"

"Think about it, William. Yes, Lily attacked those agents because she thought you were in danger. But when you directed her *not* to hurt the man in the back seat, she didn't. You stopped her. You understand what that means, right?"

"You think—"

"We hope. We hope it means if you can stop her, you can stop the others too—"

"Fellow believers!" came a call from across the yard. Quincy was striding across the grass, Rudd following closely behind, frowning. "Mr. Personality here is a little less than forthcoming with details. And I've got lots of questions."

"Tell him, Steven. It's time." Blue motioned to Quincy. "He needs to see them too."

"See what?" Quincy asked. "Damn, William. You look even more pale than usual."

"After this, Blue, you're done for the day. Time to take your medicine and rest a bit," Steven cautioned.

She looked to William. "But—"

"No buts. Rudd is going to take you home. I think he and Mr. Martin need some space anyway. William isn't going anywhere yet."

"Where is he going?" Quincy asked. "Because I—"

"Before you begin," Steven said wearily. "I need you, Mr. Martin, to just answer a quick question for me for William to hear. Quincy—that's actually your middle name, right?"

Quincy put his hands in his pockets. "Yeah . . . about that . . ."

"Why don't you tell William your first name."

"It's Rex. But here's the deal about that—"

"Rex is a family name, am I right?"

"Someone has been deep googling me."

"Named after your great-grandfather," Steven continued, looking right at William. "Dr. Rex Martin."

William blinked. Dr. Rex Martin.

From the letters. The man who helped find his grandmother in the Yucatan.

No. It can't . . .

"Even after all this time, I actually think I see some resemblance," Blue noted.

The edges of Quincy's mouth turned sheepish as he looked to William. "Apparently I'm picking up where great-grandpa Rex left off."

It was clear why Lily wanted to immediately return to the fountain after their quick dinner. There was a calming to the sound of the trickling water, spilling from a bowl held aloft by a pillar carved with owls with out-stretched wings.

William noticed it now, how often the owl was featured throughout the house. The hilts of the knives he'd found to make himself and Lily quick peanut butter-and-jelly sandwiches were emblazed with gold soaring owls.

As Steven had led the ever-excited Quincy through the hallway to the elevator, they'd passed a large painting of a resting owl.

As William had helped Blue into Rudd's car to drive to Steven's home hidden somewhere in the dense trees, he'd noticed she wore a necklace of a gold owl. As she kissed his cheek, saying she would return first thing in the morning, he'd asked about it.

"Knowledge," she'd said. "The symbol of the Corcillium. It guides us. Fear of the unknown cannot rule us. Doubt is our driver. An unflinching clarity of what we're facing gives us a foundation upon which to act. A light in the bleakest of times. Remember that, my boy."

William could barely make out the owls on the fountain, as the lights from the porch were a good distance away. The dark did allow, however, for the stars to shine brilliantly above.

"Careful, kiddo, it's dark out here," William said as Lily made another round on the edge. "In fact, why don't you come sit next to me?"

She obeyed quickly, coming to rest, as she always did, directly beside him.

"We need to talk. I know so very little about you. Where are your parents?"

Her response was her typical silence, staring out into the night. "Whatever happened, you can tell me. It's OK if it's scary. How did you end up in that valley in North Dakota? Do you remember?"

She looked down, wearing an expression of guilt.

"Hey. Whatever happened, it wasn't your fault. Just like it wasn't my fault that they took me too. Did you know they took my grandmother as well? We didn't ask for it, Lily."

"But it is my fault," she said, tears springing to her eyes.

"No it's not. Just like it's not your fault what happened to those bad men. I know you were just trying to protect me. In fact, it's my fault. And you don't ever have to do it again, OK?"

"There's a monster in the mountain."

"Honey, I don't know what that means. You have to tell me—"

The girl stood up and began to walk on the fountain again. "Lily—"

She shook her head fiercely.

He followed, keeping pace beside her. "You're going to have to tell me. I know you're tired. I am too. After a good night's sleep, we're going to talk about it. I know what it's like to be a confused kid. A scared kid—"

She turned to him and reached out. He wrapped his arms around her, and she buried her face in his neck. "We have to go there! It's my fault what happened to her—"

"William!" Quincy's voice came from the porch.

"What do you mean?" William asked. "What do you think is your fault?"

Hearing Quincy's loud approach, Lily let go and began to walk again.

William sighed, turning to the outlines of Quincy and Steven walking across the grass. "Man, I knew I was right. My Dad was right about his grandfather. I just never knew *how* right until I read those letters!"

"I'm getting the very strong feeling that none of this has happened by chance," William said. "You didn't just find me because of some sort of business deal, did you?"

"I fully intended to tell you. But you know, the explosions and kidnappings got in the way."

"Partly by chance, partly by design is the truth, I'm afraid," Steven said. "The Corcillium has been moving chess pieces for some time now. I should know, I was one of those pieces. Obviously there was a reason they kept tabs on Dr. Martin's family. Before Rex Martin died, he let the Corcillium know he'd told his son all about his research, hoping in vain that he would continue his work. No one could have guessed his great-grandson would be the one to pick up the mantle."

"It caused a pretty big rift in my family," Quincy said. "I obviously never met my great-grandfather Rex. He was dead long before even my dad was born. My dad grew up listening to his father grumble about his crazy father Rex, who told stories about people disappearing and reappearing into lightning. In fact, my grandfather took all of Rex's notes that were stored in boxes and tossed them, but my dad secretly dug them out of the trash. And Dad *really* got into it, carefully keeping them in fact. Boy, did it piss off my grandfather when he found out. Said it was a bunch of crap that ruined Rex's life. It was the beginning of the end for my dad and his father. As a final middle finger to his father, my dad made sure my first name was Rex. Being antagonistic is a family trait."

"So those letters from your great-grandfather . . . you've read them before?" William asked.

"No. I just have his private scientific notes. In them, he made several references to the fact that he was hesitant to keep anything about his actual discoveries at his home, for fear that it could be discovered and his family would be in danger. You can imagine my fascination in reading *that*. And I only found out about his technical notations when your story came out, Will. I was just a kid too. Maybe ten years old. I clearly remember talking to my dad about the kid from Tennessee who was abducted by aliens, and my dad said, 'You should read what your great-grandfather believed.' I devoured it. And by the time I made my first million, I knew how I'd be spending my money. My business goal was to get your name on the dotted line for the new campaign, but honestly, this is what I really wanted to know: If my great-grandpa Rex was right."

William felt the uncomfortable prickling of doubt. "Campaign?"

Quincy shifted his feet. "Yeah, about that. My company pioneered the app that projects hologram images from phones. We are about to launch a new version that allows you to project your image to whoever you're talking to. I regret the name, now. Beam Me Up."

William winced. "Seriously?"

"Yeah. Bad taste. I get it. But the idea all along was to tell you about my great-grandpa Rex and his studies. I had no idea the connection to your great-grandparents and your grandmother. When I got that tip that you were living in Arkansas in a trailer, I figured you could use the money and might be a spokesman for it. Don't punch me, I bruise easily."

William then turned to Steven. "He received a tip?"

Steven held up his hands. "Full transparency: We knew we would be sending our people to try and keep you safe and bring you here. But we wanted a dual approach. If Rudd had failed, and you'd gone safely with Mr. Martin, then our plan was to reach out to explain that we needed to meet with you both."

William shook his head. "I am getting the very distinct feeling that we really all are just pawns for your organization."

Steven's expression was grim. "We suspected when you surfaced, the SSA would not be far behind. Knowing what is happening here and around the world, we feared—and rightly so—that people were being abducted and returned again. But truly, all your great-grandmother wanted was to keep you safe. And so did I."

"And you can't blame him," Quincy said. "If you were my grandson, I'd want you safe too."

William flinched. "Excuse me?"

Quincy's eyebrows raised, turning to Steven, who had closed his eyes in obvious frustration.

"Well, this is uncomfortable," Quincy muttered.

The fan above the bed whirled slowly. William knew he should sleep, even if the nightmares were waiting. For once, the panic attacks were dormant, replaced by burgeoning anger.

And it was a petty anger, too. After everything that had happened, everything he'd learned, it was the smallest, most unimportant revelation.

He turned over, looking out the window of the upper bedroom of the house. After he had abruptly walked away from the fountain, he'd heard Steven call out that he would stay the night if William wanted to talk. He hadn't responded.

The two burly guards had directed him to his room. He'd paced for a good thirty minutes.

Everything. Every whisper, every rumor, every suggestion that surrounded him his entire life was true.

"I can barely hear you above the violins," he could imagine Roxy saying from the plush chair in the corner of the room.

I think I'm due a bit of rumination, Roxy.

"Really? Shall I introduce you to your grandmother? Who risked the exposure of her darkest secrets to find you? She's the only one who gets to sit around and brood. And she vacuums instead."

She should have told me the truth. I deserved to know.

"That's crap, William. She and your parents and your Grandpa Tom gave you a normal life. Now that you're in the middle of this mess, take a minute and be glad you lived in the bubble. Your grandmother risked everything to stabilize her family. And she did."

William rolled over to his other side so he couldn't see the chair.

I wonder how many other twentysomethings project their grandmother's best friend as their voice of reason.

The sad part was, he wasn't that surprised about Steven. Of course he'd heard the rumors. Once, a girl he dated had called him over to her laptop to show him a picture of Dr. Steven Richards from when he was arrested. William had gotten angry, asking what she'd been looking up. She'd just casually leaned back, pointing to the photo. "You know, you look a lot like him."

The fact of the matter was, of all the rumors, William cared the least about the one concerning his grandmother's affair, because it just didn't seem at all possible. His grandparents were in love. It was obvious by the way that Grandpa Tom doted on Nanna. He'd heard his mother say several times that it wasn't always that way, that it was practically a new development in their relationship.

Plus, it was miniscule. Grandpa Tom would always be his grandfather. Nothing would ever change that. It was simply just a final kick in the pants on a day that left his head spinning—

He heard the door handle turn quickly, and he sat up. Lily slipped through, wearing a nightgown, the whites of her eyes shining.

"Lily—"

She scurried past him to the windows. She was practically shaking.

"What is it?" he asked, sliding out.

"They're here," she said, pointing.

William looked through the glass. The moon was full, so the entire backyard was awash in pale light. He saw nothing but the fountain and the scattered gardens. Then, forms dressed in the color of night began to emerge from the trees and move towards the house.

TEN

By the time William shoved his feet into his shoes and grabbed Lily's hand, Steven was at the door, still dressed in his clothes from before.

"Get to the basement. Now—"

The sound of gunshots interrupted, and Steven waved them on.

"Just go!" he ordered, moving stiffly around the banister of the upper floor. "Quincy! Get up!"

"What's going on?" Quincy muttered as he emerged from another room looking disoriented, his shirt unbuttoned.

"Get out of there! Don't stop!" Steven barked as another round of gunfire erupted from outside.

William swept Lily into his arms as he bounded down the stairs to the first floor, remembering the elevator was just off the kitchen. As he looked back up the stairs to see if Steven and Quincy were close behind, the glass in the French doors leading to the porch shattered, inviting in the sound of a landing helicopter.

"Go!" Steven yelled. William headed for the kitchen, seeing the night revealed in the missing glass splintered by the firing of pistols from the two guards. Both were crouched behind pillars, firing repeatedly into the dark.

William ran, carrying Lily through the butler's pantry and to the large, heavy doors that concealed the elevator. He set the girl down and pulled opened the doors. Steven arrived, sliding aside the small painting and punching in a code on the keypad, then setting his thumb on the tiny screen.

They heard the scream of a man from the porch and booted feet rush up the outside stairs.

Stumbling inside as the elevator doors opened, Steven repeatedly pushed the button to descend.

As the metal doors began to close, a man in black arrived outside, sticking his foot in the opening.

William felt the heat in him, the familiar panic. He saw Lily raise her arm.

"No!" he said, yanking her hand down.

The closest to the doors, Quincy used his sizeable weight to slam his foot into the agent's shin, just as the man swiveled his weapon towards them. When he yanked his leg back in pain, the doors abruptly shut.

"Listen," Steven said as the elevator began to lower. "Do exactly as I say and we may be able to get out of here."

Before they could respond, the elevator doors opened, and Steven motioned them out. As their eyes adjusted to the dimly lit room, Steven turned to the keypad on the side of the door. As the doors to the elevator closed again, he held down his finger on the screen for several seconds, until it began to flash red.

"It's inactivated," Steven said. "William, turn around."

"What?"

Starting at William's neck, the old man began to pat him down. When he'd reached all the way to his feet, he tore off William's shoes. As he turned them over, something small tumbled out from inside one of them.

Lily reached down, holding up what appeared to be a microchip.

"Dammit," Steven said.

William's stomach sank, remembering how the agents had frisked him, even taking off his shoes.

"They must have slipped it in when they took me," he stammered.

Quincy took the tracking device from Lily and threw it to the floor, crushing it with the heel of his shoe. From above came the sound of harsh slamming on metal.

"We don't have much time." Steven hobbled across the room, opening a cabinet. Pressing a series of buttons on the top of the safe inside, he lifted out a single flash drive on a metal chain. He then moved to the only other door in the room.

Again, he pressed his thumb on a keypad, and a thudding sound came from behind it. He pulled it open, revealing only darkness beyond. "Now." He motioned them in.

They didn't hesitate. Once in, Steven closed the door. A dim light flickered on, revealing a long, dark, earthen passage stretching out before them.

"What in the world?" Quincy said softly. "Where does that go?"

Steven reached for a glass case embedded in the wall. Lifting the cover, he pulled out a hefty flashlight hanging beside a single red button. Taking a deep breath, Steven pushed the button.

"Run," he said, thrusting the flashlight towards William. "Run and don't stop. You have eight minutes. You will reach a ladder about a half mile down. Climb it and follow the path outside. It will lead you to a boat. Take it and don't stop. Do you understand? Take this flash drive. Give it to your grandmother. It must get to her."

Even in the earthen tunnel, the sound of repeated battering could still be heard above.

"Ok, let's go," Quincy said.

"Take it," Steven said, forcing the chain with the attached flash drive around William's neck.

"William, let's go!" Quincy said.

"Come on," William motioned to Steven.

The strain on the man's face was apparent, even in the dim light. "I wish we had more time, William. Tell you grandmother—"

"No," William said. "Quincy, take Lily and run."

Quincy took the flashlight from William and pulled the girl to follow.

"Let's go." William reached out for Steven's shoulder.

"There's no way I can keep up—"

"Then I guess you're going to die on the way instead of here."

"I cannot, William. I had a heart attack ten years ago—"

William ushered him down the passageway. "You've got too much to explain for me to just leave you."

"I'm already worn out—"

"Then get on," William ordered, turning around.

"You can't—"

"Do it, Steven!"

He hesitated a moment, and then climbed onto William's back. The old man was lighter than William thought, hitching him up.

"We don't have much more time."

William ran as fast as he could, heedless of how much the man jostled on his back.

The flashlight had stopped. Quincy and Lily waited.

"Don't stop!" Steven called out.

William tried to motion them to keep running, but Lily appeared to be straining to hold Quincy back until William was closer. As they met, William heard Quincy mutter something about Luke and Master Yoda.

"This is my worst nightmare," Quincy huffed. "Please don't cave in. Please don't cave in."

For several minutes they ran, with seemingly no end to the tunnel, the sound of Steven's labored breathing in William's ear.

"Hey," Quincy said, now completely out of breath. "How much further—"

"There," Steven pointed. The tunnel abruptly stopped about a yard away. When they reached the end, an iron ladder extended up. "Shine it up there."

Quincy raised the flashlight. The tunnel reaching to the surface was relatively short and ended in a circular, metal cover.

"We only have a minute or two left," Steven said.

"Before what?" Quincy asked.

William scrambled up the ladder, grabbing the lever beneath, straining to release the lid. It groaned open, and the sounds of crickets and tree frogs spilled down.

He climbed out, finding himself on a small hill. Through the trees beyond, he could see the lights of the Corcillium house. The floodlights from the helicopters flashed through the branches.

He began to order the others to follow, but already Lily was climbing out. Quincy shone the flashlight with one hand, bracing Steven with the other to help him climb. William reached down and pulled Steven the rest of the way. Quincy was immediately behind, taking a deep inhale of the night air.

"We have to keep going," Steven whispered. "Turn off the flashlight. I have to go by memory."

The abundance of moonlight helped, but it also meant that if any of the agents were nearby, they could easily be seen.

Steven led them from the hill down a path. Not nearly as manicured as the rest of the property, it was surrounded on both sides by tall grass. As they saw the glittering of water in the near distance, the earth rocked beneath them. They stumbled, and turned to see the metal cover fly into the air, propelled by flames bursting from the ground.

"Jesus!" Quincy said.

The explosion was followed by another in the distance, so loud and jarring it sounded as if a plane had crashed from the skies. Black smoke ballooned above the treetops, beginning to obscure the stars.

The lights from the Corcillium house were gone, replaced by angry flames.

In the distance, they could hear more helicopters approaching. "Come on," Steven said, trudging down the path.

"Blue. Where is Blue—?"

"My home is isolated. Rudd is with her. He'll know to take her and run."

The path veered off to split the tall grass, leading to a tucked-away dock and a small fishing boat.

"Untether the boat," Steven whispered, leaning heavily on one of the wood pillars, motioning for them to get inside.

William lifted off the rope as Quincy stepped in, lifting Lily in and helping Steven as he practically collapsed into the boat.

"There's the oar," Steven said, slumping into the seat, his head thrown back in exhaustion.

As they drifted into the water, William set the oar in, propelling them away from the dock.

"Which way?" he whispered.

"Head south. The direction we're heading."

"Shouldn't we fire up the motor?" Quincy asked.

"We can't risk them hearing."

Another geyser of flame erupted from the mansion, sending a plume of smoke into the sky.

Steven lay with his eyes closed now. "It was Blue . . . who insisted upon it. Have an escape route, she said. Make sure if we're ever compromised, nothing remains. They cannot have our records."

"But all that research. All of it gone," Quincy said. "My great-grandfather's letters . . ."

"No," Steven said, raising a trembling finger towards William. "It's all there."

William reached up to touch the flash drive on the chain around his neck. "But if they get to Blue . . ."

"Rudd is among the few to be notified when there is a security perimeter breach. They were long gone as soon as he got the alert. The one thing the Corcillium knows best is how to hide."

"How do we get in contact with any of them now?" William asked.

Steven slowly opened his eyes. "We don't."

Lynn gripped the side of the chair with such ferocity that her knuckles whitened, the veins in her age-spotted hands rising. She pushed herself to stand once again and resume her pacing in front of the French doors that overlooked the stately eastern white pines.

"If you'd like," Roxy said, flipping through the *Country Living* magazine for the twentieth time while propped up with seven pillows on the bed, "I can call for a vacuum. Best form of therapy for you."

"How could I have been so stupid?" Lynn asked.

"Stupid had nothing to do with this, at least this time." Roxy put the magazine down on her lap. "When armed government agents say for national security reasons you have to fly to DC, you go. Especially when your daughter signs the order."

Lynn's eyes flashed. "How could she?"

"Listen," Roxy said, attempting once again to position the pillows to support her lower back. "Kate is a lot of things, and things have gone extremely south in the last few years, but she still loves you. She wants you close—"

"But we aren't close to Washington." Lynn motioned to the windows. "Those are Maryland pines out there. I made Tom take me out to Boonsboro and Chestertown when he used to insist I come with him to DC. I know the Maryland countryside. We're here because it's remote and no one could find us."

"I'm not going to defend her. I obviously don't agree with what she's done. But after seeing what's happened to William . . ."

"She is simply being used as a pawn. You know better than anyone what the Suits are capable of doing. I don't understand what's happened to William, but I can tell you they'll want to silence him and make him disappear. It's exactly what they've done with us too. All under the guise of being an order from the FBI. I'm sorry, I have to go get some air."

"Don't think they'll let you go far," Roxy motioned to the door, which had been locked by the agent positioned in the hallway outside.

"They know there's nowhere to run." Lynn opened the glass doors and stepped out onto the courtyard.

The man sitting outside on an iron chair looked up from his phone. "Can I help you, Mrs. Roseworth?"

"You can allow us to leave," she said.

"Sorry, ma'am. You're here for your own security."

Liar. "I just need some fresh air."

"Of course."

She walked to the edge of the paving stones, tastefully laid amid carefully trimmed grass. After being inside for so long, she welcomed the sun, despite its already pounding heat.

Nothing, however, could dispel the chill within her.

The shadow was like a leash. She was allowed to think, to act, to do as she would, but the reminder was there, tugging at her.

"Something's controlling us," Don had said, just before they lost contact.

She had no doubt it had returned for William too.

Whatever was happening, he had to be told everything. It was perhaps the greatest debate between her and Tom in all the years since Argentum. She agonized about bringing William into the fold, believing he deserved to know the truth. But Tom insisted he be able to live a regular life for as long as possible. Knowing how heavily the truth weighed on her, she'd agreed. And now her husband, the only one who truly understood, was gone.

Some marriages couldn't survive the exposure of an affair, even if it happened forty years ago. Theirs had been strained, even sleeping in separate bedrooms for a while. After three weeks of it, she'd marched into the guest room and gotten into bed with him.

Grueling sessions with a marriage counselor had unearthed decades of resentment. The end result was a greater understanding of each other, and a professional pairing the two had never experienced before. Tom began to use government connections to see what he could uncover about Argentum. But when the official investigation discredited Lynn's claims of a vast conspiracy, Tom realized that he could no longer align himself with a government that was waging a war on the truth. He gave up his Senate seat, cutting all ties with Washington while quietly tapping into his resources. As Lynn re-established her research into the missing, she found the husband from whom she had kept so many secrets for so long was now an invaluable assistant.

Tom had frowned, however, when that package had arrived on their doorstep, containing a generic cell phone to which a single note was attached, with a phone number. Vowing to keep no more secrets, Lynn acknowledged the handwriting belonged to Dr. Steven Richards. Tom had just squeezed her hand and whispered that he trusted her. Her heart swelled for her husband in a way it hadn't for years.

Steven had sounded frantic when she called, saying he was on his way to Mexico to confirm something that she desperately needed to know. Keeping the conversation short and calm, she said she looked forward to hearing his findings and reminded him that she wanted the letters about her mother that the Corcillium had offered in exchange for her cooperation.

Steven had only said he understood.

Months later, she'd gotten irritated and used the phone to call again. A man had answered, saying that the Corcillium thought it best to keep their communication extremely limited from now on. She'd demanded the letters from her father, which the man said they hoped to provide in time. In response, she'd said that her property was off limits until the letters were provided, and to tell that to Steven himself. The man promised to relay the message.

It still made her so angry to think of her family's private details in the possession of strangers. She'd never heard from Steven again, including what it was that had made him travel so urgently to Mexico. He hadn't even ever inquired about Anne, his biological daughter, or any of his grandsons. He must have fully embraced the reclusive life of the Corcillium.

Lynn pulled her hair back off her neck, looking up to the blistering bright sky, wishing she had an elastic hair tie to lift the curls and alleviate the heat—

She held the position, blinking several times, forcing herself to keep squinting. After all, what she had just seen could have been a trick of the imagination.

But then the line above the trees took shape again, like the long tail of a kite in the wind. The swarm drifted apart, the insects separating so thoroughly that it was if they disappeared altogether. She held her breath, waiting, until they once again, for just a moment, joined together, making the shape.

The same formation that she'd seen above her own woods. The same formation she'd seen in the photographs far above other abduction sites.

Not ladybugs. It couldn't be. Moths, perhaps? What was native to Maryland—?

The answer came in the singing all around her, in the twittering crescendos of cicadas.

Someone, somewhere in these vast pines, had been taken.

As she looked down to the trees, she saw movement. Another security guard, probably on assignment to patrol the woods. She waited, slowly letting her hair fall once again. A minute later, a man moved, so deep into the trees that the green foliage almost completely blocked him from view. She saw another, then, both wearing camouflage pants and shirts, their brown ball caps curved just as William preferred to wear his. They carried rifles and had stopped to stare at her.

She lifted her hand to her chest to conceal her movement from the guard on the patio. She gave an urgent wave.

The men were so far away that she couldn't see their expressions, but neither returned the gesture. She saw one pull up something from his neck. It was black, and he raised it to his eyes.

She waited for a moment, hoping he was focusing the binoculars. She began to mouth the words. *Help me. Help me. Help me. Help me.*

The sound of shoes on grass came from behind.

Help me. Help me. Help me. Help me.

"Ma'am, time to go back inside," said the guard.

Keep the binoculars up. Please.

She waited till the guard was directly behind her, and she dramatically turned, pushing him away.

"Ma'am!"

"Get your hands off me!" she cried out, striking him again.

As she'd hoped, he reached up and took her arm gently. "Mrs. Roseworth, are you alright—"

She violently tore her arm away. *Please keep watching.*

"You can't keep us here!"

"Ma'am! That's enough! This heat has clearly gotten to you. Time to go inside and cool off. I promise you, you are in no danger at all. You need to relax."

"I will not relax!" she practically screamed.

"Lynn?" Roxy had come out to the patio.

"They have to let us go!" Lynn called out.

"That's enough," the guard said, this time forcefully taking her by the arm.

Lynn struggled but let the man lead her away. *Please keep watching. Please.*

"Lynn, what's wrong?" Roxy asked.

"Get back in the house!" the guard barked.

"Listen jerk off, you take your hand off my friend right now," Roxy walked forward.

The guard ushered them both inside, closing the door. "That was your last trip outside. Best make yourself comfortable. You just lost any privilege you thought you had by making that scene out there. You best calm the hell down. If you thought you could get one of the other agents to think I'm mistreating you, trust me, you're not that good of an actress."

Lynn gave the agent a sharp look. "Sir, you are completely unaware of what I am capable of doing."

He turned around and drew the curtain across the French doors. He then stepped through the doors, shutting them tightly.

"What the hell happened out there?" Roxy asked.

Lynn moved past her. "Did you bring any lipstick?"

"Come on. It was important to me that I look my best out in the middle of nowhere. They wouldn't let us take anything. Why? What is going on?"

Lynn rushed to the desk in the room, quickly rummaging through the bare contents inside. She found a lone pen, but no paper.

"Did you have heatstroke out there?"

"No," Lynn said, walking over the bookshelf. She searched among the row of coffee table books, finding one on beaches of the East Coast. The first page had just a small dedication to the lovers of the ocean. Tearing out the page, she hurried to the bathroom.

"OK, I'm starting to worry that you have indeed lost your mind."

"Come in the bathroom. And close the door."

"What are you doing?" Roxy asked, pulling the door shut behind her.

"Turn on the water."

"Why?"

"Because they have certainly set up cameras inside the bedroom, and microphones. The faucet will drown out our words." Lynn reached over and began to draw out large letters, scribbling back and forth on the page to darken them.

"Well, I'm going to find one of those cameras and take off my clothes and *really* give them something to look at," Roxy said, looking over her shoulder. "What in the world are you writing? HELP?"

"Turn on the shower too. There were men in the woods. Hunters. They saw me. And I bet my life on the fact that someone had been abducted from these woods."

"Wait. People saw you? And how do know there's been an abduction from here?"

"The shower, Roxy! Especially if you're going to talk that loud."

"Fine." She turned on the faucet at the sink and above the tub. "Are you sure they were hunters? In the summer?"

"They must be hunting squirrel or quail. They were carrying rifles and were wearing camouflage. One had on binoculars, and I swear he looked at me. If they're local, I bet they've noticed the swarm and came to look at it."

"Swarm? Like the ladybugs—"

"Yes. But this time they're cicadas."

"Cicadas? Are they making the same shape?"

"Yes. You wouldn't notice it unless you stood and watched for a while. I assume one of the hunters saw it. And that's why I got all dramatic out there. I hope they got worried by what they saw."

Lynn walked to the small window in the bathroom, raising the wood blinds. She looked out, seeing none of the guards walking around. She slid the paper onto the window.

She peered over the page, biting the inside of her lip. Please come in for a closer look. Please don't think I'm some crazy old woman with dementia who wandered out.

For the next hour she stood and watched, with Roxy pacing or sitting on the toilet lid. "Nothing?" she asked for the seventeen time.

"I would tell you if I saw something. No. Nothing."

"Maybe they didn't see you after all. If one of those guards walks by outside and sees that sign, we're going to get quite the lecture. Not that I care. Screw flashing the cameras, maybe I'll strip down naked, and when he opens the curtains from outside, he'll be so blinded that we can make a run for it."

"Like I said before—and just proved again—there's nowhere to run," Lynn said.

"Don't sound so defeated. This was the most excitement we've had all day. It was worth the try."

At the closure of another hour, they heard the door to the bedroom open. "Dinner," said a deep voice from beyond.

"Just one second. Waxing my upper lip," Roxy called out, opening the bathroom door.

Sighing, Lynn snatched the sign from the window and walked out.

After the food was delivered and the door to the hallway once again locked, she and Roxy sat at the table and softly spoke.

"Those swarming cicadas. If someone was taken out there, it means you were right," Roxy said, toying with a tough piece of overcooked chicken.

"It's happening at all the places where people have vanished. I developed contacts all over the world at the different abduction sites. When I saw the swarming happening above our woods, I reached out to them, asking them to take video or photographs, to see if they saw it as well. Even in Argentum, where one of the families of the missing took video above the town. It took me considerable time, but I found the shape there in the falling snow, clustering as it drifted."

"I hate to even suggest it . . . but have you thought about sharing what you've uncovered with the government? To warn them?"

"I am afraid it would mean they would kill us all. Starting with William."

"God, Lynn. There has to be another way."

"I just need to think."

"We have plenty of time for that."

Having lost all trace of an appetite, Roxy grabbed two books from the shelf and attempted to read. Two hours later, she exclaimed she was so bored that her only option was to go to bed early.

It was only beginning to darken when Lynn herself started to doze in a chair. With Roxy softly snoring, Lynn closed her eyes.

Don't go to sleep. Think. Think how to get out. Get to Stella. Get to Kate. Get to William. He has to know. Above anyone else, he has to know—

The gunshots in the distance prompted her to sit up.

"What the hell is that?" Roxy said, still deep in sleep.

"Rifles," Lynn said, sitting up. The sounds resounded again, closer to the house. They both hurried to the curtains, parting them.

The only true light came from the sole outdoor lamp above the front door to the house, and it barely penetrated the night's gloom. But it was enough to see the shapes of two guards rushing quickly past, heading in the direction of another gunshot.

"What's going on?" Roxy asked.

"I don't know—"

A loud rapping sound came from the bathroom. With Roxy clutching Lynn's arm, they walked through the dark to the bathroom. The sound repeated.

As they peered around, a flashlight illuminated a face outside the window. The light revealed a young man's face underneath the bill of a hat.

Waving at Roxy to stay back, Lynn didn't dare to turn on the light. She felt for the book page and the pen still sitting on the sink, unlatching the bolt on the window and lifting the pane.

"Are you the lady out in the yard?" the man whispered. "Are you OK?"

"Thank you, thank you for coming," Lynn said. "Thank God you saw me."

"My brother actually did. Said he didn't like how that guy was yanking you around."

At this proximity, Lynn realized this was no man. He had to be barely on the edge of sixteen, and reeked of alcohol.

"We don't have much time. I'm writing down a phone number. It's my daughter. Please, please call her and tell her where we are."

When he responded, the beer on his breath almost made Lynn flinch. "My grandpa would kill us if he knew we were up here. He's chapped our butts before for snooping around the old Scotter place. We always wonder what's going on over here, with all the men in suits and stuff. My brother didn't believe me that that the cicadas were acting weird again, so I brought him out to show him. We didn't think we'd see you too."

"Please, just take this number and run. And thank your brother."

"He's hiding under a deer tarp right now. We figured we needed a distraction to get to where you stuck that sign. What kind of trouble are you in—oh shit!"

He turned off the flashlight, snatched the book page, and took off running, quickly vanishing into the night. Lynn held her breath, peering forward.

The crickets and cicadas outside were so loud it was almost piercing. She nearly didn't hear the sounds of footsteps that arrived at the edge of the house, just beyond the window. Quietly, she slid the window shut, backing away.

For a brief moment, she saw the outline of the two guards pass the window, walking from the house towards the trees where the boy had run.

ELEVEN

She knew the sound of her heels were as rattling to the male power grid in Washington as a reporter who'd uncovered pork projects hidden in a transportation bill. *Here she comes,* they thought, her Jimmy Choos making more noise than their Allen Edmonds. It always happened as she strode into a meeting, the eyes of the mostly male faces either going straight to her chest, or disapprovingly to her blond hair. It's all real, fellas, she often wanted to declare, plopping down her briefcase.

Kate was so used to the constant evaluation, she could smell it on men like a bad cologne. It was strong in the ones around her as they moved down the hallway and into the elevator. Her white suit stood out sharply against their black pants and coats. Her frequent companions in these last, horrible days. Her own funeral procession.

As the elevator descended, she waited for a quick stop. After all, there shouldn't be many floors beneath a warehouse. Yet they continued to an uncomfortable depth.

"We're almost there, Senator."

"It's fine," she lied.

It wasn't fine, none of it was fine. The fact that she was even back here, sinking beneath the SSA's headquarters, was troubling enough. But it had been her own doing; she'd insisted on knowing more, especially given that her mother and nephew's files were missing information. There were references to absent personal letters, something about notations from her great-grandmother Freda. But she had seen little else other than the video of the questioning of her mother as a little girl when she'd been found in Mexico.

Mexico. My God.

William's file was picked over, obviously missing other documentation. "I don't want some of it," she'd demanded. "I want it all. On all of them."

As she'd awaited what was promised to be the entirety of the SSA's files into her mother and William, she'd been emailed several documents on a boy named Ryan Hardwood. On the flight back from Memphis, she'd read them in their entirety. Upon landing, she summoned her driver and dialed the number for director Mark Wolve.

"Where is this boy?" she'd said before he could even say hello.

The SSA director was somewhere down south, leading the search for her nephew and the girl. But he'd said he'd have someone escort her when she arrived.

She began to tap her foot, wondering if it sent waves of irritation through the agents. *I hope it does. Because I shouldn't be here. I should be on my way to my mother and Roxy, trying not to trip on the tail between my legs. I should be with Director Wolve, scouring every bit of information trickling in that might lead us to William. I should be with my sister's family in Nashville, trying to convince them that I am doing everything I can to find William. I should be in my office doing the job Tennesseans voted me in to do.*

She was literally going deeper down the rabbit hole that she'd denied existed all her adult life; the reason why she kept her distance from her mother and her entire family. At her father's funeral, she could sense her mother wanted make amends. Instead, she'd left the church and taken the next flight home to Washington, repeating to herself that it made no sense to return to the past she wanted desperately to avoid.

Her mother would never speak of what happened in Argentum, repeatedly stating it was for her family's safety. All Kate had to go on was the government investigators' report, which concluded that those damn Researchers had William all along, using her mother's fears to exploit their beliefs. They just used her, and it cost her father his political future.

Her kind, sweet mother, duped into something that ruined their family. Kate loved her mother, but could never forgive her for that.

And because of it, because of that denial, the painful rift between her and her family, she was now one of the most powerful women in Congress. Kate's responses—now so familiar that they were practically a campaign slogan—to questions about her mother's belief in extraterrestrial life, became her catch phrase. *I'm not here for the sideshow.*

Her conservative constituents had eaten it up. She'd barely won the election, refusing to ask her father to campaign for her. She'd restored the family's good name. The townhouse in Georgetown, the most influential committees, the praise on feminist blogs and accolades from women's groups.

All built on a lie.

The doors to the elevator finally opened, and she began to step out, when one of the agents stopped her. The panel began to flash a vibrant red, and he swiped his security badge. The light turned green. "Sets off an alarm in the hallway if you don't," he said.

He motioned down a dimly lit corridor.

"Are y'all opposed to light?" she asked.

The agents gave no response. She assumed the slip of her accent must have also grated on their nerves. One of her favorite techniques was to come off folksy, and when her opponents thought it equaled a lesser intelligence, she could slide on in with a "bless your heart," and then promptly dismantle them with fifteen years of debate and forensic training and a Stanford undergrad education.

Seeing Agent Flynn Hallow standing at the end of the hall, she readied all her sparring skills.

"A child is down here?" she demanded.

"A necessary evil, so to speak, Senator."

"That's not acceptable. If you have anything else down here, including a damn spaceship, you need to tell me."

"We keep all those in New Mexico."

"While I'm not in a joking mood, I see that you do a have a sense of humor."

"Do I?" Flynn said.

Stand back, she wanted to warn her escorts. "Let's you and I have a talk."

Flynn nodded for the agents to step away from the door where he had been waiting. Kate went to stand directly before him.

"I've read the SSA files on my mother. I know much of it is missing, as are portions of my nephew's file. I know you're keeping a lot from me. But realize that I've been reading legislation all my adult life, so I know to look in the footnotes. And in a small subsection, your name is briefly mentioned as being at the substation in Argentum where my mother and her friend Roxy were held all those years ago."

She then cocked her head. "Of the very few things my mother ever told me about that town, she described a man who looked a lot like you, smelled of cigarettes, who ultimately ordered her assassination, which she and her friend were barely able to avoid. That means you tried to have the wife of a then-sitting US senator killed. I wonder what the head of the FBI would think about that."

Flynn didn't flinch. "What makes you think he doesn't know?"

He did wince, though, when she leaned in closer. "The only reason I don't have your ass thrown in a federal prison is that for the moment, I need to know what you're hiding from me. I am tired of being lied to. I have the ears of the most powerful people in this country. And they will all know what you've done. Every single action taken by this agency. If there is indeed a child down here, I am taking him. I will get my mother and bring them both safely to my home—"

"After you meet the boy behind this door, I think you'll change your mind about that."

"Don't you dare to suggest what I will and won't do. I want the *entire* file on my family. And the fact that all this time, you had one of the abducted here—a child, no less—underground, and neglected to mention it . . . *that* was a huge mistake on you and your director's part."

"He isn't *my* director. *My* director left eight months ago, after dedicating his entire life to this work, only to be suddenly replaced by someone unfamiliar—"

"I'm not interested in your office politics."

"You should be. Director Wolve is not who you think—"

"I don't care who the hell he is, as long as I am provided what I need. Do we understand each other?"

"I understand that for longer than you've been alive, we've been trying to protect the population of this planet from a threat that no one could fathom. So if you're insulted that you don't know everything yet—that's *your* problem. I have no interest in coddling you. People are *dying*, Senator."

He pulled out his phone, holding up the array of news alerts covering his screen. "It's increasing by the hour. Hurricanes forming off the coast of

Brazil *and* across the Atlantic, just off Sierra Leone. Miles and miles of grassfires in Lesotho in Southern Africa. In Nadym—Northern Russia—a fourth of the population is sick and dying. On the borders of every major population. And many more will keep dying until the SSA worldwide can contain every single one of the abducted, and they are nearly impossible to find. So when the one behind this door was discovered, we had—and have—no intention of letting him go."

Kate held her position. "I think you're aware that if it weren't for my involvement, which is why you came to me in the first place, that you wouldn't have the swell of funding you're now receiving, nor the increased military moving in on New Orleans, California, and North Dakota. So when I say I need to know everything, what I mean to say is *the president* needs to know. Are we clear now?"

"You know the risk you take even going in there?"

"I do."

"I'm not sure of that." He put his hands on his hips. "He can convince you to strangle your own throat. It's why we don't dare to keep anyone down here longer than it takes to bring him meals."

"I've read his file."

"But, as you've deduced, the files you've received don't contain all the mountains of information we've collected. You've just read the summary."

"In two hours, I have to give a full report in the Oval Office. Thus, I need to talk to him. So I can explain to the president why he needs to be worried about the lightning that hit the earth last year and left behind that boy."

"For Christ sake, don't use that terminology," Flynn scowled. "It's outdated. See, that's the problem, why I should have been in charge of all the reports—"

"If it wasn't lightning, what was it? And please make it concise, I am running out of time."

"It's some kind of transportation. Our satellites picked up distinct lights coming from storms a year ago. They must have some kind of technology that masks their ships, but the light they use to abduct and transport is visible to us. It's always been referred to as lightning because it happens so fast. But we were waiting. We've been waiting for fifteen years. The first round of light was followed by another about a day later, also during a storm. Once again, four reports of this light at the same time, on the corners of every major population. We knew they'd first been abducted, then re-turned."

"And you got to this boy—Ryan—because he was returned close to DC?"

"Rural Maryland, actually. Just so happens there's a government-owned property with a lot of security cameras that recorded the flashes. When the second light came, we were ready and sent out teams into the woods. It didn't take them long to find the boy, just standing outside in the wet trees."

Kate looked to the door behind him.

"We expected him to be crying, hysterical. Instead, he asked for a Coke, wondered if anyone had *Candy Crush* on their phone. Turns out, as we'd theorized, he'd been missing for a day or so. Lousy grandmother with sole custody had sent him to live with her cousin for the summer, who we sus-pect runs a meth trade and hadn't reported him missing. Real nice family. When we delivered on the Coke, we asked him if he remembered where he'd been. His response: 'Yeah. With the aliens.' Since then, he's been quite cooperative. Even allowing us to do thorough . . . inspections. We've tried to find out what's been implanted inside him. But no scans, no X-rays, have found anything."

Kate nodded once. "I'm going in."

"It's just you, Senator. You understand that. It's why we have to move him down here. Because of what happens when he gets in those trances. We never know when he's going to unleash. We have no choice but to limit visitors. And always only one person at a time, never for more than a minute."

"Because he can cause people to kill each other. I know that. You can risk one life but not two. I understand."

This time it was Flynn who leaned in. "He is a thirteen-year-old re-sponsible for the death of more than seven hundred people in the metro area before we took him underground. I ask you again: are you sure—"

"Open the door."

Flynn reached into his jacket pocket and brought out a badge, swiping it.

A light flashed beside the door, which responded with a loud release of internal locks.

"Good luck," he said.

Kate opened the door, struggling at first with its weight. As she closed it behind her, she heard the jarring sound of the locks sealing her in.

The cavernous room reminded her immediately of the arcades from her youth, complete with the sounds of video games. Everything a teenage boy could ever ask for was crammed into the space. Two large-screen TVs were mounted on the wall, one displaying a violent game with people firing guns from tricked-out cars, the other showing *The Godfather*. Alongside a king-sized bed was a hot tub, against which two guitars leaned. Mounds of books lay everywhere, along with scattered magazines. Posters of naked women hung in glass frames.

And like a throne in the midst of the debauchery stood a dark blue La-Z-Boy recliner, in which sat a boy with an Xbox controller in his hands.

The smiled he flashed as she approached confirmed he was no child; she'd seen the same grin on the faces of senators and congressmen who would rather have her in their bed than on their committees. A smattering of pimples lined a face that one day might be considered enticing to women who liked reckless men. Gangly legs, hair in desperate need of a cut.

He opened to mouth to speak, but Kate beat him to the punch. "Ryan, I am Senator Kate Roseworth—"

"I know who you are." He rapidly punched the controller, hissing a "yes!" under his breath as the screen exploded in a torrent of blood and bullets.

"I'd like to talk—"

"You took your dad's senate seat when he retired," he said, almost slamming the controller with his left thumb. "You're William Roseworth's aunt, but you don't talk to your family because your mom believes in aliens."

He paused the game and chuckled. "How are you feelin' about that now?"

She'd been warned not to underestimate him. Brilliant, off-the-charts smart. Photographic memory. Spent entire days reading, and remembered every sentence.

"Ryan, you shouldn't be down here. I'm going to change that—"

"No, I really *should* be down here. No one with my teenage angst should be able to make people kill one another. It's why they sent you down here instead of Mr. Burns, and without a military escort. Because they know I could flick my middle finger and they'd unload their AK-47s on each other. They think sending a beautiful woman might make me stop. I wish I could. Don't they know all boys my age can do well is drool and mumble?"

Kate almost appreciated his bluntness, given that she knew his assessment of her was shared by many of the men who surrounded her in Washington. Instead of responding, she calmly walked over to a stool on which was a plate with a stack of pizza slices. She moved the plate to the floor.

She knew not to stand above him because that would make it seem like she was lecturing him. And she certainly was not going to kneel. So she scooted the stool directly before him and sat, uncomfortably close and at his eye level.

You are not my first Napoleon. Boys don't change, they only grow chest hair.

He leaned back further into his La-Z-Boy.

"I need to know what's about to happen. If you help me understand, I can try to get you out of here."

"You assume I want to get out of here. Well, there is one place I'd like to see."

"Talk to me and we'll see what I can do. I won't leave you down here, Ryan. I know you don't know me, but I want to earn your trust. I am told you remember everything about your abduction. Adults don't remember, but children do, am I understanding this correctly?"

"All I know is what I know. You're not full of crap? You could get me out of here, even for the weekend?"

"I will do my very best—"

"I want to go to Comic-Con. It's in two weeks."

"That might be difficult. Given what you're capable of doing, a lot of people could get hurt."

"Private tour, then. Before it starts. I get to see all the movie trailers and clips and everything before anyone else. Guarantee it, and I'll tell you everything I know."

She pulled out her phone. Even this deep beneath the earth, they'd made sure there was Wi-Fi and cell service, just to keep him happy. He was blocked from posting anything on social media or contacting anyone, but he insisted on having the access to texts in order to send demands for McDonald's and to play *Minecraft*.

She fired off a series of texts and waited.

"Done," she said, after her phone pinged twice.

"Really? Can you show me?"

She gave him the phone. "That is Alex Bright, the junior senator from

California. Deep support from Hollywood. You can see I asked for a private tour of Comic-Con for a donor's son, with full access. And, as you can read, she said no problem. Do we have a deal?"

He read it twice and nodded. "Gotta catch the last one. Can't miss it."

"I don't know if you've seen the latest grosses of the Avengers movies, but I think Comic-Con's going to be around for a while."

He shook his head. "I wouldn't count on that."

"Why do you say that?"

He looked down at the controller in his hands, obviously wanting to return to his game.

"Why, Ryan?"

He looked up at her, the smirking grin now gone. In those deep brown eyes was real fear. "You don't have any idea what's coming."

"That's why I'm here. To find out. I've seen interviews conducted with people who were abducted a long time ago. But you're the only one who still remembers. I have a million questions for you about how you were taken and what happened to you, but I have to focus on how to understand, maybe even stop, what's happening."

He grunted. "You can't."

"I know you told the agents that you communicated with . . . whatever those things are. I understand this communication was done before, by sharing memories. But I've watched your interviews, you said you didn't share memories, you actually understood them."

"Yep. Me and Earl. We shared brains."

"Earl?"

"That's what I call him. My alien, Earl. Earl's not the nicest of fellas. Earl doesn't think much of our race. Earl did some bad stuff to get into my brain. Earl is a real bastard. But when Earl connected to me, I connected to him."

"You've allowed the sketch artist to draw what happened to you. I'm sorry, Ryan. It sounds awful."

"Earl is proof that karma is real for the people of our planet," he continued quickly, obviously wanting to move on. "What we've been doing to monkeys and rats and mice for years is coming back on us."

"You mean testing."

"They think we're lower than animals. Nah, insects. If we could test weapons on insects—roaches, ants—that's what we are to them. Just a place for them to test out ways to kill. So they can use it on other worlds. Turns out there is a whole lot out there that they want to conquer."

Kate held her breath. She should have recorded this for the president to hear himself.

"How is it that you remember? And adults don't?"

"Oh, they don't think we'll remember. They put our little brains through quite the process to forget what they do to us up there. They think they're gods compared to us. But that's the one thing they haven't quite perfected yet. Kids still remember."

So did my mother and nephew when they were children. Until the government I serve took their memories away.

"Then you understand your vital role in this, Ryan. Did . . . this creature show you why the abductions have begun again?"

"Because they got it right this time."

"What do you mean?"

"Do you ever play *Age of Blood*?" He leaned over the side of the chair to dig into a container of video-game cases, pulling out one with a US soldier fighting a massive green orc decked out in ornate armor. "It's starting to show its age, but it was one of the first to let you be a general, commanding armies. And it explains the mistake Earl and his buddies made."

"Come again?" Kate squinted.

"In the game, you're a general. And if you don't keep pretty tight control of your armies, they start to unravel. Uprisings, desertion, you get the idea. Earl and his peeps obviously did not play *Age of Blood*. They thought they could take people from isolated places, juice them up with the weapon of choice, and then drop them off in different climates to see how effective they were. But they didn't keep tabs on them. No one guarded the henhouse, so to speak.

"They thought their armies would just scatter around the world, and they could test their weapons from time to time to see how people died around them. They didn't count on the government rounding them up in places like that town in Colorado and keeping them from the masses. And, they didn't count on their brains frying."

Kate tapped her fingers on her leg. "Are you talking about the comas? The ones who . . . were . . ."

"Activated? Yeah, Earl and his boys didn't count on that. Once those people got triggered to see what damage they'd cause, they'd sure as shit do it for about a minute or two, but their puny little brains couldn't handle it. Straight to coma city, and then they were just useless. So, of course, the defects had to all be gathered up. Basically an intergalactic recall."

Ryan extended his arms. "But they've been working to improve their products, and you're looking at the new and improved version. Trigger me, and I don't die. No screaming headaches, no bleeding ears, no coma. I could dance a jig for you or put together a puzzle after I command people to kill."

He thumped the cover of the game. "Thus, this time, they stole a play out of the ol' *Age of Blood* game book. No more defects. Four of us, supercharged, plopped down in every civilized nation. I watched them do it. And once our major general connects with us, he tells when to fire at will. Once he triggers us, we can do it on our own."

"You mean kill people."

"I didn't even know I was doing it. Once my agent pals moved me to Washington, they realized pretty quickly that the riots breaking out outside my building weren't just sparked by political ideology. I remember waking up from a weird dream and just watching it from my window, wondering why it seemed like the whole neighborhood was on fire. When they moved me to another location, I blacked out, and three rival gangs suddenly decided it was time for full-on warfare. It didn't take long for the Men in Black to realize something was sparking it all."

He rested his head on his fist. "He dreams, I black out, and people die. That's when I got a one-way ticket underground. It's Christmas every day down here, so they think overloading me with distractions will stop me. But I'm not in control. I suggested they sink me to the bottom of the ocean. Instead they stuck me this far underground. Apparently there's a limit to our reach."

Kate's voice was stuck in her throat. "You said, 'He dreams.' What does that mean?"

"Our major general. He woke it in me. Just like he's awakening the others. He's already met one of us in person. They're together, actually."

"Together?"

"He's got a little girl with him now."

Kate stood up so quickly she almost knocked the stool out from beneath her. "Did you say a little girl?"

"Yeah. Once they touched, I felt it. I don't know if he's connected to all of us yet or not. I guess once he's fired us all up, all over the globe, the next wave blows in. I can see by the expression on your face that the Comic-Con deal probably isn't going to happen."

She took a step towards the door. "I will do everything in my power to help you. You're thirteen, you should be at Comic-Con. I want you to get out of here—"

"You just don't want bloodshed in the streets of San Diego, I guess," he said. "Well, it was worth the try. I would have liked to have seen it."

"I'll find a way to get you there one day—"

"You don't get it," he said, those eyes haunted now. "There won't be any more. There may not be one in two weeks."

"I will come back for you, I promise," she said, practically running across the room, her heart beating loudly in her ears. As she reached the door, she heard the La-Z-Boy foot rest lower. "I know that you know, Senator, who our major general is."

He was standing now, his hands in his pockets. "I can see him. We can see him in the dreams. Like I said, I know when he first made physical contact with the girl. But I don't think he understands quite yet. He doesn't know what he's doing. I don't think he can see us. And I know what you're thinking, and you're right; he has to die in order for everyone to live—"

Ryan then shuddered and gripped the side of his chair.

"Ryan, what's wrong—"

"Go," he said, throwing his arm in an arc. "Go now!"

Kate suddenly remembered Flynn's words. *Because of what happens when he gets in those trances. We never know when he's going to unleash.*

"What is it?"

"Run past the agents if they're outside! Go!"

"What's happening—?"

"He's dreaming," Ryan said, clutching the chair. "And I can't hold him back."

Fire burned, gleefully licking the dry grass—

A storm churned over the water, preparing to launch against the city—

Two men in a dark corridor strangled each other as an elevator closed nearby—

Hospital rooms filled to capacity, the rapidly deteriorating patients now in tents outside. As always, eyes watched, including Lily's, the writhing of the black-scaled snakes all around her.

William was pulled onward. It had happened many times before. The nightmares always started in the same four locations, but periodically shifted to similar disasters in different places. Never before, though, at this speed.

First to a vast grassland, where kangaroos leapt to escape the rocking earth. Then to the skies, an angry black, on the coast of a city where a building with white sails braced as the funnel formed over the water. He was in a small medical center frantically struggling to keep pace with the people funneling in, most unable to even walk. On a farm, where men stopped herding sheep to run towards each other, pummeling each other with their fists, their faces soon bloody and gouged, their dogs watching in tense confusion.

Just as the eyes had emerged in the familiar four locations, they now met him everywhere he went. Slanted eyes, blue eyes, bloodshot eyes, eyes crusty with age, eyes watering by smoke. He saw a castle's portcullis over the shoulder of a man shot three times, screaming in what sounded like French. The Great Wall of China, perhaps, but difficult to tell; the flames were too high.

He tried to stop them, screaming at them. As the eyes flashed before him, he tried to focus on them, connect with them, order them to stop. But they quickly rushed by, as if he were on a speeding subway watching faces on a platform.

Most places he didn't recognize, including the village on the cusp of civilization, where children ran from adults who were beating, biting, stabbing each other. And when that massacre was done, the children held their breath in the hut where they hid, trying not to weep as the surviving adults approached the entrance with blood on their hands—

"William!"

He gasped for air, his throat raspy.

"William, are you alright?" Steven asked.

He sat up from where he had slumped over in the chair. He vaguely remembered the buzzing of dragonflies on the hunt for mosquito larvae and the gentle rocking of the boat tied to the dock that had made him drowsy. His screams must have shattered the near-silence of the Apalachicola River.

"I tried shaking you awake and you didn't budge. Figured you were just too tired to stay awake anymore. You weren't asleep for ten minutes when you started whimpering and then a full-on scream. It's going to be a miracle if nobody heard you. My God, did you have one of those dreams?"

William shut his eyes tightly. "I'm sorry."

"What do you see?"

"It's spreading. Rapidly. I watched it happen. I swear I even saw China. There are eyes everywhere. They must be the abducted who were returned. I don't even know if they realize what they're doing. I don't think they do."

"I'm sure they don't. It's not their fault. Just like it's not your fault."

"I'm awakening it. Whatever *it* is, within them." William shook his head, thinking of the children in the village.

"Not you, William. *They're* using you. You aren't responsible."

"There has to be a way to stop it."

"You've already proven you can, with Lily. We just have to find a way to do it with the others."

"People are dying. I don't have time to figure this out."

"I know this weighs heavily on you. Once we get somewhere safe, you can experiment with Lily. If you can stop her, you must be able to stop them too. We just have to determine how."

Steven finally lifted his hand from William's shoulder, fumbling a bit to return to his seat. He sighed as he sat, rubbing his shoulder.

"This can't be good for you," William said. "I have a lot of older people in my life. I know stiff-backed chairs are preferred. This constant movement can't be good."

"At my age, anything that isn't a leisurely walk is a stretch."

"You mentioned a heart attack. This is too much for someone of your age."

"This is too much for someone of *your* age. I'm old. Eighty-six. Every day I get, I'm thankful for. Even when every bone in my body aches, like they do right now. And I'm here with you, which is something I never thought would happen."

"That makes two of us."

"William, I owe you an apology."

"For what? For not telling me about a mistake you and my grand-mother made sixty years ago? That's none of my business. We have more pressing matters at hand. Including Blue. You're certain she's alive?"

"I am. Rudd knows where to hide her. I know she's tough. But this will weigh hard on her, to finally meet her great-grandson and then have him ripped away. All members of the Corcillium will lock down now; it's our protocol if the house is discovered. No communication for seven days. I was not exaggerating when I said we are on our own. We're fortunate the tributary by the house empties into the river that allowed us to escape."

"I have to say it again: Lily and I should turn ourselves in. I can't risk you or anyone else dying for this. We are the danger. We are the weapons. I understand why the government is so desperate to contain us. They should have us, find what was implanted in us, and rip it out."

"No." Steven tried to sit up. "We cannot trust the SSA—"

The sound of running came from across the dock. Lily was much further ahead than Quincy, her nightgown flapping around her thin body. As she arrived at the boat, her face bearing the familiar expression of concern for William, Quincy finally came to a stop, leaning over, hands on his knees.

"Are you . . . OK?" he gasped.

William nodded. "I am. I guess you could hear me?"

"We were walking back from the store when we heard you start screaming. But nobody's up there, at least nobody we saw outside," Quincy said, gathering his breath. "Another dream?"

Lily reached out and laid her hand on his shoulder.

"So there is a store up there?" Steven motioned up the path from the dock.

"About a half mile up. We saw a knockoff Dollar General. There's a crappy motel too, if you could call it that. And a gas station. While I am not a fan of returning to any motel room with this crew, it could give us a place to decompress for a minute. Plus, there's a sign in the window that the store has an ATM."

Steven frowned. "We can't. They'll be monitoring every financial transaction for any hint of us."

"Let's just say that when you get to a certain income level, you learn tricks. If I can get to the ATM, I can get cash. I'm not sure we have any other option."

William helped Steven from the boat, assisting him up the dirt road. They walked on the edge, so if they did hear a vehicle approach, they could step into the pines and hide. As soon as Steven said he felt the stiffness starting to loosen, they'd reached the cluster of buildings, which clearly only existed to provide fuel to boats and food for the people who came to ski or fish. The beat-up motel completed the image, a haven for those who drank too much on the water and needed to crash for the night. In the window of the store was a badly faded ATM sign, just above a Jeep Cherokee that didn't appear to have been driven this decade.

"I should be the one going in, I'm the least recognizable," Steven said. "You still have your debit card?"

Quincy patted his back pocket. "Only because my pants haven't blown up yet. And sorry, you've got to know the codes. And this one's long."

"This is risky. What if someone recognizes you? What if—?"

"Don't think we have a choice. Look at us. Little bit here is still in her nightgown. Anyone sees us, they're gonna call the cops. And that ended really badly last time. I'm going in."

The other three could only stand in the shadows of the pine trees, watching Quincy walk across the road and into the store. Lily held tight to William's hand.

Every minute that passed prompted more sweat and the shuffling of feet. Steven sighed repeatedly. Even Lily pulled away from William's hand so she could twist her hair tie around her finger.

Then Quincy came strolling out. He was whistling and carried two plastic sacks in his hand. He motioned to the motel.

They hurriedly crossed the road to where Quincy waited. He reached into the sack and put on a comically large trucker's hat with the words, "Deez Nuts," in bold black letters.

He winked at William, holding up a key. "The ATM is now fully drained. And we got the Presidential Suite. Old girl behind the counter is the kingpin of this monopoly. Got us a room. I think she wanted me to invite her in, but alas."

He handed William a hat. It had the grill of a Jeep on the front with the outline of a naked woman and read, "My Jeep looks better topless."

"My God." William smiled.

"I have the charming habit of being incredibly inappropriate at all times. It's this one. Room one."

With a quick turn of a key, they hurried in. The room was dark, the combined smell of mold and Lysol rising to greet them.

"Don't touch anything until we check for bedbugs," Quincy cautioned, steering Lily away from where she was about to sit on the bed. "OK. We're all winners at the Lower Florida Nordstrom. Jeans and T-shirt for William, belt for me to hold up these Hammer pants, and even something for Miss Lily here. Enough junk food to clog our arteries, and toiletries for all. And a cheapie phone. I know we can't use it, but it claims to have internet service at least."

"How much cash did you get out?" Steven asked.

"Let's just say if a local needs ten bucks to buy a Hunt Brothers pizza, they're out of luck. More money in there than I would have thought. Miss Linda needed some cash."

"Miss Linda?" William looked back from where he was peering out the curtains.

"Miss Linda Mosh from Cambria, Illinois. Miss Mosh has financial accounts I can access when necessary. Helpful to tuck away cash during tax time, and certainly helpful now. If you testify to the IRS about it, I'll deny it."

"Could I have the phone?" William asked, grabbing the clothes and a toothbrush. He needed to shower badly.

"Give me a minute," Quincy said, tearing open the packaging.

William rushed through his shower and hurriedly brushed his teeth. His beard was already becoming unkempt. Thankfully, Quincy had bought several hats, including a solid navy blue. The T-shirt was a size too small for his liking, but the jeans would do.

He stepped out, and Lily quickly ushered herself in, carrying another plastic bag, closing the door.

"Did she get something to eat?" William asked.

"Kid can tear through some Doritos. Phone is operating. The bars are low, but you can give it a whirl. And no sign of bedbugs, which is why Dr. Richards felt it was safe to use a pillow."

"Just need to rest for a moment," Steven said, his eyes closed.

"Everybody needs to rest." William held up the phone, praying that the internet responded.

"Careful with whatever you're searching. They'll be looking," Steven said.

"Just checking CNN. I want to see something."

Just as Quincy began to wipe down a chair using a thin packet of Lysol wipes from the store, the bathroom door opened, and Lily stepped out. Gone was the nightgown, replaced by a horribly bright yellow dress with grinning suns on the hem. The same color of yellow shone on the flip-flops on her feet.

"Thank you, Quincy," she said softly.

Quincy scratched his neck. "I'm used to buying Versace for women. But you're welcome, kiddo."

"Are we safe?" she asked.

William set down the phone, coming to squat in front of her. "I think so. I want you to know something: None of this is your fault. None of it. What happened back in the cotton field, and the airport, when you saved me in the car—you're not doing it. I am. I don't know how, but I am."

Lily narrowed her eyes. "But . . . I'm a monster—"

"No, no honey," William took her arms. "You're not. I know it's hard to understand. But you and I—we're . . . connected, somehow. And others like us."

"Do you make them do bad things too?" she asked.

"I don't want to. That's what I'm trying to figure out."

"You made me stop. Maybe you can make them stop too. I don't want people to get sick anymore. Why did they do this to us?"

William held his breath. "Do you remember . . . when you were taken? Up into the stars?"

She just stared for a moment, and then nodded once.

"And when they brought you back . . . what happened?"

She shook her head firmly. Tears pooled in her eyes.

"Ok." He reached out, touching her arm. "It's OK—"

"I saw you," she said, stifling her sob. "I saw you when you dreamed."

William's eyes widened. "You could see me in your dreams?"

"I had to find you."

Her bottom lip jutted out and the tears let loose. William held her, stroking the back of her hair. "You're a brave girl, Lily. But can you tell me, why did you feel like you had to find me?"

"Because of the monster," she said, the bitterness sounding harsh in her young voice. "It's waiting for us."

William's legs hung off the edge of the picnic table. The trees that lined the back of the motel were still; even the branches didn't sway, as if to indicate it was too hot for anything to move. He'd need to shower again after sitting out here.

He took another swig from the bottle of water. It was warm already.

A shape briefly interrupted the sole source of light, a bulb positioned above the trashcans in the back. Hands in his pockets, Quincy strolled towards him.

"Lily asleep?" William asked.

"Yep. Had to practically write her a contract in blood stating that if she changed into the world's ugliest unicorn pajamas, she could wear the world's ugliest dress again tomorrow. You'd think I'd bought her Vera Wang."

William managed to smirk. "She loves it."

"Poor kid. Wherever she came from, whatever life she had, she must have not had much."

"I wish I knew anything about what happened to her before, but she's clearly traumatized by it. Enough to where she won't talk about it."

Quincy leaned against the table. "Gotta be honest with you: I've wanted to know this all my life. But now that I do, I'm not feeling real good about it."

"Obviously you didn't know what you were getting into."

"I give zero shits that the papers call me a crazy conspiracy theorist. You should see my office in LA. I have the first edition of *Communion* in a glass case. And yes, I will admit, a framed *Independence Day* poster. You grow up a fat kid with no friends who likes science, and your Dad tells you about your great-grandfather's research about people disappearing into lightning, what else are you supposed to become?"

"I bet you are regretting those interests now."

"Here's the reality: I lead a pretty shallow life. I've made a lot of money on teenage girls wanting to project images of their faces to their boyfriends. I'm not curing cancer. I am surrounded by people with way too much plastic surgery driving Teslas. It is any wonder than I sought out a greater understanding of the cosmos?"

"Apparently it's genetic."

"I mean, can you believe it? Our great-grandparents discovered the first proof. And seventy or so years later, here we are. And let's be honest: This isn't by chance. The Corcillium wanted us to make this connection, but obviously without all the death and explosions."

"And it's only getting worse. That's what scares me the most."

"Will you tell me about what you see in these dreams? I think it's pretty obvious now that it's how you're connected to all the disasters, right?"

William took a long drink and started with the eyes in the storms. What he saw in the fires, the violence, the deaths in hospitals, finally ending by seeing Lily's eyes in the stone.

"And to wrap it up with a bow, there are snakes. Everywhere."

"Jesus. No wonder you wake up freaking out. But what you can do with Lily . . . that's hope, right? She says she saw you in her dreams. Maybe that means the others out there . . . can see you too. That's why you got on-line, isn't it? You wanted to see where the storm is coming. Where the fires are. Because if you can stop Lily . . ."

"I don't even know how I do it. And it's everywhere now. Global. I dream of it, everywhere. It's like a virus. Carriers in each part of the world. I can see it, but I can't communicate with them. And I'm the cause."

"And maybe the cure." Quincy raised a finger. "I know Steven thinks there's one causing the hurricanes that keep hitting New Orleans. Speaking of hurricanes: those drinks are responsible for my lack of memory of the eight Mardi Gras I've been to."

"It's a slow churning storm, but it's coming. I've seen it. It's insane to think about heading there, but I don't know what else to do. If for some reason I can find the person doing it . . ."

William turned to him. "But you've got to leave, Quincy. You shouldn't be here. Lily has to stay with me, and Steven refuses to leave."

"Well yeah, he's your grandfather. Sorry about that slip of the tongue, by the way. I just assumed you figured it out. Plus it's practically mentioned in every tabloid written about your grandmother."

"It's doesn't matter now. You need to walk away. I can't risk any more innocent people dying."

"I'm hardly innocent. While I don't enjoy being shot at or blown up, how could I go back? 'Hey Phil, will you book me that trip to the Barbados with those twins, who clearly are into me for my body and not my millions?'"

William smiled, and Quincy slapped his knee, leaving a wad of cash. "You and I could be pals, you know. I know a fellow troublemaker when I see one. I've read about your exploits in Nashville. Pissing on the hood of the paparazzo's car was particularly impressive."

"Just particularly stupid," William said, holding up the cash. "What's this about?"

"I left some with Steven too. Best that we distribute the wealth just in case something else blows up. Got to make sure that Miss Lily remains in the finest of fashions."

"Even if the reason you tracked me down was to make a buck, if you hadn't been there, Lily and I would be in some government prison, or maybe dead. We're alive, in part, because of you. But I still don't think you should stick around."

"And miss all these wonderful accommodations?" Quincy yawned. "Oh yeah, I forgot to tell you that Steven said to wake him up when we get in. He said something about experimenting with something as you slept. What's he talking about?"

"I'll explain when we get inside. It's about trying to stop the spread of the disasters. I don't know if it will work."

"Well, whatever he wants to try, I'm here to help too. Feel free to use me for my money." Quincy patted him on the back as they rounded the building.

William laughed. "Thank you, Quincy."

As they quietly opened the door to the room, they could see Lily in a hard sleep on top of the covers. Steven was slumped in a chair, his head resting on his shoulder.

Quincy walked over, whispering. "Steven, wake up—"

The door behind them flew open with a bang, slamming against the wall. The barrels of guns moved into the room.

They were on William in a heartbeat, pushing him on top of the bed with his arm twisted behind his back, rushing over to point their guns at Steven's head. They even moved in on Lily, guns drawn.

None were dressed in black.

"Mr. Martin, are you alright?" asked a nervous man, considerably smaller than his gun-toting companions, quickly shutting the door.

"Holy crap, Phil!" Quincy smacked his hands together. "My God, it worked! I could kiss you. For Christ sake, put the guns down. Bob, Tommy, come on. Guns down. Richie, loosen up on the redhead. Let go. That's an order."

William felt it, the rush inside him. A match scratched across stone. An automatic reaction that he wanted this man off him, for the pain of his twisted arm to stop.

He twisted his head around to Lily, who had sat up and was focusing her eyes on the man holding him down.

No, Lily. No!

He watched her flinch for a moment, and then go back to being just a frightened little girl.

"Hey guys, I'm serious." Quincy snapped his fingers. "Guns down! Let him up."

"Mr. Martin, we have to go," said the fidgeting man at the door.

"Everybody chill out *right now*," Quincy said. "I appreciate the cavalry, but enough. You found me, I'm safe, I'm fine. Look at me, OK? I'm not in danger. Not by these people. Get it? *Drop the weapons.*"

"Mr. Martin, please. Our car is waiting outside."

"Phil, you're my damn assistant, not the director of my security team. That's you, Richie. So loosen up on Will there, let him go."

"We've got our orders, Mr. Martin," grunted the man holding William. "The board is displeased."

"Your orders come from *me*, Richie." Quincy's face was turning red now. "And you followed protocol. As soon as I got money out of that ATM account, you knew to track it. And it worked. But I'm altering whatever plans you've been given. We need a car and a plane big enough for all of us."

"Get him out, fellas," the man ordered.

Their guns still focused on Lily and Steven, the men moved towards Quincy, motioning to him to follow.

"Hey, you don't make the decisions here. I'm the one whose initial is on the plane, remember? Phil, like I said, we need a car for all of us—"

"I'm sorry, Mr. Martin, but that's not our orders. We're bringing you in to safety. The board is really concerned. The stocks have tanked since you disappeared—"

"The board?" Quincy roared. "You can go back and tell those jack offs that I call the shots. And I'm not going anywhere without this crew. Richie, you don't understand—"

"Sorry, Mr. Martin. You know the board. Millionaires with this much at stake don't mess around. They want you brought in safely, away from these people," the man holding William said. "And ultimately, that board is who makes sure we get paid. And we need our paychecks. We're going *now.*"

The beefy security men were on Quincy, rushing him out like a president under fire.

"No!" Quincy ordered, even trying to wrench away, but the men were built like semi trucks.

The bodyguard leaned down to William. "I will have a gun on you until we are out of this place. Don't you think about making a damn move."

With a final hard press on William's arm, the man backed out, his gun still pointed at them. Swiftly and quietly, he shut the door.

Seconds later, there was a squeal of tires and a flash of headlights. What remained was a street, dark and still.

TWELVE

"You are going to burn a hole in that carpet if you walk in front of that window one more time."

Lynn stopped pacing, her hand rising in exasperation. "What else am I supposed to do?"

"You should look over this pamphlet on the Antietam Campaign Trail, as I have seventeen thousand times." Roxy took the brochure and threw it back in the drawer by the nightstand.

"What have I done? I have no idea what happened to that boy. Or his brother. Did they get caught? They're strangers, for God's sake, and I just recklessly put them in harm's way to help us escape."

"Listen, those are country boys. You know what Hank Williams Jr. says is true. Of course they survived. And if the guards caught someone trying to help us, don't you think Mr. Wonderful out there would have come in here and given us another lecture? That boy got away, Lynn. Whether or not he was sober enough to do anything with that phone number is another story."

Lynn started walking again. Morning had come, and with it a breakfast on trays served by an agent who refused to speak to them. But he had, at least, parted the curtains to allow in some natural light.

"Wonder what they'll bring us for lunch," Roxy muttered. "Food is usually the one thing I have to look forward to, so at least that's normal. Can I request Papa John's?"

Lynn hated the feeling. Even when William had first disappeared, and in those awful, dark days in Argentum, she had never felt unhinged. But she felt it rising, now, like a fever. The walls around her weren't closing in, per se, but the room felt tighter.

The weight of the shadow was growing. She felt it. It had to be tied in to what was happening to William. She had to find him. Giving the number to that young hunter may have been reckless and potentially fruitless, but she'd had to risk it.

"Roxy, I hate that you're here—"

"Nope." Roxy shook her head. "I can tell by the tone of your voice what you're about to say. You know I'd be even more angry if I'd shown up at the house and I couldn't find you. Kate is just worried; she doesn't want you caught up in what William's going through, so she holed you up here."

"They've gotten to her. I know I sound irrational, but it's true. She doesn't know the truth. She's never believed it. Anne and Chris and the boys must have called and realized I'm not answering my phone. They'll know something is wrong."

"Then it will get to the point where Kate can't leave you here without an explanation—Now, what the hell is that?"

Roxy pointed out the window. Lynn turned to the sight that once made her skin crawl. But now the large vans with the bold call letters of networks and local stations, following each other like some kind of parade, stilled her breath in her throat.

They kept coming, one after another, turning off the frontage road and heading down the long gravel driveway.

Both women hurried to the window, watching as the trucks began to stop. The passenger and driver's-side doors flew open, men and women in fashionable suits rushed alongside drivers in jeans and ball caps, gathering their equipment.

Like a tiny grand marshal, the Volvo that had led them in now parked directly in front of the home. As one of the security officers rushed out, a small woman, her hair in a fierce ponytail, waved her hand to the media to gather.

Lynn had to force herself to both breathe and not cry, watching her youngest daughter stand before the burly and enraged agent.

"This, ladies and gentlemen, is classic Stella," Roxy said with admiration.

Lynn reached for the door, seeing one of the agents running from the yard towards them. But Lynn was closer, and rushed out into courtyard with Roxy behind.

"Stella!" Lynn cried out.

As the agent began to berate Stella for being on private property, she pointed to her mother and called out to the photographers.

"You wanted proof of my mother being held against her will? There she is. And sorry, sir, you don't have a no-trespassing sign posted outside. In fact, according to this," she said, thrusting a thick file at his chest, "this home is owned by Senator Glenn Scotter, who died twenty years ago and bequeathed this home to the government for out-of-town dignitaries, which in my book, makes it government property and therefore public property. We'll do it right here, guys, once you get video of that man who wants to push my mother and her friend inside."

The agent Stella was pointing to, towards whom the photographers had swerved their lenses, had stopped at the edge of courtyard. Lynn met the guard's eyes for a moment. It was clear they were trained to secure prisoners and even kill, but not in how to respond to a swarm of reporters.

"Perhaps while this fine government employee reaches out to his agency's lawyer, we'll have this quick news conference," Stella said. "Start streaming, folks, because here we go."

As the multicolored mic flags were thrust before her, Stella put her hands on her hips. "My thanks to the news organizations who responded to my announcement. Quick introduction: I am Stella Roseworth, the daughter of Lynn Roseworth and my late father, Senator Tom Roseworth. As I indicated, this brief statement will concern the unfair seizure of my mother and our dear family friend by the government. Should you doubt it, let me ask her myself. Mom, are you being held here against your will?"

The reporters strained their mics in Lynn's direction, for she still stood a good yard or so away.

Lynn raised her voice. "Yes I am."

Even from this distance, she could see the eyes of the reporters widen.

Stella nodded. "So let me reiterate: My mother was taken into custody by the government against her will. It is unclear which agency has done this. I would not summon you all here today without proof. And so, seeing this, you will understand why I am taking my mother out of here."

Stella outstretched her hand. "Mom, Roxy, come on."

Lynn couldn't hear what the agent hissed to Stella, but she saw her daughter flinch.

"My mother is under government protection? Protection from what?" Stella said. "We're all here, sir. And we'd like to hear it."

"Which agency do you work for?" a reporter called out.

"Why is Lynn Roseworth being held here?" another yelled.

Lynn grabbed Roxy's arm and led her across the grass. As the agent rushed towards them, the photographers did as well. Trained to capture footage of riots and shootings, they saw no challenge in getting video of two seventy-nine-year-old women crossing a yard.

Stella was even quicker, bolting from the agent. He reached out for her, but running six miles a day made her difficult to catch.

As they reached each other, Stella brought both women into a fierce embrace, the media swarming like a barrier between the women and the guard.

With reporters and photographers in their faces, yelling questions while dictating the events into their phones and cameras, Stella led Lynn and Roxy towards her Volvo.

As the furious agent tried to muscle through the cluster of cameras and microphones, Stella threw open the door and ushered them into the back seat. The agent broke through, reaching for her.

She swung open her own door, his hand slamming against her window. She slid in and ignited the locks.

The agent pounded on the window, ordering her to stop.

With the cameras pointing in, Stella uttered a curse so offensive that, if it could have been heard through the windshield and above the chaos, would have caused the networks sensors broadcasting the event to scramble to bleep. Instead, the world of social media scrambled to make a GIF of it, ending with Stella throwing the car into reverse.

For a brief moment, Lynn caught the agent's eyes. She knew he was remembering her words from the day before. *You don't know what I'm capable of doing.*

Lynn nodded once to him as the car backed away.

The surreal feeling of being the only vehicle on a highway in the middle of the day, an experience usually reserved for weary overnight truck drivers on holidays, was heightened by the repeated, crackling, robotic voice on the radio.

It didn't matter the station—WNOE, B-97, WKBU—it was everywhere on a continuous loop: Hurricane imminent, evacuate the city.

And yet, with the gray skies looking down at them in disapproval, the Jeep Cherokee, with 210,000 miles and drained of windshield fluid, resulting in an army of slain mosquitoes blurring the view, continued its solo journey towards New Orleans.

The girl at the store had happily agreed to Steven's offer to trade the boat for the car, especially when he'd thrown in an additional hundred dollars. She'd pointed out that the Jeep needed new tires, but that she'd driven it just last week, and it got her back and forth to the beach.

So far, it chugged along. William had rightly feared they'd be pulled over almost immediately, spotted by a state trooper as the only vehicle on the road headed in a dangerous direction. Thus, whenever he saw a vehicle approaching in the distance on the parallel interstate, he would swerve over to the shoulder and come to a stop, telling Steven and Lily to duck. Only when the car had passed, perhaps thinking theirs was an abandoned vehicle, did they once again rise from hiding.

They could only assume that most law enforcement was assisting the Louisiana National Guard within the city battered over the last few months by the repeated hurricanes that had drained most of its residents. Steven feared that the highway, which crossed over Lake Pontchartrain at several stretches, would be flooded. But it was a safer bet than Interstate 10, which was certainly blocked off.

While the water was frighteningly close to the edges of the bridges, it was, for the time being, passable, although they sprayed through puddles so deep they had to drive at practically a crawl.

Before the phone lost Wi-Fi an hour or so prior, as they crossed from Alabama into Louisiana, William read how meteorologists were baffled by the war the weather was waging on the beleaguered city. The latest, a tropical storm that appeared out of nowhere yesterday, had climatologists scrambling to understand the errors in their predictions. They joined colleagues all across the world struggling to understand how it was also happening on coasts outside most developed countries.

William knew he'd had the dream yesterday in the boat, and had seen the storm begin to surge. Now New Orleans was bracing for another assault.

He shifted his shoulder to lean against the window. How was it happening? In the dreams, he was always so horrified when the disasters unfolded that he never gave thought to what was igniting them.

You are the conduit.

He looked back to where Lily lay sleeping in the backseat, under a blanket they'd swiped from the motel. She'd cried herself to sleep after Quincy's security team swept in. She'd kept asking, though, when Quincy was coming back. When William admitted he wasn't, she'd just clutched the dress he'd bought her.

Perhaps she'd picked up on the panic they all felt, realizing that, with Quincy suddenly ripped away, they'd lost their only chance to financially navigate the days to come. Steven knew it as well, rushing to make the bad deal on the car, even spending a bit of their remaining cash just to get them on their way at first light.

It was irresponsible what they were doing, bringing a child into this severe of a storm.

But if I can stop you . . .

How in the world was he going to even find the others like her? If what he saw in the dreams was true—the disasters unfolding around the world—it would be impossible to get to them all.

They were down to four hundred dollars, with no way to get any more cash, heading into a city that was, in essence, under siege.

The Jeep began to swerve, and William gripped the steering wheel tighter. He could see the wind blowing across the water, forcing waves over the bridge.

"If we can just make it over this, we should be clear of Lake Catherine. No more waters to cross," Steven said. "If we're lucky, we'll make it to Little Woods, find a place to hunker down before it hits. Hopefully the houses are abandoned."

William nodded. "You know a lot about New Orleans?"

"Spent a lot of time there over the last decade. There are quite a few Researchers there—or at least, were there, until the storms started. It's actually where I met Neve years ago. . . ."

"I'm sorry. I don't even know how to express how sorry I am."

"Nothing to say. It wasn't your fault. She, Kevin . . . they knew the risks. Especially in the hysteria that followed your return all those years ago. We all wore scarlet letters if we outed ourselves publically. Everybody went underground, even deeper than we had before. Your great-grandparents got the true first taste of what the SSA can do. To think, all those years ago, I sent their daughter on the same dangerous path to find you . . ."

"You sent her?"

"She never told you? Any of it?"

William turned on the wipers. "She insisted that I have as normal a life as possible. I don't think I could have comprehended what she went through . . . what Blue went through . . . until I read it, and saw it for myself. But she deserves to know. All of it."

"I wanted her to know. I still do. It's why I'm now determined to stay alive to make sure I at least deliver on that. It is the least I can do for Lynn."

William shifted in his seat.

"Sorry. Probably makes you uncomfortable to think of someone else in love with your grandmother."

William tapped the steering wheel. "She certainly loved my grand-father."

"That she did. It's important you know that, in the end, she chose a life with him over one with me."

"You never married?"

Steven smiled sadly. "If you had known your grandmother in those days you would understand that once you met Lynn Roseworth, no one would ever compare. Then to see her, all those years later, be so brave, risk so much for our grandson, and still be so beautiful—"

"OK, I get it."

"I wanted her to have her father's letters. And when I learned her mother was alive, I was determined to deliver both to her. I don't have much time left, after all."

William looked over quickly. "What?"

"I'm dying, son. Congestive heart failure. Pretty advanced. Didn't think I'd even make it down that tunnel. I'm at the end of my days, but I've got to see this through. I intended to go with Lynn to find you in Colorado, but the Suits got to me first. I've never forgiven myself for putting her in such harm's way. And now I feel I'm doing the same with you. You must under-stand why I have to see this through. We have to determine how it is you can stop Lily. Because whatever is in your grandmother, if you trigger her . . ."

She'll die.

Steven continued. "She hasn't been activated yet. But I fear it's coming.

But if you can control what's within her, maybe even prevent it from awakening, then there's a fighting chance she'll survive."

"But I don't know how. I can only assume I trigger all of them in the dreams. I can stop Lily, but I can't even communicate with the rest. I don't have the slightest idea how to figure that out."

Steven looked in the rearview mirror. "We're a good distance off the lake now. We need to get off this main road. Cops could be around, making sure no one's still here."

The rain started to heavily pelt the car as they turned down a neighborhood street, where yards were already flooded.

"We better start squatting somewhere quick," Steven added.

William spotted a shotgun home built on a slightly higher elevation and pulled in. He ran up to the front door, knocking loudly. When no one answered, he went around to the back. Finding it unlocked, he entered, calling out if anyone was home. He was greeted with silence.

He ran back out to the car, finding Lily still passed out as he lifted her, covering her head with the blanket to shield her from the rain. He carried her in, finding a bedroom. Gently laying her down, he sat on the edge of the bed.

"So what now?" Steven whispered from the doorway.

The raining was hitting hard now. All his life, the pattering sound had made William drowsy.

"Need to try something. Give me a little bit."

"I'll try to scrounge up some food. Don't know how long they've been without power here." Steven quietly closed the door.

William lay down beside Lily, his arms behind his head. A familiar anxiety rose in his throat. For a year now, he'd fought falling asleep. He began to breathe, long and slow. He should have told Steven to give him a few hours. It could take that long to even fall asleep—

A moment later, he hovered above the churning waters, the storm barreling around him.

He realized it then. He wasn't asleep. It had never been a dream.

It explained why he was so exhausted, so internally bruised afterwards. His body wasn't resting. It was being infiltrated.

He struggled to take control. It was apparent at once he had made a mistake—he was a blade of grass trying to slow down in a rushing river. He looked around wildly, the winds and water pummeling him.

For a second, he saw the eyes, and then they were gone in the torrents of rain. He tried to find them, but he could already feel the familiar pull, wanting to take him elsewhere.

The eyes. He had to get to them.

He jumped.

At least he tried. It was terribly awkward, more of a collapsed leap than anything. All he could think to do was see if he could move on his own.

He leapt again. With each movement above the water, whatever bound him held tight, as if he were stretching invisible chains.

He tried to run. That, too, was a disaster, as if he were attempting it waist deep in snow.

As he inched closer, he caught a glimpse of not only the eyes, but a face. For the briefest of moments, he saw where she was.

The wind ripped at his skin, the water drenching him. The woman's face and the hospital behind her were gone in a torrential wall of rain.

The doctor dropped her chart.

It clanged to the floor, echoing in the empty hallway. She reached for the wall behind her, steadying herself.

Had she momentarily blacked out?

She was certainly that tired. Irrationally tired. No-business-treating patients tired. But was she delusional tired?

Because it sure felt like, for just a moment, she'd fallen asleep standing up. She'd literally had the damn dream standing up. The crazy dream, where she was watching the hurricanes form, the waves fighting against each other, all of it rushing towards New Orleans. And, as always, hovering over it all, was William Chance.

She'd finally told Shelia about the dreams yesterday, and her friend had laughed until she cried. She loved to watch Shelia laugh like that, especially in these dire hours. Her face crinkling up, her hand rising to her heart to momentarily cover up her nurse's badge on her upper chest.

"Jane, my heart, my heart," Shelia gasped, in between laughter. "My heart is going to burst if you don't stop. You mean the hot alien dude?"

"Trust me, he was never my type growing up. Which is what makes this so ridiculous."

"I don't know, girl. How long has he been showing up in these dreams of yours?"

Jane had sheepishly admitted it had happened on and off for about a year. Shelia had slapped the table so hard she almost knocked over her coffee.

She wanted to share in Shelia's laughter, to think it was funny too. After all, it was ridiculous. Of course she was dreaming about hurricanes, they haunted the nightmares of every person still in the city. And the dreams were becoming more frightening each time.

"Wait, wait, Dr. Doogie," Shelia had stammered when she finally caught her breath. Shelia relished in calling Jane by the nickname she'd earned by becoming the youngest resident in the hospital's history. Now everyone on staff, even the janitors, called her Doogie Howser. "I want this dream. But in my dream, it's going to be Denzel. Malcolm X Denzel. And he's gonna be floating just like your William. I don't even care if I drown, if Denzel is with me."

Jane had laughed at that, but then the ambulance had screamed up to the emergency room with an older couple that'd refused to leave the city. The man was in the throes of a heart attack, and his wife had soiled herself because their bathroom was flooded. Nothing was funny from that point on.

She'd slept since then, hadn't she? She truly couldn't remember. There were so few doctors left to go on rotation.

And, she'd been walking; it wasn't like she had stopped to lean against the wall or something. She hadn't passed out, otherwise she'd have been on the floor with a wicked headache.

But she hadn't injured herself either when she'd blacked out before. And substantial time had passed then.

Had it been a year now since that happened? A fellow runner had found her lying on the edge of the tree line along the Mississippi levee trail. She'd been so confused. She'd just gone for a long run. How had she ended up practically in the trees?

When the runner told her it was noon on Sunday, Jane had panicked. She'd gone for a run at one in the afternoon on a Saturday. She'd been lying there an entire night and morning.

The cops had been called. She'd undergone a full physical checkup. No drugs in her system, no signs of an attack. An MRI showed no tumors, no brain abnormalities. Everyone had come up with theories. *You pushed yourself too hard, you collapsed. Your blood sugar was too low. A car sideswiped you and thought you were dead and left you.*

Why, then, weren't there bruises? How can I have simply no memory of being gone for an entire twenty-four-hour period?

Jane hurried down the hall to the nurses' station. Shelia was there, sipping what must have been her sixth cup of coffee of the day. There weren't many nurses left either.

"Word is the National Guard is going to force us to move," Shelia said.

"They can't. There are too many terminal patients. They can't be removed from their life support, even for a minute."

"They say they'll airlift them out."

"During a hurricane? That's impossible. What does Dr. Parker say?"

"That even our backup generators aren't designed to run this long. That we'll be lucky to have an ounce of power once Hurricane Nancy is done with us. Is it just a tropical storm? Or was that the last one? How are we supposed to keep track?"

"Listen." Jane leaned in. "Remember when I blacked out last year?"

"Of course. I about came unglued. We were supposed to go out that night and you never showed."

"It just happened again, I think. Standing up."

"Whoa, girl." Shelia touched her shoulder. "Go lie down now. Dr. Wraf just came in; I thought for sure he'd skip town. Go lie down. I'd tell you to go home, but that honestly isn't an option for any of us. I'll wake you if something happens."

"You know it will. But I don't think I have much of a choice. I just checked on the head trauma patient in room seven."

"Go now, before the next crisis flares up. Please. You know I'll come for you."

"I think, at the moment, everyone is stable. But that could change in a minute."

"If it does, Dr. Wraf can handle it. Dr. de Riesthal and Dr. Stankewicz are still here too. If it gets bad, I'll wake you. Seriously. I think you are just pushing yourself too hard and your body reacts in a scary way. Go. Now."

Jane squeezed her friend's hand and headed down to the doctor's lounge. It was empty, of course. None of them had the appetite to eat anyway.

The hospital had become the last lifeline for the desperate who had waited too late to escape.

If the coming hurricane was as bad as its predecessor, it could be the end for all of them.

Jane lay down on the cot in the on-call room adjacent to the lounge. Mom must be frantic, she thought. Dad too. She'd been able to send out a text a few days ago that she was alive and in the hospital, but then all communication had gone dark. They hadn't wanted her to even come to undergrad at Loyola, but she'd fallen in love with the school and the city. She'd then quickly enrolled in medical school at Tulane and had never wanted to leave.

Even after the fourth hurricane this year. Even after the levees failed and the mayor ordered an entire evacuation. Even after the CEO of the hospital ordered the patients out, leaving only the sickest of the sick and a bare-bones staff of doctors and nurses. Even after her mother had called, sobbing, begging her to leave.

She was too ideological, Dr. Wraf had lectured her. Too young, too naïve, too much potential to get trapped here. You could die, Jane. We all could.

Jane couldn't explain why she stayed, beyond her true desire to stay with her patients who had no family and other loved ones.

She also couldn't explain that mentally and physically, she simply couldn't leave. Something kept her here.

She turned over in the dark, closing her eyes. No more thinking about the choices she made. Shelia could come in any second with word of the next disaster. She needed to sleep while she could. She said a silent prayer that the dream bypassed her this time. . . .

When she woke, her jaw hurt, which meant she'd been grinding her teeth. It signaled a long sleep.

She slipped off the cot, frantically pulling her hair back with the hair tie she always kept on her wrist. As she rushed to brush her teeth with the spare toothbrush she kept in her locker, and wash her face, she glanced at her phone, which now only served as a way to check the time and date.

Seven a.m. She'd slept the rest of the afternoon and night. Next to her phone was a note in Shelia's handwriting. *You needed it. It's been quiet.*

She hurried out into the lounge, quickly glancing at the back of a man leaning against the frame of one of the windows being hammered by the storm outside. Even the plywood nailed up outside was thumping like someone was pounding on it. It must be calmer inside, though, if Dr. Wraf was taking a break.

"You guys shouldn't have let me sleep that long—"

Jane looked back quickly, realizing Dr. Wraf never wore a ball cap.

When the man turned from the window, she reached over and pinched her hand. *You're still asleep. You're still asleep.*

"I didn't want to wake you," the man said hesitantly. "I figured seeing my face after being asleep might make . . . things . . . even stranger."

William Chance looked much older than she'd seen in her dreams. Certainly he'd aged from how he'd looked on the poster board of cut-out pictures that Julie, her best friend from high school, once hung in her bedroom. She'd tacked him alongside that guy from the Disney musical. She distinctly remembered Julie searching all the teen magazines and online websites for a picture of him smiling, but she could never find one. He clearly didn't like having his photo taken.

"You can't be in here." It was all she could manage to say.

He exhaled, leaning on a table. "Probably not. But security is pretty light."

She suddenly snapped into clarity. She'd seen him on the news before the power went out. He was on the run for some reason. He'd been kidnapped, right? By some kind of fanatics. It explained why he'd appeared again in her dreams. The subconscious mind was a powerful thing.

"Do you need help?" she asked. "I saw . . . you've been in trouble, right? I don't know how you ended up here, but there are still police in town—"

He shook his head. "No. I'm . . . as fine as I can be. I came here to try and find you."

Don't say that. God, don't say that.

"I know this is really strange. But I know you. And I think you know me."

"The whole world knows you," Jane said, trying to keep her voice in a calm, detached, doctor tone. "I'll ask again, are you in need of help? The last I saw, you were . . . kidnapped? Are you safe?"

"None of us are safe. That's why I'm here. I know you, but I don't even know your name."

Jane took a small step backwards. She'd had her fair share of mentally ill patients. There was certainly strong speculation that a young man who vanished and then reappeared in a violent confrontation with law enforcement might be dangerously off balance.

"Why don't you take a seat, Mr. Chance. You've obviously been through a lot, and it could do you some good to get a thorough examination. Are you on any medication I need to know about?"

He rested his hands on his hips, his shoulders broadening, the vein in his neck rising.

"Listen, please know this is as weird for me as it is for you."

"I seriously doubt that."

"I didn't think I could find you. I couldn't, actually, until a few hours ago. I still don't truly understand how. But I did. And . . . I know you've seen me in your dreams. Just like I've seen your eyes and, eventually, your face. It's how I found you. We don't have a lot of time because that storm out there is getting worse. I assume you had a moment, maybe about a year ago, where you have a block of time that you don't remember. Am I right?"

She flinched. "How do you know that?"

He took a hesitant step towards her. "I don't know how to even start having this conversation with you. Something happened to you that you don't remember. The same thing happened to me, a long time ago. What you need to know is that . . . you're causing the hurricanes. And I'm the one who is making you do it."

Run. Run now. This guy is insane.

Jane bolted. As she darted across the room, she realized she misjudged the distance between them.

"Wait," he said, reaching out, taking her arm.

The jolt was so strong she felt the room tilt. For a moment, all she could see was the storm blowing in from the gulf. It was all around her, ripping and tearing at her and everything in its path—

She yanked her arm back. "You need to step back," she stammered.

William looked as stunned as she. He held up his hand, examining his fingertips.

"I don't know what you're talking about, but you need to stay the hell back—"

Something smashed against the windows outside—a limb, or perhaps a piece of a nearby house. The howling was shockingly loud, and more debris began to crash outside.

He continued to look at his hands, his voice low. "That's it. How I can stop Lily."

He raised his head. "Give me your hand. You can stop this. We can stop this. People are going to die if we don't—"

The battering against the window was so intense, even the hurricane-readied glass began to crack. The walls and floors shook.

William rushed forward and grabbed both her arms. She began to fight back, when she found she could not wrest her eyes from his. She was unable to even blink.

The glass shattered as the storm roared in.

THIRTEEN

The men in suits were waiting for her outside the Oval Office. They stood at attention as she exited, their director towering over them.

"Senator—"

Kate kept walking. "Give me a moment, Director Wolve," she said, heading out into the hallway.

The Secret Service agents eyed them cautiously as they strode past. As they walked into the adjoining hallway, she stopped.

"The president made it clear we were to discuss this only in private. Is your car waiting?"

"It is," he said.

As they brushed through the West Wing, one of the SSA agents quietly called to have the car pulled around. They went out a set of double doors to a private exit, where the Secret Service was sweeping their vehicle. Kate could hear the tapping of the director's shoes as they waited for the nod of approval to enter.

As they slid into the backseat, he turned to her. "Is he on board?"

"He is frustrated, he is angry, he is not one hundred percent sold, but yes," she said.

"How much does he know? You were only in there for an hour—"

"He is still poring over everything."

"Should you have left—?"

"I would have loved to have stayed. But I have yet another crisis on my hands, thanks to the inability of your men to keep my mother safely protected."

"I've already explained—"

"You were the one who convinced me that she was some sort of danger to people! I had *my own mother* practically arrested and quarantined—"

"As we've explained, if all of the abducted are being activated, then at some point, she will be too. You've seen what they can do. We have no idea what she is capable of doing."

"And yet my little sister was able to lead a parade of reporters in and waltz her right out?"

He sighed, silencing his phone buzzing in his suit coat. "Frankly, we never anticipated what your sister had in store."

"My sister Stella is a journalist, Mark. Have you met many? They are resourceful and, even more, they are relentless. She knew the last thing you'd expect was a press conference at your front door. What matters is they have to be found. She is my mother, for God sake. I want her and my sister safe, regardless of how pissed off I am. And Jesus Christ, where is my nephew?"

"We'll find them all. We just needed more men, which is why the president had to get on board. The National Guard—"

"I had that authorized days ago. They've already mobilized in California and North Dakota. They're obviously already in Louisiana, but how you intend to find one person in a state besieged by hurricanes is beyond me. As much as I hate the fact that you have a child trapped miles beneath the earth, at least the streets of DC don't have to become a military zone."

His phone rang again, and he handed it to one of the agents in the front seat. "Can you see what Agent Lucas wants? He's called five times. OK, Senator, this is important: You believe that the president understands the seriousness of this now?"

Kate scrolled through the mountain of texts on her own phone. Her communications director had also called repeatedly. Everyone wanted her response to her sister's claims that the government was holding their mother hostage.

Once again, her mother was telling the truth.

"Convincing a sixty-eight-year-old former marine that people are being abducted and returned to earth as weapons is not an easy sell, Director.

Which is why you incorporated me in this, knowing that if I believe it, then the president will too. I understand how you think I'm your pawn in all this. But I can promise you this," she said, raising a finger. "I went into that boy's room on my own. It was my life that was in danger. But I did it of my volition."

She'd never been more terrified in her life. Ryan had told her that her nephew had been dreaming, that the violence was about to start. She'd slipped out to find the agents stationed outside choking each other. As she'd hurried by, one of them sprang after her, his eyes wild. She'd reached the elevator, the doors barely shutting to keep him from following. He'd pounded on the doors and screamed like an enraged animal.

"The president saw the video of what happened in that hallway," she said softly.

"Agent Hallow warned you for a reason—"

"Director, I'm sorry, you need to take this." The agent in the front seat handed him the phone.

"Rick, just find out—"

"Director, it's about the boy. He wants to talk to the senator."

"What?" Kate sat forward.

"Agent Lucas?" Mark put the phone to his ear. "What's going on?"

Kate watched as the director shook his head. "No way is she going back down there. Not after what happened."

"What's going on?" Kate asked.

She watched as the director's eyes widened a bit. He nodded. "Agent, hold on. Senator, Ryan says your nephew has found another of the abducted."

"How does he know this?" she demanded.

"He says he's seen them."

"Does he know where they are?" she asked.

"He says he does, but in exchange for that information, he wants you to go with him to San Diego," Mark said, not hiding his frustration. "I don't know what this means, but he'd like Iron Man to give him the tour."

Jane knew she should be dead.

She'd heard the glass shatter, felt the weight of the hurricane winds, saw the chunks of wood and metal fly through to pummel and slice her and William Chance apart.

She'd shut her eyes instinctively, bracing herself.

Instead, the southernmost wall, on the other side of the room, shuddered with the impact. The plaster wall of the old hospital cracked like an eggshell, exposing the wood studs and insulation, until it too was torn apart by shards of splintered plywood, rock, and whatever else the winds carried.

Yet she and William remained untouched, as was everything behind them, even though they were directly across from the windows that had blown apart when the storm barreled in.

The winds had turned. *They* had turned the winds.

When she met William's eyes, she saw a mixture of astonishment at what they had done. There was no discussion, no stammering; just a basic understanding.

We did this.

And in that realization came silence, and the equally jarring sight of sunlight slowly peering through the dissipating storm.

Within seconds, the cries started coming from the hallway.

William touched her arm. She felt the jolt again, so strong it was almost electrical. *We have to go.*

The cry of her name from further down the hall broke her from the connection.

"I . . . can't," she said.

Go. I'll find you.

As she hurried away, she realized William hadn't opened his mouth to speak.

She immediately found the hurricane had showed its force in every room with a window. Walls had collapsed, water gushed in, debris covered the floors, the humidity was rushing in with the stank smell of ruin.

Fearing the worst was coming, hospital staff had moved all the remaining patients to interior rooms. While the generators staggered to keep operational, the hospital was now also open to the outside, with hundreds of gaping wounds. The glaringly bright sunlight revealed the impossibility of keeping patients here.

She'd forced herself to stop thinking about what had happened as she and the staff rushed to keep people alive. Over the next frantic hours, she'd seen glimpses of William, his hat pulled low, helping to clear debris from exits for the mass evacuation. No one had questioned who he was in the chaos; he appeared to be another example of a New Orleanian trying to once again rise above the horror of the hour as he helped to clear the halls and doorways for the gurneys and wheelchairs.

When the National Guard arrived, Dr. Wraf ordered all of the staff out as well. The patients were now fully in the care of the military. Shelia had run past her in the hallway, saying it was time to go. Jane told her that she'd meet her at the staging area outside the city. Jane had then grabbed Dr. Wraf, telling him she needed to check in on her own home before leaving the city. Exhausted and having heard repeatedly from staff who insisting on seeing what remained of their own properties, he'd only nodded and told her to hurry. Who knew when the next storm was coming, he'd said.

William lingered at the end of the hall.

She'd walked past him as she made her way to the underground parking garage. The storm had flooded the lower levels, but her parking space was near the exit ramp, high enough to escape the water.

"Jane," William called out as she reached her Honda.

"I need you to stay away," she said, holding up her hand.

I don't like this any more than you do.

"How are you doing that?" she demanded. "How are you doing any of this?"

"Wait, can you hear me? What did you hear?"

"I don't know if you're throwing your voice or what—"

Can you hear this?

"Whatever it is you're doing, stop it."

"I swear to you I'm not meaning to do it. I'm just as shocked as you that you can hear me."

She pressed her key fob, opening the car door and throwing in her purse.

"Just please come with me. I parked my car outside on the street. A white Jeep Cherokee. I just need some time with you to explain. Just hear me out. I think . . . that all this can stop."

She looked back to him. "No one can stop a storm."

No one can talk without speaking words either.

She winced. "Stop."

"I don't even know it's happening," William admitted. "Honestly, I can only figure this out with you. And the others. That's why I have to talk to you. Show you Lily."

"Lily? Who is Lily?"

"When you meet her, you'll understand."

She studied his weary face. "I'm not getting in a car with you."

"That's fine. I'll wait for you outside. Just follow me. It's not far."

He took off jogging up the ramp, past the now-permanently opened security arm. She slid into the car, and exhaled.

She wanted to peel out, take a sharp right, and meet up with the National Guard caravan. She'd find Shelia and make her get in the car. *You're not going to believe the crazy thing that happened back there. I think I was drugged or something. Or maybe sleepwalking?* She would leave New Orleans. Maybe she'd take her parents' advice and relocate in another city, one that was far inland—

I'm just outside.

Jane gripped her steering wheel. Her every instinct was to drive as far away from this man as quickly as she could.

She began to tremble as she found herself putting the car in reverse and heading out of the garage. In the exhilaration of the moment when William had touched her and the storm changed course before her very eyes, she'd failed to realize her ability to take control of her own actions was gone.

She'd followed the Jeep to a row of shotgun homes, growing angrier by the minute. She'd even tried a few times to take a sudden hard left or right, to break away. But her body had refused to listen. *My God, had he injected her with something while she was sleeping?*

When they pulled up in front of one of the homes, she knew her face was flushed in anger. She quickly turned off the car, practically jumping out to begin her full-on tirade.

Then the little girl had flown out of the front door and scampered towards William, her neon-yellow dress brighter than the pouring sunlight.

"The sun is out!" she said, jumping into his arms. "You made it stop!"

He smiled at her and shook his head. "Not me. Her."

They both turned to Jane. "Lily, this is Jane."

The little girl shyly waved. Jane instinctively smiled back at her, and then shook her head. "William, we need to talk. Privately."

"Let's go inside," he said, carrying Lily across the lawn.

Jane once again felt the horrible sensation of something propelling her to follow, a heartbeat before her own consciousness could even register what she actually intended to do.

Now the anger was turning to fear.

Inside, a senior citizen at the door had quietly introduced himself as Steven and shut the door, locking it. Her heartbeat was pounding now, as the old man made sure the small opening in the curtain over the front window was closed.

"Let me go," Jane said.

William set Lily down. "What?"

"I don't know what you've done to me, what you slipped me or whatever, but please let me go. Now."

William looked genuinely confused. "I'm . . . not sure what you're talking about."

"I am a doctor. I know there is no medical explanation for what you are doing to me. No one can control someone else's movements. Unlock that door and let me go."

"Steven, unlock the door," William said, holding up his hands. "Please believe me that I am in no way trying to do this. I'm trying to understand it as well. Are you saying that you're compelled to . . . follow my directions?"

"I didn't want to follow you here. I tried to drive away and I was physically unable to do so. I didn't want to come in this house, but my body isn't listening. And I am on the verge of screaming for help."

Lily slowly approached her. "I got scared too when it started happening to me."

"What are you talking about?" William asked.

Lily looked from him back to Jane. "I don't think he means to do it."

"Lily." William kneeled down before her, his eyebrows raised. "Are you saying you've been forced to follow me?"

"I want to go with you. But . . . I can't say no, either. It's like . . . I don't want to hurt people. But when you're in trouble . . . I have to do it."

"Hurt people?" Jane demanded. "I don't know what's going on, but you need to let me, and this little girl, go. Right now."

"Don't be afraid of him. He's not doing it, it is," Lily said. "The monster in the mountain is."

"Seriously, stop this right now—"

"I would if I could," William said. "I don't want to be doing any of this. I just know what happened to Lily and me . . . happened to you."

"What are you talking about?"

"Jane . . . do you remember if you went missing . . . about a year ago?" William asked.

Jane flinched. "I didn't go missing . . ."

"But something happened. A period of time you don't remember. Am I right?"

She swallowed. "Did you have something to do with that?"

"No." He shook his head. "But I know what happened."

Jane whirled to Steven. "Are you one of those people who kidnapped him? Is that what this is? Did you also do something to me?"

"Young lady, I haven't ever laid eyes on you before just now. And I am so sorry that you're caught up in this. We will explain everything to you." He motioned with his chin towards William. "Listen to him. Even if he doesn't direct you to do so, you should probably sit down."

The headlights of the Jeep Cherokee, clouded by years of oxidation, made for even a dimmer view of the shockingly dark neighborhoods, void of electricity. They drove at a slow pace, hoping to conserve as much gas as possible, as there was no way to know how far they would have to go to find a working station. It also meant no air-conditioning; the slight breeze coming from their glacial pace offering little comfort.

"Let's hope the military isn't close by, looking for survivors. If so, we're in trouble," Steven said.

"Jane said the city had all but emptied before the last storm. The National Guard only returned for them at the hospital." William took off his hat to try and dry his sweaty hairline.

"You're sure . . . you're absolutely sure you can find her? Because that is one strong-willed, frightened young woman. It wouldn't surprise me if she hit the gas and did not let up until Mississippi."

"I can feel her. She's still in the city."

"How can you know that?"

William maneuvered around scattered trashcans in the street. Even the headlights seemed insignificant in the black.

"It's the touch."

"Touch?"

"I realized it in the hospital, right before the hurricane hit. When I physically touched Jane, I knew it. I could feel it. I had complete control over her abilities. Together . . . we *moved* the winds in the room from striking us. And then stopped the storm."

"My God," Steven said softly.

"It's the same with Lily, once we made a physical connection. All I had to do was think . . . tell Lily to stop, and she would."

"You can communicate with her telepathically?"

William glanced at him. "It sounds ridiculous. But yes. I didn't realize the extent of it until I touched Jane. Once we made that connection . . . not only can I talk to her . . ."

"You can actually control her movements. Even if she doesn't want to do it. William . . ."

"I know."

"It's incredible. Is that by design? Or did they even realize this could happen?"

"I don't think so. In fact . . . I don't think they're happy about it at all."

"How do you know?"

"They're clearly controlling me when I dream to connect to the others, to spark their weapons. But back at the shotgun house, when I entered the dream, or connection, whatever you want to call it, and I tried to move on my own volition to find Jane, there was heavy resistance; a strong feeling that I was defying them. I got that same feeling when Jane and I stopped the storm: an anger from afar."

"Son, I know you are shouldering a lot. And we're all scared as hell. But this is the first sign of hope."

"Hope?" William's forehead wrinkled. "I have to physically touch them to stop their abilities. The others like us are all over the world. How I can begin to stop them all?"

"I've spent a lifetime of defeat after defeat. Heartbreak after heartbreak. When you get to my age, you celebrate the signs of possibility. And speaking of signs, that one reads we're in Uptown. She said it's where she lived."

"I vaguely remember these streets," William said as a strand of beads in a magnolia flashed momentarily in the headlights. "My parents used to take us here all the time for the kid-safe parades in Mardi Gras. It was one of the few times I could blend into a crowd without being identified. Quincy actually made a joke about drinking too many hurricanes and not remembering the times he'd been here."

"Bizarre to wish that someone who is practically a stranger was still here," Steven said.

William smiled sadly. "I didn't even know who he was before all this."

"We used him. I'll admit it now. We didn't know what it would take to get you where you needed to go. With Quincy, though, your options were endless. We'd hoped the realization that both your great-grandparents started on this path would help you see past his . . . eccentric ways, and his insulting job offer. I've seen his YouTube videos and read his interviews. He believes in stuff that even *I* find farfetched. I wonder, now, what he'll do with what he knows. If he goes to the FBI, tells them where we're headed . . ."

"I doubt that. He saw enough to know to stay away from any government agent."

"That's true. He's probably holed up in some posh hotel or maybe a boardroom, being grilled by his board of directors on how to handle this PR crisis. Eventually, though, they'll have to alert his shareholders that he is alive, in order to reverse the plunging stock. His company took a big hit when he disappeared. And once that's out, the FBI will come to him. We don't have much time."

"But even if we do convince Jane to come with us, which sounds almost impossible given her reaction to what we told her . . . I believe the others are on the East and West coasts. And that's just in the United States. They're all over the world. I can't get to them all."

"I learned this in those terrible days when the Suits raided my home and I was on the run for the first time: You take one day at a time. One hour at a time if you must. And I know it probably isn't much of a comfort, but as long as I'm breathing, I'm with you."

"Here," William said, taking the chain with the flash drive off his neck. "Take it. Should we ever get to Nanna, it needs to come from you."

Steven accepted it, putting it around his neck. He held the flash drive in his hand. "Just don't forget it, if something happens to me. I haven't taken my meds for a day or so now."

"Jane is a doctor. Maybe she can help."

"How far away are we now?"

William could feel her, just as he could sense exactly where Lily was sitting in the back seat.

"I need to turn there. Wait, wait. It looks flooded. I'll find another way around. You OK Lily?" He looked over his shoulder.

She nodded, perspiration on her forehead.

"I know it's hot. Want to lay down?" William asked.

"That's OK."

She had to be hungry, and they were down to the last of the chips and peanuts they'd bought at the gas station in Alabama.

"We'll find some food and a place to rest once we hit the road. A place with air-conditioning," William promised.

"William, there's something else," Steven said. "Are you prepared . . . if Jane refuses to come with us . . . ?"

"To force her to come? I hope to avoid that."

"You realize you may not have that chance. You have no idea how far your control over her reaches. I don't think she will come willingly. You saw how she grilled us. You're asking someone who believes only in science to believe science fiction."

"There." William pointed, his headlights flashing on another shotgun. "The one with the white trim."

The house, like all the others, was completely dark. Jane's Honda was parked in the drive.

He pulled up, aware he was blocking her in. William took Lily by the hand as they exited the car. When she started to drag her feet in weariness, he lifted her till they got to the door.

They knocked. After a few moments, they heard a muffled reply from inside. William opened the door.

"Jane?"

They walked in, the humidity of the room almost overwhelming. He set Lily down, hating to use what was left of the phone battery for light. Holding it out, he saw a glimpse of Jane lying on the couch, apparently asleep.

The light revealed the two men standing over her, dressed in black suits.

He felt the injection in his neck. Steven grunted while Lily cried out.

William whirled around with the light, the movement causing such dizziness he almost fell.

Before he hit the ground, he swore he saw, just for a moment, the face of his Aunt Kate standing in the corner, watching, with her hands covering her mouth.

FOURTEEN

He was so groggy at first that it was difficult even opening his eyes. Even when he could focus enough to sit up, he immediately had to lie back down, the nausea so strong he feared he might vomit.

Drugged now, twice. Not just him, but Lily too. Injected with God knows what. It can't be good for a little girl.

William sat up again, slowly this time. There were no windows, so the only light came from fluorescents above. The queen-sized bed took up much of the space, as if it were hastily crammed in. Books were stacked in columns, even on the floor. A *Sports Illustrated* issue covered a nightstand. A small TV was placed in the corner, with a connected Xbox.

It took him a moment to realize everything was tailor-made for him.

He heard the beeping of a code and the loud release of bolts in the door. The door opened slightly.

"Will."

He hadn't imagined it, that last moment in Jane's house. Even for a moment, it was a face he instantly recognized—his eighth birthday party, Sunday dinners around Nanna's table—his aunt Kate was there for a while, often in a business suit, fresh off a plane. And when she wasn't dressed for a meeting, she was in a Predators jersey, playing football with him and his brothers, a cautioning hand when they were in public, scanning for photographers in the crowd. The family's pit bull, William's dad had called her, ready to bite anyone who lunged at them and wired not to let go.

Until Grandpa Tom resigned from office, and the aunt he knew became someone else.

Very much looking like a US senator, in her dark blue suit and glasses, she walked over to him, her arms outstretched.

"Don't," he said, holding up his hand.

She paused as he groggily stood. "You're with them, Kate. You let them do this."

"Honey, I didn't want to. It's the last thing I ever wanted. And I'm not with *them*. I want to keep you safe. Keep everyone safe."

"Safe? You call drugging and throwing me—wherever we are—safe?"

"This is the safest place right now, I promise you."

"And you've locked up a little girl and a doctor too? And Steven, is he here too?"

"They're two of the deadliest people on the planet, William. And you know it as well as I do. This had to happen. As for Dr. Richards, he's being questioned right now."

"Thinking about maybe pegging this one on him too? Since the murder charge didn't stick last time?"

"William, please. I had nothing to do with that—"

"Why are you even here, Aunt Kate? How do you know about any of this? How did you know how to find me?"

"I've been trying to track you down for a year now, William. Obviously, since the disaster in Little Rock, I've moved heaven and earth to locate you. People have come to me with information that assisted in that effort."

"People? Such as government agents dressed in black? The same ones you used to deny existed? I remember the fights you had with my mom over the phone. You denied everything that Nanna said."

"I made a lot of mistakes. But I understand now. It's why we've desperately been looking for you—"

"We've?" William winced. "So you're now aligned with the SSA? Because news flash, Aunt Kate, they weren't trying to look for me. They've tried to *kill us all*."

"I wouldn't let anyone lay a single finger on you, and you know it. I've done it all your life. I know this has been horrible for you, and I'm not happy about it—"

"This is bullshit."

"Hey," she said, snapping her fingers. "I'm know you've been through hell, but son, I've changed your diaper, taught you to tie a bowtie, and taken red-eye flights to make your eight a.m. Little League baseball games—"

"You turned your back on us!" William outstretched his hands. "Your own family! Your own mother! And now you try to play the doting aunt?"

"I don't expect you to understand. You have every right to blame me. But I never stopped loving any of you."

"This is how you show your love—"

"Yes, this is how I show it," she said, taking a step towards him. "You are no longer on the run. You are under constant protection. I can at least tell your mother and father and brothers that you are with me and there is no need to worry while we try to figure out what to do next."

"You don't get it. There isn't time. If you keep me locked up in here, I can't stop this. I can't stop what's coming. You want to keep your country safe? There won't be a country if you keep me down here."

"What is best now is that you and the other three are safe and taken care of, and I swear I will make sure you have everything you need—"

"The other three? You've found another?"

Kate bit her lip. "I will tell you everything in due time. Everything I learn I swear I will share with you. I will keep nothing from you. I'm just trying to protect my state and my country and family—"

"You know about Blue, then? Do you know about that, Aunt Kate?"

She blinked. "Blue?"

"They didn't tell you that, did they?" William said, motioning outside the door. "Ask your friends in the suits about Blue. Ask your government about Blue. Then see if you can ever look any member of your family in the eye again. Until then, leave me the hell alone."

William turned away from her, his fingers laced behind his head.

"Will—"

"Ask them. Ask them about Blue. See if you think your family is safe in the hands of your government."

She sighed. She went to the door, her hand pausing on the handle. "You know I love you, even if you hate me right now. But I can't put family before country."

When he didn't respond, she quietly walked out. A series of bolts sealed behind her.

The anger burned, and in it, he sensed Lily immediately. He felt the rise in her as well.

He took a deep breath and blew out through his nose, repeating it over and over. He closed his eyes.

William?

In a heartbeat, he was with her. She sat on the edge of a bed, clutching a large pink stuffed hippo. On the walls were posters of unicorns and teddy bears. A small table beside her bed was covered in LEGOs. Another custom-made prison.

Lily. I'm here.

Come get me.

I'm trying, honey. But I have to figure out how.

I'm scared.

I know. But just stay calm.

Please come get me.

I'll come for you, I promise, as soon as I can.

He hated to make a vow he might not be able to keep, and hated even more to leave her.

As soon as he broke the connection, he attempted another.

Jane was pacing in a room similar to his, but obviously much less prepared. They didn't know enough about her to try to personalize her cell.

Jane.

She flinched, looking around. Even with her hair pulled back in a messy ponytail, wearing the same scrubs for God knows how long, William couldn't help but notice what he first thought when he saw her: Dr. Spencer was a beautiful woman.

Jane, it's William. I'm here.

"What?" she almost cried out.

Listen, try to talk to me just by thinking. They're watching us every second, I'm sure of it. Please. Just try.

She opened her mouth to speak.

Just think. Try—

William?

Yes. I'm here.

What is going on? My God, where are we?

I don't know. I'm in a room just like yours. The agents found us. The same agents I told you about before. They somehow got to you before I could. I don't know how. They want to keep us isolated.

They can't do that. We haven't done anything wrong. . . .

He sensed the apprehension as soon as she said the words. They'd spoken for hours at the abandoned home in New Orleans. She'd fought every claim he made, about the disappearance she didn't remember to what she was capable of doing with the storms.

But at last, she couldn't deny it. She knew what she'd seen. She'd just said she wanted to go to her home. He'd of course agreed. He'd told her not to even give him her address. That as further proof, he'd just find her that night.

He'd been too late.

I'm trying to get to you. And Lily too. The agents brought us here. I don't know where.

They just can't keep us locked in here. They have to provide us a lawyer.

William almost laughed. She didn't understand that the rules of the normal world didn't apply anymore—

Hey, William. You there?

William's eyes flew open. What was that voice?

Dude, I know you're there.

William focused once more on Jane. *I'll find, you Jane. I'll do everything I can.*

He could see her frantic expression. *William—*

As he left her, he began to seek, until someone found him first.

There you are. Hello, General.

He was barely a teenager, swallowed in a La-Z-Boy recliner. In his hands were a game console, and the sounds of explosions and bullets came from a television. His hair was thick and unruly, and he wore a wrinkled Foo Fighters T-shirt and sweat pants.

So what's going on in your side of the X-Men dorm? Your room isn't nearly as tricked out as mine. But just make a bunch of threats, you'll have a keg in there in no time.

You can see me?

Si, compadre. Once you opened up the communication channel, as I call it. Your room's pretty lame.

William took a step back to steady himself. There would be no need to try and find the third of the abducted. The government already had him.

Where are we?

Somewhere in DC. The boy squirmed in his chair, leaning to the right in a desperate attempt to stay alive in whatever game he was playing. *Deep DC. So far below that we can't kill people. At least, that's what they hope.*

Who are you?

The boy cursed, slapping the console on his thigh. The sound of an electronic death came from the television. *I can't ever get past this stage. But all I got is time. So, I'm Ryan. Here's my insta bio: thirteen, troubled youth, ability to kill. A pretty disturbing superpower, thanks to the star lords. It's why I reside in the Taj Mahal of unwashed teenagers; they think if they keep me happy, I won't kill people on the surface. And I have you to thank for this arrangement, I guess. And what's the story with the hot doctor?*

William scowled. *You can listen in?*

Oh sure. You and me are tight. You just don't realize it yet. Each time you dreamed, opened the floodgates, reached out to the others, I was right there. Now that you're my suitemate, looks like I can come to you, too. Which is nice, since I get no visitors, except for your aunt, that one time.

You led them to us?

We probably shouldn't be allowed to wander around killing people. It's not our fault, though, that we were picked up by the bastards and made to be weapons of mass destruction. I do wonder if we'll survive, though, what's coming.

What do you mean?

Ryan began playing again, swerving in his seat. *I remember. I remember everything. I bet your little friend, Miss Lily, remembers too, but she's too scared to talk about it. You and Dr. Sweetness are grownups, so they scorched your memory, it's what they do to adults. But us kids remember. Oh wait, you were a kid when you were taken, right? So you must remember.*

William frowned. *Everything I knew was wiped out by the same agency that is locking us away.*

Well, don't be too grumpy about it. I wish I didn't remember. I know what they did with us, how we're different than the ones before. When they trigger us at the end, we'll be just fine. Not like the old models, with their bleeding ears and blown up brains. . . .

William's stomach cramped.

Nanna.

Listen, Ryan, don't say anything to them about how we communicate. I have to find a way to get us out of here.

You can't stop it. The US might be in slightly better shape with three of us underground, but, as you probably have figured out, it's happening all over the world. All you have to do is read any news website and you'll see it. Hate to say it, but if I were in their position, I'd lock us up down here and throw away the key. And we're down deep. Level forty-two deep. There's no way out.

Just please don't reveal that we can communicate.

Sure. Just don't be a stranger, OK? I think we're going to be down here for a long, long time.

I promise.

The boy was gone, the connection broken.

William knocked over two stacks of books and kicked a trashcan across the room. He pounded his fist on the door, yelling to be let out.

Lily stirred, and Jane stood. He saw them, as clearly as he could see Ryan, also rising from his chair.

He knew he could unleash them all. But it would do nothing. It would only prove why they need to be buried in a taxpayer-funded tomb.

He slumped down in a chair, his head in his hands. He might be able to control their abilities, but it wouldn't help them escape. There was no way for him to attempt to contact anyone—not Blue, not Quincy. Aunt Kate certainly wouldn't tell his parents or brothers where he was.

There was no way out. And everyone he loved would die because he couldn't stop what was coming.

And what would happen when it did? Would the dream just suddenly seize him, connecting him to all the abducted all over the world, triggering them all at once?

If there was something in him that he could rip out, he would do it, even if he had to claw through his own skin. . . .

William stared straight ahead. For several moments, he held his breath.

Then he closed his eyes.

The darkness was vast, so different than when he was trying to get to Jane across the angry gulf. This time, there was only black. He knew instinctively that what he was attempting wasn't allowed.

He wasn't supposed to enter the dark voluntarily.

When he took that first step, he felt it immediately: the anger looming in the distance, coming to pull him towards the disasters. He wanted to cower; its coming fury like a wave of heat.

The dreams were how they designed it to happen. He was theirs, their vehicle, their way to get to the others to connect. Establish a web, unite them all.

He was never to be in control, to navigate the way to the others on his own.

He turned from it and plunged into the dark.

How much time passed, he didn't know. It felt like hours, but it could have been just moments; pushing through blackness as thick as tar. But at last, he found her.

She looked tired. He hated to wake her if she were sleeping.

As he reached her, Nanna opened her eyes.

"How many cups is that?"

Roxy scowled, raising her right eyebrow at Stella. "Don't judge, young lady. It's been a hell of a couple days. More excitement than I've had since, well, you know, the damn aliens."

She expected a sigh or some retort from Lynn, but she'd just spaced out, sitting in the chair in the hotel room and staring out the window. Roxy had hoped she'd finally fallen asleep when her eyes had closed, given that Lynn had barely slept in the government safe house. But it appeared now she was just in a deep state of zoning out.

"No judging here. You've just mentioned, more than once, the coffee isn't that good," Stella said from where she sat across the room from her mother.

"Oh, it tastes like the Mississippi River, all right. But at least it has caffeine. Still no sign of discovery?"

Stella reached back and parted the curtain on her side of the window. "Not yet. But I'm afraid it's only a matter of time. I feel terrible that I haven't been able to respond to Anne or Chris or the boys, but I'm hesitant to make any calls, given the kind of tracking technology my sources say the FBI has at their disposal. Anne is blowing up my phone as we speak."

"I know I've said it already, but brilliant move, kiddo. Long live the fourth estate. And good thinking ditching the Volvo for a rental car. Although I was unaware that you'd changed your first and last name."

"I did a series of reports on how easy it was to buy fake IDs once. Had one made myself to prove it. I always wondered if one day it would come in handy."

"If you're worried about being tracked by cell, shouldn't you be worried about that laptop?" Roxy pointed to the computer sitting on Stella's lap.

"It's got a pretty strong firewall, and everything I do is encrypted. I feel safe using it. As soon as we come up with some kind of plan, I'll email Chris and Anne. They're already so worried about William, now they know Mom is in some sort of trouble too. If I wasn't so mad at my ass of an older sister, I would reach out to her for help."

Stella turned to Lynn. "Sorry, Mom. I know you don't like me talking badly about Kate. But my God, signing that order? That's low, even for her."

"Stella, now's not the time," Roxy cautioned, waiting for Lynn to inter-ject.

Instead, Lynn just kept staring. When Roxy saw she hadn't blinked, she walked over. "Lynn?"

Lynn slowly held up her hand.

"Mom?" Stella asked. "Are you OK?"

Lynn's fingers folded, with only her index finger remaining extended.

"What are we waiting for exactly?" Roxy demanded.

Lynn closed her eyes. When she opened them, they were filled with tears.

"Mom!"

"I'm OK," Lynn said softly. "It's William."

"What?" Roxy asked, pulling up a chair. "What are you talking about?"

Lynn exhaled. "I know where he is."

Roxy reached out and put her hand on Lynn's shoulder. "Sis, seriously. You're scaring me a little."

"I'm fine. He found me. I just need to think."

"Found you?" Stella asked. "What do you mean?"

"Stella, I thought I heard you say that you trusted your laptop. Can you send secure messages?" Lynn asked.

"I can," Stella began, exchanging worried glances with Roxy. "But I don't understand."

Lynn dug into her pocket, bringing out the flash drive. "I'm going to need access to my files."

"And they thought making two little old ladies leave their purses behind would keep us from causing trouble," Roxy said. "Now, back to how you think you communicated with William—"

"I don't think I did. I *did*," Lynn said, reaching for Stella's laptop. "It was more . . . of a connection than communication. I could barely understand what little he said. I couldn't respond, I didn't know how. I have to make sure . . . that it's all here. It's my only choice."

"Choice to do what?" Stella asked.

Lynn inserted the flash drive.

FIFTEEN

Two hundred and seventy-two text messages in two days.

As she had done dozens of times in the last week, Kate resisted the urge to call her chief of staff and explain why she'd gone completely off the radar. *Sorry, Rachel. It's just that the world is about to end.*

Instead, she sent a quick apology, promising to explain more about why she was so unreachable. What she wanted to tell Rachel was to go home to her loved ones.

Did you see the hurricane now forming in the Bering Sea, heading for Alaska, Rachel? Or how the southern tip of Greenland is burning? Or maybe how hospitals in Valparaiso are overrun, completely freaking out the Chilean government? But that, of course, has been momentarily overshadowed by the shooting massacre in Buenos Aires. The world is quickly realizing these are not isolated events.

Kate's phone dinged again. Make that two hundred seventy-three.

Anne again. Her older sister's texts were the hardest to ignore.

Kate! I know you're getting these. Stella's not responding, you're not responding. I can't take this. If you care at all for your family, please call me. I have no idea where William is. It's been two days since that video of Mom and Roxy leaving that house with Stella. We got into Maryland last night and no one will tell us anything. You must know something. Please, Kate. Please call. I can't take this.

Kate's fingers hovered over her phone. *My God, what would I say? That Mom is hiding from me too? That I know your son is in a government cell miles beneath the earth, and they won't even let me see him?*

It still burned, thinking about how after she left William's cell, she was briskly escorted out of the SSA's building and ushered into a waiting Town Car. She'd demanded to see Director Wolve, but was told he would be calling her any moment now.

That had been forty-eight hours ago.

She'd repeatedly called. But the director of the SSA was out in the field, his secretary explained. Kate's calls to his cell phone had gone to voice mail.

When she'd demanded to see her nephew, she was told it was too high of a security risk at the moment.

They used me and now have no need to keep me in the loop.

And he wasn't the only one.

She'd learned the president had been having hourly updates, and her presence hadn't been required. When she'd inquired with his chief of staff, she'd been told that the president intended to bring her in at the appropriate time. With that, her access to the Oval Office was shut down.

So she'd made a phone call she never thought she'd make again. The car had arrived two hours ago.

Kate didn't wait for her door to be opened when they arrived at the SSA's warehouse headquarters, brushing into the building as soon as her escort had punched in the code and allowed the screen to scan his eyes. Another code and another scan in the small front lobby, and they walked briskly through.

She stopped walking at the sight of all the camouflage.

The sprawling first floor of the operation was more chaotic than before, as men and women clad in army fatigues moved between computer screens and television monitors, each showcasing a different disaster somewhere in the world. At each work station were SSA employees, looking more dour than usual.

She watched as one grizzled-looking soldier, an AR-15 strapped to his back, grilled a woman in a black suit about video of a hospital room. When the woman didn't immediately respond, he shoved his finger at the screen.

"Senator, this way," her escort said, placing his hand on her arm. It was more of a forceful touch than she would have liked.

Kate gave the operation another look as he led—no, whisked—her down a hallway. After several turns and another retinal scan, they arrived in a nondescript office.

Inside, Agent Flynn Hallow leaned over two laptops.

"Senator. I'm glad you called—"

"I want to see my nephew," she said, throwing her purse on a chair.

"That's beyond my ability to allow at this point."

"Then what about Steven Richards? I was told he was found with William and the others. Has he been useful?"

"Not at all. He refuses to speak or eat. He won't even change his clothes. He's a very ill old man, that's obvious, but won't tell us even if he needs medicine. He's just down the hall."

"I'll want to see him. But first, why is Director Wolve not taking my calls?"

"It's General Wolve, not director."

Kate blinked. "Come again?"

Flynn stood with a hunch, looking even more haggard in the dim light. "I didn't know anything about him when he was suddenly assigned to lead the SSA late last year. Prior military, his records showed. But there wasn't anything prior about it. Everything became clear when the military arrived two days ago, and our director ditched his black suit for his old dark navy one, featuring quite a few medals. I can see by your expression that everything is suddenly coming very clear. Feel free to take a seat."

"I'll stand, thank you," Kate said. "I'm not involved in the strategic planning of director personnel in government offices, but it's certainly not unusual for a member of the military to be asked to step in to lead an obscure agency—"

"Please, Senator. It's called infiltration. It was their plan all along. We were all snowed. I figured you deserve to know, given your role in it. And why you won't ever see your nephew again, or your mother, if they find her. Which they will. They won't stop until they do."

"They? It's your agency—"

"The military is now running the show, Senator. We're just worker bees doing their bidding. My counterparts across the world are reporting pretty much the same story. Every military in every nation in the world is scrambling, just as ours is, to collect the abducted, now that the SSAs have delivered our findings. We should have known better. Of course, only the US has found the host, the conduit. It means we have the means to control. Even direct, if the occasion calls for that."

Kate felt the dread spread across her. "Obviously the priority is to stop the abducted before they are activated. . . ."

"You have been too long convinced that you hold the cards. You are blind to what even your president has been convinced to do. Yes, contain the abducted, stop the disasters. But just imagine what they can be used for. What wars can be won, who will emerge the true superpower if we, and only we, have someone to control them all."

The agent leaned forward. "Senator, you have helped deliver the key weapon in the greatest arms race of all time."

The van drove down the street, slowly enough for the photographer behind the wheel to glance down at the map on his phone. *No way is this address right. There's nothing out here.*

Still, he double checked out the address on the printed-out email and compared it once again to the map. Hell, it was the same.

The crowd confirmed he was at the right location, which stirred a sense of relief and dread. It had been a long day, and if this became the lead story at six o'clock, he'd have to stay out here until it was over, which meant driving all the way back to the station, droping off his gear, handing over his P2 cards with all this video, then another hour and a half commute home. The McDonald's bag from lunch winked at him. *See ya at dinner.*

He rolled down the window as two people walked past, signs under their arms. "Hey, is she here yet?"

"Supposed to be any minute," a woman responded.

He pulled over the lumbering van. No need to raise the mast yet, the news release said this was where they were supposed to meet and then walk to the location. It better not be far. The LiveU, that enabled anyone to go live from any location, was as heavy as the old three-quarter-inch gear.

Strapping it on his back and grabbing his camera and tripod, he saw people were already holding up their signs, like runners stretching out before a race. He grabbed a few establishing shots and then some tighter close-ups on the bold writing: "WE WANT THE TRUTH." "THE TRUTH IS OUT THERE." "THE WORLD DESERVES THE TRUTH." "WHERE ARE OUR MISSING?"

He made sure his lavalier mic was ready to go because he wanted to capture the natural sound when those freaks started chanting. Hell, they'd probably let him pin the mic to their shirts to get good, close sound. Whichever reporter was rushed down here would appreciate it.

Better get close ups of the T-shirts, too. He saw more than one that were homemade, with the picture of that redhead dude who everybody thought got abducted by aliens when he was a kid. "BEAM ME UP, WILLIAM," one shirt read. "TAKE ME TO YOUR WILLIAM," read another.

He saw the crowd begin to crane their necks as a car with tinted windows pulled up. One of the people, who he decided was clearly an organizer, based on her shaved head and her Stranger Things T-shirt, rushed over and talked to the driver.

"OK!" the woman shouted out after a moment. "Follow the car to the meeting space!"

It was only when the crowd began to walk that the photographer realized just how large it was, given that he'd been unaware of all the people who were now coming from a side street.

Were there two hundred . . . no, three hundred people? Jesus.

None of it will matter unless she shows.

He kept pace, getting tight shots of the feet, medium shots of the walk. No one was chanting, so the mic stayed in his gear bag.

The van stopped, and the crowd began to gather around it. He pushed to the front, seeing Jason from Channel 11 and Sarah from the Fox affiliate jockeying to do the same. Only photogs had been sent, no reporters, given that no one knew if this was just going to be a loony parade.

As the crowd settled in, the passenger door opened, and a Birkenstock-clad foot extended. He could hear a few sighs of disappointment as an old woman with a head full of crazy hair stepped out, wearing a quilted vest over a denim shirt. She reached for the door to the back seat and pulled it open.

The crowd let loose.

"Shit," he whispered as people stepped into his frame. He struggled to turn on the LiveU. He moved forward, zooming in as he scrambled to hold the phone up to his ear.

"She's here," he blurted out to the assignment editor who answered. "I'm streaming. Get one of the reporters down here pronto."

The cheers and applause intensified as Lynn Roseworth made her way through the crowd. Jason had already begun to assemble a mic stand, with

Sarah hurrying to attach her mic flag to it. He'd have to just stick the lav on it, which would make his news director pissed that his station wouldn't have representation in the shot, but there wasn't time.

The streaming technology wasn't always perfect, but the signal would be good enough to give the other stations that chose to ignore the cryptic news conference email a true case of the craps. Ever since the old broad had been found at that house in Maryland and her daughter claimed she was being held against her will by the government, Lynn Roseworth had been on the radar of every media outlet in the world.

The email had hinted at her appearance for the protest in the warehouse district in DC. His assignment editor had just rolled her eyes and told him to check it out.

And there she was. Freakin' Lynn Roseworth.

He hustled to get right up in front, and in the process accidentally bumped the shoulder of the other old woman who had stepped out of the car.

"Watch it, jerk off," she said.

"Roxy," he heard Lynn quietly chastise.

"That lens nearly took me out!" the woman said. "We want you here, but don't crawl up my ass."

Liking her already, he whispered an apology. To his delight, the woman moved up to the mics.

"OK, listen up. Thanks, everybody, for coming. Lynn will be making a very brief statement—oh, looks like another friend in the media, make that two now, are coming on up, so while they're getting ready to join us, I want you all to share this everywhere. Stream this on your phone. Put it on Snapchat or whatever crap you prefer. Hurry up with those cameras, guys. Alright, alright, don't run people over. Just put that mic with the others. OK, you rolling? Alright, ladies and gentlemen, may I present Lynn Roseworth."

The crowd erupted again in cheers, and the photographer panned over. What did the email say again? What are they protesting, even? Something about government cover-ups or some other insanity.

He turned away as Lynn stepped up to the mic. He clicked his camera onto his tripod, thankful that he'd hauled it along. These people were old, who knows how long it would take.

When he focused on Lynn, he was surprised at the sharpness in her eyes, the grace of her approach.

"Thank you all for coming on such short notice. I am not comfortable doing this, but I have no choice. Most of you know—from your interest in the unexplained disappearances of so many people around the world, to the many of you who I have corresponded with personally—that I have not made any public statements since the discovery of my grandson fifteen years ago."

She took a deep breath. "But that does not mean I have stopped in my pursuit of the truth. Many of you know this, as I recognize some faces."

"We love you Lynn!" one woman cried out.

"And what I said, all those years ago, about there being a vast government conspiracy, is as true today as it was then. And it is now time for the people of the world to know that truth."

Lynn gestured behind her, pointing her finger down an alley to a darkened warehouse, barely visible. "It's difficult to see, but in that building, just down that alley, is an agency that goes by the name of the SSA—the Sky Surveillance Agency. For decades, they have used taxpayer dollars to study the disappearance of people all over the world. People abducted by extraterrestrials."

He could hear the collective gasp by the people huddled around him.

She then held up what looked like some sort of government document. "My late husband, Senator Tom Roseworth, joined me in my research later in life, and he was able to find proof of this organization buried deep in the appropriations for the FBI. He was also able to obtain internal emails referencing the rounding up of missing people who had been returned to earth."

"Jesus Christ," a man in the crowd muttered.

"These documents are now listed in an article published at this very moment on the website of my daughter, the journalist Stella Roseworth. Anyone, across the world, can see what we've found. Including how much the government has known and what it hasn't told us."

A few people in the crowd began to boo. "I called you here today," Lynn said, her voice elevating, "to protest. To let the government know that we demand these truths. That we demand to know more about what they've uncovered. If you will, go to them right now. Let them hear you. That we want the truth. We demand the truth."

The old lady beside her began to yell out the chant, pointing down the alley. "Let them hear you! We want the truth! We demand the truth!"

The crowd picked it up immediately, raising their signs as they began to pour down the alley towards the warehouse. The photographer unlocked his camera from the tripod, feeling the crowd almost push him over. Already, Lynn Roseworth and the other lady had slipped into the mayhem.

As the crowd spilled down the alley, a government car slowly made its way down a parallel street. Inside, the silver-haired representative from the great state of Texas rolled down his window and frowned.

"What this hell is going on here?" Congressman Flip Smith asked. "Maybe this is a bad time to be doing this."

"It's actually the perfect time. I want to know more about this agency before your government erases its existence," said the man in the seat next to him.

"Nothing is getting erased until I get some answers. I'm the chair of the Committee on Homeland Security, for Christ sake. What are those people yelling?"

"Well, according to the news alerts now completely taking over my phone, it's about just-now-released documents that this agency had knowledge of the abductions of people. What does it say, Flip, that I got a tip about this but you didn't know?"

"Apparently I'm so clueless I could fall up a tree. And I don't like it. My people in Austin expect me to be in the know, not spanked cross-eyed. Which is why I so appreciated your call about this. Like I said before: Any time you call, about anything, I'm yours. Which is why I arranged for this. They're expecting me, but they're not going to like a civilian showing up too. They can't deny my security clearance, though, and, like I said, you're coming with me."

His companion just nodded.

"Well, crap on a stick." Flip craned his neck. "Those damn people are all over the front now."

"We can get you in, Congressman," said the security detail from the front seat.

"Well get out there, boys. Make us some room."

As soon as the Lincoln parked, the driver and the guard from the front seat hustled around to open the door for the congressman and his companion. Sandwiching the two between them, the men, both over six feet tall and weighing a combined five hundred pounds, parted the crowd with little effort. The attention of the growing masses was too fixated on chanting and streaming from their cell phones to pay much attention to who was trying to pass through them.

The only entrance was a single metal door, and a pull on the handle proved it to be locked tight.

Flip was already on his phone. "Yes, this is Congressman Smith, and I have an appointment right now. Yes, now. Yes, I am aware this might be a bad time for you, given the circus outside your building. But unless you want me to turn around and start talking to the press, which I can wave over at any moment, I'd open up the damned door."

After a few moments, the loud sound of multiple locks came from within the door, and the congressman's guard yanked the handle. The door swung open.

"Go over to that parking garage and wait for me, boys!" Flip said, making sure his companion slipped in before the last member of his detail shut the door. "It's a good thing you wore that hat and those sunglasses; that crowd might recognize you."

"I'm usually not discreet. But I thought it was a good idea today."

The congressman walked over to the harried woman sitting behind a pane of glass, the phones around her ringing nonstop. "I assume you're the one I was on the phone with just now?"

"Sir, I'm sorry, but this is just a bad time. Can we reschedule—?"

"This security clearance says no." He pulled out his badge from inside his sports coat.

The woman frantically looked down at her phone, which was lighting up with more calls coming in. She raised her hand to her upper chest, which was turning a bright shade of red.

Flip pressed his badge against the glass between them. "If you can't read this, I'll bet I could call the head of Homeland Security down here to see if he can—"

"Just one second. I'll buzz you in, but you have to stay right by the door until I can get you an escort. And I don't have the other gentleman on the list."

"He's with me," Flip said. "Open the damn door."

As she buzzed them through, she knocked on the glass. "Wait for the escort! And I need his name for our records!"

The congressman was already through the door. His companion turned to her, flashing a smile. She stared back at him, tilting her head a bit, struggling to recall how she knew him.

Quincy Martin knew the look well, and stepped through before she could put a name with the face.

Roxy swatted at the reporters who had been shouting questions at Lynn as they made their way to the car.

"Thanks for coming, friends! Keeping speaking truth to power! But I told you Lynn wasn't taking any questions!" Roxy called out, jabbing at one reporter. "Nice spray tan, by the way!"

"There she is," Lynn said, hurrying to the car. She opened the door for Roxy to climb in and followed, while camera lenses pressed up against the glass.

"Drive, Stella!" Roxy yelled.

But the car was already lurching forward, horn blaring to part the crowd.

"Mom, look," Stella said, handing a laptop back to Lynn.

"Stella, focus on the road. Don't hit anybody," Lynn warned. "I know a lot of these people."

"I'm afraid the site might crash! It's already had so many hits!" Stella said. "But for now, it's still on. Mom, you did it. After all this time, you did it. Dad would be so proud. So will Anne. Once she sees this, she'll understand why we couldn't text or call her back."

"Anne would want us to find William, that's all Anne would want," Lynn said. "Did you see him, Stella? Did it work?"

Stella held up her binoculars. "Like clockwork. Just like you planned, Mom. When the protest reached the front of the building, he had Congressman Smith drive him up. I watched them go in."

"I still just can't believe it. That nut job Quincy Martin really does know William," Roxy said.

"I was really afraid that I misunderstood William. But he kept repeating his name. That he might be able to help. Thank God you were able to track him down, Stella."

"It wasn't easy. Just like it isn't easy driving through this crowd. Wow, Mom, you can really bring them in."

Lynn looked out the window. "I knew they would come."

"Well, I guess we all know now what you've been doing all this time," Roxy said, not disguising her aggravation.

"Obviously, I couldn't let you or anyone know what Tom discovered about the SSA. If they knew what we found, they would have come for anyone who knew. But I promised myself that all those families that I found . . . all those people that I communicated with who had missing loved ones . . . that I'd tell them. I'd tell them everything."

"Quite the bomb you've dropped, sis." Roxy patted her leg. "Now that we put the match to this bale of hay, what do we do to actually get him out?"

Lynn looked back to the warehouse. "I don't know. William hasn't reached out to me again, and I can't figure out how he did it."

"Don't know why I'm having trouble believing that William could speak to you with his mind, given the events in my so-called golden years," Roxy said.

"Tell me again what Quincy said, Stella," Lynn asked.

"That he has a powerful congressman in his pocket that could get him in, and they would get William out. And now that I've seen Flip Smith here, he wasn't exaggerating. There's no one more connected. Mom, you remember that Dad and Flip were buddies, even if they were on other ends of the political spectrum. Quincy hopes that when Flip sees that the grandson of a US senator is being held against his will, he'll use every resource to get him out. And that Quincy intends to broadcast it all on social media from his phone if he has to."

Stella laid on the horn. "Move, people! OK, once we clear this, we've got to haul butt. Hang on ladies."

When the crowd thinned, Stella hustled down the alley. "Mom, get out my phone. I think we take a left here and that will get us to one of the avenues."

"Yes, take that left."

"The freeway shouldn't be too far—"

Stella slammed on the brakes at the sight of the black cars blocking the street and the men in suits waiting outside. She changed gears to back up, only to see a large black SUV pull up directly behind them.

Kate was horrified at the condition of the man. She'd only ever seen him in photographs and video of him being released from jail when the kidnapping and murder charges had been dropped. He was old fifteen years ago, but appeared in good health.

She guessed Dr. Steven Richards was in his late eighties, and looked every bit of it. His breathing appeared labored, his clothes were disheveled, and he was in bad need of a shower.

"My God." She turned to Agent Hallow.

"I told you, he won't talk or cooperate. Hasn't since they seized him in New Orleans. Won't eat or do anything."

"Dr. Richards," Kate said, walking across the room to where he sat slumped in a chair. "Dr. Richards, look at me. My name is Kate Roseworth. I'm Lynn's middle daughter."

He raised his head, his eyes bloodshot. "Well, of course you are. You look just like her. You even have her hair."

Kate had never discussed the affair her mother had with the man in front of her. Or that he likely was the father of her sister Anne, making him the biological grandfather to her nephews, including William. There was no denying the resemblance.

"Sir, I have a lot of questions for you about my nephew. But I'm very worried about your condition."

"That's because I'm dying, ma'am."

"Agent, get a doctor in here—"

"That's all I'm saying as long as he's in this room. As long as I'm in this building and anywhere near these bastards," Steven said, his breath raspy.

"We've tried to help him," Flynn said.

"Please just talk to me, and I'll get you out of here. You clearly need medical attention. And we are running swiftly out of time."

"Excuse me, Senator. I need to step out," Flynn said, looking angrily at his phone.

She turned back to Steven. "Sir, please—"

"I won't. I won't talk here. They're listening to everything I say. I won't betray what I know." He raised his hand to pat at his chest.

"Trust me, I am understanding more every minute that no one in this building can be trusted. But my nephew is here. They won't let me see him, and I have to understand what you know about him, the girl, and the other woman you were with."

"Aren't you the one who didn't believe? Wouldn't support your mother?" He squinted one eye.

Kate swallowed. "I've made some real mistakes. But all I want now is to get William and the others somewhere safe. Where we can figure out what to do. I saw Will for just a moment, he told me I needed to find out about Blue. Do you know what that means?"

"I'm sorry, I won't talk here. I won't."

"Agent!" Kate said, standing up. "Agent Hallow! I'm taking this man out of here now—"

The door opened and Flynn stepped in, his face furious. "No one is going anywhere."

"This man is gravely ill—"

"There's a protest outside. Led by your mother."

"What?" Steven asked weakly.

"I'm sorry?" Kate demanded. "What did you say?"

"It doesn't matter now, anyway," Flynn scowled. "They found her. They're bringing her in now."

SIXTEEN

"Why is this elevator going so far down?"

The congressman turned to Quincy, who was intently watching the display descend to an alarming number: *15, 16, 17 . . .*

"You think the director of this agency keeps an office nineteen, no, twenty floors below a damn warehouse? We were supposed to wait for an escort to take us, that's why the secretary buzzed us in. How could you possibly know what floor that the director's office is on?"

"We aren't going to the director's office, Congressman."

"Then why did I have to swipe my security badge just to get this thing to go down? In my experience, that type of access is only necessary for military offices and weapons storage."

"Congressman, do me a favor from this point on," Quincy said, fighting the urge to cover the politician's mouth with both his hands. "Just accept the two million my PAC will spend on attack ads on your much-younger opponent and please just be quiet for a moment. You will see why we're going this far down in a moment."

"While I certainly appreciate your support, I have a strong feeling I'm being played. This protest comes at just the same moment that you need to get into a secure government building? I thought all you wanted to know was about this SSA agency—"

"Oh, I do. But trust me, as someone who's a champion for the rights of Americans, you're going to want to see what's down here."

"The rights of Americans—"

The elevator kept descending. The display read floors *31, 32* . . .

Forty-two. Go to level forty-two, William's aunt Stella had told him in that first bizarre phone call. He'd been stunned when he checked his voice mail and heard Stella's urgent message to call her.

He'd quickly returned the call. An hour later, he was on a chartered NetJet heading to Washington, leaving behind a seriously pissed-off board of directors that was waiting on an explanation for his disappearance. It had not been easy to slip away. But money talks, as it always did. His head of security—former head, he should say, as he was now on his way to the Caymans for a permanent vacation—was now rich enough to buy his own island if he wanted.

38, 39. . . .

Stella had explained that the location William's grandmother had pinpointed on a map ended up being a government-owned building that her own records showed was owned by some obscure agency called the SSA.

"Can you possibly get in if we create a distraction?" Stella had asked.

"And how does your grandmother know this?" he'd replied.

"Trust me, you wouldn't believe it."

"Listen, sister, I've been on this crazy train for a while now. Did William say anything about a little girl?"

40, 41 . . .

One call to Congressman Flip Smith, and a promise to heavily fund a reelection effort, and here he was.

He knew he needed to find William first. Make sure he was OK and ready to run. But Lily was down here too. And he didn't want her to wait a half second more.

42.

As the doors opened to an empty hallway, the panel on the elevator began to rapidly blink red. The same flashing pattern was repeated outside the doors that lined the corridor.

"Wait," Quincy said. "No security?"

"Why would there need to be security?" Flip asked.

"Because there are civilians down here, locked away without being charged with a crime. And this agency doesn't want anyone to know."

"Quincy, what the hell is going on—?"

As soon as the congressman stepped out, a piercing alarm resounded.

The doors to the elevator began to swiftly shut, and Quincy stumbled through.

"Good God!" Flip said, covering up his ears.

"Go!" Quincy said, ushering him down the hall to the first door.

"You sure as hell never mentioned that you were told civilians were being kept down here!" Flip yelled. "What aren't you telling me?"

"Use your badge!" Quincy pointed as they arrived at the first door. The keypad flashed like an angry migraine, the sound hurting almost as much.

The congressman fumbled with the card and pressed it against the light. It immediately switched to green, and the alarm ceased.

"I bet we don't have much time now," Quincy said. "I bet we have company real soon. We should have swiped it at the elevator again. Some kind of final clearance system."

"Clearance to what? I am fed up at this point—"

"I'm stepping inside. So you check your email, Flip. On the way down, I sent you a link to a Stella Roseworth's website. She's a journalist and the daughter of your old sparring partner, Senator Roseworth. She just posted a full report on this agency that includes some documentation of what they do. Looks like her dad did some digging before he died, based on what his wife discovered."

"His wife? You mean Lynn Roseworth? This isn't this alien crap again, is it?" Flip shook his head. "Jesus, Quincy. Is this all because you got caught up with those alien-obsessed nut jobs that kidnapped Roseworth's grandson?"

"He's not kidnapped. He's here. With a little girl."

"Roseworth's grandson is down here? Isn't he supposed to be missing? And a little girl?"

Yes. A little girl. The same one he wanted to ditch by the side of the road just a few days ago. A girl who clung to him in the back of a SUV after they narrowly escaped an explosion. A girl who held his hand while they ran through the blackness of an underground tunnel. A girl who slept on his shoulder while they drifted down a river in the dark, looking desperately for a place to find food and shelter. A girl who beamed with happiness after he bought her a cheap dress, and delighted in even worse pajamas, asking him to tuck her in. A girl he couldn't stop thinking about as he was forced back to Los Angeles—the fear on her face as he was dragged out of the room.

When he found out she was somewhere inside a government warehouse, he whispered it over and over, tapping his finger on the armrest of the chair on the plane.

I'm coming. I'm coming. I'm coming.

Quincy hurriedly opened the door and exhaled.

Lily sat on a bed, surrounded by a trove of American Girl dolls that she had placed around her like a shield. As he stepped into the doorway, she practically plowed over them.

He could feel her tears wet his shoulder after he swept her up.

"You went away. Why did you do that?" she said, her voice muffled in his shirt.

He found himself nuzzling his face on the top of her head. "I didn't want to, kiddo. But I had to get away from the men who took me. One of them I had to pay a whole lot of money to sneak away."

She looked up at him. "I still have your dress on. They brought me new clothes but I didn't care."

He smiled, his vision blurry.

The dreams were coming constantly, an insistent barrage, making sleep useless. William could feel its hunger for him.

Hunger and rage, just as he experienced when he first sought out Jane during the dream, and again when he reached out in the vast, unexplored darkness that opened in his mind as he tried to find Nanna.

Anger at his defiance. And it grew in intensity each time he found a way to block it.

It took Jane to show him how.

He hadn't thought of it when he communicated with the others. When he'd finally found Nanna, he was exhausted, barely clawing through the dark to cry out to her. It was if he were yelling at her underwater, knowing she couldn't understand his words. He'd extended his hand, feeling as if he were a rubber band about to snap. She'd stretched for him. With a single touch, a brush of their fingertips, the connection was so strong that he saw exactly where she was, and in turn, knew she could do the same. He could barely speak.

"Quincy," he'd said in that second. "Tell Quincy Martin. Level forty-two."

The band broke, and he spun back through the black and into the fluorescent light of the room. He was so tired, he'd closed his eyes, only to find the dream waiting.

So he'd reached out to Lily, but she became so upset at his eventual departure that he worried he was doing more harm than good letting her know he was still there. Ryan, too, became agitated when he had to leave.

Jane, however, gave him no choice. When he checked on her welfare, she made it clear that he was not allowed to break their communication until she said so. With a doctor's precision, she'd begun to grill him on the dreams: what he was seeing, what it might mean when he saw the eyes of the other abducted, how he had broken through the dream to get to her, and what was at stake for all of them.

They'd ended up talking for hours, exhausting every possibility, every option to escape the holding cells and the mental commands from the dreams to unleash the disasters waiting inside them all.

You said it came for you almost hourly now? You've fought it off since we've been talking? she'd asked.

He'd realized it then. *No, actually. Not since then.*

She'd nodded, looking every bit the calculating doctor. *Like a spinal cord epidural.*

What? he'd asked.

We use them as a pain inhibitor. Perhaps when you open these channels to us, it blocks its ability to get to you. And, as a result, only you can control us. Well, best keep at it to keep it from getting to you. Plus, I need to vent.

She was angry. Furious. She hated the idea of something having control of her. Hated that she was locked up inside a room.

I survived medical school. Someone should only be in prison once in their lives, she'd said.

He'd grinned. She'd smirked.

Then she was back to business, asking more about when the dreams had come to him, and asking for details about the moments since the agents arrived at his trailer in Arkansas.

He'd told her everything, wishing there were something—anything—humorous to mention, just to see her smile again. He was desperate for something to break the tension of the last days.

When their meals had come, they'd broken the communication. After eating, he'd tried to read, worrying that there was no way Nanna could make sense of what he'd said.

The dreams had reached him so suddenly, he stood up in alarm.

The room was too small for any type of real exercise, but he knew from before that physical exhaustion often kept the dreams at bay. He did pushups until he couldn't lift himself, but then lay on the floor, closing his eyes.

The dream waited.

Desperately, he'd stood. He'd reached out to her.

Come on in, Jane replied.

He could almost hear a hiss of anger as their communication blocked out everything.

Tell me everything, he'd said.

Everything?

Talk to me until there's nothing left to say. I'm so sorry that you're caught up in this.

She'd leaned forward. *Now that I've touched you, I can sense where you are. You think your grandmother can too?*

It's different for adults, I think. We have to touch first. It's like it burns a connection into us, that's the best way I can describe it. But Lily and that boy Ryan, who I told you is down here with us? They could do it before we ever make contact. He thinks it's because they're children, and they're somehow tuned in more precisely than adults. Ryan says we're right beside the Potomac River, beneath some warehouse. I hope my Nanna knows that."

"If she knows where you are, and we're deep under the earth beneath some warehouse, how in the world will she ever get us out?"

"I'm gambling that she—or probably my aunt, she's a reporter—can get word to a friend. It's a long shot, but he's well connected. If he can get out of his own mess, he might be able to buy his way down here."

"Even if he gets in, how do we get out?"

He'd just hung his head.

She'd then remarked on how tired he looked, and suggested he try to sleep. He'd replied that sleep is when the dreams came.

Then just stay with me. If it can't reach you in these . . . communications of ours . . . then just sleep. We won't have to talk.

He'd laid down on the bed, watching as she closed her own eyes. He was asleep almost instantly.

The unbolting of the door forced him awake and out of his bond to her. His grogginess suggested he had slept for a good amount of time.

The door opened, and Lily's small face peered around.

His eyes widened as she rushed to him, throwing her arms around his neck.

"He came back," Lily said softly.

William reached out and firmly shook Quincy's hand. "I can't believe it. . . ."

"We gotta get out of here."

"There are others, we need to get Jane—"

"I'm here."

She stood out in the hallway, next to an older man in a suit, with an American flag pin on his lapel. "Imagine my surprise when Miss Lily was standing in my door, along with the rest of these gentlemen," she said.

"Jesus Christ," the man in the suit said, looking at William. "It is you."

"Will, this is Congressman Flip Smith. I'm a longtime supporter of his. I told him I needed a tour of this agency that happened to be in a warehouse. Listen, we don't have much time—"

"Congressman, thank you. There's another boy down here," William said, walking into the hall. "We have to get him out. And Steven must be here somewhere. We have to get them both."

"There's only two doors left at the end of the hall. Look. One reads 'staircase' above it," Quincy said, pointing. "We didn't get to that one."

"I actually need someone to explain to me right now why you people are all down here," Flip said. "None of us are moving one more inch until I am told the whole damn story—"

The ding of an elevator that shot down the hallway was obviously set at an incredibly high decibel to alert anyone standing in the nearby corridors.

"Oh crap," Quincy muttered.

"I don't know where Steven is. But Ryan is just down the hall," William said, turning around to run when the sound of rushing booted feet pounded towards them.

A squadron of soldiers in black spilled out around the corner, the infrared lights on their long guns flashed as they blocked the hall.

"Drop to the floor! Drop now!" one shouted. "Mr. Chance, we don't want anyone to get hurt!"

"Listen here!" Flip stepped forward. "I am Congressman Flip Smith, and you best lower those weapons! You get your damn general down here—"

"Sir, drop to the floor! Hands on your head!"

William immediately felt Lily stir, and he reached out to touch her shoulder.

"Mr. Chance! I'm not warning you again—"

"You know what we can do!" William barked. "Stand back! I don't want to hurt any of you!"

He could tell the soldiers had been warned.

"What do you mean, what you can do?" Flip demanded.

William knew Jane had come to stand directly behind him, remembering her question about Quincy finding them. *If he can get in, how can we get out?*

He hadn't answered her then.

With a quick reach backwards, he found her wrist and held tight.

SEVENTEEN

From the first-floor windows, purposely made to appear dingy from the outside to conceal the agency within, Kate watched the protestors rush away in the sudden onslaught of rain.

Her mother was not with them.

She looked back to Steven, whose breathing had becoming disturbingly labored in the far corner of the room. He'd confided that he had advanced heart disease. Even with all the pain and resentment she'd felt for years about the man, it pained her to see this kind of suffering.

"Hang on, Dr. Richards," she said. "I demanded that they bring a doctor."

"Is she here?" he responded in a whisper.

Once again, Kate glared at the door, furious that Hallow had locked it behind him. All of the threats she wanted to make were useless. It didn't matter what elected position she held. All she was now was the daughter of the woman who had revealed an agency's once clandestine location to the world—

The door handle turned, and Flynn stepped in, quickly shutting it.

"Where is my mother—"

"I am only doing this because I have nowhere else to stash them at the moment," he said. He then held up a finger. "And I certainly wouldn't be hiding them in here if I had any other choice."

He turned and pounded twice on the door. The agents outside opened it.

Kate had rarely seen hatred in her mother's eyes, and it stilled her breath to see it as she stepped through, careful not to even brush by Flynn Hallow.

"I remember you, asshole," Roxy said, holding tight to Lynn's hand as she rushed in behind. "I hoped you'd died a long time ago."

"Hello, Mrs. Garth," Flynn responded.

Roxy almost ran into Lynn, she had stopped so suddenly.

"Mom," Kate said, watching her mother's angry expression turn to shock.

"Kate?" Lynn said softly. She hesitated, then strode across the room to fiercely embrace her.

"Mom, I'm so sorry," Kate said, burying her face in her hair. "I am so, so sorry."

"What the hell, Kate!" Stella brushed through the agents gathered outside. "Did you do this? Did you order these agents to take us—?"

"She did not," Flynn said. "Agent, close that door and lock it. If the military out there realizes you're in here, we're all in for it. Right now, your nephew is causing a real shit show down there—"

"Where is he?" Lynn demanded. "Take us to him right now."

"I can't do that, Mrs. Roseworth. What he's done—"

The building shuddered as the rain outside turned from a pour to a gush. The windows began to rattle.

"What in the world?" Roxy said.

The trembling of the glass turned into a sudden shaking.

"You've . . . brought . . . quite the storm, Lynn."

All heads turned to the man quietly tucked away in the back corner, who was struggling just to raise his head.

"Steven?" Lynn said in a whisper.

Kate steadied her. "Mom—"

Roxy threw up her hands. "Who else is in here? Barry Manilow? Ross Poldark?"

"What . . . how . . ." Lynn stammered.

"I tried, Lynn," he said, his breath barely supporting words. "I tried to tell you—"

The windows cracked so loudly that everyone flinched. Kate instinctively moved her mother away, just as one of the windows shattered.

The air outside seem to take a deep breath before it bellowed.

Glass, wind, and rain flew in. Kate covered her mother, hearing Roxy and Stella cry out.

"Open the door!" Flynn bellowed, pounding on the door.

The other window burst as the agents opened the door. The wind was so strong now, Kate could barely stand. She held tight to her mother as the agents pulled Stella and Roxy from the room.

"Steven!" Lynn cried out.

Kate looked to see the man slide from the chair to collapse on the floor.

"Get out of here!" Flynn yelled.

The wind beating at them, Lynn broke from Kate to teeter towards Steven, barely making it far enough to kneel beside him.

"Mom!" Kate screamed above the winds. She stumbled, seeing Steven weakly raise his hand to his chest and pull out something on a thin chain. With a jerk, he broke it free. He placed it in Lynn's hand.

Lynn leaned in close to him as he became limp, her hair blowing wildly.

"Mom! Now!" Kate reached her, pulling at her to stand.

"We can't! We can't leave him!" Lynn said.

Kate forced her to stand, propelling her through the door. In the moment she herself slipped through, she looked back, seeing the water pour in, soaking the dead man's body.

The hallway outside was in complete chaos. Lynn had been pulled into the crowd of agents already surrounding Roxy and Stella, with Flynn screaming at them to get out.

One of the agents saw Kate emerge and grabbed her. She heard her mother yell for her as they were propelled down the hall.

"Mom!"

"Keep moving! To those stairs!" Flynn shouted.

"What is going on out there?" Kate yelled to the agent who had her arm gripped tightly.

"There's a damn tornado! Coming off the water on the other side of the building—"

"Kate!" Stella called out as she was forced down the hallway with her mother and Roxy.

"I'm coming! Agent Hallow! Flynn!"

The agent's face, usually so sour, was now frantic. "We're going to be lucky to make it to the garage—"

"William, Ryan. All the others down there, we have to get them out—"

"Where do you think the storm came from?" he snapped, practically shoving her through the opened door.

The frustration in the soldiers was evident in their jugular veins, strained after several minutes of holding their weapons erect. The order to contain the threat at all costs had not included the fact that a US congressman and an famous billionaire would be standing with them.

The strike team leader dared to inch forward. "I'm not going to tell you again to get on your knees with your hands up in the air!"

The hallway trembled. William again repeated what he'd already stated three times before. "Turn around and go back up the elevator. No one has to be hurt. Let us go."

Another tremor shook beneath their feet.

"What the hell was that?" Quincy whispered.

William could see the soldiers' eyes flicker from the walls around them back to the scopes of their weapons.

He didn't dare to move, fearing not only that the soldiers would react badly, but of potentially disturbing Jane. She'd begun to tremble, and he didn't dare let go to break the connection.

"Mr. Chance, you know we can't let that happen. There is no way out for you—"

"Enough!" Congressman Smith pointed. "I mean it! Soldiers, lower those weapons now! We're going to talk this through—"

The crack resounded like thunder, rupturing down the south wall, between the soldiers and civilians. It started first at the ceiling, jarring through the concrete. Water at first leaked and then began to spray.

The soldiers were so jarred they momentarily turned their weapons to the splitting walls.

Like a hundred pipes exploding at once, the Potomac broke through.

The last glimpse William saw of the soldiers showed them rushing back towards the elevator before they were lost completely behind the gushing leaks. Lily gasped as the frigid water swept over their feet and down the hall.

"Run," William said unnecessarily, turning to take Jane by the arms. "Jane, we have to move. We have to move now!"

She blinked and then stared in astonishment at the rushing water. She looked at him in outrage. "What did you do to me—?"

He forced her down the hall, seeing Quincy carrying Lily and pulling the congressman reach the first door to the right. He then fumbled with something inside the politician's coat, pulling out a small card and pressing it against the keypad. Quincy pulled the handle, revealing stairs beyond.

"Take them all up!" William said. "I'll be right behind you once I get him out. Keep that door propped open."

"You'll need this," Quincy said, holding out the badge. As soon as William took it, Quincy ushered the clearly shell-shocked congressman through.

"Go on." William motioned to Jane.

Her angry eyes were fixated instead on him. "You should have told me!"

"I didn't have a choice. Once you get up a few flights, I'll reach out to you to stop it—"

She breezed past William. "Never again. You'll never use me again."

"Jane—"

"Open the door!" she yelled, standing in front of the last door.

William sloshed across the hall, holding the badge against the keypad. Seizing the handle, he yanked open the door.

Inside the cavernous room, the boy stood on top of a stool, trying to balance himself above the rising waters.

"William!" he yelled. "What's happening?"

"Hold on Ryan!" William called out, waiting for Jane to hold the door open so it wouldn't lock behind him. As he began to move through the waters to reach the boy and carry him out, a crashing came from down the hallway. A roar of water followed the thudding sound of falling concrete.

He heard Jane cry out as a torrent of water crashed into her, sending her careening through the opening and forcing the door to press against the inside wall.

"Jane!" William scrambled towards her, battling the increasingly strong current plowing through. After being nearly knocked over, he had to steady himself to keep from plunging beneath. When she didn't surface, he rushed into the current.

What have I done—?

The water began to change.

He thought at first it was just the fierce current that was altering the color of the water, going from the brownish muck to a whitish silver. But he quickly realized it was the water itself separating, allowing for the woman to emerge.

"My God," William whispered.

Dr. Jane Spencer rose from the water that now split around her, like an island rising in the midst of a river. While she was soaked through, not a drop of the water now touched her.

It was obvious that she was enraged.

The water continued to rush in, but parted before her. William could see straight to the floor of the room beneath her; it appeared as dry as a sidewalk in summer.

She gave him a quick look of such intense anger that he almost stepped back. "Now," she said.

William did not hesitate, rushing over to Ryan, who was gaping, his hands on top of his head. He lifted the boy off the table, finding that the divide in the water around Jane had splintered off and was reaching towards them. When the split got close enough, William practically threw Ryan between the parting waters and then jumped into the clearing as well.

They rushed to catch up to Jane, who was now out in the hallway, the water almost up to her neck but cascading around her.

"Holy Moses," Ryan whispered, looking back and forth at the water rushing around them.

The water parted for them to approach the door to the stairwell and William flashed the badge. Jane led them through and up the first flight of stairs, finally reaching a point where the water was beneath them but rising every moment.

"Jane—" William said, reaching for her as they climbed.

"This is not me. This is not me. I want it out of me. I want it *out*."

He took her hand. "I'm sorry. I'm so sorry. You'll freeze if we don't get out of here now."

She snatched her hand away, hurrying up the stairs and away from him.

In the nearby parking deck, the security team for Congressman Flip Smith waited to die.

The two men, fiercely devoted to the politician, did not like the fact that he had entered the building with the smart-ass tech billionaire before they could sweep it, but Flip insisted it was a safe government facility.

They also didn't approve when he directed them to discreetly wait for him in what appeared to be an empty and practically abandoned old parking garage across the street. "I'll call you when I'm ready," he'd said.

So they'd come here, parking on the second level. Their position gave them a view of the protests. They'd watched with some amusement when a hell of a storm had blown in, scattering the crazies like leaves. Not long after, the wind and rain had picked up to such an alarming degree, they saw street signs starting to blow off their poles. Even their car had rocked a little, and they were thankful for the concrete around them.

The rain had started to come down with such force they could barely make out the people and soldiers rushing from the building and heading into a warehouse across the street, which obviously doubled as private parking. Seeing that, they'd opened the car doors to go and find the congressman, only to be practically blown off the deck. When they saw the top of a funnel hovering over the Potomac on the other side of the building, survival instinct kicked in.

They ran to the stairwell inside the parking deck, covering their heads and crouching down, reverting instantly to the children they once were, practicing tornado drills in their elementary school hallway. Waiting for the entire ancient garage to collapse around them, they shouted the Hail Mary to each other.

Minutes later, the storm began to diminish. The walls stopped shaking, the winds ceased howling. Their necks sore, the two men dared to venture out.

The parking deck was covered in shattered glass and leaves. The men ran to their car, finding it intact but covered with a fine coating of dirt. They jumped in, speeding towards the first ramp, and almost drove right into the congressman and a group of people running up.

At the sight of the beleaguered Flip Smith soaked from the knees down, the men jumped out of the car, leaving it running. Beside him was the billionaire, carrying a little black girl. A stunner of a woman, soaked more than any of them, walked alongside a tall redheaded man who looked familiar. A kid followed, shivering.

"Congressman! Are you alright?"

"No," he responded. "I am not. But I am not hurt."

"That storm came out of nowhere! Flip, we tried to get to you!"

"We're getting the car. Got to get these people warmed up," Quincy said, motioning for the others to follow.

"What happened out here?" Flip asked. "What did you see?"

"It came out of nowhere! In the middle of the day! We were afraid that whole building was going to collapse on top of you, but I guess the funnel turned. You should have seen it! You know I check the weather all the time, sir, and I promise you there was no warning at all about a storm."

They'd never seen the Congressman look so old. "There's a lot I don't understand—"

The revving of an engine came from behind them, following by the squealing of tires. They turned to see the Town Car heading down the ramp.

Quincy slammed on the brakes beside them, rolling down the window. "This is kind of a crap move, Flip, but we're kicking you off the ride. I think you're ready to get off."

"Sir, get out of the car—"

"No, John, let them go," Flip said, holding out his arm. "He's right. I don't want to have anything more to do with this."

Quincy quickly glanced back at the people in the car. "Probably a good call," he said, driving out into the brightening daylight.

EIGHTEEN

It was fitting that it was the four of them again.

Kate vividly remembered sitting, then standing, then pacing in her parents' kitchen fifteen years ago as her mother recounted her time at the University of Illinois, the work she had done into missing people, and why, on that very night, she had gone to meet secretly with the professor who was suspected in William's disappearance. Kate had gotten so angry realizing what her mother had done that Roxy had chastised her harsh reaction, and she and Stella had bitterly argued outside. When her mother had driven off into the night, Kate felt the first pang of doubt that she didn't truly know her at all.

Fifteen years later, it was she who had to explain. Yet this time, they were trapped in some room, in yet another warehouse that hid government offices inside.

Her mother's eyes were so filled with sadness that Kate had to avoid looking at her. Stella was furious, and Roxy wore an expression that was a blend of empathy and disapproval.

When Kate had finished explaining everything she knew, there was a familiar silence, the same, heavy, uncomfortable quiet that followed when Lynn had told her own story all those years ago.

"Regret isn't even the word," Kate said, feeling like she'd repeated it so many times now that it had lost its meaning.

"Dammit, Kate," Stella said, standing and walking to the locked door, shaking the handle. "Isn't it a little too late for that?"

"Stella," Lynn said wearily.

"She's right, Mom," Kate said. "I delivered you right to them. I did the same with William. I thought I was doing the right thing. For the country, for my family—"

"That's crap," Stella snapped.

"Stella, enough," Lynn said.

"Listen to your mother, girls," Roxy said. "We can't exactly call in a family counselor right now. Let me tell you something: When everyone thought William was dead and everything really went to hell, your mother didn't drown in the mess this family can be. She got on a plane and flew to the middle of literally nowhere and faced something horrific. Don't you dishonor her by squabbling right now."

Stella took a deep breath. "All I can think about is Anne. She's surely seen Mom at that protest, and that a storm hit the building. She has no idea that her son was beneath that building too. And that her father—"

She covered her mouth. "Mom, I'm sorry—"

"Tom was her father," Lynn said. "In almost every sense of the word. Steven just helped bring her into the world, that's it."

Her voice broke a bit when saying his name. She looked to Kate. "Why was Steven there, Kate? How did he end up with William?"

"I don't know. In the brief time that I got to speak with him, he was so angry . . . he wouldn't say much, especially with the agents nearby. He was really sick, Mom. When that storm blew in, I think his heart just couldn't take it."

Roxy reached out to place her hand on Lynn's leg. "What did he give you?"

Lynn reached out to place a flash drive on the coffee table in front of her. From her pocket, she pulled out another to set it beside the other. "To think . . . we once coveted our paper files. There were mountains of them. Now we scurry around with these to contain our secrets. Steven will never know what I found, and I doubt very much the SSA is going to provide me a laptop to learn his."

"Bastards," Stella muttered, once again shaking the door handle. "They better be scouring that building to make sure William is OK. You said he was really down there deep. He should be safe from that storm, right?"

Kate nodded. "I hope so. It didn't appear the building collapsed. Agent Hallow said something about *him* creating the storm—"

The sound of a series of bolts unlocking came from outside, and the handle turned. Stella took a few steps back as a tall man with gray hair stepped in the room, wearing a heavily decorated military uniform.

"Now, who the hell are you?" Roxy asked.

"This is Mark Wolve," Kate said, crossing her arms. "Apparently, he's a general. You look a bit different out of your black suit."

"Unfortunately, deception is sometimes necessary to serve our country," he said. "I am told none of you were injured leaving the building? The underground tunnel leading to our parking garage was intended to provide security, but I'm thankful it was there. Otherwise, none of you could have escaped—"

"Not all of us did," Lynn said sharply, sliding the flash drives into her pocket while standing. "My grandson. Is he alive?"

The general exhaled. "The area where he was being protected is now underwater."

Roxy gasped, but the man held up a finger. "But a plane rented by Quincy Martin is now airborne. Security footage from the private airstrips at Dulles International show five people entering a hangar. Your grandson was easily identifiable."

"Well," Roxy said, quickly composing herself. "Looks like stashing innocent people in government cells underground doesn't always work, now does it."

"Innocent?" The general raised an eyebrow. "Who do you think brought that storm? Who do you think is bringing widespread disease and murders? And raging wildfires? That little protest you staged to sneak him out has now unleashed the most dangerous people in the United States."

He looked over to Kate. "Perhaps it's sinking in now. Why the military had to infiltrate the SSA. This is way beyond people disappearing. What's happening now all over the world is a full-scale war on the people of this planet. And William Chance was our only chance of stopping it. And now you've set him loose."

"Strange," Kate said, taking a step towards him. "Agent Hallow let it slip that the military had even greater designs for him and the others. Are you worried because you think he's dangerous, or because you've just lost your most powerful potential weapon against your enemies?"

"Agent Hallow spoke out of turn and is now relieved of his duties."

"Small loss there," Roxy muttered.

"It frankly astounds me," Lynn began, "with everything that is happening, all over the world now, that the focus of our military is to use my grandson and the others in a war on other countries. Can you truly be that blind to what's happening?"

"I'm not spending a lot of time on this, given that should your grandson trigger you, ma'am, then God knows what could happen to anyone near you. I can see by your expression that you understand. The world's militaries have joined the small pockets of SSA agents in scrambling to find the individuals causing these disasters. What do you think power-hungry governments will do with that? Take North Korea—besieged by hurricanes. If they find the person causing them, what would they do with that kind of weapon?"

"My God," Lynn's hand rose before her. "This isn't an attack on just one country. This is a global crisis—"

"And the United States will *not* fall. We had a real chance of stopping this until you undermined every effort to protect this nation. Four of them were gathered. We had a chance of determining what it is inside you that's making this happen, maybe even remove it—"

"You can't," Lynn said, biting her lip.

The general stopped. "Whatever you know, Mrs. Roseworth, you're going to tell us. Including the location of Don Rush and his sister Barbara. I think you understand why it's vital we find him as well. You're all going to tell us *everything* you know. Every one of you will do exactly as I direct from now on."

"You don't know us well. None of us takes orders from men very well," Roxy said.

"We're tracking that flight carrying your nephew. We have suspicions as to where they're going. And it's where you're going to go to convince your grandson to turn himself in. That storm is just a taste of what he can do with those people. He has to be stopped. Don't you see: He's gathering them, just like we think *they* want him to do. He is not who you think he is at all."

NINETEEN

The devil was coming.

Juan Rodriguez knew it, judging by the intensity of the smoke smudging the skies, smearing the sun. He watched it from the flatbed of the Ford, repeatedly jarred by the perilous terrain of the dirt roads woven among the orchards. The others attempted to continue sleeping, their mouths covered in cheap surgical masks, but not him. He'd actually slept last night, given it was his turn for the single bed. He'd collapsed into it and didn't stir until the sound of the truck arriving.

And the truck always came, even as the valley burned.

"We just can't let it all die," Patrick said a few days ago, clapping him on the back.

Juan looked from the skies through the sliding window of the truck to see the back of Patrick's thick neck. Even in a loose-fit unbuttoned shirt, a fat roll still extended just above his collar and beneath his short-cropped gray hair. The fat always spilled over when Patrick strained his neck to wave to his wife, honking the horn while driving by their sprawling ranch home. That was before he sent her and their daughters away when the flames appeared on the horizon.

Patrick had not, however, demanded his workers flee as well. At least not all of them, including those housed in his rental property, nestled deep in citrus trees. He even allowed them to turn on the single window air-conditioning unit at night. But when his truck arrived at dawn, that unit had better be turned off.

To the inhabitants of his rental, he offered triple the pay if they stayed. "Stupid to tell everyone to leave." Patrick had spit out his chew when he'd extended the deal. "You can't force a man off his land. This is my land! Government can't take it. That's what they want to do, you know. I've got a twelve-gauge waiting for them if they step one foot on it."

Juan and the others had just stared at him, doing the calculations in their minds. *Mama could get that hip surgery. Maybe even get Tommy across the border, if the price hasn't gone up.*

"Damn fires probably won't even make it here! Where do they think they're going to get their damn orange juice if we cut and run? Screw them and their blockade. You can keep people from coming in, but my ass if they're going to force us out."

So of course Juan had stayed, even when the video on their grainy television showed weary firefighters battling what the graphic on the bottom of the screen repeatedly labeled "FIRE CRISIS." At the beginning, all the reporters talked about was finding the ignition source for the fire that was cutting a swath through the fertile farmland, burning tens of thousands of acres. But now, all anyone focused on was how even with the military's assistance, the fire kept raging, even springing up in areas not even close to other flames.

It was no wonder Juan dreamed of fire.

And he could feel the devil coming to watch it all burn.

Juan said a prayer to Mother Mary to keep away Diablo. The devil wouldn't rise from hell with horns and red skin; he would look like every other entitled white man. He would have red hair, blue eyes, and pale skin. He would be handsome and tall. Juan feared he'd see him every time he closed his eyes to sleep.

Juan knew the devil was responsible for the night he didn't remember, and for turning his dislike for Patrick into hatred.

It had been a year now since Juan had woken with Patrick kicking him. Tasting dirt in his mouth, Juan felt the kick to his hip. He had rolled over to another kick, Patrick's fat face leaning over him, blocking out the sun. "I don't pay you get to get drunk and disappear!"

"*No comprende. . . .*"

"Listen," Patrick had waved his fat finger in Juan's face, "If you ever, I mean ever, pull a bender like that again and not show up for work *for an entire day*, I'll ship your ass back to Tijuana and give you to the border patrol myself. Understand that?"

Juan had scrambled to get on the truck, apologizing profusely.

The others had later explained as they'd stripped the clementines. Juan had gone out for a smoke before bed two nights ago and never returned. Patrick had rolled up this morning to find him lying outside on the ground.

"Tequila!" Mateo had joked.

Juan did like his Jose Cuervo, but only touched it on Saturday night when there was no possibility of work the next day (Patrick kept a Bible in the bed of his truck and thumped it often when talking about the merits of a hard day's work). Juan had disappeared on a Tuesday night.

Later came the dreams of fire, and the white man watching him. Juan knew the dreams were a warning from his Heavenly Father that the devil was near, and that he needed to protect his soul and himself.

So when Mateo had privately shown him the Smith & Wesson 629 he'd purchased from the alley behind the 7-Eleven, Juan had asked how he could get one as well. Mateo had made it happen, and Juan kept it with him at all times, contained in the side pocket of his cargo pants. The devil could come anytime, and Juan would be ready. And if Patrick decided to kick him ever again . . .

When he had such thoughts, he'd pray to Mother Mary for forgiveness and quickly pat the weapon.

Juan slid forward when the truck suddenly veered off the road and came to a rough stop beneath the citrus trees. He and the others knew what to do. They scrambled to lie down, throwing the filthy blankets Patrick kept in the bed of the truck over themselves. Even under the heavy blankets, they could hear the whirl of the military helicopter pass over and then fade away. When the sound was gone, the truck lurched forward.

It happened at least once a day. When they were picking in the orchards, all they had to do was make sure they remained deep in the foliage. Patrick always kept the truck parked beneath the leaves so it couldn't be seen. At night, Patrick would choose one of them to go with him as he used one of the few back roads not blocked off by the military to make the delivery.

"Trust me on this," Patrick always repeated. "These oranges are like solid gold. Stupid celebrities in LA will pay twelve times over for the last of the true fruit from the valley, just for the bragging rights. Got to keep the money flowing until these fires die down. Government can't take everything from us."

The truck turned into the grove and pivoted underneath the widest of canopies. Juan and the others slid out, their muscles already stiff from the jarring ride. One by one, they grabbed the ladders and set off for the trees.

Thankfully, Juan's ladder opened easily underneath a particularly thick patch of mandarins. It didn't always happen, for the ladders were constantly used and moved. As he climbed to the top, grasping the first fruit, he heard the commotion beneath.

Mateo was shaking his own ladder, angrily trying to pry it open. *Don't*, Juan wanted to cry out. *Treat it gentle–*

With a loud crash, the ladder fell to the ground in two succinct parts, the worn-out hinges spilling out in the grass, nuts and bolts forever lost. Mateo stood above it, astonished.

Patrick moved like a bull from where he leaned on the truck. "Damn fool!" he charged. "Son of a bitch! You're gonna climb that tree like a fucking monkey! No place for me to buy a new ladder at this point. You know how much money you cost me, monkey? That's all you all are, a bunch of monkeys."

When Patrick shoved Mateo, Juan reached down to his pocket. The gun felt heavy resting against his thigh.

Patrick reached up and pulled down an orange, shoving it in Mateo's face. "You're worth less than this. You know that? What it's going to cost me to smuggle in a new ladder is coming out of your wages. You *comprende?*"

Patrick began to peel the mandarin with his hands. Each peel he removed, he then whipped at Mateo. "Just consider each one of these peels a dollar not in your pocket. One, two, three. Get up that damn tree! Climb it boy!"

With a swift move of his leg, he kicked Mateo towards the tree, chomping into the orange.

Juan had seen Patrick do it before. It horrified him each time Patrick swallowed the mini fruits whole. The farmer was clearly proud of his ability to do so. Juan imagined the fruit slipping past Patrick's tongue, causing him to choke. He thought about it having a bitter taste, perhaps because of a white mold on the inside. Or better yet, a black widow spider had chosen that particular fruit and was at this moment about to strike the inside of the farmer's cheek.

Juan pictured the mandarin as a tiny sun, fiery to the touch.

Patrick clutched his throat and gasped. First it was just his left hand, but then his right flew up as well. Juan saw a bit of Patrick's tongue emerge. *Was it scorched black?*

Juan dropped the orange in his own hand when the smoke began to leak from Patrick's mouth. When the black mark began to show between his sausage fingers on his even fatter throat, Juan began to rapidly climb down. By the time he'd reached the ground, Patrick was already lying in the grass, rolling around like a pig in the dirt.

Juan and the others rushed over, horrified at the smell of singeing flesh. Patrick's neck was opening up, burning from the inside out.

"Help me," he gasped, unable to stop the widening hole. They saw a flash of the trachea, and for a moment, a bit of flame from inside his throat. His eyes bulging, Patrick thrashed to his side, and then stopped moving.

They all scooted back as a small, completely burnt orange rolled from the gaping hole in the dead man's throat.

For several moments, they stood in silent astonishment. Then Mateo was moving, yelling for the others to help move Patrick's body into the back of the truck. "We dump him," Mateo ordered. "Close to where the fires are burning! No one will ever know!"

Juan could only watch them carry the body, his hand struggling to make the sign of the cross. His heart was heavier than the untouched pistol in his pocket.

The cable networks were clearly struggling to keep up. CNN, FOX, MSNBC, their beleaguered anchors repeatedly trying to stay on top of each unfolding disaster.

Quincy repeatedly flipped between the channels on the large-screen television mounted in the front of the plane.

FOX branded their coverage "Crisis on the Coasts." Their blond anchorwoman stood in front of a wall of monitors, each highlighting a different disaster. "The Pope is calling for worldwide prayer in the wake of what you're seeing here—"

Flip.

"Our Mumbai bureau is reporting the president of India is calling for a mass evacuation of the southern tip of the nation in the wake of the wildfires there," read a CNN anchor. "I'm sorry folks, I know it seems like we're moving minute by minute to new developments, but that's how quickly this is unfolding. We have to go now LIVE to Rome where the Pope is prepared to speak to the masses flooding the Vatican—"

Flip.

The MSNBC anchor team sat in front of a panel of gathered journalists. "Kimberly, we're hearing from the White House the same message, aren't we? The president is urging calm, repeating what he's said often in the last twenty-four hours, that the hurricanes have stopped—"

"Except for that freak storm just outside Washington," the reporter said. "He also points out the violence that has sprung up in other countries has been largely avoided here in the last few weeks here. But he can't say the same for the wildfires out west or—"

Flip.

"Quincy, can you at least mute it for a minute?" William said, standing up from where the two sat.

"Good idea. I don't know much more I can watch."

"I can't stop thinking about Steven. And my Aunt Kate. Did they make it out of that warehouse before the storm tore it apart? And my grandmother, my aunt Stella, and Roxy . . . did they get away safely in time from that protest?"

"I wish I had the answers, Will. I can only imagine once that storm was spotted, that building cleared fast. Your aunt is an important person, and Steven is valuable to the SSA, they'll want to keep them alive. I know the plan was for your grandmother and the rest to bust out once they lit the fire of that protest. They knew they had to get away to avoid being captured again. I know you want to reach out to her to know for sure."

"I do. But . . . I have to talk to Jane first."

"OK. I better make sure there's going to be a place for us to even land in all that smoke."

While Quincy went to talk to the pilot, William turned to slowly walk down the aisle.

He could feel Jane's simmering anger as he approached. She sat in the back, in between Lily and Ryan, her hands moving protectively to land on both their knees.

"You don't need to be afraid of me," William said.

"You'll understand I'm having a hard time believing that, knowing at any moment you can just choose to activate us. Even without telling us."

"I swear to you, back there in the warehouse is the *only* time I've ever purposely triggered you. All the other times . . . in those dreams . . . I wasn't in control."

"I believed you. I really did, William. But for all that talk in the hospital about stopping the storms, you brought it. You used me to do it. I'm already completely torn up about all the deaths I've caused in New Orleans—"

"That wasn't your fault, Jane—"

"But you knowingly just did it back there. How many other people died?"

William shook his head. "I had to get us out. I have to show them."

"Show them what? All you've done is demonstrate you can use us to cause complete destruction. What do you think this looks like now? We're on our way to California. I know it. It's where the wildfires are burning—"

"I have to show them that I can stop it," William said. "I'm sorry, Jane. I really am, making you bring that storm. I put my own family in danger. They were nearby after that protest, even if Quincy said the plan was for my grandmother to drive far away. But don't you get it? If I can find the man causing the fires, find a way to touch him and stop him, then we'll all be together. And we can show them that I can stop it all. At least in the US. Then, if there's a way, I'll go all over the world to stop the others."

Jane sat forward. "I want to believe you. I really do. But it's just hard after what you did. You should have warned me."

He approached them, kneeling down. "I need you, Jane. I need you to wake me up."

"What do you mean?"

"I have to find the man causing the fires. Like I did to find you . . . I have to go in. To the dreams. If I'm successful, I want to then try and find my grandmother too. But if *it* gets me first, you have to wake me up. If it truly takes hold of me, it will not let me go. This wasn't in their plans. I was only supposed to connect with you through the dreams, that was it. They never intended us to actually find each other."

"How do you know that?" Jane asked.

"The anger. I feel it every time I defy them, whether it be reaching out to you on my own or stopping the disasters. They obviously intended me only to control you under their direction. I don't think they ever anticipated how much control I actually have."

Jane shook her head. "How am I supposed to know if it takes you?"

"He screams," Lily said softly.

"Can you do it? You'll have to force me awake. It might take . . . the connection between us to do it. We know . . . when we're together, it can't reach me."

"Earl isn't going to like that," Ryan said.

"Earl?" Jane raised an eyebrow.

"One of the bastards up there," Ryan pointed up. "He spent a lot of time in my head, and vice versa. So I know they see us as lower than rats in a maze, and they're just watching to see how successful we are on our world in destroying each other. Whatever works, they'll just duplicate it elsewhere. We're just a testing site. If they didn't count on William having this much control, once they have him, they won't let him go."

William stood and walked over to one of the seats. He sighed, hearing Jane rise and come and sit beside him.

"It comes at me all the time now," he said. "It will be quick."

She nodded.

He slowed his breath. Before he shut his eyes, he thought of the flames, and the eyes.

Before he could even begin to venture into the dark, it had him.

Jane watched him flinch, and she instinctively reached out to squeeze his hand. William then seemed to calm, the tension in his face softening.

My God, she thought. *How is this happening to us?*

Even though she was still angry with William and harbored a real worry that even he wasn't truly in control of himself, she did believe him. That he wanted to stop this.

She looked back to Lily and Ryan, who were both now looking out the windows. Just two kids. Handling this as an adult was one thing. But children? She could only imagine what it would be like to be a hormonal teenager and wake up one day to realize you could make people kill each other with a flick of your wrist. Or what about Lily? Close your eyes and give people diseases. How can a child even comprehend that? And somewhere, out there in the smoke, was someone who was burning the very world around him.

And let us not forget yourself, dear doctor. Who ruined the city you love with wind and rain? How many people died in those hurricanes you summoned? How many homes and businesses were destroyed when you had the dreams of storms?

She knew it wasn't her fault. It wasn't William's fault. They were only instruments in the hands of what—*aliens?* She couldn't even say the word. It was all too ludicrous. *You are a woman of science, of facts and proven theories.*

Yet you summoned hurricane winds to batter a warehouse. You brought down the rain to drown a building. You parted the waters from the storm so you could walk through. And before all that, you had psychic communications with a man in another room, blocking repeated attempts by an outside force to control him. You could see his astral projections, for God's sake, while you were locked in some room miles beneath the earth. What bit of science explains any of that?

"It doesn't," she whispered.

It all paled in comparison to knowing each time she's had the horrific dreams of the storms, that she was, in fact, bringing them. That they weren't dreams; it was William connecting with her unknowingly from afar, triggering whatever weapon was inside her. She distinctly recalled his confused and frightened look in the dreams.

She looked back at him. It sure would be easier to hate the unwilling commander of all their destructive abilities if he weren't a genuinely honest guy who happens to look like Prince Harry.

When he jerked, wrenching his face towards her, she actually gasped in surprise. William thrashed to the other side, his eyes squinted and his hands clutching the armrests. He began to shake.

"William!" She took his face in her hands, only to have him pull away. His teeth were chattering.

"Jane, what's happening?" Ryan cried out.

"What's going on back there?" Quincy yelled from the cockpit.

Jane took a deep breath. She closed her eyes, trying to recall the sensation of when William had come to her repeatedly in their government cells.

She felt it immediately, a pathway. She saw him.

William was in flames.

He struggled to move, as if he wanted to go further into the fire. But his arms, his wrists, his legs, all were enveloped in long, slick stretches of tar. The substance then split, climbing up his back and wrapping around his throat.

A moving mass sprang from the corner of her eye, shooting out and immediately enveloping her in writhing wall of shining black scales.

As it closed in around her, she wanted to scream. Pure rage emitted from the twisting and thrashing, a wrath so pervasive that she choked, unable to breathe.

Just a glimpse of William then, a fragment of his face, trying to get through. She could see his fingers, then a hand. She grasped it with both her hands. At the moment they touched, it was if a million flashbulbs went off before her eyes.

They gasped for air. Jane tried to get her bearings as William nearly fell out of his chair.

"What happened?" Quincy said, standing with Ryan and Lily in the aisle.

"It was waiting," he said with a delirious look in his eyes. "You came for me."

"Are you alright? What was that?" Jane demanded.

"Oh God," he said, covering his eyes. "It had me from the second I entered. I couldn't stop it. I couldn't get away. It took me . . . all over the world. I saw their eyes, and the disasters started. Over and over and over . . . I couldn't stop it."

"I saw you . . . in flames. That . . . *thing* . . . had you."

"I couldn't get away . . . but I could divert. Just for a moment. I found him, the man in the flames. But he's afraid."

"Of course he is. He's surrounded by fire," Jane said.

"No," William said. "He's afraid of me."

TWENTY

The smoke was relentless. Outside the window of the Gulfstream, it looked to Kate like the entire world was burning. The footage from television didn't do the fires justice; everything below the plane was gray and ash.

Across from her sat an armed soldier, who, uncomfortably, kept a fairly constant gaze upon her. If she were to swivel around, she would see the same arrangement was made for her mother, Stella, even Roxy.

"What do you think I'm going to do? Flip someone over my shoulder? Maybe a karate chop?" Roxy had complained when they'd boarded the plane six hours prior, and she was forced to sit in her own section under the watch of the soldier.

Stella had lectured everyone intensely about the freedoms of the press and pointed out that journalists in the United States cannot be taken prisoners of the government. She'd been shown her seat at the back of the plane.

Kate had raised her own hell on the flight, demanding to speak with her staff, even invoking the name of the president. Mark Wolve had just given her an aggravated look, ordering the soldiers to keep them silent as he drew a curtain separating him and his staff from the rest of them.

Only her mother had said nothing, sitting, folding her hands in her lap, and looking out the window. Four soldiers were stationed around her.

Kate wanted to stand and tear the curtain open, demanding to know where they were going. But she knew if she dared make a move, that soldier would be on her in a heartbeat. Even when she did turn around to check on her family, he cleared his throat as a warning.

She thought about praying, something she hadn't done in perhaps a decade or more. She'd prayed at her dad's funeral, hadn't she?

Dad. Would you be ashamed of me? Would you understand I did what I thought I had to do to protect the nation? Or would you frown that I had put country before family—

The curtain abruptly parted, and Mark stepped through, carrying a laptop. All the soldiers snapped to attention. "Corporal Rice, your seat."

"Yes sir, General Wolve, sir." As the corporal went to stand in the back of the plane, Mark sat down, opening up the laptop.

"General, what is Blue?"

The man continued to look at his laptop. "That doesn't matter right now—"

"My nephew said to ask about Blue. And I have. And no one seems to want to answer that question."

"You have to understand something, Senator. I am no longer here to answer all your questions anymore."

"Must have been a heavy hit to the ego to cover up those four stars under that black suit."

He slowly looked up. "When the lightning first arrived last year, and the SSA updated the director of the FBI, he thought it best to contact my boss at the Pentagon. I was quietly transferred over to make sure that what happened fifteen years ago didn't happen again."

"Yes, things are much better this time."

He turned the laptop, displaying a flashing red stripe stretched across CNN's homepage, the banner reading, "WORLD UNDER SIEGE."

"Let's just start with the United Kingdom. Hurricanes off the coast of Scotland. A terror attack in Southampton. Wildfires in East Ireland. Hospitals in Kingston upon Hull flooded with calls from people suddenly in the final stages of cancer, heart disease, you name it. And do you know when all this started?"

"There have been reports of these disasters sporadically in different countries for the last six months—"

"They started ten minutes ago." He scrolled down on the site. "Let's check in on the Middle East. The coast of Yemen: Hurricanes. In Pakistan, Islamabad started burning like someone poured gasoline on the streets. Northern Kazakhstan: All of the residents of the Hotel Hizhina died when a car drove up and tossed in a truckload of bombs into the lobby. Lebanon:

Overwhelmed with people barely able to breathe because of chest infections. In the last ten minutes."

Mark pointed to a map of the world. "It's the same now on every coast of Africa. Australia's been battling these disasters for days now, but it's now happening on the corners of every continent and heavily populated country. China, Russia, they have multiple accounts of the same disasters. On the four corners of the largest populations."

"People are dying in all these countries, and you're worried that we won't be able to keep up with competing regimes? You have alien technology using our planet as a weapons testing site—"

"We have to make sure that there's an America left if Syria finds one of the four."

"My God, General, shouldn't basic survival of our people be at the top of your list of concerns—"

"I'll tell you what I'm concerned about. What I've been concerned about since the moment I was assigned to take over this shadow agency: that the SSA is operating in every nation in every world practically unchecked. So everyone has the same intelligence, and once the four are identified, their militaries will be thinking the same. That's what worries me."

"But they can't be controlled. They can't be used as weapons—"

"Unless we find William. And all the different branches of the SSA around the world have the intelligence that he is considered the conduit. So don't think we're the only ones after him all this time. Imagine if another superpower gets to him first. We did have him, until your family got involved. We suspect your nephew is operating not by his own will. We tried to bring him in, remove whatever it is within them all to stop this. Now, he's left us no choice."

"I know him. He's smart, and he's trying to stop this. He's worried about what they can do."

"He's a college dropout who mows lawns and can control people with unstoppable weapons. I'll keep the security of this nation in our hands, if you don't mind."

He looked out the window. "We are at the end of this, Senator. You will have to choose whether to uphold your sworn duty to serve the people of this country or put your family first. I think I know how you will choose."

"You don't know anything about me."

"Really?" He raised his eyebrows. "No husband. No children. No family of your own. Your entire life is devoted to amassing power. If the world survives this, you could be president one day. And that, of course, will all depend on whether or not you can make some hard decisions."

"What I can do? I have no way of finding him. Surely you aren't thinking of using me as some kind of bait? Because I can tell you, he's not especially fond of me at the moment."

"Of course not. But your mother, your sister, your family friend back there. That's a different story. He's quite fond of them. Which is why you will convince them to help us bring him in. Just so it's clear, the commander in chief agrees this must be done. If you'd like, I can get him on the phone."

Kate crossed her ankles. "Funny, General. I've used the same threat myself in the past when I've needed someone to follow my direction."

"Then you understand that our president is not a man to piss off. He's been made aware that while the San Joaquin Valley has been evacuated, there are still people inside. It's been difficult to track with the fires, but thermal imaging shows a small pocket of people moving. We've been keeping watch on them. We'll be landing at Beale Air Force Base and then taking helicopters to their current location. We have men stationed nearby."

"How can anyone exist in that?" she asked.

"The fires ignite in random locations, but it's clear whoever is starting them has no grasp on what he can do. There are still pockets that haven't been touched. And in one of those areas, we've identified a farmer who we think has been secretly working illegals until the fires reach his land. We think that farmer is our fourth. And we just need your nephew to get to him to know for sure. It's the only reason we haven't moved in on your nephew's plane, which landed about an hour ago. We're tracking him at this moment."

"You can't just let my twenty-two-year-old nephew wander into a wildfire, for Christ sake. He'll never survive—"

"Senator, we are keeping watch on him from various fire trucks that he no doubt believes are fighting the fires. Frankly, I'm growing weary of chasing your relatives. If you need another reason," he said, scrolling to the second major headline on CNN's page. "SENATOR'S WIFE OFFERS PROOF OF ALIEN COVER-UP."

The general glowered. "I just haven't determined yet which member of your family is more of a threat. You must convince your mother to speak with us. Tell us where Don Rush is; he could be a real threat if your nephew activates him. As could your mother, obviously. And she hinted that she knows what is within them that gives them this weapon. We must know that."

"I told you, she won't discuss it with me. She says she will only tell William."

"Which is another reason why we must contain him. But realize this, Senator: He has the ability to activate them. We know that the ones abducted in the past year survive even after they unleash their weapons. But all those returned from the abductions all those years before . . . do not. I know you've read the files. If he triggers your mother, all those around her could die. And she, for certain, will."

"Are you sure?" Quincy asked, looking over the steering wheel. "You're sure he's out there?"

The landscape beyond the windshield was completely covered in a dark haze. From their perch on the rim of the valley, it was impossible to see where the fires started and ended. Twice now, a fire truck had gone screaming past them.

They'd gone unnoticed once again because of Quincy. An older-model pickup truck was waiting for them at the private runway. He'd had it delivered using one of his private accounts, just as he had done to rent the plane, knowing his corporation was desperate to find him and would be monitoring all his accounts they were familiar with.

They'd rushed from the plane into the truck, afraid of seeing the rest of Quincy's security, which he hadn't paid off or, even worse, government agents. But they'd gotten away without incident, hoping the truck allowed them to attempt to blend in with the farmers who could only drive by the fires and watch their livelihood burn.

"I can sense him," William said. "But I don't know where. Out there, somewhere. But we can't just drive into that smoke—"

The pressure was suddenly so strong in his head that he doubled over. He covered his head, struggling to keep the dream from seizing control to draw him in.

"Fight it," Jane said, her hand on his back.

After a few moments, he sat back, his face hurting from the strain. He felt Lily's hand on his arm. He reached up and patted her hand.

"I'm OK."

"Jesus, that's what it feels like?" Quincy asked.

"It does now. It's constantly trying to draw me in."

"I don't care what happens," Jane said. "It's the only way to block it—"

"I'm not putting you all at risk any more than I already have," William said.

"If it can't touch you when we're connected, what harm is there if it can see us?" Jane was demanding now. "As long as we're not in the dream and you're controlling the communication, who cares if it's blocked but knows we've connected? I'll happily do it. And give it the middle finger in the process."

"I do like her," Quincy said, flicking his thumb towards her.

William looked back. As she had worn it since that first day in the hospital, Jane's hair was pulled back in an efficient ponytail. Not a stitch of makeup allowed a scattering of freckles to show. Her eyes caught the light, showing gold and green among the brown.

"I don't want to risk it," he said, turning once again to the smoke. "Maybe it's just holding back and now it can even penetrate our communications. Quincy, just look for a way to get in."

They continued along, Quincy occasionally flooring the gas when it looked as if the smoke was about to conceal the road.

"Wait," William said suddenly. "I feel him closer. He's not far. He's through there."

"You mean through those miles and miles of black smoke? How are we supposed to get through that?"

Jane leaned forward. "Are you sure, William?"

He nodded once. "It's almost like a scent. I know it's him."

"Quincy, stop the truck," she said.

"What—"

"Just do it."

As he hit the brakes, she opened her door and jumped out.

"Jane?" William asked.

He watched her scramble to the front of the truck, standing before the smoke.

Quincy tilted his head. "What is she doing?"

William felt it, the swell of her. "Jane!" he said, reaching for his door handle.

She turned back to hold up her hand in warning.

The winds rattled the truck, sweeping in with such force that Ryan and Lily rocked in the back seat. William braced himself, watching the winds tear at Jane's shirt and blow her hair wildly.

As the wind rushed past her, the smoke cleared.

Stumbling, she fought against the gusts to make her way back. Ryan tried to open the back door of the quad cab, but the force outside was too strong.

She saw it too. With a single look in the direction of the winds, the force bent around the truck, calming while still pummeling the smoke. As she jumped in the truck, the torrents once against picked up outside.

"Drive Quincy!" she said.

Rain hit them, falling in waves. Quincy slammed the gas, turning down a split in the road and barreling onto the path through the smoke. The winds made it nearly impossible to stay straight.

"I can't keep on the road!" Quincy yelled.

"I can feel him. We're not far," William said.

"Can you calm the winds or something?"

"It has to be strong enough to keep the smoke blowing away," Jane said.

"Crap," Quincy muttered, keeping the gas pedal to the floor, the smoke barely at bay around them as the winds cleaved a path. The rain was now falling so hard that the wipers couldn't keep up.

William reached for Jane. She nodded.

"Are we clear?"

"Almost! OK! Now! Now!"

The moment he laid his hand on her leg, he felt it coming, like a freight train whose brakes had failed.

He felt it slam against whatever invisible barrier he and Jane forged together in their communication. As in those times isolated from everything but each other in the SSA's confinement, he didn't just see Jane, but the emitting brightness around them. He saw Lily and Ryan in the same manner, the outside world fading away in a tunnel created only for them.

He dared to look away from Jane for just a moment.

The blackness thrashed, a horde of thick, twisting strands of viscid oil. It pummeled against the barrier, hammering to get through. And from the distorted feelers began to emerge something from which the tentacles were born.

Once again, he was seven years old, his hand dropping from his grand-mother's fierce clutch in a dark hallway. He could barely see the creature ratcheting itself to its full height—

William yanked his hand off Jane's leg, shattering the connection.

Jane gasped, her eyes blinking. "It was on us."

William stammered for breath as Quincy righted the truck, the winds around them calming.

"Ok, we're through," Quincy said. "Fires haven't gotten this far yet."

"What is it?" Jane asked. Lily looked over at her in fear. "*What is it?*"

The girl then turned to William, sadness in her weary face.

The pull, the sensation of the other was immediately so strong that he jerked back to look out the window. "He's right here. I can feel it. Wait, what's that? Right there."

"That's a truck hauling ass," Quincy said. "It's coming right through that orchard. It's headed for the road."

"Get in front of it. He's in that truck."

The grayness had begun to dissipate, revealing lush, untouched or-chards in the near distance. Quincy once again slammed on the gas pedal, easily reaching the beginning of the dirt road the other truck was barreling down. He parked, completely blocking the way.

William slid out to walk to the center of the road. As the truck came to a stop a yard away, the driver began to lean on the horn. William held up his hands. "I just need to talk to you," he called out.

The driver waved at him to move the truck. William shook his head, yelling out again that he wanted to talk. He started to walk when he saw movement just above the truck's roof.

A worker leaned on the metal, aiming a gun.

William felt the bullet whiz by, miss his shoulder by a breath. He cow-ered, waiting for the second bullet to strike.

Instead, he felt Ryan.

The man with the gun was tossed from the truck, hitting the ground hard. Two other men jumped from the bed, rushing to him as he tried to stand. One pummeled him in the face, the other punched him in the gut. The driver of the truck jumped out of the cab, walking towards the beating.

"Ryan, stop!" William yelled.

"You made me do it!" Ryan responded.

My God.

Just as he had done with Lily. With Jane. The instinct to protect himself, to kill or hurt, happened in a heartbeat.

He ran towards the fallen man, blocking Ryan's commands. The three men stopped their assault and staggered back, clearly confused by their own sudden, unexplainable violence.

As William reached them, the man in the dirt scrambled for the pistol that had fallen a few feet away.

"No! I don't want to hurt you!" William said.

"Diablo!" he gasped, clutching his stomach as he lurched for the pistol.

William scrambled to reach it first, sticking it in the back of his jeans. "Listen, please."

"*Mary, madre de la gracia,*" the man responded, struggling to kneel. "*Protegeme. Mary, madre del la gracia . . .*"

Touch him. Just once.

William reached down and put his hand on the man's shoulder. The man hissed at the connection between them. He scurried away from the shock, the electrical current that startled William at its intensity. "Diablo! *Mantente alejado* Diablo!"

"He saying to stay away, devil," Jane said, she and the others cautiously approaching.

"Can you tell him we're not here to hurt him?"

"*No querer hacer dano,*" Jane said.

"Diablo! Diablo *demonio!*" The man pushed himself back in the dirt.

"He thinks we're all demons. . . ." Jane stopped, looking over her shoulder. "Do you hear that?"

"Mary, *madre de la gracia,*" the man continued, tears in his eyes.

"Hear what?" Quincy asked.

"That buzzing. What is that?" Jane asked.

"I don't hear anything."

The sound of tires tearing across dirt came from the near distance. "Someone's coming," William said. "Jane, can you tell him—"

"William Chance!" came a voice on a bullhorn from deep within the trees. "Drop to your knees and put your hands on your head!"

They looked to the grove, seeing the shapes running. Soldiers in camouflage, their weapons out, barreling towards them.

A drone then buzzed over, just as the approaching vehicles grew louder and greater in number.

"Get behind that truck!" William ordered.

In the increasing noise came the sound of helicopters, lifting over the swell of hills nearby. From the road, Marauders came to a grinding halt, the doors flying open and more soldiers rushing out.

"William Chance! The entire perimeter is surrounded. Please put your hands on your head and direct the others with you to do the same."

The soldiers in the groves were quickly approaching, the others that had swarmed around Quincy's rented truck were lining up as well, their weapons fixed on them.

"Mr. Chance! This is your final warning. We do not want to hurt you or any of those people. Your family is here. They want you to stop this," boomed the voice.

He saw it then. The soldiers waved four people out from one of the Marauders.

William's heart dropped, seeing his aunts Kate and Stella surrounded by soldiers. He watched them both turn back to help two women out.

At the sight of Roxy and his grandmother, his chest tightened.

"No!" he bellowed.

They had them. All of them. Regardless of everything he did, everything he'd done, they were still in harm's way.

"Mr. Chance! Now!" the bullhorn bellowed.

He saw some of the weapons turn towards his grandmother.

William closed his eyes.

Fire exploded, the very dirt erupting in fire, so tall it reached to the tops of the trees. The leaves caught fire next, the fruit exploding with the heat. As the soldiers near the grove stumbled away, the trunks sizzled and began to ignite.

The flames encircled William and the others, now rising so high that the sight of the hovering helicopters was lost.

William breathed, beginning to walk towards the flames, keeping his connection strong with the immigrant. The presence was there, again on the boundary, angrily trying to penetrate, knowing William was controlling another.

Burn, burn, burn, he could almost feel it commanding.

With the heat of the flames so strong that it began to singe his eyelashes, he again closed his eyes.

Like the sudden shutting off of a gas valve, the flames immediately died, and as if a downpour of rain suddenly fell and then evaporated, the leaves and charred trees smoked but no longer burned.

The only sound was the spitting of dying embers.

"Listen to me!" he yelled. "This can all stop! Right now!"

"Mr. Chance!" the voice on the bullhorn called out. "Your family wants you to turn yourself in—"

"You saw how quickly I put out that fire! Watch your satellites! Above the fires in California!"

"William! Do not move! Drop to your knees!"

William slowly began to step back, holding up his hands. "Are you watching? The fires? There were storms in Louisiana and we stopped them! There's no more violence in Washington! Watch your satellites!"

He braced for the command to fire, the sting of bullets. The seconds it took to scurry back to the others felt like a lifetime.

The immigrant man cowered behind the truck, and William swallowed, compelling him to come towards him. With fear in his eyes, the man stumbled forward, straining to keep William from touching him.

The man stiffened as William reached deep within their connection with a simple command.

Stop. Stop the flames.

The man slumped, and William knew. All across burning San Joaquin Valley, the flames began to snuff out, as if a torrent of water had been tossed upon it. While he could not see it, William had no doubt that all that remained was scorched earth.

"Did you see? It's over! The fires are out!" William called out.

He could see in the distance several of the soldiers clustered around large satellite phones, pointing excitedly.

Conferring with a soldier on the phone beside him, the man with the gray hair raised the bullhorn to his mouth. "William. No one wants to hurt any of you. You all need to come forward and surrender yourselves."

"We can control it! All of it! No more people have to die!" William yelled.

"People are still dying, William!" the man responded.

"That's impossible," William whispered to himself. He then cupped his hands to his mouth. "It's over! All of it!"

"William, whatever you're trying to do, it's not working. People are still dying! We just checked with the hospital at the edge of the hot zone!"

"Lily!" William called out, motioning for the girl. She cautiously approached as William let go of the immigrant, who staggered back, running for the truck.

He reached out and took her hand, feeling the furious dark, pounding just beyond their connection. William reached deeper within Lily, commanding her to stop the sicknesses.

Nothing came from her. The weapon inside lay dormant.

"I'm sorry," he heard Lily say.

William looked to the girl. "Lily, I don't understand. . . ."

"William, you have five seconds to get to the ground!" the bullhorn screamed.

Suddenly he knew.

It struck him like a hammer. Each time he entered the dream to see the sickness at the hospital, and looked beyond to the stone formations beyond, he would see eyes. Eyes still in the stone. Even though Lily was with him.

He kept his focus on Lily. "That isn't you, is it?"

"I tried to get Ava out," Lily wept. "But she was trapped. And I was so scared."

"Lily, who is Ava?"

"William! Drop now! All of you, drop now!" the voice commanded.

"I don't know how I got out. I promised her I would come back for her. I tried to tell you . . ." Guilt and anguish washed over Lily's nine-year-old face. "My sister is in the mountain. With the monster."

William wanted to ask more, but a red laser light from a high-powered rifle appeared on Lily's forehead. He stepped in front of her, the light now squarely on his stomach, and dropped to his knees.

TWENTY-ONE

Through a child's eyes, the mesas did look like mountains.

They'd arrived by helicopter at the military encampment at the Theodore Roosevelt National Park at dawn, in time to see the sky awaken the silver of the sage, the bluish gray of the sandstone, the gold of the clay. It would have been a breathtaking view: the morning sun on the expansive canyons where broken towers of stone loomed over the vast emptiness. The swath of all-terrain military vehicles, forming a barrier to prevent anyone from entering what the locals had come to call the death zone, was like a camouflaged stain on the earth.

William looked out the eastern window, the other helicopters sweeping in like a flock of blackbirds. As he leaned forward, the soldier in front of him stirred, his finger moving an inch or so closer to the trigger. The four other camouflaged men did the same, their eyes constantly focused on him and the girl beside them.

The fact that he and Lily were even allowed in the same space was an almost impossible feat.

As the military swarmed them in the orchard, William had reached out with his mind to the others: *Show no aggression. I won't let you be harmed.* Before they were all ushered away at gunpoint, he could see the immigrant's terrified expression at the voice inside his head. Jane tried to stay with Ryan, but they were quickly separated.

It cut deep to see Lily's terrified face as she was surrounded by soldiers. Quincy swiftly lifted her in his arms, yelling that his only mutant ability was to eat a double quarter pounder. Not daring to actually touch Lily, the soldiers hesitated and then began to motion Quincy away with their rifles.

William had been quickly directed towards a Marauder. He'd strained for any sight of his grandmother or family, but was almost immediately ushered into the military vehicle. Waiting inside was the tall gray-haired man who'd held the bullhorn.

"My name is General Mark Wolve, and from this point on, you're going to do exactly as I tell you."

William had listened to his furious berating: how he'd put the lives of countless people in danger, that he was an instrument of a kind of weaponry that was ripping the world apart, that the government had tried to protect them all and he'd undone everything on the whim of an immature twenty-two-year-old mind—

"We can kill everyone," William had said quietly. "Everyone here. You. Every soldier. Just like that." He snapped his fingers. "I didn't allow us to be taken because you had a sniper set on the girl. I did it because I needed a way to get to North Dakota as quickly as possible. Inadvertently, by separating us, you've positioned us in different locations within your military operation. Before you could put a bullet in my head, I could unleash all their weapons. No section of your soldiers will be unaffected. We will survive. You will not."

The general's eyes were furious. "So you'd unleash the weapon inside your grandmother? Knowing how it would destroy her? I'm supposed to believe that?"

"I wouldn't have to. I have complete control over the weapons within the others. You saw the precision I had with the flames. I could activate all of it on your operation, and my family would be untouched. Speaking of safe, I need proof that Dr. Steven Richards is unharmed."

The general's lips had formed a thin line. "We offered to help him. Give him the medicine he needed. In the end, he refused assistance."

"In the end?" William asked.

"Yes, Mr. Chance. The end."

William fought the urge to launch across the helicopter at the expressionless man. "Now that we've established the rules, you're going to order the helicopters to take all of us exactly where we need to go. I'd like to try and end this. And I need the girl with me."

His directive had not gone over well, but the show of force with the flames was still fresh. After an hour of heated discussions, the helicopters had taken off. The general had even agreed to allow Lily to ride with William, but had explained that the rest of the Roseworth family would be on the helicopters carrying Jane, Ryan, and the immigrant. If William decided to activate any weapons while they were airborne, his family would perish as well.

William had just nodded and reminded him that the longer they delayed, the more people would die.

Steven.

He'd spent much of the flight thinking about his biological grandfather. What he'd endured in his life, the sacrifice, the scrutiny. How all he wanted in the end was to tell his grandmother the truth about her family. And to help William. Without Dr. Steven Richards, he wouldn't even be alive at this moment.

I'm sorry, Steven. I'm sorry I didn't get to thank you.

They'd flown at a relentless pace, stopping only to refuel. The general had traveled with him and Lily, constantly questioning them. William had been completely forthcoming about everything, explaining that all he knew to do was to try and find Lily's twin, Ava, in the national park. As had happened with the immigrant, whose name he now knew to be Juan, he hoped he could sense Lily's sister when he got close enough to her.

A chill ran through him, thinking of Lily alone in the darkness of these ravines, wandering beneath the mesas and buttes. He considered entering the dream to try and find Lily's sister, but after the last disastrous attempt, in which Jane had barely rescued him, he feared he would not escape its grasp again. Whatever *it* was, there within the stone.

He looked out the window again as they began to land, the true size and vastness of the sprawling rock formations coming into a clearer view. Out there, somewhere, was another little girl identical to Lily.

It had never been Lily's eyes he'd seen in the stone. It was her twin who continued to emit the diseases when Lily came in search of him. Only when Lily at last found him did he inadvertently wake the weapon inside her in order to protect himself.

Lily had sobbed in explaining the guilt she felt that she had somehow gotten free of the mountain and could not rescue her sister. That by finding William, she hoped he could help her free her sister.

He remembered her words at the fountain. *We have to go there! It's my fault what happened to her . . .*

As the Black Hawk came to a landing along with the others upon the stone he could feel them all: Jane, Ryan, Juan. Nanna, too.

The door was thrust open, and William scooted to the edge of his seat, prompting Lily to do the same. The soldiers reacted by raising their firearms.

"Tell them," William yelled to the general above the sound the blades of the helicopter outside. "Tell them we go where we please."

General Wolve clenched his jaw. "I need ten minutes, Mr. Chance, to be debriefed—"

"You've been in constant communication this entire flight. You have two minutes."

The general tore out the door, and William remained on the edge of the seat. He closed his eyes.

Jane.

There was a brief pause.

I'm here, William.

Are you alright?

As any of us can be. Your grandmother was with me. They placed her in my helicopter, but they wouldn't even let us talk. They've already ushered her out, but I've been told to stay put. She kept telling them that she needed to speak with you.

I'll find her. I promise I will not allow any of you to be harmed—

Don't do that. Don't say that, William. No one knows what could happen next. You've successfully convinced them to fear us, which I suppose buys us a bit of time. If you're going to promise . . . just say that you'll be careful. If what we saw in that dream is out there . . . whatever it is . . .

I know. Watch over the others.

There was another pause.

Just come back.

William looked out the door. Two minutes were up.

He took Lily's hand, the soldiers scrambling. They formed a perimeter around them as he and the girl stepped out on the rocky earth.

They'd landed behind the military blockade he'd seen from above. The activity around them—the rushing soldiers, the men and women in suits huddled around laptops—came to an abrupt standstill.

The general stood under a tent among a crowd of camouflage and black. At seeing William emerge, he strode over.

"Let's go over the ground rules—"

"All due respect, General, you aren't making any rules. I have to find the girl. That's all. And I must see my grandmother. Now."

"I know you think you have us by the balls—"

"I don't, sir. We all have the same end game."

The man leaned in. "Do we? Because my understanding is that you're the one triggering all of this. And you've successfully gathered all of them in the United States to you. How are we to know for sure that you fully control of your own actions? Or is something else pulling your strings? And I'm just pouring a can of gasoline on a burning house."

William mimicked the gesture, stopping just an inch from his face. "Because it's my family—all the people I love—who have suffered for generations to get to this point. You could put your whole damn army in front of me and I'd find a way through."

The general stared at him for a moment more, and then motioned for him to follow. He reached into his pocket to bring out a phone, quickly dialing and barking orders to bring Lynn Roseworth to the perimeter. Once he hung up, his turned to William. "We need to formulate a plan here. How do you intend to stop the girl out there?"

"I have to find her first. And make physical contact. Like I did with the others, I should be able to contain her abilities."

As they walked, the crowds parted. They passed through several tents, all with the same reaction.

Moving beyond the last tent, William stopped, surprised at what he saw on a solitary table.

In a cage on the table, multiple rats scurried on a wheel or amidst pieces of shredded newspaper. Lily recoiled at the sight.

"What is that?" William asked.

"We'll explain in a moment. Let's keep going. But it reminds me, how did she—how did both those girls survive out there all this time? And how did she escape?"

William felt Lily's grip tighten as they walked. "She doesn't remember anything."

"This feels bad, Mr. Chance. Really bad. I don't trust this at all—"

"And given what your agency and government have done to my family, the feeling is completely mutual."

"Let's just hope you meant what you said, that we all want the same conclusion."

Among the parked vehicles were two ATVs positioned at an angle, almost touching, preventing anyone from walking beyond. Standing before them were four women, encircled by soldiers.

"Well played, General," William said softly.

"Just a reminder of what's at stake should you decide to make a move that we don't agree with."

He passed by his aunts, prevented from touching them by the surrounding soldiers. He saw Kate put her arm around Stella as he passed.

"Screw this," he heard a familiar voice say. "Let me see that boy."

William attempted to take Roxy's outstretched hand, but the soldiers gently pushed her back.

"No contact, that's non-negotiable," the general said from just a footstep behind him. "And that goes for everyone."

Only one person did not turn to him at his approach, as her gaze was fixed on the broken landscape.

"Nanna," William said.

"William, come stand with me."

"Mrs. Roseworth, you know that is not going to happen," the general said.

At that, she did look over her shoulder. "You will give me a moment with my grandson. And then you can have all the time you want to bark."

William heard Roxy grunt in satisfaction.

"We're here for one reason only, and that is for you both to reveal what you know so I can formulate a strategy—"

"Then stand between us if you wish, General. But you are only wasting time," Lynn said.

William flashed his raised eyebrows at the general, motioning at the space beside his grandmother. The soldiers around her parted for the general as he huffed over, putting his hands on his hips to further the divide between grandmother and grandson.

"Understand this first," the general said. "No one can go any further than the points of these vehicles. Do you see there?"

Not far across the mesa on which they stood was another cage. There appeared to be movement inside it.

"More rats?" William asked.

"Indeed. The cages mark the perimeter of the area in which people have died. When the waves of sickness come, there is no warning. In the last week, when the diseases intensified, we set them set up at different locations and intervals to warn us. If the bastards keel over, we run and don't look back. So far, it hasn't reached this far.

"But it also means we cannot go in search of the source. We even attempted by helicopter. The last radio communication was from the pilot saying he couldn't breathe. It crashed less than a minute later."

Lynn raised her hand to her neck. The general continued. "Drones show us nothing but dead animals and birds out there. No one has walked out of this area alive. That is, except for that little girl. She was quite the discovery. We certainly didn't intend on letting her leave—"

"What do you mean, let her leave?" William said, Lily peering around his leg.

"Please, Mr. Chance. A nameless little girl wanders out of a hot zone that is under complete surveillance by the military and you think we weren't alerted? We were about to seize her, take her to the DC headquarters or quarantine her, even if she wasn't emitting the diseases. But then she saw you on that parks investigator's phone. When she indicated that she had to find you—you, of all people—we knew for certain that it was happening again. And that we had to find you. Who do you think arranged for them to fly to Arkansas? We were with them the entire time, watching, observing. She led us right to you. We, of course, misjudged what she was, in fact, capable of. And you, for that matter."

William could barely contain his budding anger. "So many people didn't have to die."

"Understand that we're in the same place today that we were eight days ago, when that girl was discovered. We cannot venture in to determine what is causing the diseases. We'd hoped that girl would find you and explain to you what was occurring, so we could take you both safely into custody to determine what could be done to stop it. But reckless fanatics changed our course."

"Fanatics," Lynn said softly. "You refer, of course, to the people who have wanted to expose the truth that you so badly wished to contain."

The general jutted out his jaw. "All that matters now is stopping it. And you and that girl are going to show us how."

William reached down and lifted Lily, leaning in to her. "I know your sister's out there. I can feel her. But I don't know exactly where. Does any of it out there . . . look familiar?"

Lily shook her head. "It was so dark."

He held her tighter. "The bottom line is we don't know. There's simply no way of finding her unless I can get closer—"

"You're wrong, my boy," Lynn said. "There is a way."

"What is it?" the general demanded.

Lynn's sad eyes turned to William. "I should have told you. When I first suspected it. But I couldn't. The truth was too difficult for even me to share."

"I don't understand," William said.

"There's nothing that can be taken out of us, William, to erase the danger we pose. There's nothing implanted inside you, or me, or that sweet girl in your arms. We *are* the weapons. They changed us, William. Down to our very DNA."

"How could you possibly know that?" the general said.

Her eyes flickered to him. "Because I am a Researcher, General. While you and your agents and soldiers were either trying to contain or use us as weapons—I was trying to understand how to make us safe again. And it was there, in the very skies above my woods."

"Nanna." William stepped towards her, but the general held up his hand and the soldiers moved in. "Nanna, what do you mean?"

"They swarmed when you first disappeared. The ladybugs. I thought it was some bizarre reaction to the abductions. But in the last year, they started acting strangely again. I've seen it documented, in photographs or video, all over the world, in all the sites of abductions and where they are returned to earth. It only happens for a moment, and you have to know what to look for. Sometimes you see it in swarms of flies, in locusts, in lady-bugs, or even in snow or rain. Whatever is indigenous to the area or its weather patterns. Look closely above and you will see it. The shapes of DNA strands."

"Impossible," the general fumed. "The very best minds in the world scoured those sites for anything like that."

"None of those people *live* at an abduction site. Or know that a year ago, when I felt the first tremor, the first inkling of control over me, I saw it for the first time, before my very eyes. I saw it again in Maryland just a week ago—in the form of swarming cicadas—where I suspect the boy, Ryan, was taken. I can tell by your expression that I am correct. The cicadas took the form of the strand."

The general stammered. "What does it mean?"

"I believe . . . it's how they mark what they've done to us. What each person taken or returned is afflicted with. It's how they've engineered us. Ultimately, where to position us."

William looked out. "So you think . . . out there . . . wherever Lily and her sister were returned to earth, there will be some indication? In the skies—"

A high-pitched sound tore the air, echoed in several locations through-out the camp. A harsh light began to pulsate not far away, positioned next to the cage where the movement of the rodents had now come to an abrupt stop.

"Go! Go!" General Wolve yelled. "It's coming! Get back now!"

William sidestepped the general, taking his grandmother by the arm while holding tight to Lily. In the chaos, one of the soldiers broke loose, jumping into one of the ATVs on the perimeter, calling for the general to follow. He fired it up, clearly hoping for a faster escape.

"Major, no!" the general cried out.

The man looked over and then reached up to his throat. A second later, he began to convulse, his skin changing to a yellow pall.

As they ran, William caught a glimpse of Lily's face as she craned her neck to look back towards the mesas. He'd seen the girl look so frightened for so long, it was startling to see her calmness, her expression void of fear. For a moment, she looked at him, her eyes conveying a simple message.

William thrust Lily towards his grandmother. "Nanna! Take her!"

He practically dumped her into his grandmother's arms, turning and bolting back towards the perimeter.

"No!" the general yelled.

"William!" he heard his grandmother cry out.

He choked back the bile rising to his throat, seeing the soldier's body now slumped against the window.

It took only moments to reach the ATV. He stopped, bracing himself, his eyes clenched shut.

Nothing. He felt nothing. No pain, no convulsions. The waves of sickness that killed the soldier had no effect on him.

It's how they've engineered us, Nanna had said.

Lily's look explained it all. She hadn't been afraid because she knew she was immune. A carrier of the disease couldn't be killed by it.

As the conduit of it all, neither could he.

Swallowing his revulsion, he slid the body of the soldier, devastated by disease, out of the ATV. Its engine vibrated, stuck in neutral.

The fleeing crowds had stopped, all now positioned behind the first cage they'd passed. Even without being able to see inside, he knew the rats inside were alive. The wave hadn't reached that far.

Of all of them, Lily would be the only one to survive the journey ahead, but he had no intention of taking her where he had to go.

He climbed in, positioning the gear to reverse.

No less than two minutes later, the phone inside the ATV began to ring.

"Send in your drones, General," William said.

"You're going to turn around and get your ass back here—"

"Send them throughout the area looking for a swarm. I'm driving blind here. I'll need directions how to navigate the canyon as well."

He could almost feel the spittle of the general's words through the phone. "You get back here *now*. There is real belief that you used that little girl in your arms to send out that blast so you could get away. And if you think I'm joking, then know right now she has about fifteen high-powered rifles pointed at her."

William winced at the image. "You know I wouldn't have risked my family—"

"I don't know a damn thing but that I have another dead soldier and a furious leader of the free world. You turn around right now or things are going to get worse. If you don't believe me, then perhaps this will convince you."

The phone was jostled, and another voice came onto the line.

"William, it's Aunt Kate."

"Is Nanna OK? Are you and Stella all right? Roxy?"

"We are. William . . . we don't have much time. I've talked to the president. They're considering drone strikes, to just wipe out the entire area. I am trying to convince them to let you try and stop this. But they very much believe you're not acting of your own accord."

William paused. "Convince them otherwise. You know I'm the only one that can control them all. If they wipe me out, then there's no stopping what's happening all over the world."

"They know you can't do anything unless you make physical contact with them. William, there's no way you can do that in time. You can't get to all of them."

"But I can protect the US. Tell them that. Tell them that we could be the last ones standing. Because I'm sure they're listening in to this call right now."

"I'll do my best, William—"

"I don't know if you heard Nanna, but she's figured out how to find the girl. I got lucky in California that the man causing the fires ended up near to me so I could directly track him down. This canyon is too vast and too broken for me to just drive. I need help. I need those drones to search for the swarm. Ask Nanna."

"William, please be careful—"

"I will. Kate, there's one last thing. I know that Dr. . . . that Steven died. But he was carrying something that you all need to see. It explains what I told you to ask about. It explains Blue."

"Mom has it, William. He gave a flash drive to her. She hasn't been able to look at it yet."

"Nanna saw Steven? Before he died?"

"He lasted long enough to give it to her—"

Kate's voice was abruptly cut off. He could hear her arguing, and the general's voice came on the line. "Just know that the final move will be ours, William. You do anything we don't like, it's all over."

"The guns come off the girl, General. Now. That's a deal breaker. We are on the same side here. I promise you, if I do anything that concerns you, take any maneuver you wish. But I won't drive a foot further until I know those guns are down."

"There's a whole lot more at stake for you than just that little girl if you try to pull something over on us."

"Understood. But the guns. Now."

He heard the general cover up the receiver and bark commands.

"It's done. But know that these drones are armed."

"I realize that. And General, I'd pull everyone back as far as you can. I'm not in control of Lily's sister. It could spread rapidly."

"Is that's what's coming? Dammit, son, if you're holding out—"

"I'm not. I just don't want my family or any other innocent people that close to a wave like that again. And frankly . . . it concerns me that it *is* what's coming next. The positioning of those carrying the weapons . . . it isn't effective."

"Effective? What the hell does that mean—?"

"It only affects the borders of the populations. It doesn't impact the majority of people."

The general was quiet for a moment. "I shouldn't disclose this . . . but what does it matter at this point? Our fear is that they are trapping every population. Storms on one border; fires, sickness, violence on the others. They'll be no way to escape; every damn country will be paralyzed, unable to flee. We'll be ripe for the picking, if that's their intention. Alright, the drones are up. I'm putting one of my geographic experts on the line to guide you where you can drive. A final warning, William: You do anything questionable, and we're coming right for you."

"I wouldn't blame you."

A pause, then another man's voice. "Sir, this is Corporal Sava. We've studied the terrain. First thing you'll have to do is backtrack off the plateau."

William followed the orders, driving the ATV for an hour across the bone-dry and at times brutally uneven terrain. The corporal explained that a drone above him would guide him to Interstate 94, which would lead him into the canyon. William clearly understood what that drone carried that could be dropped at any moment.

"We've got nothing," General Wolve practically shouted when he snatched the phone from the corporal. "Everything is dead out there. The girl is useless so far, she only says it looks like a mountain. You said you've seen it, can't you give us anything?"

"I wish I could. What I've seen is replicated a million times out there."

"Dammit. Are you even in the canyon yet?"

"I can see the interstate now. Driving as fast as I can, but it's rough out here."

The corporal got back on the line and directed him down the blessedly smooth pavement, utterly deserted by order of the military. It reminded him of driving on the abandoned Louisiana highway, with no one but a dying old man and a terrified little girl as company.

"William," Wolve's voice shot through the speakerphone. "We think we've found it."

"What do you see?"

"It's isolated. Apart from the others. And we're seeing it now. There's something above it, moving. Your grandmother says it's how the beetles looked above the trees. Stand by, we're figuring out how to get you to it. It's in the middle of nowhere."

William pressed the pedal further, thankful that the gas gauge read nearly full.

"Mr. Chance, you should be passing over the Little Missouri River now," Corporal Sava said. "You'll have to start slowing down. You're going to have to take what looks to be East River Road. There's no exit, you'll have to off-road onto it."

He could feel the proximity of Lily's sister growing stronger as he exited once again onto the jarringly bumpy earth. As he jumbled onto the road, he accelerated.

"You'll stay on this for a while. But get ready to off-road again," Sava said.

Clearly designed to be a sightseeing destination, the road provided stunning views of the sprawling Badlands and the towering mesas beyond. A half hour on the road, the feeling of déjà vu began to creep in.

"Alright, at that next curve, you're going to have to just head northeast. I can tell the terrain isn't smooth."

He steered onto grasslands, thankful for the military vehicle's stabilization as he rumbled through the wildflowers and wheatgrass, nearly colliding more than once with a petrified tree. As he approached a particularly isolated butte, the smell of rotten meat hit, and nearly caused him to gag. A herd of dead buffalo, at least twenty strong, lay surrounded by a swirl of flies. He lifted his shirt over his mouth, trying not to breathe.

He vaguely remembered from his junior high geography class that buttes were typically smaller than mesas and plateaus. But the solitary imperial formation, building from the earth with sheer walls and topped with a staggering array of jutting rock, was massive.

He'd seen it so many times over the past year, but only for that fleeting moment, as the dream took him from the hospital into the stone itself.

It defied logic to think that anything could be alive inside.

His throat clogged, and he wished there was water nearby. Thudding across the earth, he at last came to park before it.

"Ok, proceed with caution." The general was back on the phone. "Take the satellite phone with you. There should be a rifle in the back. Grab it. We're watching. Keep talking to us."

William unplugged the phone and stepped out, opening the back of the Humvee to find carefully mounted rifles. Beside them rested two service pistols. Preferring the idea of concealing a weapon more than approaching obviously armed, he slid one into the back of his jeans.

The heat blasted him as he squinted, looking up at the blinding blue sky above. In the near distance, he could hear the whirling of the drone.

If he didn't know what to look for, it could have been easily missed. It was, after all, further up into the sky than insects should be. Yet the swarm was unmistakable. Whatever diseases killed below somehow did not wipe out the creatures above.

He watched the swarm change and twist. For a moment, he saw it take shape, right before it broke apart again.

"My grandmother was right," William said into the phone. "Tell her she was right. I see it. I see the strand."

"OK. Careful now. Keep talking."

"I'm walking up."

The dream had shown him the crevices left behind by erosion, the redness of the scoria. Around it, nothing grew. Nothing thrived.

How could a child be inside?

"Any sign of the girl? You might have to walk around."

"Nothing yet."

The fissures scattered across the rock appeared to deepen as the outcroppings began casting lengthy shadows as the sun dropped.

"Something's happening," William said.

"What is it? Talk to us."

He took a suddenly step back as he realized he was not seeing a darkening contour, but a widening division splitting the rock before him. It made no sound, no cracking of the earth. Fluidly it parted, not offering a formal passageway, but wide enough to step into.

"It's opening."

"The rock? Opening? OK, back away. We're flying the drone closer—"

The phone suddenly went dead. The buzzing of the drone ceased as well, and seconds later William flinched and whirled around as it came crashing to the earth.

"General?" William said.

The phone's screen was black. He pressed the power button, but it failed to respond.

He looked from the dead device to the rock.

His heart thudded in his chest, thinking of the online material he'd furiously read while flying to the disaster site in an effort to educate himself about the terrain on which he would ultimately travel.

The nation's twenty-sixth president, for whom the park was named, had loved the Badlands, describing the rocks as characters that were fantastically broken. Roosevelt's quote was repeated on most websites.

"... so bizarre in color as to seem hardly properly to belong to this earth."

He reached out for Lily's sister. He could feel her, less than a yard or two away.

All he had to do was touch her. Touch her and it would be over.

He stepped into the opening, the darkness beyond beginning to lighten. He hesitantly moved inwards, reaching out to touch the sides of the rock to steady himself. He swallowed a bit of revulsion when the walls felt clammy, not unlike a sweaty palm.

The opening continued to brighten, revealing walls the color of liquid metal, littered with scores of lights embedded deep in broken lines. It was when he turned back, hoping that the glimpse of daylight from the familiar world would give him strength, that he realized his mistake.

Only blackness, now shining with thousands of tiny lights, was behind him. He imagined Lily running through the lights, somehow free, desperate to escape, emerging to the clean night air outside.

She hadn't understood how she'd escaped, and it was suddenly clear why. She hadn't found a way out. Without her understanding, without her realization, she'd been sent.

To see if she could find him. To bring him in.

"What the hell is happening?"

Kate looked up from the blank screen that had been, just moments ago, displaying the image from the drone above her nephew. General Wolve was practically screaming now.

"Get that drone back up! Or send another that way!"

"Sir," a soldier said, turning around another laptop screen on the table. "They're all down. All the drones we sent in. They just crashed."

"Jesus! Did you try that phone again?"

"It's dead sir. It's like something wiped it all out."

"Dammit!" The general strode away. Kate quickly followed behind.

"General—"

"We've been had, Senator, just in case you're slow on the draw," the general said. "And your nephew has left me no choice."

"My nephew isn't doing this—"

"How the hell do you know?" He momentarily whirled around. "How do we know he isn't being controlled? That all this is *what they intended?*"

"Let's cut to the chase. You know how the president feels. You drop bombs on that mesa, you are wiping out the country's only chance at stopping—"

"General Wolve!"

Two men emerged from the tent, running towards them, representing the general's split command, the soldier dressed in camouflage, the agent in a black suit. The SSA agent held out a laptop.

"Sir, you need to see this."

The agent pointed to the screen, which displayed white pinpoints over a satellite view of the United States. "This is from our weather radar that picked up the light transmissions a year ago. Since the four appeared, there's been nothing since. In the last five minutes, there have been ninety-two. Just as storms literally formed all over the world. At the same time."

"Ninety-two?" The general took the laptop to examine it closer. "My God, the entire middle of the US is covered. Do we have a visual yet?"

"Just outside of Philadelphia International in a wildlife refuge. Federal worker happened to catch it on his phone. He counted more than a thousand."

"A thousand what?" the general demanded.

"People sir. They just appeared in lights from the storm. We're already getting reports from the other agencies. They're returning, sir. All over the world."

"Kate!"

She looked over to see Roxy waving. "Kate, come quick! It's your mom!"

Her stomach lurching, she hurried around the general to see Roxy now standing before her mother, who had remained near the cage, looking out beyond the edge of the barricade.

"What's wrong?"

"It's Mom," Stella said, reaching down to take her mother's hand.

"What's wrong?" Kate asked. "Mom's, what's—"

She stopped, holding her breath. Her mother was as unmoving as a statue, her eyes, usually a sparkling blue, had rolled back into her head, revealing nothing but white.

"My God," Kate said softly. "General!"

She broke away, seeing soldiers running out of the tents where the others had been quarantined. She knew without asking that the girl, the doctor, the immigrant, and Ryan all now stood erect, their eyes a horrible white.

"General!"

"Get them in the air!" General Wolve shouted. "And keep guns on those people! Get ready!"

"General, please listen—"

He shot Kate a furious glance. "Back away, Senator. You won't want to see this."

"General, don't—"

He snatched a phone brought to him by a subordinate.

"When those jets are in position, fire when ready," he directed.

TWENTY-TWO

The fear was old and buried, yet returned with the smell of trapped air, a taste of metal, the curving of the walls with layers of carvings beginning at the ceiling and scrawling across the floor. A hum rose from deep within.

William watched as the passageway lengthened like a spinal cord, adjusting and uncoiling. Though his earliest memories had been stolen, it still felt disturbingly familiar: the lights throbbing within the walls, the greenish tint of the air as if he were underwater, his lungs absent of air and unable to reach the surface.

He thought of Nanna, a little girl at five years old. Of Jane. Of Lily and her sister. Of Ryan and Juan and all of them, ripped from their lives and forced down murky throats into whatever waited within the dark.

He wished for the immigrant's weapon, to see it all burn.

Find the girl and get her out.

When it at last stopped reshaping itself, he crept down the passage, his right hand close to his hip to quickly reach for the pistol. An opaque light shone from beyond, blurred by the ever-present fog. His entire body clenched as he passed through the clearing mists.

He was wrong to assume that whatever had landed here had somehow taken refuge inside the ancient rock formation in order to hide itself. His inability to determine how high the ceiling rose, to comprehend the vastness of the space, proved that it had adapted over time, shedding its original skin, replacing it with rock and dust and clay, existing here longer than the time it took for the waters to erode the canyon outside.

The cavernous walls soared like tidal waves, their deep hollows and rising mounds frozen just before impact. The slender knolls appeared to breathe, rising and falling, reaching into the darkness above where they merged together at a zenith, reaching down in a thick, pulsating appendage towards the machine below.

It too was riddled with the harsh, grotesque inscriptions that lined the walls of the artery that brought him here. Dim, throbbing lights infected every inch of its sprawling girth. It took up nearly the entire center of the chamber, not with defined and sharp edges, but organically; a tumor from which the infection grew.

In its core was the girl.

He could feel her more than he could see her, as the curved pod she lay within was coated in a thick film.

Reaching her would mean crossing a floor pockmarked with hollows and peaks, like a churning sea suddenly frozen. Ridges, like raised veins, scrawled across the surface, giving the only semblance of a passage to her.

As he began to cross, he dared, at last, to open the channel to her mind.

Ava, I'm here. My name is William. I'm coming.

Don't slip. Don't think about what's within those deep crevices. Find a way to break her free. Just one touch—

No.

He almost stopped, he was so surprised by her response.

Your sister, Lily, brought me. To find you.

He could feel her tremble, see the outside of her form flinch within the encasement.

Run.

Ava—

Run!

The chattering of a thousand swarming rattlesnakes preceded it, slowing and stretching. It rose from behind her: a mud-stained shell of a snapping turtle swollen to the size of a monolith dome. Skin beneath parted to reveal shapes narrowed and long like drowned canoes at the bottom of a polluted river. A maw opened slightly beneath, its saliva thick as dripping tar.

The air around it moved in sways of thrashing locks, thousands of coils born from beneath the shell and lifting like a leviathan free from the water. While most of the tendrils were free to flail, other, larger cords stretched out to sink into the ground and walls. It was everything beneath them, above them; the very air now in their lungs.

The choking fear at seeing its ascension was blasted away by the euphoria.

It was almost agonizing in its return, that barely remembered sensation from the dark, terrifying night in the hospital, his grandmother awkwardly rushing him down a hallway. She'd ripped him from the blissful consciousness. He'd almost protested, until he saw the creature emitting the feeling, and whatever joy he felt dissolved into wretched despair.

The feeling had happened more than once that night: it came again from the scattering, horrible things in the hospital waiting room, and then finally from the multicolored lights from the ships in the sky that promised exultation if he just stepped out of the truck and walked into the beams of light.

The light.

The light in the trees. He remembered. At last, he remembered.

Forget Brian and Greg and their stupid game. Jerks. They can have their stupid tent; it means they don't see what I see. What was it, that far into Grandpa Tom's woods? I'll get there first before they even notice it. They'll feel bad for not letting me in.

I hope Mom doesn't get mad about my muddy socks. Everything's so wet from the rain, but I've gotta see it. That light is so bright!

I hear Brian, he's calling my name. I know it's him. I can always tell the difference between him and Greg running in the house. Brian always dragged his feet more. Well, I can run too, Brian. I'm faster than you. I beat you.

It almost hurts to look up at it, but it feels so good. Like the sun. It's like I can fly! I am flying! Look, Brian, I'm above the trees! Can you see me?

The light's gone. I'm cold. I'm in the dark, I'm somewhere else. I can't see anything! Brian! Brian! Something's coming. I want to go back. Brian, something's coming—

William staggered back, and the ecstasy struck him again. All his pleasure sensors were firing at once, resulting in a painful erection. He was protected and loved and cared for. All he had to do was step into the machine, where more joy awaited.

He walked without fear of slipping now, even though the path was barely a foot wide. He was safe and secure.

His mind, however, was screaming.

It has you! It has you! Get to to the girl!

But the drenching comfort showed there was nothing to fear, certainly not in the machine.

It's not a machine! It's part of it! Flesh and metal! Blood vessels and lights and straining membranes inserting into cords. God, something's rising—

It emerged like a pocket of air bubbling up from a putrid swamp. As he reached it, a pod surfaced, directly beside the one containing the girl. The grime covering it began to peel back; it was large enough to step inside.

No! No! Don't go in! Get to her—

He stepped in, and a rush of gas blew across his face. As he lay down on the spongy interior, the gap from which he entered had already sealed, the film on its surface thin enough to see the chamber beyond.

Fight! Break out! It has you!

Even when the hundreds of penetrations began to sink into his skin, he did not flinch. Somehow, there was no pain. His hair rustled across his forehead as more gas sprayed at his face, and the extreme pleasure faded to a restful calmness. The pod trembled, and he could feel it rising, detaching.

It slowly rose, and with it much of the thick moisture that coated the pod began to slide away. He watched as the floor of the chamber faded away and a tendril, like a curving stalk of a bindweed, lifted the pod into the air, slowly turning. The walls were now a mixture of deep shadows and brilliant lights, all fully awakened.

As the pod completely shifted, he could see the girl far beneath him in the shadow of the rising head of the creature. A single neck, as thick as a subway train, supported the feelers that erupted from its maw and the waves of tentacles flailing from beneath its scaled dome. Several of the black coils reached for him, inserting into the sides of the pod.

He could hear the puncturing of the walls around him, and the smell of it, of rock and spoiled water, reached his senses just as the thin outshoots of the pod sank in and his skin began to stiffen. He gasped at the infusion jolting into his bloodstream, exchanging with his own bodily fluids.

It was within him now, just as he was within it.

And he understood. It needed him to understand, to complete its task. It needed more than a connection; it needed a complete fusion.

His eyes closed, and opened to stars.

Millions of them, flying past as the scientist traveled the vast deep. Inside its cocoon, carrying memories of smoke and death, of battles fought in skies among ships the sizes of cities. Of wars that nearly obliterated not only its own kind, but that of the civilizations that refused to surrender to them. Of centuries of hatred between races that showed no sign of dissipating.

To not only survive, but ultimately conquer, a new form of warfare was necessary.

The first scouts had found it; a planet of blue and white, its only companion a solitary moon. So it came to see for itself, traveling across the stars to finally pass through the atmosphere and into air and water. Abundant, overwhelming life. From above, the scientist observed what the others had reported: a race of people with inferior yet remarkable intelligence and, vastly more importantly, containing a complex origination system.

The world was covered in different landscapes and temperatures, proving an ideal location to test how their weaponry would work in various conditions.

It chose a great barren canyon, its craft obliterating a once-towering mesa and landing in its sudden absence, altering itself it take its form, down to the very grains of clay and stone. Once completed, the scientist sent forth a telepathic message to the others: *Bring them to me.*

Hiding behind the storms that were necessary to blanket their arrival, the testing began almost immediately, conducted on the very first of mankind to be taken. More people, then; samplings, dissection. At last, a single, successful manipulation, with extraordinary results: The very building blocks that gave them existence, the strands of molecules and chromosomes, if adjusted and twisted, affected the makeup of the very air around them.

The experimentation continued. Few survived. But those who did, who had been changed themselves, each commanded a power: fire, storms, death, and disease.

The testing began, small, slow. The specimens released into varying locations. From within the canyon, it watched their environments, seeing how each was affected by their return. Diseases spiked. Storms leveled homes. Murders increased. Even the food, for many, became deadly to eat.

And the scientist was pleased.

No longer would it be necessary to send their kind into battle, to eviscerate valuable natural resources in order to wage war. Once perfected, the very populations they wished to remove would be taken, altered, returned, and activated.

In the end, all their enemies would ultimately kill their own kind.

But almost immediately, the scientist discovered the fatal flaw. The abducted, when their weapons were activated, could not withstand it. Their fragile brains faltered, leaving them incapacitated. And when the time came to see how far the specimens had traveled, the scientist made an astounding and enraging discovery: Even their pathetic governments had realized the danger they posed and corralled them, limiting the scope of the sampling.

Furious now, the scientist ordered all of them removed, even the one— the boy—who it intended to thrust them into the next phase of testing. None of its kind knew what it had done, how far it had gone, to complete the task.

Take them away, the scientist had ordered. *They may still be of use.*

It was much later when the scouts—the scurrying, smaller of its kind that quaked in his presence—alerted the scientist that a few of the abducted were not in their ships. Including the boy named William.

Enraged, the scientist retreated into its work, knowing full well that the boy was alive. Only it, and it alone, could know this.

Longer experiments, more extensive manipulations, taking year after year, examining the strands of DNA that they had taken from the boy himself. The conduit was too valuable to abandon.

Then the scientist unraveled its mistake, the fatal miscalculation born of pride and arrogance. It ordered the scouts to begin the reaping once again.

The boy would be grown now.

This time, nothing would be left to chance. No great swaths of people. Only four of each population, on each border of the population. All of them with the correct alterations, tied to the boy.

It pained the scientist to realize what must be done, as distasteful as it was. It was now time to see if its theory would, in fact, prove to be the missing link.

The scientist itself would have to be altered. Manipulating its own genetics, it intertwined the boy's DNA into its own.

It would be shunned amongst its own kind if any were to learn. But when the work was done, the connection was complete. Even the boy's dreams belonged to it now.

Each of the newly taken was brought to him. Their manipulations had been improved as well, a sliver of the boy's genes added to each.

When the four were in place, on the corners of the populations, it reached out for him in the darkness of his mind. And in turn, the boy had found the others.

When the scientist willed the activation, the boy, in turn, willed it. The newly abducted not only survived but thrived.

It was careful with the boy's mind, as pushing him too far, too fast, threatened to ruin him. Already, he could feel how he was struggling, at times, with the inability to breathe. In time, it learned how to push him to the others around the world. And when all the others were linked, the time had come to bring the boy in.

There was just one glaring problem: Despite their genetic and tele-pathic links, the scientist could not control him while he was awake. Influ-ence, yes. Move him to a central location amongst the four to enrich their connection. But the boy would always wake from the dreams untouchable, as of late, for days on end.

It was why the girl had to be released. To see if, in fact, she could lead him back. If the emotional attachment to her sibling would serve as a beacon.

Unexpectedly, the boy began to usurp the scientist's control. Reach out to others on his own accord. And most troubling of all: The boy's physical touch of anyone that shared his DNA enabled him to disarm their weapons as well.

A defiance that could no longer be allowed.

"They're in range, General!"

"Do not hesitate!" General Wolve shouted. "Fire at that mesa with everything you've got—"

"General, please!" Kate grabbed his arm. "William could be our only chance—"

"Realize this," he said, pulling her in closely. "We're all dead. Do you understand that? If we don't do that, your mother, the others, will kill us all. All those people taken all over the world into those ships fifteen years ago, *they're returned*. And they've been placed all over the world, in all the gaps between. This is what they intended. Unless we take him out."

Kate looked helplessly at the screen where a feed of the mesa was coming in from a satellite. From its vantage point, she could even see the F-15 fighter jets emerging from every direction.

"Fire!" the general bellowed.

They watched the jets approach, knowing they carried Tomahawks.

Oh, William.

She gasped as the planes suddenly exploded, all at the same moment.

"What the hell is that?" the general screamed. "What just happened? What fired on them?"

"Sir, it doesn't look like anything did," the soldier at a computer stammered. "It looks like they just smashed into something."

"There's nothing to hit, only fucking air!"

"Unless when those drones went down, when William's phone died, something went up that we can't see," Kate said. "Something those pilots couldn't see either."

The image on the screen just showed the undisturbed mesa, with the burning remains of the wreckage lying on the edge of an imperceptible barrier.

The boy felt the intrusions into his body. There was a dullness, a numbness. When a sudden infusion ripped into his body, there was at last pain, his eyes burning in the light.

He didn't remember his name. Only that it considered him a boy. And it was both angry and pleased with him.

He saw them. All of them, all of their faces at once. Four in every large population, in smoke, in storms, in death and disease. But now there were hundreds more, in clusters, standing together. Who were they? Why were their eyes that milky white? Who was the beautiful woman with brunette hair? The girl with black skin? The old woman with curls of white?

He knew that, just like him, they had no thoughts, no memories, no concerns. Blissful, unmoving. Waiting.

For him.

It guided him. Beyond their minds. Into the fabric of their bodies, their veins, their cells. Deeper still, to the foundation of their existence.

It was there that the irregularities of the molecules were apparent, as if each of the strands of curving phosphates had been infected. While the purity, the original designs of the DNA strands, were still intact, they had been corrupted, twisted. The irregularities were visible, like a plague that was still not yet complete.

A flicker of memory flashed, of what he had done with the four in igniting the weapons within them. He understood it now; the very essence of how he, alone, could command them all. He was the missing part of the distortion.

With his intrusion, he would complete the disjointed nucleotides, just barely, enough to awaken what had been placed within them all.

All it took was a blink, and it would be done.

Who was the woman? Who was that girl? The old woman, who was she? Why did it pain him to see her most of all?

He was inside her. She felt familiar somehow. He was somehow not just within her, but part of her. Where she began, he ended. What originated in her, continued to him. Not a mother. A grandmother.

"Nanna," he whispered.

Nanna, Lily, Ryan, Juan. And Jane. Beautiful Jane, weary from passing through the storm in the government cells beneath the earth. Climbing the stairs to escape, wet and cold. William had reached her, and she responded in anger.

"This is not me. This is not me. I want it out of me. I want out," Jane had said.

He remembered what he came here to do.

William felt the monster's approval as he took control of all the DNA strains in all the abducted. Just a slight adjustment, and the activation would occur.

Instead, he began to break.

Beginning with the molecules, then the chromosomes, smashing the pervasive alterations. In doing so, he sensed how his own DNA had been placed inside the infected strands, and obliterated it.

To the furthest edges of the world he reached, finding the four in each population. From one nation to another; a flash of light sprinting around the globe. The relief from all those who had been taken washed over him as he then began to exit their bodies, their original DNA strands almost gleaming in response.

But before he could completely break free of them, the rage from the creature blasted him like a furnace, so hot it felt as if he were on fire. He felt the infusion again, this time a hundred times stronger.

Everything faded. He was a breath away from becoming a husk of himself; a mindless tool to once again reach into the abducted and twist the very fabric of their being to reignite their weapons.

His hand, however, had already reached behind him and pulled out the gun.

There should be five bullets. All he needed was one.

"You're free, Jane," he whispered.

He raised the gun to his own head, and fired.

SEVEN DAYS LATER

TWENTY-THREE

The two vans pulled up to the small house deep in the palmetto trees.

"Are you sure this is it?" Stella asked, stepping out.

"It's the address," Kate responded. "Mom, are you sure—"

Lynn was already out of the van, walking towards the house.

"Is this it?" Anne called out. Chris had hurried around to open her door.

"My God, it's hot here," Brian commented, stepping out and shading his eyes.

"Son, your seventy-nine-year-old grandmother seems to be doing quite fine in this heat. Greg, help her," Chris motioned.

"Hold up, Nanna!" Greg said, the last to step out of the van.

Lynn was already at the stairs, climbing.

The door opened, and a man with a shaved head walked out. He extended his hand to Lynn. "Hello, Mrs. Roseworth. My name is SJ Rudd. But everybody calls me Rudd."

"It is nice to meet you," Lynn said. "Please tell me . . ."

"I think it's probably best that the rest of you wait outside. She really only needs one visitor at a time," Rudd said.

"Mom?" Kate asked, her two sisters coming to stand beside her. "Are you OK?"

Lynn nodded quickly.

"We'll be right outside," Stella said.

Rudd opened the door. The house was a typical bungalow, hidden, just as described, in the Florida Everglades. A bachelor pad, mostly. Except for the quilts thrown on the recliner and several other chairs.

"She gets cold," Rudd said. "Even in Florida."

Lynn stopped. "Does she still . . . remember?"

"Oh, she remembers all right. And even if she didn't, all she'd had to do is look at you. You'll see, the resemblance is pretty uncanny."

"Where is she?" Lynn's voice was thin.

"Right through here." Rudd walked down the hall to a pair of French doors. He knocked softly on the glass. "Miss Blue?"

He opened the door, and the woman inside turned her wheelchair.

Lynn raised her hands to cover her mouth.

"My girl," Blue said softly.

Lynn walked across the tile floor, her eyes swimming. She then rushed over, leaning down to embrace the old woman gently.

"I won't break. I've waited my whole life for this," Blue said. "Did you know it rained last night? A bad storm, my girl. Lightning. Lightning took you from me. And you see? It brought you back."

Lynn sobbed. Rudd scrambled to bring over a chair, but Lynn was already on her knees.

"Mama. You're really here."

"I always have been," Blue said, petting her hair. "He did it, in the end. Steven. That sweet man. He brought you to me."

Lynn uncurled her hand, a flash drive in her palm.

"Did you bring them, Lynn? Your daughters? Your grandsons? My family?"

Lynn nodded, wiping her eyes. "They can't believe it. I can hardly believe it."

"I just . . . I just wish William was here," Blue said, her voice cracking, her hand caressing Lynn's cheek.

"Yes," Lynn said, kissing her hand. "I wish he were here too."

"We're free, you know. It's over. He did that for you. For all of us."

Lynn stood, holding tight to her mother's hand. The window was without wooden grilles, allowing the morning sun to shine through, absent of shadow.

EPILOGUE

The palm trees towered overhead against a sky bleached with thinning clouds, shifting islands in blue. A whiff of the ocean snuck through the haze of the smog, blowing across Wilshire Boulevard, prompting Quincy to open the sunroof and inhale.

"Nice day to begin your global empire, girls," he said, looking in the rearview mirror.

They were such exact images of each other, nearly impossible to tell them apart. He insisted every day that Lily wear red hair ties, and Ava blue. He suspected, occasionally, they switched them and went the entire day just giggling as they responded to each other's names.

But the school insisted that there be no variation for any of the students, so they both wore the plaid headbands, their hair pulled back tight. Have to make sure everyone is on the same playing field, the admissions director had said.

So you won't know which kid's dad owns Google and which kid's mom is the CEO of Warner Brothers? Quincy had asked.

He knew they had concerns about his girls. There were no official transcripts, just the test results from the tutors. *The best in LA,* he mentioned more than once. Yes, there was no medical history, no recommendations from anyone other than their therapists and doctors, and of course the tutors, who said they were brilliant despite their years of no education.

They were small, too. About the height of third graders, even though they were entering fifth. The admissions director had even inquired if they would feel out of place.

"Do you want the twenty million dollar new technology center or what?" he'd responded.

Yes, Mr. Martin. Thank you. Here's your admission letters. Is there anything else we should know? What their life was like before the adoption?

Oh, there's plenty to know, Quincy had thought. It's been one heck of a three years.

The private investigator he'd hired had finally tracked down that the girls' mother was a crack addict and their father was in prison. They'd lived for a time with their aunt, who slept during the day and operated a fairly successful cocaine operation at night. They lived in a trailer on the outskirts of Medora, North Dakota. The girls had never gone to school and resided in the drug community where others kids watched TV all day and scrounged for food. When the girls had just disappeared one night while playing outside, the aunt hadn't even contacted police.

No. Nothing much to say about it, Quincy had answered.

"I know! 'Immigrant Song'!" he said, scrolling through his phone. "It's our fight song!"

Just as Led Zeppelin began to howl the Viking anthem, Lily turned from the window. "I don't want to do this, Quincy. We want to stay at home."

Ava had just nodded.

"It's time, you Goddesses of the Air. Mrs. Ratchett and Mr. Temple say you need to be more socialized. As much as I enjoy our little compound, the world awaits. Plus, who's going to take over my companies if you don't get that PhD from Harvard?"

"It's fifth grade, Quincy," Lily mumbled.

"We all start somewhere. And there, my sweets, is where you begin."

The tops of the whitewashed buildings of Lankard Academy could be seen above the palm trees. A sweeping fence circled the vast campus, rising from perfectly manicured grass. Mercedes, Teslas, and Range Rovers formed a two-lane parade, jockeying to pull in to the entrance.

In the Lexus convertible beside them, a blond woman in a tennis visor shouted, despite the Bluetooth in her ear. In the back seat, three blond girls, all wearing the same uniform as Ava and Lily, stared into their iPhones.

"I swear to God, Debbie, I'm going to be late," the woman yelled. "This school is going to have to hire traffic control. Just reserve court six. And listen, I'm just going to say, for the record, I don't buy it. Not for a single second."

Rolling his eyes, Quincy began to close up the sunroof, until the woman laughed irritatingly loud. "I mean, aliens? Come on. I mean, I have a few cleaning the pool today, don't get me wrong!"

Quincy didn't have to crane to hear her, but he did anyway. "I mean, yes, like we've talked about, it's super weird all those missing people came back. But they weren't taken by aliens, I don't care what Marsha says or what the *Washington Post* reports. It's just mainstream media trying to get clicks. It's just crap."

He couldn't make out what the other trophy wife was saying, but Mrs. Blonde shook her head, her ponytail waving wildly. "And what's so strange about wildfires? Although it did *totally* interrupt Mike and my wine country anniversary. So what if people were sick and fighting everywhere? It happens. It's the world. I hate it for those people who died, but it happens."

Quincy rolled down his window. "Hey lady," he yelled.

She looked over, and he winked. "It's all real."

He punched the gas and swerved in front of her. She honked her horn twice.

"I'll probably have homeroom with one of those girls," Lily said. "We aren't like these rich kids."

"No, you're richer. At least I'm richer, and so by default, you're richer. And like we talked about, if anyone questions it, just tell your last name. It's MARTIN. As in QUINCY MARTIN."

Lily rolled her eyes. She'd adopted so many of his mannerisms.

I wish I could keep you home. Cover you in Lilly Pulitzer clothes. Find a way to fill your room with more toys, if that were possible. Be there every second some snobby girl asks who your parents really are. Or more importantly, be a voice for Ava when she refuses to talk.

It hadn't been easy. None of it had. It's why they lived in almost constant isolation that first year. Daily sessions with therapists who had signed nondisclosure agreements and were paid more in a week than they normally made in a month. Night terrors, sobbing, fear of the dark, refusal to speak. And that was just Ava.

Lily had been forced to become her sister's mouthpiece, grappling daily with the guilt she felt. She'd had to be coaxed to stop doing everything for her sister.

Quincy had given them everything. Ice cream for breakfast. Private trips to Hawaiian islands. He tried to show them that there was good in the world, even though he had a hard time seeing it himself.

He'd found it in them.

He knew they were his the moment that Ava had woken screaming again, about six months into their stay. He'd rushed into her room, knowing she refused to be touched by anyone except for Lily. When he'd sat on the edge of the bed and she'd reached out for him, he vowed to never let go.

It was that night when she'd explained what she'd seen in those final moments inside the mountain. How the man from her dreams, the one who brought her the comfort of knowing she wasn't alone in the never-ending nightmare, stood in the same kind of cage that had trapped her for so long.

How, in just one moment, she felt different. Something in her had changed. And the man from the dreams had done it. The burden she'd carried, the dreams of the diseases, were gone. It was over.

She remembered pressing her hands against the filmy substance that ensnared her as she watched the man pull a gun out and point it to his head—

"Quincy, you're holding up traffic," Lily said.

"Oops, sorry. Hey, where's the valet?" He smiled at her.

They pulled up in front of the school, amid a sea of children in perfectly coiffed ponytails and dry-cleaned uniforms. A woman in a drab suit and sensible shoes walked briskly up to his Mercedes.

"No need to get out, sir. Just let them out, and the line won't stall—"

Quincy began to open the doors for the girls. "That," he said, pointing to the building under construction on the corner of campus, "means everyone else can just move around me." A sizeable sign stood in front reading, "The Quincy Martin Center for Technology."

"Oh." The woman forced a smile. "Of course."

"Quincy," Lily chastised. "Don't make a scene."

"Men open doors for ladies." He reached down to give her bear hug.

"Ladies don't need men to open anything for them," she said, returning the hug.

"I do adore you, Lily girl," he said, with a final kiss to her forehead.

Then he followed her around to open Ava's door.

"And you, pretty face, are going to knock it out of the park," he said, sliding Ava's backpack over her shoulder. He leaned in and whispered, "I stuck your phone in the side pocket. You need me, I'll be a hologram for you in a second."

"Do you promise, Quincy?" she asked.

He knew she wasn't talking about the phone.

Ava had made the same request almost every day since the night she explained how it ended. How she watched the monster move in so close to William that she feared it would tear him apart in those horrible jaws. Even at nine years old, she'd understood why William held the gun to his head. If he were dead, there would be no way to ever reignite them all.

But then William had turned the gun from where he held it against his temple and began to fire at the monster, right into its eye.

She'd been with it for so long, she'd become part of it too. The hundreds of veins that had so long ago lodged themselves into her skin meant it was a part of her. She knew it was completely armored, nothing could penetrate it. But the eyes, those large slashes of darkness, were as vulnerable and jelly-like as her own.

William had fired over and over into them, and she felt the pain in the monster's head. It screamed again, this time in confusion and disbelief. By the time William had run out of bullets, it could no longer see, but was still very much alive.

And that's when she felt him, reach down to her and ignite the weapon within her. But this time, instead of being directed out into the world around her, it was focused entirely on the monster itself.

She felt the others too, from the dreams, including her sister. The tendrils of the creature burst into flames. Winds suddenly rushed around them, fanning the fire that now burned its horrid face and neck. She felt the diseases from Lily join the ones she sent as well, turning the skin from oily black to a fading gray.

The lights around her had gone out. The tentacle holding William's pod dropped as the monster fell, its horrible face smashing against the floor, thrashing for a moment before it lay in silence.

Then, she felt no connection to the others. The disease, so much a part of her that she could taste it, was gone. She felt lighter.

She forced her way through the filmy prison, stepping out to see the other pod had crashed. A single hand reached out from it, and a red-haired man stumbled free.

"You know the deal," Quincy said, his hands on her shoulders. "You go to school. You get good grades and you talk and you show everybody what you're made of, and I promise. We'll go see William again."

Lynn gripped the armrests of the seat as the plane landed. Even in her plush surroundings, she felt her nerves jitter as the wheels of the jet touched the surface of the rural airport. She looked out the window at the holy-wood trees rushing past them, thrilling for a moment that she was seeing them for the first time after reading about them all her life. The slow-growing trees provided the hardest wood in the world, which explained why the species was endangered. Her daddy had told her about them, mar-veling in their existence. He hadn't lived to see them, though.

She certainly thought she never would either.

"I finally get that Caribbean vacation."

She looked from the window to the Roxy. "I can barely stand it."

"I do wish, however, we were staying at a resort. One of the Sandals places, where the couples do three-legged races in the commercials. I'd like to wear my bikini and stun them all."

"You're a mess."

"It's about time we got here."

That was true, Lynn thought, as the jet came to a stop. *I've counted the days, the hours even, to come here.*

They walked down the aisle of the private jet and waited as the flight crew prepared the stairs.

"I hope you enjoyed your flight, Mrs. Roseworth," said the pretty flight attendant. Like all the staff, she wore a green hologram of a Q on her lapel.

"I certainly did. Thank you. This is incredibly nice."

"It is Mr. Martin's favorite jet, after all," the woman said. "And we've come to enjoy making this trip. Looks like we're ready for you."

They walked out the door and down the stairs. The sunlight was al-most blinding, the air tasting as beautiful as the crystal blue sky above them. It took her a moment to adjust to the brightness, to see the woman standing before the Jeep.

She waved, her long brown hair pulled back in a ponytail. Lynn and Roxy returned the gesture as she hurried across the dirt towards them.

Jane hesitated. "Is it OK to hug someone you only met once, inside a helicopter?"

"You are my family," Lynn said, bringing the woman into her arms.

As Jane stepped back, she wiped tears from her eyes.

"And I may not be blood, but I'm part of the circus," Roxy said.

"I hear you're the star attraction," Jane said, hugging her as well. "William says he was raised by two brilliant grandmothers. He can't wait to see you."

"I can hardly wait," Lynn responded.

As the flight attendants went to pick up their bags, Jane motioned to the ragged Jeep. "You'll have to forgive your transportation. You know your grandson."

"It's his preferred mode of transportation," Lynn said. "His grandpa was the same way."

"And let me just say," Jane said, taking her hand and leading her to the passenger side. "I'm so sorry that it's had to be this long before you could come. William has just hated it."

A familiar sting of anger flared. *I've hated it too.*

Hated that she'd had no contact with William in the past three, long years. She thought of him every day, and longed to see him for a million reasons. She wanted to hold him, run her hands through that thick, unruly red hair. See those eyes, the brilliant color of blue.

Blue.

"I know it's impossible for your mother to make the trip," Jane said, hurrying over to help Roxy inside.

"Her health isn't great. But she's made the transition to Tennessee really well. Anne is staying with her while we're here."

Jane settled into the driver's seat. "It's remarkable, isn't it? That she's even still alive. I would like to meet her. But I suppose that will probably never happen."

No. It hurts to realize it, but no.

It had all happened so quickly that day. She'd come out of the strange trance to find herself feeling light, as if a burden the size of a grand piano had been lifted off her shoulders. Stella, Roxy, and Kate had surrounded her, repeatedly asking if she was OK. They told her that her eyes had rolled back in her head and she hadn't moved. She'd replied she was fine, and asked about William.

They didn't know. Then came the excited cries from the tents nearby.

Not long after, the helicopters started taking off, carrying the others, still under heavy guard despite the overwhelming proof pouring in across the globe: The disasters had stopped, almost immediately, all over the world.

Lynn had insisted that she remain, but the general was not having it. The danger was still too real. Roxy actually sat herself on the ground, stating that she would not move her considerable behind until she knew William was safe.

After an hour, the general had stridden over with his phone, telling them all to gather around. "Our drones can go in now," he said, pointing to the screen.

His finger extended to the video of a red-haired man walking towards the Jeep. Holding his hand was a little girl who looked remarkably like the one who'd been rushed away with Quincy.

With that, the general summoned the soldiers to have the women taken to a helicopter. "I don't have time to deal with you," he said, practically shoving them all inside. "What our crews found inside that rock forma-tion . . . Not to mention that thousands of people around the world have suddenly returned."

For two days, Lynn and Roxy were kept in quarantine at the nearby military base. They had wisely kept Roxy with Lynn rather than face her wrath. All the women could do was watch television, news reports of how the government had swept in to gather the returned in order to study them and make sure they posed no threat, and to handle the growing throngs of family and loved ones who rushed the hastily arranged confinement cen-ters, to see if they could locate their missing.

When Kate finally arrived, with a furious Stella in tow, it was with news that they could leave. When asked where William was, Kate's face had just turned sad, handing her a piece of paper.

"He doesn't want us to know," she said.

There was no question it was his handwriting.

You're together, and that's what matters. Aunt Kate said that Steven gave you a flash drive. I'm sorry you have to find out this way, but you have to read it. And then find a man by the name of Rudd in Florida. Ask the Researchers.

Give me some time. I love you. Nanna. You were right. You were right all along.

- William

So, of course, she had read what was contained in the files. The next day, after she conferred with a man named SJ Rudd, her entire family had arrived in Florida to make the discovery that had stunned them to their very core.

Still, in all her joy, William was gone.

Every month or so, they would get a message delivered to them by a government official. Always in William's handwriting, stating that he was somewhere far away, and had to make sure he wasn't a danger—

"Are we ready?" Jane asked, buckling her seatbelt.

"Bags are all in," Roxy said, sliding in. "I hope my back doesn't give out riding in this thing."

Quincy had warned her about the conditions of where William and Jane were living, when he'd first broken the news to her over the phone. "Me and the girls went to see William, Lynn. Now, don't be mad. William's just testing the waters, to see what would happen if he was around more of the others, besides Jane. Everything was fine. And when he's up for more visitors, you are going to take my plane. No questions asked. But I'll warn you, it's remote. Seriously remote."

Lynn had demanded to go immediately, but Quincy said he was sworn to secrecy. William had not reached out. Then, six months later, Quincy Martin himself had come, with those darling girls in tow, and asked Lynn to summon her entire family.

"I suppose I should say congratulations, first," Quincy had said, holding out a picture of a baby with a fuzz of red hair. "You're a great-grandmother, Mrs. Roseworth. William and Jane had a son."

He'd then turned to the woman in the wheelchair. "And that means you, Miss Blue—"

"It's Freda, Mr. Martin. It's what your great-grandfather called me."

"Means you're super, super old."

They'd been outraged and thrilled all at once. William's father and brothers had practically flipped the table, they were so angry that no one knew. Quincy had just held up his hands. "William knew you'd all be mad. But he's still not convinced he isn't a threat. Even though the world has stopped being a crap show for a while now. But my plane is ready for you, Mr. and Mrs. Chance, and your sons. But for now, that's all William wants as visitors."

Lynn had been heartbroken, confiding in Quincy that she felt that William blamed her somehow. But the big man had only taken her hands in his own. "Don't you see it, Lynn? He's afraid. He's afraid that somehow, he'll awaken whatever's in you."

"But it's not there anymore," she'd said. "He changed us. Changed us all back to what we were. It's gone."

Anne and Chris had returned with the boys two weeks later. Lynn tried to show a brave face. "The baby is so beautiful. But he's not coming back, Mom. He said he never will."

A year later, Quincy had sent his plane with a simple message for her: "William wants his grandmother to meet his son."

So Lynn and Roxy had boarded Quincy's luxury plane and headed for, of all places, the eastern Caribbean. He warned her again that this was no tropical paradise.

She'd understood William's reasoning: He wanted a place so remote that no one, especially the world's press, desperate to understand the return of the missing and the disasters, could ever find him. Or his new family.

Lynn looked at the woman driving the Jeep. "You work as a doctor here? Who takes care of the baby?"

She gave Lynn an amused smile. "William does, of course. *It takes a village* is a way of life here. You'll see."

They drove on rough dirt roads, the branches of trees sometimes smacking the sides of the Jeep. The sight of butterflies weaving among the leaves helped to calm Lynn's racing heart.

"There are paved roads that lead to the resorts, and I'm sorry we can't take them," Jane yelled.

"Where do you live?" Roxy asked from the back seat.

"We're not far now," she said, pulling onto an even rougher road, blanketed by shadows. Navigating the potholes, apologizing profusely to Lynn for the bumping, she took another turn and stopped.

William had forbidden his father and brothers from taking pictures, but they'd described the home. A shack, Brian had complained.

But it wasn't. In fact, Lynn could tell it was sturdy. William had always taken to manual labor.

"I'll admit, it's not much to look at," Jane said, sliding out.

It seemed to be made of reclaimed wood, with a dark blue paint. "It can be challenging at times, getting around. But the resorts and hotels need doctors all the time, so they often just bring a boat for me," Jane said.

She helped Lynn step out of the Jeep. "I understood most of your work is with the indigenous people?"

"It is. It took us awhile to earn their trust. But after William helped re-build so many of their homes, they started allowing me to help treat what-ever ailments would arise. They built most of this home. And when Will is working on homes and I'm at the resorts, they come here to watch the baby."

Lynn forced a smile, trying to swallow her jealousy of other people car-ing for the great-grandson she'd never met.

"You'll meet them, Lynn, we want you to meet them all . . . well, look who's up."

The screen on the front door opened. William stepped through, carry-ing a large toddler with a shock of red hair.

Lynn couldn't stop the tears. Jane reached out and touched her arm, Roxy resting her hand on the small of her back as William walked off the porch.

"Nanna, Roxy," he said, lifting the boy a bit higher. "I want you to meet Tommy Christopher Chance."

Lynn covered her mouth; the boy smiled. It was like looking at William at one year old. She stepped forward and embraced them both, kissing the boy's face and then William's.

"I have missed you so much," William said.

"He looks so much like your mother," Lynn said, wiping her eyes.

"I think he looks just like you," William said.

"Let's go inside, have some lunch," Jane said. "Will, let your grand-mother carry Tommy."

Lynn held her breath, taking the boy. She waited for tears, maybe a cry of unfamiliarity. But he just looked at her with interest and smiled.

After the dishes were washed, and Jane and Roxy were deep in a conversa-tion about how to survive without pizza, William asked Lynn to take a walk. It was time for Tommy's nap, but he was all laughter and showing off in full force. So William had scooped him up, slathered him with sunscreen and bug spray.

They'd taken a trail from the house to the beach, which opened up to a breathtaking sight of white sand and stunning hues of green and blue. "I know it looks like paradise, but it wasn't at first. I pretty much expected Jane to leave every day for about six months. But you'd be surprised at how quickly you get to know someone when there's no TV, no internet, and no phones. And the pregnancy was *not* planned."

"She seems really wonderful. But surely her family is upset about this. . . ."

He took a deep breath. "Don't be angry, but they've been here twice now. And they're not happy. But her parents understand as much as they can. Even with everything that's public now, it's hard to believe that your daughter was caught up in it."

"It's been hard for a lot of people. My phone doesn't stop ringing. All those families reunited. And new families formed. You know the adoption was finalized."

William smiled. "To think of Aunt Kate with a seventeen-year-old son. I guess she really took a liking to Ryan."

"He's a really good boy. He fits in nicely into the family."

"I'd like to get them here one day. Stella too. Strange to think of Kate as a mother."

"She's a great one, too. Ryan had nowhere to go, and Kate just made it very clear that she'd promised to come back for him. Stella told me about the other man. Juan was his name?"

"Back in California. She found out he has his own farm now. He obviously doesn't keep in touch, given that he still thinks I'm the devil."

"Well, he's wrong about that. I'm so proud. You ended it. For all of us."

"No, Nanna. You did. It was always you. No one else but you even figured out about the ladybugs. If the government had, I don't know if they would have even allowed us to live. I still get a bit nervous when I see a bunch of them crawling together. But at least they don't swarm into the sky."

Lynn shook her head. "I remember thinking it simply couldn't be. But I saw it above the trees. At first, I thought it was how they marked the locations of abductions. But now I think . . . it's how they communicated what they had done to us. How they had altered us."

"I saw the same above that formation in North Dakota. I knew then and there that nothing would ever save all of us. We'd changed. In the end, it was how I knew, when I was trapped in that . . . thing . . . , that perhaps I could change everyone back."

Lynn stopped, the breeze blowing her hair. "I know that's why you stay here. Why you always will. Because you reversed what they did to all of us, but you didn't do it to yourself, did you?"

William looked out over the beach. "I failed. I couldn't do it in the end. My plan was to alter what they'd done to us, and then remove myself, to make sure no one could ever be switched back. But I saw the chance for revenge, and I took it. It died, and I was out of bullets."

Lynn exhaled, leaning into his shoulder. "I'm glad. We all are."

He shook his head. "We all live with the mistakes we make, don't we, Nanna?"

"Yes we do," she said softly.

They'd reached a shaded edge of the beach, where a pair of refurbished lounge chairs sat almost tucked in the woods. "And here is Tommy's favorite napping spot. And I say that with complete sarcasm."

"I remember another red-headed boy who hated to take naps, too."

"I need to check on a build just down the way, see if the pillars of this dock we're working on held overnight. Think you could rock a baby to sleep?"

"I have some experience with that."

As Lynn settled in the chair, William handed her the baby, who was already starting to whine. She held him, already humming in his ear.

"I'll be right back," William said, kissing her on the forehead and jogging down the beach.

Tommy raised his head and began to cry. Lynn swayed back and forth.

"Blackbird singing in the dead of night," she sang softly.

With William rounding a bend in the beach and disappearing, Tommy began to wail.

"Take these broken wings and learn to fly . . ."

The boy was strong, trying to push himself up, reaching for the direction of his father.

"All your life, you were only waiting for this moment to arise," she sang a bit louder.

He'd reached full tantrum mode, his sweet rounded cheeks flushed, his eyes narrowed fighting sleep.

"Blackbird singing in the dead—"

The thunderclap jolted her as she saw the lightning bolt flash on the horizon. The boy screamed, and the lightning flared again. A strong wind picked up, tossing the trees around them. As his little fist curled almost painfully on the sagging skin of her arm, the crack of thunder resounded across the water, now beginning to churn in the distance.

My God. My God.

Lynn leaned in, their foreheads touching. "Listen to me. No sir. No sir, you will not."

His eyes, the deepest of blue, then began to close. He laid his head on her shoulder, whimpered once more, and sighed.

Lynn looked across the water, now calming. She closed her eyes.

A storm was coming. But it would not be today.